T0363661

ABOUT THE AUTHOR

Kaneana May studied television production at university, graduating with first-class honours in screenwriting. She went on to work in the script departments of television drama programs and became a scriptwriter on *Home and Away*. She turned her attention to fiction writing and in 2019 was shortlisted for ARRA's Favourite Debut Romance Author Award for her novel *The One*. Her second book is *All We Have Is Now*. She balances out her love for coffee, cake, cheese and champagne with early morning bootcamp sessions or walks along the beach. Kaneana lives on the Mid North Coast with her husband, three children and their enthusiastic labrador.

For more about Kaneana, check out kaneanamay.com or join her over on Facebook or Instagram where you'll see her sharing loads of her life, loves and writing.

Also by Kaneana May

All We Have Is Now

The one

KANEANA MAY

mira

First Published 2019
Second Australian Paperback Edition 2021
ISBN 9781867221975

THE ONE
© 2019 by Kaneana May
Australian Copyright 2019
New Zealand Copyright 2019

Except for use in any review, the reproduction or utilisation of this work in whole or in part in any form by any electronic, mechanical or other means, now known or hereafter invented, including xerography, photocopying and recording, or in any information storage or retrieval system, is forbidden without the permission of the publisher.

This book is sold subject to the condition that it shall not, by way of trade or otherwise, be lent, resold, hired out or otherwise circulated without the prior consent of the publisher in any form of binding or cover other than that in which it is published and without a similar condition including this condition being imposed on the subsequent purchaser.

All rights reserved including the right of reproduction in whole or in part in any form.

This is a work of fiction. Names, characters, places, and incidents are either the product of the author's imagination or are used fictitiously, and any resemblance to actual persons, living or dead, business establishments, events, or locales is entirely coincidental.

Published by
Mira
An imprint of Harlequin Enterprises (Australia) Pty Limited (ABN 47 001 180 918), a subsidiary of HarperCollins Publishers Australia Pty Limited (ABN 36 009 913 517)
Level 13, 201 Elizabeth St
SYDNEY NSW 2000
AUSTRALIA

® and TM (apart from those relating to FSC®) are trademarks of Harlequin Enterprises (Australia) Pty Limited or its corporate affiliates. Trademarks indicated with ® are registered in Australia, New Zealand and in other countries.

A catalogue record for this book is available from the National Library of Australia
www.librariesaustralia.nla.gov.au

Printed and bound in Australia by McPherson's Printing Group

For Alex, who will always be
'the one' for me.

For my mum, who had total faith that, one day,
I would become a published author.
Thank you for championing me every step of the way.

1

Darcy glances to Ben, the cameraman who has been assigned to her for the day. 'Ready?'

He nods. 'Rolling.'

'Okay, Bonnie.' Darcy smiles, picking up a pen so she can make notes on Bonnie's application form. 'Can you tell us a bit about yourself?'

The woman is visibly uncomfortable and Darcy's first thought is that she'll probably look awkward on screen, but then Darcy glances at the monitor to her left and sees there's a lovely vulnerability to Bonnie's nervousness. Maybe she shouldn't cast her off too quickly.

'I'm Bonnie Yates, I'm thirty-three and I own a photography studio up the coast.'

Darcy already knows this due to the detailed application all the girls have completed. Today is more about getting a sense of how easily they talk in front of the camera and how they interact with the other girls. Thirty-three is getting on the *old* side, but they do need to cast at least one or two older contestants.

'What about your living arrangements?' Darcy queries. 'Do you rent or own? Do you have housemates?'

'I bought a townhouse about eight years ago. It's just me.'

There's a sting in Darcy's heart at hearing the sadness entwined in Bonnie's words. She should be used to the contestants' loneliness by now; this is her fourth season working on *The One* but she's still not as tough as she should be. She can handle desperation, but for some reason loneliness makes her want to hug them.

'So, we want to know a bit about your dating history,' Darcy says. 'Have you ever been in love?' In the early days of her job, she used to feel like she was rudely prying, but she's asked the question so many times over the last few seasons that it now just falls from her lips.

'Yes.' Bonnie nods, her face serious as memories likely fill her head. 'More than once. I fall hard and fast.'

Even though there's a raw honesty about the words, it seems she's hoping they'll only lightly skim the subject and she won't have to reveal too much history. The show needs girls who will fall in love fast. Darcy scrawls on the paperwork. She's developed her own code of scribbles in case the girls get a glimpse of what she's writing.

'You've said here that you're not sure why your relationships haven't worked?' Darcy refers to the application form in front of her.

'My sister filled that out,' Bonnie says, a slight annoyance in her voice that she tries to hide with amusement. 'I know perfectly well why the relationships haven't worked out.'

This surprises Darcy.

'I'm always more in love with them than they are with me.'

Oh, this just about breaks Darcy's heart.

Bonnie must realise this because she quickly bolsters a smile. 'It's okay. You don't have to feel sorry for me.'

But Darcy does and suddenly has a longing to call Drew. She left home this morning when he was still asleep. 'You mentioned your sister,' Darcy comments. 'What's your relationship with her like?'

For the first time since the interview started, Bonnie glances at the camera self-consciously, her brown eyes almost hidden by a forest of lashes. 'We're close.' Her voice is higher than it was before.

Darcy recognises the opportunity. 'Were you annoyed she filled out the application for you?'

Bonnie glances at the camera again and tucks a dark strand of hair behind her ear, allowing herself a moment to pause before answering. 'Carla just wants me to be happy. She's married with kids and can't understand how anyone can be happy without that.'

The tone in Bonnie's voice isn't lost on Darcy. 'Can they?' Darcy knows she's treading on dangerous ground. Of course the answer is *yes!* But why is there a natural instinct to feel sorry for anyone who is unable to have children or hasn't found a partner to share their life with?

'Can we be happy without being married and having kids?' Bonnie clarifies.

Darcy wonders whether she's repeated the question purely to give herself more time to answer. She nods, curious to know her response.

Bonnie exhales on a breath of laughter. 'I hope so.'

Bonnie can hear how nervous she sounds. A pounding hangover has wedged itself right behind her eyes. She's trying her hardest not to stare down the barrel of the camera, but it's too big and intrusive. She's starting to realise what it must be like for the shy brides she photographs. It's actually much harder to relax and pretend the camera isn't there than she thought.

Darcy, the field producer interviewing her, is younger than she is, which in itself is depressing. Thankfully she isn't wearing a wedding ring—that really would be rubbing salt in the wound, but maybe crewmembers take them off before spending the day with over a hundred single women looking for love.

'So, we'd meet Carla, her husband and kids on your hometown date?'

'Hometown date?' Bonnie echoes and as she draws her eyes away from the camera, they lock with the cameraman's for a split second. She can't see the rest of his face but can tell by his gentle brown eyes that he's friendly. She finds comfort in this but then cringes, wondering what he must think of her and all the other women signing up for a show like this. 'Sorry, I haven't thought about that.' She can't even think about taking home a guy she doesn't know yet and introducing him to Carla. Her sister would jump the gun, assume Bonnie was the only woman for him. She'd be pushy and aggressive. Bonnie's chest tightens at the thought of how much screen time they'd be allocated. 'We could go to my best friend's place?' Bonnie suggests, knowing Paige would be a much safer option. 'We've been friends since we were at school.'

But Darcy brushes away the suggestion of Paige. 'Is there a reason why you wouldn't want to take the suitor to meet your sister?'

Bonnie feels very aware of the camera and the man standing behind it but forces herself to keep looking at Darcy. 'No.' She shrugs. 'I'm sure my sister would love it.' That is probably the biggest understatement she's ever made; Carla would almost die with excitement at being involved in *The One*.

Darcy studies her face for a moment, as though trying to decide whether or not to push the subject. But then she glances down at her question sheet and moves on. 'Have you done much travelling?'

'I always thought I'd travel but somehow I've never even left Australia. I was so determined to set up my business and make it a success that I kept putting it off. I've barely had any time off work in ten years.'

'Wow.' Darcy shakes her head. 'That's impressive.'

'Or just stupid?' She wonders if she'd do things differently if she had known that she'd have a successful business but still be single.

'So, are there any places you'd really like to see?'

'Anywhere. Everywhere.' Bonnie is struck with a feeling of inadequacy about her lack of worldliness. She wishes this wasn't being recorded. Her throat narrows at the thought of someone potentially picking through her interview and deciding what to broadcast on national television.

'Can you describe your ultimate fantasy date?'

Even though Carla had prepped Bonnie with questions like this, Bonnie feels herself inwardly sigh. 'Honestly? Trackpants, takeaway, good wine and Netflix.'

Darcy smiles politely, her pen scrawling something on the paper. Bonnie's head cranes a little as she tries to see what's being written, but Darcy pulls the paper a little closer.

'Not exactly what you're after?'

'It's fine,' Darcy assures her. 'It just gives us an idea of what type of activities you crave in a relationship and what dates to put you on if you're chosen for the show.'

Bonnie tenses at the reminder that this is an audition.

'Filming a date of you and the suitor watching TV probably won't be very exciting. Is there anything else you'd like to do?'

Bonnie considers, aware that regardless of what she says, the dates on *The One* are going to be extravagant and over the top.

'How would you like to be swept off your feet?'

Bonnie knows Darcy is waiting to be dazzled and feels like she's about to let her down. 'I just want to find someone who wants nothing more than to hang out with me. Of course I want the romance. I want that giddy feeling in your stomach and that longing to be with them when you're apart. But I've been in enough relationships to know that eventually those feelings fade. What I want is to be with someone who, at the end of their day, wants to come home to me.'

Darcy doesn't say anything, and Bonnie is fairly confident that she's just screwed up her chances of getting on the show. Her relationship ideals must sound so boring. Earlier today on their drive to the audition, Carla had been beside herself with advice. Bonnie's last-minute acceptance of her audition spot meant Carla, a dedicated *The One* viewer, had to squeeze everything she knew into their five-hour drive from Port Macquarie to Sydney. Carla insisted they'd cast bright, bubbly personalities, and Bonnie feels nothing but the opposite of that. Now she'll have to go back home and face Ollie and her mistakes of last night.

She should feel nothing but dread, but there's a tingle of hope that tries to dance inside her body. She feels her teeth biting into her bottom lip, and pleads with herself to stop thinking about him.

She sits a little straighter, pushing her hair over her shoulder as she waits for Darcy's next question. But Darcy seems momentarily lost, probably hypnotised by Bonnie's boringness. The cameraman, his face covered with a scruffy beard, tilts his head to the side so she can see more of him. He offers a little smile before moving back behind the camera and Bonnie realises her response must have been so pitiable that even he feels sorry for her.

⌒

Bonnie's words offer Darcy a reassurance she didn't know she needed. But she'd be lying if she didn't admit that some days she wonders if she missed out on the big romance. She's known Drew since primary school. She wasn't swept off her feet, they just happened to hook up at a party when she was sixteen, then did it again at another party, and then started going out. They fell in love but it wasn't a magical, earth-shattering experience that some people go on about. Their relationship is certainly at the trackies and takeaway level and most days she's okay with that. But some days she wonders what else is out there...

Ben, the cameraman, shifts and she glances up at him, but his eyes are still on Bonnie. Darcy assumes he's subtly giving her the hint to keep things going.

'Okay, so special talents,' Darcy says, reading the next question. 'Are there any hobbies or activities you'd like to tell us about?'

Bonnie's face splits into a smile, a rumble of laughter in the back of her throat. 'I'm sorry, but whenever I hear "special talents" I can't help but think you're expecting me to do fire twirling while hula-hooping in a bikini or something.'

Darcy almost snorts at this. Some of the videos that applicants send in are very close to that description. She feels Ben's body shake with laughter next to her.

Darcy waves the question away. 'Fair enough, let's move on.' She quickly refers to her checklist of questions. 'What do you like to do for exercise?'

Bonnie shrugs apologetically. 'I walk sometimes, but it's usually followed by a glass of wine. It's not really something I enjoy.' Bonnie's grim, as though waiting execution.

Darcy can't help but like her. She seems so real and down to earth, which are qualities they don't often get in applicants. 'Do you have a favourite recipe you'd like to cook for the suitor?'

Bonnie rubs her forehead. 'I feel like I'm a total disappointment here but no ... I don't cook.'

Darcy wants this girl on the show. She likes Bonnie's honesty and knows they could have fun putting her on dates she'd be clearly uncomfortable with. Darcy imagines the audience will love her frankness. 'I think that's all we need,' Darcy tells her. 'If you go back to the holding room, we'll come and grab you for some games shortly.'

The look on Bonnie's face suggests she's just been told she'll be thrown into a tank of sharks. Darcy has to stifle more brewing laughter.

'Great,' Bonnie says politely. 'Thanks for your time.' She gets up and moves to the door.

Darcy scrawls a thick asterisk on Bonnie's application before turning to Ben. 'I like her.'

'Yeah.' He nods. 'She seemed pretty awesome.'

Carla is waiting in the driver's seat of her Pajero as Bonnie walks out from quite possibly the longest day of her life. Carla's face is bright and expectant. 'How'd you go?'

Bonnie slumps into the passenger seat next to her, noticing the back seat is filled with shopping bags. 'It was awful.'

'Come on, it couldn't have been that bad?' If Carla had just auditioned, it would probably rank as one of the best days of her life.

'It was worse than I imagined. Three hours of hideous games with about thirty cameras recording our every move.' She reaches for Carla's water bottle and takes a swig, still trying to shake her hangover that has only gotten worse as the day has worn on.

'What did they make you do?' Carla doesn't try to hide that she's a diehard fan.

Bonnie groans. Where does she start? 'The highlight was probably having to put ourselves in order from youngest to oldest, based on how we looked. Without talking.'

'Really?' Carla's wide eyes reveal she's enjoying this too much.

Bonnie grimaces as she remembers walking straight to the back of the line. It hadn't even been comforting to learn that she wasn't the oldest. Two other women were older than she was. Two out of one hundred.

'Did you try to get lots of screen time, like I said?'

Bonnie makes a face. 'Do you even know me?'

'What were the other girls like?' Carla's whole body is twisted in the seat, facing Bonnie, eager for every word.

Bonnie considers. 'Skinny. Young. Blonde.'

Carla, a skinny, young, (dyed) blonde herself, screws her face up at this. 'Oh, come on, it's not that bad anymore. Diversity is the new blonde.'

Bonnie smiles at this, impressed her younger sister even knows the word *diversity*, let alone how to use it in a sentence. 'There was a slight mix of girls, I guess, but they were all attractive and mostly very loud.'

'Any D-grade celebrities?'

'Maybe?' Bonnie shrugs; she wouldn't know any if she fell over them.

'What about your interview? How did that go?'

Bonnie remembers the way the producer had smiled politely at her as she scribbled on her pad of paper, even the smile of sympathy the cameraman had offered. 'I was dull,' she says, grimacing. 'I think they even felt sorry for me.' She wonders if the crew are now off having a great big laugh at how pathetic she was. Mimicking her answers, mocking her desperation to find love. She feels sick.

A text message chimes on Carla's phone. She retrieves it from her handbag, glancing down at the screen.

Bonnie stares out the window, watching as some of the other girls emerge from the studio. 'Let's get going.' She wants to be as far away from here as possible.

'You were out with Oliver James last night?'

Bonnie's head moves sharply back to Carla, who has clearly just read this information on her phone. Maybe she shouldn't be rushing back to her hometown. 'We just had a couple of drinks and caught up.' Bonnie tries to sound casual, but Carla sees straight through it.

'Faith McKinnon just sent me this.' Carla holds up her phone for Bonnie to see. It's a photo of Bonnie and Oliver near the pool table. They're standing much too close, smiling, lustful. There's no way she can argue innocence.

Bonnie swallows hard, her lips remembering Oliver's. She tries to think of something to say but words escape her. She'd wanted Oliver, he'd wanted her. 'Please make sure that photo is deleted.'

Carla knows her well enough to know something more happened. 'Bonnie, he's engaged.' Her tone is more sympathetic than Bonnie had been expecting. She'd assumed Carla would be angry.

'I know.' She can't hide the sadness in her voice.

'Oh, Bon.' Carla's face fills with concern. 'You still love him?'

Bonnie quickly shakes the question off before it has a chance to settle. She will not let herself even think about loving a man who is engaged to somebody else. 'We were just drunk, catching up on old times.' She shakes her head. 'It shouldn't have happened.'

Carla looks stricken.

'I didn't sleep with him,' she hastily adds. But she would have if Sophie hadn't shown up when she did. The knot in Bonnie's stomach pulls a little tighter.

'Is that why you agreed to audition?'

Bonnie had outright refused when Carla turned up a couple of weeks earlier, announcing she'd secretly sent in an application for Bonnie to be a contestant on *The One* and that she'd made it through to the auditions. Bonnie almost choked. She might have been lonely in love, but she wasn't desperate enough to try to find it on a reality TV show.

But that had been before Oliver James moved back to town. Before she'd had something, some*one* to run away from.

2

Penelope's phone vibrates. She knows it's him ringing again without even checking the screen. Her throat tightens, knowing a text message with a blur of words will arrive within minutes. She won't read it. She's learned that the hard way. His words make her doubt her decision. Instead she looks out to sea and tries to focus on the calming waves rolling in onto the shore.

Warm memories try to come to the forefront of her mind. Her skin prickles at this, craving the sweetness of such thoughts to take over her body. But she forces her mind to take control. She clamps her eyes shut and makes herself focus. A cold ocean breeze comes whipping and chills her to the core.

As a waitress brings her a small pot of green tea, Penelope hears a soft sob and turns her head to the table beside her. There's a woman of a similar age to herself sitting alone with a glass of wine, her face etched with sadness. She catches Penelope looking at her and is visibly embarrassed. Her hands move to wipe away tears and push hair off her face. Penelope feels bad for catching her in such a moment and tries to look away.

'Sorry, I'm not usually like this,' the woman says, calling Penelope's attention back.

Penelope gives a small smile, ready to turn away and offer her some privacy in the small cafe by the sea.

But the woman goes on. 'My mum died a month ago.'

'Oh, I'm sorry.' Penelope's heart stings, as it always does, remembering the pain. It rushes back a little too quickly today.

The woman waves away the condolences; she's no doubt been offered the same sympathetic expressions for the past month. 'I think I must have been in shock when it first happened because I've been fine.' She reconsiders her words. 'Maybe not fine, but coping.'

Penelope nods. 'It's horrible when the reality of it sinks in.'

'Your mother died too?'

Penelope hadn't intended on telling this woman anything about her own experience. 'A while ago now.'

'You must have been young?'

Penelope can tell she's studying her face, probably trying to determine how old she is. 'Seventeen.'

The woman's eyes fill with sympathy. 'What a horrible time to lose your mum.' She shakes her head, realising what she's said. 'Oh, you know what I mean. Any time is awful, but at seventeen you should be out partying and having fun.'

Penelope feels her face strain, thinking back to those dark days. Looking back, she realises she missed out on pivotal milestones in her teenage years but she's glad she hadn't cared about it at the time. She hadn't been longing for nights out with her friends, parties till dawn or to fool around with guys. All she'd wanted was more time with her mum. Seventeen years hadn't been enough. She'd greedily wanted more, decades more, but as it had been coming to an end, all she'd wanted was another day, another hour.

'I guess I should count myself lucky. I'm thirty-five. I got double the time you did,' the woman says, somewhat chastising herself.

'There's never enough time.' Penelope's still trying to come to terms with that.

'I thought we had years before I'd have to say goodbye,' she says, leaning forward to have another sip of her wine. 'She just turned sixty-two.'

'That is young.' Her own mother had been only weeks away from turning thirty-nine, but it wasn't time to compare.

'Dad called me at work and said, "Your mother's dropped dead on the golf course". At first I thought he was joking, not that it's something you'd ever joke about, but he just sounded so together.'

'He mustn't have really processed it.' Penelope remembers calling a few of her mother's friends to tell them after her mum died. She hadn't even been teary. The words had come out of her mouth as though she was talking about a character on a television show.

The woman shakes her head. 'No, I guess not.'

They sit in silence for a moment, their eyes drawn to the ocean. Both thinking of death and loss and grief. What could have been, what will never be …

The woman lets out another sob, her pain still raw. Penelope can hear it, fresh like a newborn baby's cry.

'I'm sorry, I'm such a mess.'

'Please don't apologise.'

The woman wipes at her face again, a little rough this time, seemingly angry with herself. 'I got sent home from work.' She shakes her head, ashamed. 'So unprofessional.'

'We all have bad days. I'm sure your boss would have understood.' Penelope hears her phone vibrate again and tries to ignore the longing in her heart to answer it.

'I guess.' She swallows hard. 'I always feel like I'm letting them down. I only work three days but I'm constantly running late and scooting off early, asking for extra time off.' She drains the last of her wine. 'Do you have kids?'

Penelope shakes her head, not trusting her voice. She tries not to let her mind wander.

'I never feel like I have enough time to get anything done, let alone have a minute to myself.' She glances at her empty wine glass and suddenly looks guilty. 'I know it doesn't look like it,' she indicates around her, 'but I've never done this before.'

Penelope knows that the woman feels like she's being judged, but if she tries to tell her how much she doesn't care what this woman does with her time, she's only going to sound rude, which wouldn't be her intention at all.

'When my boss told me to go home, I couldn't actually face it. The kitchen still has breakfast dishes all across the counter, the floors need a vacuum, there are so many piles of washing that I don't know what's clean and what's dirty.'

Penelope wants to ease the woman's mind, but she's had conversations like these before and knows how it goes. Penelope doesn't have kids, so she doesn't understand what it's like to have constant mess and no time. 'You should enjoy your time out then,' Penelope says as kindly as she can, hoping to put a full stop on their conversation and turn away.

'Are you a local? I haven't seen you around before.'

Penny shakes her head. 'New to town.'

The woman's face lights up. 'Oh, welcome!' She looks genuinely pleased at the possibility of friendship. 'What street are you on?'

'Weatherley.'

The woman considers this a moment. 'I didn't know anything had sold along there?'

'I'm renting one of the furnished units,' Penelope says, feeling a little unsettled at giving out so much information.

She looks relieved that she's gotten to the bottom of it. 'My husband works at the local real estate,' the woman explains, 'so I usually know when new people have moved to town.'

'I'm renting privately.' Penelope's words are clipped.

'Join me?' The woman indicates towards the wine. 'I thought I might have another glass.' Her eyes are hopeful and friendly.

But Penelope doesn't let herself be tempted. 'I really better be going.' She begins to gather her things.

'What a shame.' The woman's face falls. The rejection seems to hit her harder than Penelope had anticipated and for a moment she feels a stab of guilt.

She offers a polite goodbye before hurrying off, craving a walk, a release from once again feeling like she's let someone down. She digs into her bag for her phone, forcing herself not to look at the screen. Instead she flicks open the back, rips out the SIM and chucks it into a bin without letting herself give it a second thought.

3

'I ran into Parko today,' Drew says as he gets out of Darcy's parents' shower and wraps a towel around his waist.

'Yeah?' Darcy leans towards the mirror as she applies some mascara, getting ready for a little family barbecue to celebrate her dad's birthday. She'd finished audition week on *The One* and even though she could have slept the whole weekend away, they'd decided to drive up to their hometown. She curses under her breath when some mascara clumps at the end of her lashes. She bought a new brand last week and every time she uses it, she ends up spending more time pinching the clumps off than she does applying it in the first place.

'He said there's a position coming up.'

Parko is the head of PE at Gloucester High, their old high school. 'What? Here?' Her fingers are now black with mascara.

'Yeah,' Drew says, leaning across her to grab his toothbrush. She prickles as he drips water onto her dress. She steps to the side, straddling the toilet to give him space.

'For you?' She's confused.

'Yeah, why not?'

Darcy almost laughs. 'Because we live in Sydney. It'd be a bit of a commute, wouldn't it?'

He's started brushing his teeth, but pauses for a second, watching her reflection in the mirror. 'It's probably just going to be a ten-week block. It's mine if I want it.'

Her heart starts racing a little faster, nervous about where this conversation is going. 'But Drew, you have a job.'

He spits out a mouthful of foam, burying his head in the sink rather than looking at her. 'You know how much I hate that school.' The all-girls school has proved to be nothing but a challenge for Drew who resents the teenage girls who let him know they have the world at their fingertips because of their parents' bank accounts. 'I need a change.'

'Okay,' she says slowly, wanting to be more supportive than she's feeling. 'So, I'd just stay in Sydney and you'd be here?'

'Yeah, I mean I'd come down some weekends and you could come up here.'

He's suggesting long distance?! 'If you're really keen to give up your job, why don't you look for something else in Sydney? Even if you can't find something permanent, you could teach casually for a while?'

'Because teaching back here would be awesome.' His eyes are bright as though he's a kid talking about Santa Claus. 'I already know heaps of the families, Parko said he'd be happy for me to help out with the footy coaching and, who knows, it could lead to a full-time position.'

A full-time position? Here? He's got to be joking. But at the look on his face she knows he's nothing but serious.

'Don't you miss it?'

Frankly, no. She loves her family but not one part of her wants to be back in Gloucester for more than a long weekend. 'Not really.' She'd spent the afternoon at Lauren's place. They've been friends since preschool. Lauren is now married with kids and a mortgage, and Darcy had watched her friend with amused admiration. The mess, the noise, the chaos. Lauren was certainly dishevelled but appeared as though she actually enjoyed it. Darcy had left wondering if she'd be able to spend her days like that, and she's still plagued with doubt. She knows Lauren's happy with the life she has, but in all honesty, Darcy felt suffocated just being at her place. Knowing she gets to drive back to her life in Sydney tomorrow is liberating.

Drew's jaw tightens, and she sees a flicker of disappointment cross his eyes. She knows he wishes she could feel as fondly towards their hometown as he does.

'I think I'm going to take it.'

'What?' Darcy's indignant. 'So I don't even get a say?'

'Don't be like that.' He's annoyed. 'It's ten weeks. You won't even notice I'm not around. You've barely been at home all week and it's only going to get worse as the job goes on.'

He's right. Every season of *The One* has had her working twelve-hour days, but she still wants to see him each night before crashing into bed. 'Drew,' she begins, searching for the right words.

'I know it'll be hard,' he says, stepping in close, 'but we'll make it work.' He kisses her on the forehead, signalling the conversation is over.

Darcy takes another gulp of her champagne. It's the only thing stopping her from starting a fight with Drew. She keeps going over the discussion they had. They're a couple. They're supposed to discuss things and figure them out together. The more she thinks about it, the angrier she becomes. How could he just dump this on her in her parents' bathroom? He knew she wouldn't make a scene. If they'd been at their place in Sydney she would have yelled and stormed off and probably even slammed the door.

She sees her mum approaching, laying the last of the salads on the table, now just waiting on her dad to finish barbecuing the meat. By the look on her mum's face she knows Drew's shared his news.

Darcy braces herself as her mum sits down beside her. 'I just heard about Drew's new job.' Her mum's voice is steady, fishing for Darcy's reaction.

Darcy meets her eye, and in that moment, her mum knows exactly how she's feeling.

'Oh, darling, I'm sorry.' She places her hand on Darcy's, giving it a light squeeze. Darcy can smell her mum's lavender hand cream. 'It mightn't be as bad as you think.'

Darcy notices her own fingers gripping tightly onto the bottom of the champagne glass and forces herself to loosen them. She wants to tell her mum that things haven't been great with Drew recently, that the last thing they need is more time apart, but she's not about to get into that kind of conversation with the rest of her family only metres away.

'Drew seems really excited about it.' Her mum looks at her with hopeful eyes, reminding Darcy that Drew's happiness is important. Maybe she should be more understanding.

'Yeah, he does,' Darcy murmurs as she watches him talking animatedly to her brother and his wife. She hasn't seen him smile like that in months. She should be relieved but seeing him happy only highlights how unhappy he's been … living with her in Sydney.

It terrifies her to the pit of her stomach.

Bonnie is leaning over her desk with invoices sprawled out in front of her when the door to her studio pushes open. She looks up and her heart skips a beat at seeing him, but it's quickly followed by an ache, knowing that her longing to be with him won't be fulfilled. 'Ollie, you shouldn't be here.'

But he ignores her words and moves towards her, his face unashamedly crestfallen. 'I came to see you the other day.'

Her body stiffens. She knows he's waiting for her to explain why she closed the studio the very day after they'd caught up. 'I had an appointment in Sydney,' she says, hoping he doesn't notice the squeak in her voice.

He pauses as though giving her a chance to elaborate. 'Everything okay?'

Bonnie grimaces, realising he assumes it was a medical appointment. She can't look at him and instead begins sorting some prints on her desk. 'Yep, yes. I'm fine. All okay. Better than ever. Nothing to worry about.' She can't stop the verbal outpour, anything to hide the truth. Imagine if he knew she'd auditioned for *The One*. She can feel her cheeks burn with humiliation. She honestly doesn't know what she'd been thinking.

'I miss you, Bon.'

Those few words mean more than they should. It doesn't even bother her that it sounds ridiculously clichéd. For a moment she can imagine herself murmuring that she misses him too. She longs to take a few steps forward and let him take her in his arms. She could nestle against him. She can almost feel the heat radiating off his body. Just the thought of how good it would feel strangles her breath.

'Does Sophie know you're here?' she forces herself to ask.

Oliver shakes his head, anticipating the same thing running through her mind. 'I left my phone at work, so she'll think I'm still there.'

Bonnie nods a little absently, still trying to get her head around Sophie being able to track Oliver's location and him seemingly being okay with that. She can feel his gaze on her, causing her shoulders to tighten. She looks up and her eyes fall on his lips. She can still taste him.

'So, are we okay after last week?' His eyes, pale blue with more clarity than a diamond, stare back with unsettling hope.

Part of her had been thinking they could both pretend nothing had happened. But the simple words *last week* refer to much more than old friends catching up over a drink. *Last week* alludes to lust and passion, the raw ugly truth that Oliver cheated on his fiancée.

And Bonnie is the other woman.

'Yeah, we're okay,' she's quick to say. 'It shouldn't have happened. You're engaged, I get it.' Bonnie doesn't know why she's holding out hope for her high school boyfriend; this will be his second marriage since their relationship all those years ago. He spent more than a decade married to Amy and bounced straight out of that relationship into an engagement with Sophie.

His hands twist uncomfortably. She can still feel the heat that had radiated from them when he'd touched her. She had never felt lust like that before, she'd never wanted anyone like she'd wanted him. She has to gulp down on a lump forming in her throat.

She constantly needs to remind herself of Sophie. 'Did you tell her anything?'

'No,' Oliver assures her quickly. 'Nothing at all.'

Bonnie nods but she can't deny her heart sinks a little. If Oliver wanted to be with her, he would have told Sophie and ended things straight away. He isn't here to declare his love. He's probably here to declare his regret.

He bites at his bottom lip before saying, 'I'm just trying to figure out what to do.'

'There's nothing to figure out, Oliver. I won't tell anyone. Sophie won't find out.' She immediately thinks about the photo Carla showed her the other day. She hopes it isn't going to find its way to Sophie. She'll have to talk to Carla about Faith McKinnon deleting it.

'So, you don't think I should tell Sophie?'

Bonnie isn't exactly sure why he's asking her. Does he genuinely want her opinion or is he fishing to see if she wants something more? 'Do what you feel comfortable with,' she manages, knowing she can't feel guilt over being *the other woman* and then encourage him to lie about it too.

'Right,' he says slowly. 'But you'd prefer no one found out?'

Her stomach churns at the thought of people around town hearing about it. She's a businesswoman, a respected member of the community. How many wives would want to book a photoshoot with her if they thought she was a husband snatcher? 'I can't say I'm in a rush to have anyone know.'

He looks at her for a long time, causing Bonnie to look away. Just being in the same room as him makes her heart race too fast. She can feel herself getting hotter.

'I wish …' he begins.

There's something about the way he's looking at her that makes her whole stomach flip. She should tell him not to say any more, it's too dangerous, but she can't help herself. 'You wish what?'

'I wish there was a chance for us.'

A flicker of hope and then images of a life with Oliver come spiralling faster than she'd thought possible. Friday nights on the lounge with takeaway, barbecues and Pictionary with Paige and Andy, lazy Sunday mornings in bed … A dog, kids, a bigger house …

But the images come to a screeching halt because there's Sophie. He's engaged to someone else.

'I can't believe I let you get away all those years ago.'

Bonnie can barely breathe. Her chest throbs.

'I've missed you, Bon. I've thought about nothing but you since last week.'

Her throat feels like it's closing over, no words can escape, she wonders if she's still breathing.

'I know I'm engaged to somebody else, but it feels wrong.'

Bonnie grips the side of the desk to steady herself.

'I know it's not fair to ask how you feel about me, but I want you to know that I'm going to break up with Sophie. It's wrong of me to be with her when I feel this way about you.'

Thoughts collide inside her head, but she ignores them, letting her heart leap and soar with hope. A future with Oliver suddenly seems possible. 'I have feelings for you,' she admits, solemn, but then she finds herself smiling, laughing, everything in her life suddenly shifting. 'I have more feelings for you than I did when I was a giddy love-struck teenager.'

Oliver's whole face lights up. 'Really?'

She nods, euphoria starting to take over.

'The other night made me realise how much I've been missing you for all these years.'

'I know,' she agrees. 'Being with you just feels so natural.'

She can feel herself floating. She moves forward, her body being pulled to his. 'You know it won't be easy. This town is small. Everyone will have an opinion.'

'It might not be easy, but it'll be worth it.' He reaches out, his hand taking hers.

And just like that she melts. They stare at each other, neither saying a word. Bonnie can hear the seconds on the clock ticking over. She feels magnetised to him, her body wanting to be against his. He clearly feels the same, drawing her closer.

'We can't, Ollie. Not yet.'

'I want you, Bonnie. I want you so bad.' His eyes remain steady on her lips as he pulls her against him. She can feel how much he wants her.

Her own aching desire is pulsing through her. She can feel herself becoming a little breathless, but she stops herself. 'You have to end things with Sophie.' She tries to step back but he holds onto her, leaning in for a kiss.

'Ollie, no!' She's firm now.

'Sorry.' He shakes himself and lets out a deep breath. 'You just turn me on so much.'

Bonnie feels herself redden at this, but she bites down on a smile.

They both stand there staring at each other, Bonnie's giddiness reflected in the twinkle of Ollie's eyes. It's as though they both know their worlds are about to combine.

'You better go,' she tells him with a smile to indicate there's plenty of time to do everything he wants to do to her.

This fills his face with a grin. 'Soon, okay … soon.'

He walks off, leaving Bonnie with a promise she's going to let herself fall asleep with.

4

Darcy's desk is covered with applicant profiles, Post-its and highlighters. They have to dwindle the one hundred girls who auditioned for *The One* down to the final twenty-two contestants. Darcy needs to present her choices and reasons for them in a production meeting scheduled for later today.

'Have you compiled the list yet?' Alice's voice cuts sharply through the office as her heels clang against the concrete floor.

Darcy immediately straightens in her chair. 'Almost.' Her voice catches in her throat. 'We're still finalising the last few—'

'I don't want to hear the details. Just get it done.' And just like that she's gone.

'She's terrifying,' Mel, the new girl, whispers.

Darcy nods. 'Yeah, that doesn't ease up either.' Earlier in the week Darcy had approached Alice in hopes of a promotion. 'This is my fourth season doing the same role,' she'd begun. 'I was hoping there might be a chance of moving up the ladder? I know I'm ready for some new challenges.'

'Is this about money?' Alice had said, her permanent frown harsher than usual. 'Because no pay rises have been approved for this season. They simply don't fit into the budget.'

Darcy had wanted to say that she felt as though her career was stuck in some kind of stalemate. She was after progression, new responsibilities, even a fancier title. But instead she'd let Alice talk over her.

'The new girl starts this week. I'll need you to show her what to do. I can't afford to lose you from the field team at the moment.'

Darcy's heart had sunk. The sleepless nights rehearsing the conversation had all been a waste.

'How about we re-evaluate things at the end of the season?'

It was probably the nicest thing Alice had ever said to her, yet Darcy now wonders whether it's merely a carrot she will dangle in front of her over the next couple of months before tossing it in the bin.

Darcy shakes her head and turns her attention back to Mel. 'All right, let's run through the list again.' She begins to lay the photographs of the girls they've chosen so far out on the desk. 'We've still got four positions up for grabs.' She splits the pile of leftover photographs and hands them to Mel to look through.

'Have we got enough legitimate contestants?' Mel asks as she starts thumbing through her pile.

'We call them wifeys,' Darcy says absentmindedly, pausing at a photo of a fiery redhead. She needs to help Mel get up to speed with the lingo. Alice will crucify her if she doesn't talk the talk. 'And no, possibly not.'

'What about her?' Mel pulls a photograph from her pile. 'I reviewed her interview. She seems likeable.'

Darcy nods, noticing that Mel has one green eye and one blue. 'Yeah, I liked her too.' But Alice doesn't care for the nice ones. She'll only want to know that they have plenty of girls who will create drama. 'But we need to make sure we have enough girls who will drive the ratings up.'

Darcy's mobile starts ringing. She leans across the desk to see who's calling and grabs it when she sees it's her friend Ed. 'Let's try to find another wild one, a kooky one, a fish out of water and a wifey,' she tells Mel.

Mel nods and heads back to her own desk with the pile of photographs.

'Hey, Ed,' Darcy says into the phone, her eyes moving to her computer screen and the two new work emails sitting in her inbox.

'How's the new season going? Got your puppets all lined up and ready to perform?' Ed's heard more details about the female contestants over the last three years than a guy should ever have to listen to.

'Ed! Finding potential soul mates is serious business,' she reminds him. 'But no, not yet. Hopefully by day's end.'

'If it makes you feel any better I'm trying to edit together a rainy wedding with a couple that barely looked at each other all day.'

Darcy chuckles. Ed films weddings for a living and always has amusing stories to tell.

'How'd you go asking about the promotion?'

'Yeah, not going to happen. She said we can re-evaluate at the end of the season.' Darcy makes a noise to indicate she doesn't believe that's going to happen.

'Don't be like that,' Ed tells her. 'You'll just have to prove to her that you deserve it.'

'I know.' Darcy feels like she deserves it, but will Alice ever see how much she busts her arse?

'You and Drew want to come over for dinner? I told Sienna I'd grab some groceries. Thought I'd buy one of those store lasagnes. Keen?'

'Can't.' She tilts her head towards her shoulder, wedging the phone in place so she can type a reply to the first email. 'Drew's heading back to Gloucester after school today.'

'Already?'

'Already,' she confirms, trying to ignore the irritation that her boyfriend rushed through his commitments with his current school so that he can get back to their hometown.

'You okay?'

Darcy's heart stings at his question but she refuses to let herself think about it properly. Alice does not tolerate personal issues or emotions at work. Darcy is well practised at switching any personal phone calls to sound like location enquiries for dates she's organising if Alice happens to walk past her desk.

'Why don't you come tonight anyway?'

She loves that Ed can gauge her mood so easily, realising that she needs his company. She's about to say yes when an email from Alice chimes in her inbox and her eyes scan over the request. 'Thanks, but I've got so much going on here. I won't get away till late. I might need a wine later in the week?' Once she's locked in the contestants, things at work should calm down for a few days.

'Okay, but we're here if you change your mind, okay?'

'Thanks, Ed.' He's the best friend any girl could hope for.

Hours later, Darcy's arse aches as she finally stands up to leave the production meeting.

'Wow,' Mel murmurs. 'That was intense.'

Alice had been in a real mood and challenged every girl they presented for the final twenty-two. After much debate, they have eventually settled on the final contestants. Within the next few days the successful girls will be notified and have forty-eight hours to sign on to the show. They'll be put into lockdown in a hotel in the city before the season premiere next week. Darcy should be feeling relieved, but she has a lack-of-caffeine headache and an armload of work to get through.

Her mobile lights up with a text message from Drew as she reaches her desk.

The car is packed. Just waiting to say goodbye before I hit the road.

Darcy cringes, glancing at her long to-do list. The meeting really chewed into her afternoon. She won't get out of the office for hours yet.

Her fingers fly over the phone.

Totally swamped, can you drop by here to say goodbye?

It's out of his way and he'll be annoyed. It takes five long minutes for him to reply.

Ok.

Forty minutes later Drew texts her to say he's outside. 'Can you cover me?' Darcy asks Mel.

'Of course. If anyone asks, you're on a very important task.' She smiles. 'Hope there aren't too many tears.'

Darcy moves from her desk and down the hall, immediately feeling a lump forming in her throat. She hadn't thought about crying but of course this is sad. Drew's leaving. He won't be there when she gets home from work, he won't sleep next to her tonight. After almost five years of living together, he's going back to live with his mother. The lump gets higher and higher. She forcefully swallows it down. *It's just for ten weeks*, she reminds herself. *Ten weeks. It'll be fine.*

She pushes through the office doors and steps onto the street. Drew's waiting, his hands shoved in his pockets. 'Traffic was hell,' he tells her, making sure she knows.

She tries to ignore his mood, leaning in to kiss him. 'I'm going to miss you.'

This throws him. 'I'll miss you too, Darce.' He wraps his arms around her. 'But I'll see you in a couple of weeks and we'll talk every day.'

Darcy nods, her voice shaky as she says, 'I know.' But it doesn't seem like a big deal to him.

'I've taken the bins out, but you'll need to grab some milk and there's laundry in the machine that needs to be hung out.'

Darcy prickles that the last things he needs to say to her are about housekeeping. Their relationship has come down to garbage, groceries and washing. She's only twenty-five; this isn't right. She checks the time on her phone, deciding she can spare twenty minutes and stay behind even later tonight. 'Want to get a coffee?' They can snuggle on the bench seat of the cafe around the corner and soak up their last minutes together.

'Nah, better not. I told Mum I'd be back for a late dinner. You know what she's like—she'll stress if I'm driving for too long in the dark.'

Darcy feels her neck tighten, knowing Sheila would have made him a roast and apple crumble—two things Darcy has attempted to make on several occasions, but somehow can't make quite as good as Drew's mum. 'Okay, have a safe trip and make sure you give me a call when you get there.'

'Of course.' He leans in and they kiss. She's ready to savour the moment, but it's over too soon; their lips part and he's walking off down the street towards his car. 'Love you,' he calls with a wave. She can see the excitement in his eyes.

'Love you too.' She waves back. She plans on watching until his car disappears down the street, but her mobile buzzes. Work is calling.

5

The yoga studio looks quaint and welcoming. Deep green shutters against a white cottage, a lavender bush growing under one of the windows, a cat lazing sleepily near the doorway. Penelope's body is craving the release. She's been practising each day in her small unit, but she wants someone else to guide her today. She needs to hold on to their voice and instruction as she pushes her body until it floats away.

She hears chatter as she steps up onto the veranda. A welcome sign hangs on the door. She pushes it open and it creaks.

A few ladies are already there amid a hum of conversation. Penelope smiles a hello and goes to set up away from the group. The instructor, who she spoke to a few days earlier, comes over and welcomes her to the class, telling her they'll get started in a few minutes.

Penelope sits on her mat, stretching her legs out in front of her. She loves the stillness of yoga, the subtle moves being able to extend not only the body but the mind. She easily blocks out the chatter around her and begins focusing on her breath. She feels it all the way down in the pit of her stomach. Her eyes naturally close as she begins to concentrate on her body. She hears the door creak open and absentmindedly thinks the instructor really should fix it considering it's a place of quiet Zen.

'Am I late?' The voice is panicked. 'Oh good, you haven't started yet.' She answers her own question as she pads across the floor. 'I thought I was going to be late again.'

'You're just in time,' the instructor tells her.

'If it's not one thing, it's another,' the woman goes on. 'The kids were right off this morning. The kitchen has mess from one end to the other, but I just had to tell myself to get out of there today. Sometimes you just have to walk away from it. I'm sure this will make me feel better.'

Penelope tries to ignore the woman and the noise she's bringing into the studio. *Breathe in, breathe out. In ... out ... In ... out.*

'Oh, it's you!' the woman says.

Penelope focuses in a little tighter. *In ... out ... In ... out.*

'Excuse me, hello?' The words are a little louder now and project towards Penelope.

Penelope opens her eyes and turns her head. The woman is familiar, but it takes her a second longer to place her. It's the woman from the seaside cafe, the one whose mother died. 'Oh, hi,' Penelope says.

'You found our little sanctuary.' She smiles, apparently pleased to see her again.

Penelope nods. 'Here for my first class.'

'Oh, it's great,' she enthuses. 'Mind you, I can't do half the stuff she tries to get us to do.'

'Okay guys, we might get started,' the instructor calls from the front of the room. 'If I can get you to stand on your mat to begin.'

Penelope pushes up to stand as the woman sets up beside her.

'We could go grab a coffee after this,' the woman whispers to her.

Penelope offers her a polite smile in return but knows that instead of embracing the calm and letting herself get lost in the class, she'll spend the next hour coming up with an excuse not to go for coffee.

6

Bonnie's fingers fly over the keys, replying to an email, when the door pushes open. She looks up and her breath is immediately knocked away.

Sophie Nix.

Oh God, she isn't ready for this. Bonnie had expected Oliver to break up with Sophie days ago, but he'd texted to say she'd gone away for work and he'd need to wait until she got back.

So, she's back.

Bonnie thought Oliver would have messaged to warn her but the last text he'd sent was two nights ago, explaining in great detail what he'd like to do to her the next time they were alone. Her face reddens just at the thought of it.

'Bonnie, hi!' Sophie says, looking only slightly tentative about being there.

Bonnie stands as a sour taste fills her mouth. She hasn't mentally prepared herself to come face to face with Sophie, especially when she doesn't know what Oliver has told her.

Bonnie glances down at her outfit and grimaces for not making more of an effort. She'd had a family photoshoot earlier on the beach at sunrise. She'd thrown on tights and an oversized top and pulled her hair into a messy ponytail on the top of her head. She hadn't even bothered with mascara.

'Great space,' Sophie coos as she looks around the studio, tossing her bouncy hair.

'Thanks.' Bonnie stands a little straighter, totally unsure how to move through this conversation.

'I've been asking around and have heard nothing but good things about your work.' Sophie leans a bit closer, a grin creeping onto her face as she confesses, 'I've also been stalking your business page— checking out all your photos.'

This makes Bonnie feel more uncomfortable than it should, as though Sophie has been going through her underwear drawer. But maybe the discomfort comes from Bonnie's own guilt that she's planning on sleeping with Sophie's fiancé the second he breaks off the engagement. Bonnie's eyes drop to the floor, shame creeping through her body.

'You've got a great eye,' Sophie goes on, every inch of her face animated. 'Every photograph I've seen is brilliant.'

'Thank you.'

'I want to book you to photograph our wedding.'

Bonnie feels like she's been winded. This girl has got to be joking, doesn't she? She feels her hands shaking just at the thought of having to look through her camera lens at Ollie dressed as a groom.

But then another thought screams through her head: *Why hasn't Ollie broken up with her yet?*

'And Oliver's okay with it?'

Sophie is blasé at this. 'Trust me, he won't mind. I asked him how he felt after we ran into you at the shops the other week and he said it wasn't weird seeing you at all.'

Well, that feels like a slap in the face.

'I know some people are funny with exes and everything, but you guys were together *years* ago.' Sophie waves away Bonnie and Oliver's relationship like she's swatting away a fly. 'And you know what guys are like. He's happy for me to organise everything. This morning he joked that he'll take care of his bucks and I can do everything else.' Sophie shakes her head and rolls her eyes, but her face is filled with loving amusement.

'This morning?' Bonnie hears herself echo as images of Sophie and Oliver in bed together spin into her mind. Why had Oliver been having a conversation with Sophie about their wedding this morning when he should have been breaking up with her?

'So, are you available June third?'

'Wow, that's soon.'

Sophie shrugs. 'Why wait, right? I just picked up the most amazing wedding dress in Sydney. I didn't think I'd take something off the rack, but it fits me like a glove.'

'You were dress shopping?' Bonnie wonders if Oliver knows.

'I had to go down to tie up some work things but then I thought, why not?'

Bonnie feels lightheaded but somehow autopilot takes over. 'So, June third. Let's take a look. I get booked really early these days.'

Sophie suddenly looks nervous.

Bonnie fixes a smile on her face but her heart feels like it's beating outside her chest. She prays she's already booked as she moves to her diary. She flicks through the pages and notices her hands are dry; she really should take the time to moisturise like Carla says. The pages settle on June third and Bonnie almost cries. She should tell Sophie no—she doesn't feel comfortable doing it—but she's too gutless to say so. She should come up with an excuse but all logical thoughts vanish from her mind and instead she says, 'Look at that, I'm free.'

'Yay!' Sophie cheers, raising her arms in joyful celebration. 'Great, lock us in.'

Bonnie's hand shakes as she writes *James/Nix wedding* in her diary.

'I can pay a deposit now if you like?'

The deposit is usually non-refundable, so Bonnie doesn't feel right about taking one when the groom-to-be is supposedly calling off the wedding. 'Don't worry about it,' she says. 'We can fix the payment up later.'

'Thanks.' Sophie claps her hands together. 'Better be off, I've got an appointment to get to.' She smiles a little mischievously as though she's about to go pick out wedding night lingerie.

Bonnie manages to make her way through polite farewells and watches as Sophie saunters out of the studio. She doesn't normally swear, but what the fuck is going on? Does Oliver want to be with her or is this some sort of game to him? She picks up her phone and sends a text: *Your fiancée just booked me as your wedding photographer.*

'Have you seen this?' The words spit from Darcy's mouth before Ed's even fully opened the door.

Ed sees her holding her phone screen towards him and nods. 'I wondered how long it'd take for you to turn up.'

'You'd think they've never had a young female producer before.' She could have called Drew to bitch about Zoe Eggins, her university arch nemesis, but Ed was also subjected to Zoe on a daily basis at university and knows the extent of Darcy's feelings.

'Well, she is pretty young to be the producer on Australia's longest running serial.' Ed shrugs, quoting one of the many tag lines.

Darcy moves to the kitchen and pulls open the fridge to inspect if there's any wine.

'Not the answer you wanted?' He grins, already pulling two wine glasses from the cupboard.

Darcy passes him the wine. 'Sometimes I forget you're a man who doesn't understand the female need to bitch.'

'Not all females feel the need to bitch,' he counters.

When she doesn't say anything, Ed looks up and sees her face. He seems to realise she *needs* him to say something horrible about Zoe. 'Do you remember on the first day of class when Zoe got up there, dressed in her power suit, and said she was only going to direct and produce as though all other roles were beneath her? I mean, what a *cow*.'

Darcy can't help but laugh. 'I remember it more clearly than I'd like.' She takes one of the glasses of wine. 'She's been annoying me since that first day. I finally thought when we'd finished university that I'd be rid of her, but here she is, all through my newsfeed with my dream job!'

'I thought your dream job was to produce a new TV show?' he says a little pointedly.

He's right, but … 'I'd certainly settle to be producer on *Smith Street*.'

Ed sends a sympathetic look but isn't about to let her dwell on Zoe's achievements. 'Remember all those getting-to-know-you games they had us playing on the first day of university?'

Before he can even go on she begins to feel better; she knows what he's going to say.

'Everyone was a bit unsure because it all seemed pretty daggy but when you were singled out, you just went with it. You didn't care that you looked like an idiot.'

'Hey!' Darcy protests as she perches on the stool at the kitchen counter. 'You're calling me an idiot?'

'I was going to say that from that first day everyone liked you. They knew you were down to earth and fun.'

Unlike Zoe.

Darcy remembers Zoe had sat in the corner, refusing to join in. When she was told it was part of their participation grade, she got up but looked as though someone had stuck a ruler up her arse. 'It was fun,' Darcy remembers fondly. She's always been a sucker for any kind of game. 'Mind you, maybe if I'd had a little less fun, my grades would have been as good as Zoe's—and I'd be the one landing the big gigs.'

'Oh, please,' Ed says. 'Want me to get out my violin?' His sympathy levels have clearly reached their peak. 'Who wants to go to university to just study? We're never going to party like we did back then.'

It's depressing to think that, but she guesses he's right. They'd had so much fun over those three years. Among their studies, there had been a constant stream of parties and impromptu drinking sessions and staying out all night. As she moves to the cupboard to find some food, she tells him, 'I remember you so clearly from that first day.'

A crease forms between Ed's eyes as he collapses onto the lounge. 'Oh yeah, what is it you remember? My good looks?'

Ed is a good-looking man. Tall, broad, with green sparkling eyes and a smile that brightens any room. But it hadn't been his looks that caught Darcy's attention. 'I thought you looked like a nice guy.' She remembers thinking she could be friends with him. He seemed like the kind of guy that was fun but genuine, silly yet serious.

Ed frowns, unimpressed with her answer. 'You do know if I said the same thing to you, you'd think it was the worst compliment in the world—you'd twist my words and make out that it meant you were very *unattractive*.'

Darcy's amused at this and reconsiders her words. 'So true.' She finally finds half a bag of corn chips and settles back against the bench. 'So, what first impressions did I make on you?'

'Killer legs,' he answers without hesitation.

She feigns offence—'Typical guy!'—but then hides her grin behind her glass of wine.

He rolls his eyes at seeing how much she likes the compliment, and gestures for her to chuck him the packet of chips.

'Where's Sienna?' Darcy asks, throwing the packet to him.

'Who knows?' He shrugs, stuffing some chips into his mouth. 'I've given up asking. There's always some meeting after school, photocopying to be done or setting up for the next day.'

Darcy gets it. Even though Drew technically knocks off at three o'clock, some nights he doesn't get home until hours later.

'She gets the shits if I call to check how long she's going to be,' he says.

'Teachers.' She shakes her head in mock disgust. 'What bastards, educating the children of the world.'

'Touché.'

Darcy moves to the lounge and flops next to Ed.

'How's Drew? You coping without him?'

It's only been a few days since Drew left, but it's nice to have Ed ask. Every time she's spoken to Drew, he's given a running commentary on who he's seen and what they're up to. She's trying not to take how much he's enjoying it personally. He did call today asking if she could get away for the weekend so that had been a nice surprise. 'I'm meeting him this weekend in the Hunter Valley.'

Ed raises his eyebrows. '*Ooh-la-la.*'

'I know!' Excitement sparks at the thought of having a weekend away—a *romantic* weekend away. 'I'm going to head straight up after work on Friday. He's booked a last-minute deal.'

'I bet he got a good one.' Ed is well aware of Drew's penny-saving ways.

Darcy wouldn't expect anything less and rolls her eyes. Drew's fixation on saving is one thing that grates on her.

Ed changes the subject. 'How's the new season of the show?'

'The final twenty-two get notified tomorrow.'

'Are the chicks as desperate as last year?'

The girls that had been cast last year seemed to get more desperate as each episode aired. The suitor, Simon, had been totally freaked out. Darcy had spent plenty of time trying to assure him they weren't as bad as they seemed.

'The *chicks*,' she echoes, 'seem a little more normal this season.'

'You don't sound completely sure about that?'

Darcy's thoughtful as she considers the stuff she's read in some of the applications. So many sound like they'd do anything to have a real chance at love. When she reads all their stories and situations it reminds her she's lucky to have Drew. Some of the applicants have been single for so long that it makes them sound a little psychotic.

'They all seem okay before the cameras start rolling,' he teases.

Even she has to smirk at this. 'Ain't that the truth.' It never ceases to surprise her how the 'competition' for love brings out extreme character traits. 'But you know the audience loves the crazy ones the best.'

'The poor guy.'

'Well, that's debatable.' Her eyebrows arch.

'I don't envy him for a second. Dating twenty-two women at once? Sounds like a nightmare to me.'

Darcy imagines what Ed would be like as the suitor and finds herself grinning. She knows he'd find the whole thing overwhelming and end up saying really awkward things.

Ed looks up and sees her expression. 'I know what you're thinking. If it were me, I'd make a total arse of myself.'

'Stop talking,' she tells him, turning away to try to soak up the picture of him as the suitor. 'I'm enjoying this too much.'

Ed ignores her request. 'You know I'm a one-woman man. Can you imagine trying to remember what you'd told each of them? I'd constantly be putting my foot in my mouth, saying, "Haven't I told you this already? Oh, no, that's right, I told one of the other girls I'm dating."'

'Awkward,' Darcy agrees, knowing that's actually happened quite a few times on set.

'What's he like? The guy?'

Darcy thinks about Joe. She's only met him once for about two minutes. 'He seems okay.'

'Good-looking?'

'Well, that's the stupidest question you've ever asked. Of course he's good-looking.'

'Yet he still can't get a girlfriend?'

Darcy shrugs. 'He's had a few girlfriends but nothing serious for years.'

'Can you imagine watching an ex on a show like that? Urgh.' He groans. 'Horrendous.'

'Have you forgotten? The only ex I have is Nick Simmons.'

Ed snorts. 'Yeah, I'm still not sure he *really* counts.'

Darcy had dated Nick Simmons for about six weeks in year eight. They kissed, held hands and spoke to each other *occasionally*. It certainly wasn't a romance to write about. She hadn't even kissed another guy until she started going out with Drew two years later.

'You're lucky, Darce. Not everyone ends up with their high school sweetheart.'

'Yeah, I know.'

'Come here,' Ed says, pushing out of the lounge and moving to his edit suite set up in the corner of the room. 'Check out this romantic brilliance. This couple met and married within the year.' He hits the space bar and the screen fades up from black to a close-up of gorgeous white calla lilies.

Darcy relaxes into the chair next to Ed to watch another one of his masterpieces, quickly feeling that she missed out on a big romance that so many others seem to get.

Bonnie's just about to start the car engine after a long day at work when the passenger door opens.

'I can explain,' Oliver says, presenting her with a bunch of flowers and sliding into the seat next to her.

Bonnie eyes the bright bunch of gerberas, her heart wanting to swell at the romance of them, but she quickly reminds herself of her heartache only this morning when she had to take a booking for Oliver's wedding to someone else. 'Well, get on with it then.'

'God you're sexy when you're angry.' He leans closer to her, his hand reaching towards her, his fingers tangling in her hair.

She quivers at his touch, heat rushing through her body, an immediate desire to have his hands all over her. She gulps down some air. It takes everything she has to grab his hand and remove it from her skin. 'Ollie, I'm serious. What's going on? Why are you buying me flowers when you're still engaged to Sophie?' She tosses the flowers on the backseat.

He slumps back in the passenger chair. 'Look, she only got back from Sydney late last night. It wasn't the right time to break up with her.'

Bonnie tries to ignore the image of Sophie crawling into bed with him. She isn't the kind of girl who would own daggy PJs but sexy lingerie. Actually, she probably just sleeps naked. 'How about this morning then?' Now an image of Sophie naked at the breakfast table flashes into Bonnie's head.

'I had to rush to work for a breakfast meeting.' Ollie drags a hand down his face. 'I'm the new guy, remember, I can't afford to show up late just yet.'

A wave of frustration surges through Bonnie. 'Ollie, are you sure you want to break up with her?'

'Of course I do. Why would you say that?' His eyes are wide, searching for her answer.

Bonnie shrugs. 'I just assumed when you left here the other day you'd be going straight home to break things off. I didn't think I'd be sitting here almost a week later still not sure what's going on with us.'

'I told you, she went away. I couldn't break up with her over the phone.'

Bonnie gets that. No one deserves a phone break-up. 'She's back now and she's spent the day making bookings for your wedding.'

Oliver clears his throat, his eyes casting downwards.

'You didn't mention how soon your wedding is ...' Bonnie fishes.

'Soph wanted a winter wonderland theme and I just said okay. It wasn't a big deal to me.' Oliver exhales. 'We were still in Sydney at that stage. I didn't know I'd feel this way when I saw you again.' He turns back to her. 'I want to be with you, Bonnie. I really do.' His eyes stare into hers, the same eyes she fell in love with when she was seventeen. Memories and emotions bound tightly together.

He leans towards her until their mouths are only inches apart. 'Please, can I kiss you?'

She should say no, she should tell him they can kiss when he's a single man, when Bonnie isn't the other woman. But instead of answering him, Bonnie leans forward, her lips meeting his. It's an instant relief as their tongues collide, sliding in and out of each other's mouths. The reprieve is short-lived, however, because Bonnie quickly finds herself wanting more and Ollie clearly feels the same way. His hand moves onto her waist and up under her shirt, his fingers creeping up her stomach before cupping her breast. She reaches for the button in his jeans, but her elbow hits the horn and blasts out a loud *hooonnnk!*

Bonnie, short of breath, pulls away, realising she's just done what she's been filled with guilt about for the last couple of weeks.

The whole reason she ended up auditioning for *The One*. She cringes, trying to push memories of her audition away.

Oliver reaches for her, his head leaning to the side, going in for another kiss.

She shakes him away. 'Ollie, no. We can't.' He still belongs to someone else.

'We can.' He nods, his hand touching her face, and pushes up out of his seat to move closer to her. Sophie seems to be far from his mind.

Bonnie is firm. 'You're still engaged.'

'I'll end things tonight.' His hand slides along the inside of her thigh.

Bonnie's body squeezes in anticipation of what his touch will do. She's desperate for him to make her shudder with relief but turns her head and pushes his hand away from her. 'Go home, Ollie. Come see me tomorrow.'

7

Penelope stands in line, ready to order a green tea smoothie, when the waft of coffee infiltrates her nostrils. Today that's all it takes and suddenly she's eight again with her mum standing at the small kitchen bench, busily packing school lunches, half dressed for work, eating a piece of toast.

'Miranda, hurry up!' her mum calls. 'We'll have to get going soon.' Her mum casts an eye at her. 'Imagine how long she's going to take when she's actually a teenager!'

Penny smiles, warmed by the familiarity of Miranda spending the majority of the morning perfecting her fringe before school.

She hears her mum flick the kettle on and move to the cupboard to get herself a mug. She sighs, and Penny looks up from her bowl of cornflakes, already knowing the cupboard must be empty—a common occurrence in their house.

'The mugs have gone walkabout again!'

'I'm not helping!' Miranda calls from the bathroom, ready for the coming request.

Penny pushes off her stool, resigned to her fate.

'Come on, Pen, let's find these mugs!'

Penny follows her mother around the house as her mother sings to the tune of 'We're Going on a Bear Hunt'. *'We're going on a mug hunt, we're going to find a lot of them! I'm a coffee addict. Sixteen cups a day! Sixteen cups a day!'*

Penny joins in the singing, giggling as she picks up a mug from next to the lounge, another perched on top of the TV, one on the windowsill, and two more on her mum's bedside table.

'There's one in here,' Miranda calls, pushing open the door, ready to hand the mug over.

'Come on, Miranda, join us!' her mum chants. 'We're going on a mug hunt, we're going to find a lot of them ...'

'If you'd just take them to the sink when you finished, we wouldn't have to do this every second day,' Miranda whines.

'That's the problem, I don't finish them.' She holds up the mugs as proof, each one at least a third full.

Penny heads back into the kitchen, the smell of cold coffee filling her nose as her mum dumps her load of mugs on the bench then leans down and kisses her on the forehead. 'Thanks, Pen.'

If Penelope closes her eyes, she can still feel her mum's lips against her forehead.

'What can I get you?'

It takes Penelope a moment, but she realises she's now first in line and the cashier is waiting to take her order. 'A coffee, please.'

The young man raises his eyebrows at her, pushing his shaggy hair out of his eyes. 'Flat white, long black, cappuccino, latte ... Any preference?'

'Oh,' she stammers. She's never actually ordered a coffee before. She recalls the last one he mentioned. 'A latte?'

'Sure.' His word is drawn out, and Penelope can feel him staring at her like she's a little odd.

A few minutes later, the barista hands her a latte and sends her on her way. She carries it as though it's precious treasure and waits until she's settled on a park bench in the sun to take a sip. The moment she tastes it on her lips, memories of her mother come tumbling back, each sip like a lost page of a diary. She wants to be greedy, but savours each mouthful, forcing herself to remember more.

She knows tomorrow and each day afterwards she'll be drinking coffee. Before now she'd always avoided it, thinking it would bring pain, but now she wishes she'd discovered this porthole back to her mother years ago.

8

'So, you're just waiting to hear from him?' Paige's hands are still clutched around the menu as she looks worriedly at Bonnie. The two friends are meeting on their lunch break.

'I guess so.' Bonnie shrugs. 'It feels kind of tacky.' She hadn't slept at all last night, thinking about Ollie calling off his engagement. Bonnie doesn't know if he was going to tell Sophie about his feelings for her. They hadn't gone into any of those kinds of details and now her gut is all twisted.

'Less tacky than sleeping with him when he *was* still engaged,' Paige points out.

Bonnie supposes that is something. 'I was so close to doing that.' She shakes her head at herself. Her body is still craving his, her mind wanting to ignore the practicalities of how a relationship with him is going to evolve. 'Being around him makes me feel so young and …' She leans forward to whisper, 'Horny.'

Paige laughs at this. 'You couldn't keep your hands off each other when you were teenagers. Things clearly haven't changed.'

'We're far from teenagers now. I should know better than to kiss a man who is engaged to someone else.'

Bonnie ignores the chime of a new email from her phone as she sees the waitress approach, notepad in hand. She's paid no attention to the menu in front of her and is forced to make a quick decision on what to order for lunch.

After this, Bonnie regards her friend's expression. 'What is it?'

Paige gives a reluctant sigh. 'I'm worried about you getting involved with him straight away.'

Bonnie knows she should give Ollie some time to get over his relationship with Sophie, but the truth is she doesn't trust herself. If he comes to her this afternoon to say he's ended things, she'll be locking the studio, taking him out the back and ripping his clothes off.

Worry is etched across Paige's face. 'I don't want you to get hurt.'

Bonnie reaches out and squeezes Paige's hand. 'Things with Sophie might get a bit nasty, but it's Ollie.' Her voice goes soft as soon as she says his name. 'I don't think I've ever stopped loving him.'

Her phone now beeps with a message. 'That'll be Carla,' Bonnie says before she even checks it. 'She messages me every day to see if I've heard from *The One*.'

Paige grins at this. 'I can't believe you auditioned for that.'

Bonnie covers her face with her hands. 'Neither can I.' She has nothing but guilt and desperation to blame.

Paige checks her watch.

'What time is your appointment?'

'Not till two p.m.'

Bonnie can see her friend is nervous. 'It'll happen this time.' Of course Bonnie can't guarantee that, but it's been heartbreaking seeing Paige and Andy go through round after round of IVF.

Paige's mouth turns upwards at this, her desire to be a mum so clear. 'I know, but there's so much riding on it this time.' They've decided it will be their last attempt.

'We have to stay positive.' Bonnie leans across the table to squeeze her hand. She wishes she could offer more than hope.

Half an hour later, after two coffees and an oversized burger, Bonnie leaves lunch bloated and uncomfortable. She blames Oliver for the stress eating.

She is turning the corner on her way back to the studio when she spots Oliver and Sophie sitting outside at a cafe. Seeing them throws her for a second. Why are they together when Oliver was supposed to break things off last night? Tension immediately forms in her neck. But then, as she takes in the scene, she relaxes a little. Oliver's back is to Bonnie and Sophie is looking down, her hands in her lap. Bonnie's stomach churns. He must be breaking up with her now.

She goes to turn back the other way, but it's too late. Sophie looks up and even though she's wearing dark glasses hiding much of her face, Bonnie knows she's seen her. She's queasy, wondering what Oliver has said.

'Bonnie, hi!' Sophie calls, her voice warm and floaty. Frustration comes flooding in. He hasn't told her.

Oliver turns. His eyes are dull and his face is pale. She finds herself softening. Breaking up with Sophie Nix clearly isn't an easy task.

'We're celebrating,' Sophie says, a twinkle in her eye.

'Sophie,' Oliver begins, a little panicked.

'Relax.' She smiles. 'Bonnie can keep a secret.'

Bonnie feels herself stand a little straighter.

'We're pregnant,' Sophie shrills, then clasps her hands over her mouth. 'I still can't believe it.' She shakes her head. 'Pregnant, pregnant, pregnant!'

Bonnie feels all the blood drain from her face and pump to the pit of her stomach, heavy and unbearable. She can feel Oliver's eyes on her, but she can't look at him.

'Champagne for Ollie, but only juice for me.' Sophie grins, pointing to the champagne glasses.

'Wow,' Bonnie manages. 'Congratulations.' All morning her heart had been floating blissfully above the clouds like a helium balloon, but just like that a pin has pricked it. All the air rushes out quicker than she thought possible, leaving nothing but a shrivelled mess she has to shove back into her chest.

'It was a shock,' Oliver says quickly, seemingly needing her to know he hadn't planned this. Bonnie can still feel him staring at her, wanting her to look at him, but she can't. She won't be able to hold herself together if their eyes meet.

'You should have seen how shocked he was!' Sophie laughs. 'It was like he didn't know you could fall pregnant from having sex!'

An image of Oliver and Sophie having sex jumps straight into Bonnie's mind, making her feel like someone has their hands wrapped tightly around her throat.

'He came home from work last night in this really weird mood. I'd had a special cake made from that new bakery on William Street and kept trying to get him to open the box. In the end I had to tear it open myself to show him the "you're going to be a dad" icing.'

Bonnie feels sick knowing her tongue had been in Ollie's mouth, his hand on her inner thigh, while his fiancée was waiting at home to tell him she was pregnant.

'It was the best tasting cake I've ever had,' Sophie gushes. 'I'll definitely have them do our wedding cake.'

Bonnie feels like she's having an out-of-body experience, as though she's looking down from above, watching this horrible little scene play out.

'And now I just don't know what to do about the wedding.' Sophie sighs dramatically. 'I don't know if the dress I bought will fit me in a couple of months, so maybe we should wait and have the wedding in a year? It would be nice to have the baby in the photos, wouldn't it?' Sophie, light and breezy about their predicament, looks to Bonnie as though seeking professional advice.

'Quite the decision,' Bonnie finally manages.

'What do you think? You're an expert on weddings.'

Except for the fact that Bonnie has never gotten close to having her own.

She wants to slam her face against the nearby brick wall. She can't be talking about this. 'Personal preference, I guess.' Her voice wavers. She isn't going to survive through much more of this conversation.

'Sophie, don't hassle Bonnie about it,' Oliver says.

'What? I just want her opinion. I've tried talking to you about it, but you've barely said two words.' She turns back to Bonnie. 'Poor thing is still getting his head around having a *B-A-B-Y*.' She grins, amused, and rests her hand on her flat tummy as though it's bulging.

Bonnie fights the urge to blink, fearful that tears will spill over.

Thankfully Sophie's mobile sitting on the tabletop comes to life. She grabs it quickly. 'It's Mum—she's probably checking up on how I'm feeling. Worst morning sickness ever,' she declares happily, unaware that true morning sickness doesn't leave you smiling. She steps away. 'Hi Mum ...'

'I'm sorry,' Oliver says quickly, standing to be on Bonnie's level. His hand reaches out to her but she swats it away.

'Don't be ridiculous,' Bonnie hisses, somewhat surprised at how angry she sounds. But how can he try to make physical contact when his pregnant fiancée is only metres away?

'Sorry,' he whispers, completely heartfelt. 'When I left you yesterday I wanted my life to be with you, I did, but this ...' He shakes his head, somewhat lost for words.

It crushes her hard and fast. 'Yep, I get it,' she says quickly. 'It changes everything.'

'I don't know.' Oliver looks exhausted. 'I don't know what to do.'

'You're with Sophie and you're having a baby. You're allowed to be happy.'

'But I still have feelings for you ...' Oliver tapers off.

Feelings don't win out in a situation like this. She knows Oliver well enough to be sure he'll stand by and support his child no matter what. 'Don't,' she urges. She knows a baby will tie Oliver and Sophie together for the rest of their lives. That's exactly what happened with Liam. She gave him her heart and he went back to his ex-wife, the mother of his son. 'I'm taking myself out of the equation.'

Without giving him another look, she walks off. She stays strong and steady until she reaches her studio, but the moment she shuts the door, the tears come fast.

9

'So, where do you have to meet him?'

A smile edges its way onto Darcy's face. 'Olive Garden Estate.'
Her romantic weekend away with Drew is only a couple of hours
away.

Mel's impressed. 'Nice.'

From what Darcy's seen online it looks *very* nice. 'It has a spa.'
Her eyebrows dance suggestively.

'Okay, gross,' Mel says. 'I don't need to know all the details.'

Darcy laughs, feeling lighter than she has in ages. Here in Sydney
there are always things to do or friends to hang out with. Up in
the Hunter Valley there will be nothing to focus on but the two of
them. Well, perhaps some wine, good food and the two of them.

Mel eyes her. 'Look at your face,' she squeals. 'You're thinking
about having sex, aren't you?'

Darcy has to bite her lip, a guilty grin trying to make its way upwards. The truth is she's excited about having sex somewhere other than their bedroom. They used to have sex any chance they got—outdoors, in toilet cubicles, in her parents' pool, on his mum's dining room table, even at the movies one time. But these days they move from their own couch to the bedroom to be more comfortable. They've become old in their relationship, but hopefully this weekend away will kick-start some romance. Maybe it'll even spur on some sexting to help survive the long distance for the next couple of months.

Darcy checks her watch; it's just before three. 'Hopefully we can get through this meeting by four and I'll be able to scoot off.' The top twenty-two girls were sent confirmations earlier today, so Mel and Darcy have been getting contracts ready and prepping for production to start. Darcy actually feels like she has a handle on everything.

'You're optimistic. When do we ever get out early?'

Darcy shakes her head at herself. 'I know. I probably just jinxed us by saying it out loud.'

Alice comes striding into the room. Darcy prickles; her presence is always unsettling. 'Be prepared to sleep here for the whole weekend,' Alice declares, her voice booming as though she's trying to talk to someone in the building across the road. Her face is grim, her eyes unnerving, reminding Darcy of a vicious animal. 'Joe has met someone and pulled out of the show.'

Darcy and Mel exchange looks. This is the worse jinx Darcy could have ever imagined.

'We won't be leaving here until we find a replacement suitor.'

'What about his contract?' Darcy says. 'He's already signed on.'

Alice's icy glare is enough to make Darcy feel like she must be the most incompetent person she's ever had to work with. She still isn't used to it, even after four seasons of working together.

'Of course he's signed a bloody contract but do you really think the audience will like someone who clearly isn't invested in any of our contestants? If he's fallen in love, he's fallen in love.' She talks about the subject with utmost disgust.

This has got to be the worst timing. All the successful applicants have already been notified. When they chose the top twenty-two they considered Joe's preferences and the character traits he was looking for in a partner. What if the girls they chose aren't appealing to whichever last-minute suitor they cast?

Darcy's eye catches the clock on her computer screen change from 2.59 to 3.00. The bell at Drew's school would be ringing. Drew thinks he's heading away for a dirty weekend.

Little does he know.

'But everything is booked, Darce.'

Darcy leans against the wall, her mobile to her ear. 'I know and I'm so sorry.'

'It's not like I'll be able to get my money back.'

She knows that. He's told her more than once that it was non-refundable. 'Why don't you ask Silas to go—make it a boys' trip instead?'

'I don't want to go with your brother!' He sighs, frustrated. 'It's the Hunter Valley!' She knows what he means. The Hunter Valley is either a couples' destination or a girls' weekend away.

There's silence for a moment. Darcy knows each second that ticks by counts. She needs to be back in the office working. 'If I could get out of it, I would.'

He makes a sound that infuriates her.

'There's nothing I can do, Drew.' She's struggling to stay in control. 'The bloody suitor pulled out. Without him there's no show.'

More silence before Drew asks, 'So they need absolutely everyone to figure this out?' He sounds doubtful that her role is important enough to be required.

'If I walk out of here, not only will I lose this job, I'll probably never work in the industry again.'

'Would that be such a bad thing?'

Darcy bites down so hard on her lip that she's sure she's drawn blood. He used to think her career aspirations were fun and impressive, but that was before the reality of the industry. His opinion changed very quickly, his support slipping dramatically fast.

'There's no point arguing about this now.'

'Sorry.' He pauses. His tone softening, he says, 'I was just really looking forward to seeing you.'

'I know. Me too.' He only left on Monday, but it's the longest they've been apart in years.

Darcy looks up and sees Mel gesturing to wind it up. Alice must be looking for her. 'I'll call you when I can.' She knows this isn't offering him much, but she's scared of making promises she can't keep.

'I'll drive down there anyway. Maybe you can come up tomorrow and we can have at least one night together.'

Darcy can see Alice pacing the room, words flying from her mouth. Even though Darcy can't hear what she's saying, the terrifying wrath vibrates. She knows there is no way she'll be heading to the Hunter tomorrow.

'Darcy! Get in here!'

Alice's voice paralyses her for a split second. 'I've got to go,' she hurriedly tells Drew. She can hear a shift in his breath, he's about to say something, but she cuts him off. 'Love you.' She hangs up, knowing how his face would be pinched with frustration. To him, she's choosing her career over him, and that's never going to be okay.

10

'Okay, so what do we know about him?'

'Thirty-two, an only child, furniture designer, ready to settle down,' Mel says.

Even though Darcy and Mel spent hours going through the original shortlist of suitor applicants from when Joe had applied, making phone calls and checking availabilities, Alice has been instructed by Nigel, the head honcho of the network, that the new suitor is Ty Peterson. It doesn't matter that he hasn't filled out the application form that resembles something of a PhD or gone through three rounds of interviews and psychological testing—Ty had gone to school with Nigel's son which is enough to fast track him to the finish line.

'He was engaged,' Darcy adds, wishing she had some toothpicks to keep her eyelids open, 'but the girl dumped him and has pretty much disappeared.'

'Disappeared?' Alice repeats dubiously. 'I hope he's not a deranged psychotic killer.'

Darcy cringes uncomfortably. She'd said something similar to Mel as the circumstances do sound cagey. 'We've contacted friends and family. No one really knows what happened, but I did speak to her old boss who said the girl has relocated.'

'Oh, geez, what's wrong with him?' Alice flicks through the notes Mel and Darcy have compiled.

'Everyone thought they were happy, but he got home from a mate's bucks weekend and she had her bags packed, ready to go.'

'She must have been having an affair,' Mel muses.

Darcy thinks maybe they just weren't as in love as everyone thought, but she's so tired she doesn't bother saying anything. The quicker they get through this, the quicker she can go home and get some sleep.

'At least he's good-looking,' Alice says, her expression implying she doubted that would be the case since Nigel made the final call. She drops the folder of notes onto the desk. 'Okay, so we're running with Ty Peterson.' She doesn't seem overly thrilled, more resigned to Nigel's request.

Despite her exhaustion, Darcy flickers with excitement, the prospect of both a shower and her bed flooding to the front of her mind. She hasn't heard from Drew since she hung up on him almost twelve hours ago. He must be furious with her, but she can't muster the energy to even begin to think about how she's going to make it up to him. She slides her feet under the desk, blindly searching for the shoes she'd kicked off hours ago.

'You'll need to schedule the publicity shoots ASAP,' Alice says, glancing at her watch, which would tell her it's almost four a.m. 'Get him in first thing. We might be able to get something out to the press by day's end.'

Oh God. Darcy is going to cry.

'You want us to do that now?' Mel clarifies, her voice unsteady. They had gotten into work around eight a.m. which means they've been there for about twenty hours straight. It's hideously illegal, but who would protest and risk not only their job, but the rest of their career?

'I'm going to pretend you didn't just ask me that ridiculous question.' Alice doesn't look at either of them. 'Email me through the schedule as soon as it's done. I'll be in my office.' Alice barely seems tired. If anything, she seems more motivated than normal, almost like she's thriving on the pressure. It makes Darcy wonder what Alice would be like if she were a producer on the news. Would natural disasters, world chaos and murder be like hitting the jackpot? In that case, maybe reality television is the best place for her.

Alice leaves the room but Darcy and Mel both sit there for a moment, frozen with the knowledge they have hours of work ahead of them. Sleep is a faraway fantasy.

'Doesn't she have a home she wants to go to?'

Darcy looks down at the long list of things she needs to complete. 'Some days I seriously question my career choice.'

Mel laughs. 'What, only *some* days? I feel like I question it at least once an hour, every work day.'

Darcy grimaces, wondering whether she's committed enough to be successful in this industry.

Bonnie glances at herself in the reflection of her computer monitor as it fires up for the day. Her eyes are puffy after spending too many hours last night pathetically sobbing for a relationship that didn't even get the chance to start. Her head aches with a dull hangover, her belly is bloated. She'd spent much of the night in the bath with a bottle of wine and a tub of ice-cream.

But today is a new day and she's back at work, waiting for her first clients to show up for their newborn shoot.

She clicks on her emails to load when there's a *beep, beep* from the street. Bonnie looks up to see Carla radically swerve in to park. She's waving frantically from the driver's seat.

Bonnie's heart jumps into her throat. What's happened? Is her mum all right? Carla's kids? Her feet move fast, her head spinning as she runs out the door and onto the pavement.

Carla pushes open the driver's door. The car is parked with its tail still sticking out on the street. She rushes around to Bonnie.

'What is it?' Fear is laced through her breath.

'You got in.' Carla's breathless, her hair and makeup not done. Bonnie absentmindedly admires how beautiful she looks, unable to remember the last time she saw her sister not 'done'. Her hair, makeup and clothes are always immaculate. Seeing Carla like this is oddly comforting. 'What?'

'I just logged into your email and you got in. They chose you as a contestant on *The One*.'

Bonnie's head spins at this information, her thoughts colliding. But for some reason she asks, 'How did you log into my email?'

Carla waves this away. 'Your password has been the same for the last ten years.'

Bonnie really should stop using the same password for every account.

'Hello? Why are you not screaming with excitement right now?' Carla's face is grinning wide, a stark contrast to her panicked arrival.

Is Carla right? Should she be shrieking with joy? *The One* producers want her? They want her on the show? Bonnie thinks back to her audition. She thought she'd failed epically. 'Are you sure?'

'Yes!' Carla reaches for her phone and pulls up Bonnie's email account. There's a stack of emails. She hasn't checked it since yesterday, before lunch with Paige. The idea that Carla can just log into her account at any time is certainly unsettling. 'Look!' Carla thrusts the email from *The One* under her nose.

Bonnie's eyes scan the email. It's true. She's been selected as one of the final twenty-two girls to appear on the show.

Bonnie gulps. She can't deny she isn't a little bit flattered.

'You have to let them know by Monday, then it's pretty much pack your bags and you're out of here.'

Out of here?

That actually sounds appealing right now. But broadcasting her desperation to find a man across the whole nation? Is that really something she can do? 'I can't go on that show.' Bonnie shakes her head, her hands hiding her face at just the thought. 'I don't know what I was thinking auditioning.'

'Don't be stupid, of course you can.'

'What about the business? I can't just up and leave in a matter of days.' Bonnie glances down the street, wishing the Myles family would turn up so she'd have an excuse to get out of this conversation. She notices the hairdressers have gotten a new sign. She really should take the time to make an appointment for a cut and colour.

'I can help with the admin,' Carla says matter-of-factly. 'I can reschedule bookings for when you get back or refer them on to other photographers.'

'I'm a small business, Carla. I can't afford to turn work away.'

Carla screws up her face. 'Yes, you can. I've seen your bank account. You can easily take two months off work.'

Bonnie wonders when and even why Carla has seen her bank balance but knows there's no point asking because Carla probably believes it's her right as Bonnie's sister to check on her finances.

'Look at it like a holiday. You'd get out of this place for eight weeks.'

'A holiday where awkward dates are televised for the whole country to see. Not to mention living in a house with a bunch of women who are dating the same man. No thanks.'

'This guy could be your one true love.'

Bonnie has to laugh at this. She highly doubts it. 'The show will probably make me out as the pathetic older spinster.'

Carla's face drops and Bonnie can tell her sister's tactic will be to sulk, a well-practised move that she used as a kid and now uses in her marriage to get whatever she wants. 'It makes me so sad that you carry on like this. You're a beautiful woman and you're kind and smart and caring. You have to let other people see that too.'

Bonnie closes her eyes for a moment as Oliver spirals into her mind. He sees her for who she truly is. She wants a future with him, but that's not possible anymore.

'I want to see you happy. I want you to have what I have.'

Bonnie wants that too but keeps her face neutral. If she gives Carla even the remotest bit of hope, Bonnie won't have a chance at standing her ground.

'I'd love to have you and your hubby over for dinner. The kids would love cousins. Do you know how many times Lily asks when Aunty Bonnie is going to have kids?'

'Why don't you tell Lily the truth—that Aunty Bonnie might never have kids?'

'Don't be like that. You've got to believe in a happily ever after for yourself.'

Oh, geez, she's going to start all the positive-thinking talk again.

Bonnie had happily gone along with Carla's vision boards, and she does believe that you can attract success and happiness. She'd effectively done that for her business. She just always seems to bomb out when it comes to her personal life.

'This is your chance. You owe it to yourself.'

Maybe she does owe it to herself, but is she ready to put herself out there when she'd almost handed Oliver her heart again?

'What is it?' Carla says, realising there's more to it than resisting going on live television. 'Is this about Oliver being back in town? You haven't seen him again, have you?'

'No,' Bonnie lies.

Carla eyes her warily. 'Maybe being away from here will be good for you.'

Bonnie knows she means being away from Oliver. Her heart squeezes tight. As much as she doesn't want to admit it, maybe her little sister is right.

11

Penelope adds a book to the pile she has stacked at her feet. She pulls another from the shelf and flips it over to read the back cover. The local library is surprisingly well stocked and much larger than she'd imagined.

A dull thumping in her head, just across the back of her eyes, tells her she needs a coffee. The addiction has taken hold so quickly. The noise from the kids' section isn't helping either. There's been singing, dancing and even instruments playing for the last half an hour. Maybe she'll grab a flyer on her way out so she knows what times to avoid in future.

She pulls out her new library card and makes her way from the non-fiction area to the front of the library. She'll go buy a coffee and flick through some of the books she's borrowing. Her skin is craving sunshine.

On the new releases stand she sees a book by his favourite author. She wonders if he knows there's a new one out. She picks it up and begins to read the back. It's not her thing but reading it would feel like spending time with him; she could imagine what he'd think of the characters and the action-adventure plot. She could pretend … but at the last minute she puts it back on the shelf.

Penelope borrows the armload of books and heads towards the exit at exactly the same time that the woman from the restaurant, the same woman from her yoga class, comes out of the children's area. A grubby toddler sits in the pram and a little blonde-haired girl walks behind her.

'Hello, again,' the woman says.

'Hi.' Penelope smiles, reminding herself to be friendlier than what comes naturally.

'Did you finish your deadline?'

Penelope pauses for a second, but then remembers the excuse she'd used last week after yoga. 'Yes, all done.' What a stupid excuse to use when she's not even working. But thankfully the woman hadn't pressed for details. The excuse had come too easily; Penelope had used it many times before when deadlines had ruled her life on a weekly basis. She hugs the books she's carrying a little closer to her chest, trying to ignore the longing for her old life and her old job. Days spent hunched over manuscripts … transporting herself into different worlds … searching for new authors …

'I'm Lara,' the woman says, interrupting Penelope's stream of thought. 'I realised we haven't properly introduced ourselves.'

'I'm Penelope.'

'Well, it's nice to meet you,' she laughs. 'Oh, this is Molly and Harry,' she goes on, pointing to her kids. Snotty-nosed Harry stares up at her with big blue unsure eyes, and Molly hides behind her mum's leg. 'We've just been to story time.'

'I heard that going on. Sounded like fun.' Penelope attempts a smile at the kids, but it feels unnatural and forced.

'Oh, it's hideous noise for everyone else I imagine,' Lara says. 'They probably need to stick a big warning sign on the door so people know when to avoid coming in.'

'It wasn't that bad.'

Lara reaches for something in her bag, which is strapped onto the back of the pram. 'So, you're settling in okay?'

'Yeah, it's all great. I like it here.' Penelope suddenly feels very conscious of the books she's holding, and uncomfortable at the thought of Lara paying attention to any of them. She shifts the large pile to the side, hoping Lara won't spy any of the titles.

'Oh, good.' Lara, having retrieved a tissue, wipes at Harry's nose. The snot makes Penelope's stomach turn.

'We're just going down to the park. Want to come with us?' Lara's face is welcoming. 'There's a great coffee place on the way.'

Penelope can see how much this woman wants to be friends, but she can't bear the thought of it. 'Sorry, I can't today.' She doesn't even bother giving a reason why and instead tries to ignore the familiar thudding of guilt in her gut.

'No worries.' Lara forces a smile, but Penelope can see the hurt and knows Lara won't extend the hand of friendship again.

12

'This is Ty Peterson.' Alice strides into the meeting room with the new suitor a few steps behind.

The atmosphere in the room changes, both Darcy and Mel sitting a little straighter. He's even better looking than his photos suggested.

'Hi.' He waves, a little unsure. Joe had been loud, friendly and outright flirty—basically a replica of the previous suitors. Ty seems different—cautious and tentative. Darcy had been hopeful but concerns quickly surface.

'This is Darcy and Mel,' Alice tells Ty. 'They're our field producers so you'll be spending a fair bit of time with them. They'll organise your dates, help choose which girls to take through and if you have any problems they're the people to see.'

'Thanks.' Ty nods, nothing resembling a smile even close to touching his face.

Darcy sucks in a long breath. This guy is going to need a lot of media training.

'Have you got any questions for Ty?' Alice looks to the girls.

'We've already done our final castings,' Darcy says. 'Most of the girls have already signed their contracts and sent them back to us so we've got a basic idea of who we'll be presenting to you.'

Ty's face is blank, dull even. Normally the suitors are excited, often greedy with nervous anticipation, at the mention of the smorgasbord of women they're about to date. It's a relief he's good-looking because his personality seems as flat as a pancake.

'We know that not everyone will be your ideal contender, but they'll make for an exciting show,' Darcy continues. 'We just want to know if there's anything in particular you're looking for in a partner?' They'll have to try to figure out who is going to be wifey material for Ty.

Ty looks sad at this question and eventually he shrugs. 'I thought I knew what I was looking for, but it turns out I was wrong.' He jams his hands into his jeans pockets. 'Whatever you find will be fine.'

'Okay.' Darcy hides her concern behind a cheery smile.

'Don't you worry, we've got you some good ones.' Mel's enthusiasm is admirable.

'I'm ready to get married,' Ty offers, perhaps sensing their alarm. 'I want someone who wants that too.' Darcy's mind immediately goes to his ex-fiancée, the woman he was ready to settle down with. She'll try to find a photo to see what she looks like. If one of the girls doesn't sign on, maybe they can find a lookalike to put on the show. That kind of thing always sparks some emotion.

Alice fidgets, tapping away on her phone despite the conversation going on around her.

Darcy, used to such rudeness, keeps her attention on Ty. 'We've read your file and it doesn't seem to say much about the types of dates you're keen to go on. Is anything a no-go zone?'

Ty considers this and then admits, 'I'm not huge on sharks.'

Darcy has already scheduled whale watching for the first one-on-one date. She smiles, knowing the chances of him going on a date in a shark cage just increased dramatically. The suitors never want to appear weak when it comes to crunch time and part of Darcy's job is pushing them to their limits.

'I also wanted to double check about your ex,' Mel says. 'We've tried unsuccessfully to get in contact with her just to make sure she isn't going to create any waves and contact you once the show begins. You were engaged, right?'

Ty's face drains of colour. 'She doesn't care I'm doing this. She made it very clear that it's over between us.'

'Mel,' Alice says sharply, her eyes narrowing before casting Ty an apologetic look. 'Sorry about that.'

Darcy cringes in anticipation of the talking-to Mel will be getting later. Mel wasn't trying to cause trouble, but there'll be no point in trying to tell Alice that.

Mel keeps her mouth shut for the rest of the meeting, letting Darcy take the lead through all the questions.

'It was nice to meet you both,' Ty tells them finally. 'I'll try to make your job as easy as I can.'

Darcy offers a smile. Maybe she shouldn't be so quick to judge him. 'It's our job to make this as easy as possible for you.'

They watch as Ty and Alice leave, then Mel, her eyes glinting with respect, says, 'Damn, you're good at your job. I'm hoping it's contagious.'

Darcy's flattered at this and can't help but laugh. But then the small hint of pride floats away. If she's that good at her job, why is she still in the same role after four years?

∾

Bonnie is closing up for the day. It's been chaotic trying to shift bookings and rearrange her schedule for the next two months. Most of her clients had been okay about her sudden decision to leave town for an extended period because of 'personal reasons'. She's had to be evasive about *The One* because of the confidentiality contract she'd signed and emailed back after almost a bottle of wine on Saturday night.

She hears the door push open and turns, expecting Carla, who insisted on going out and buying new outfits for Bonnie to wear on the show. They both knew Carla would do a better job at choosing so there was no point arguing with her.

But it's not Carla at the door, it's Oliver. His face is pale and his forehead creased with nerves. 'Hey,' he says.

'Hi.'

He's wearing a blue business shirt that reminds her of the school uniform he'd worn for years. A time when she'd been his girlfriend, a time when she had ownership of him. Now, she has nothing.

'Can we talk?'

She wants to say no. Her heart is too fragile to handle this conversation. She'd wanted to disappear without a word.

'Sophie called me,' Oliver says before Bonnie's had the chance to answer his question. 'She said you're going out of town for a couple of months?' He fails to mention that the reason Sophie called is that Bonnie won't be able to photograph their wedding.

'An opportunity came up and I've decided to take it,' Bonnie says, rather formally, like he's a client rather than ... well, she doesn't actually know what he is to her. An ex-boyfriend, an almost lover?

Oliver cocks his head to the side, full of doubt. 'Really?'

There's part of Bonnie that wants to break down and tell him how devastated she is. But tears will flow if she describes the future she'd imagined with him by her side and that wouldn't be fair on him. He's going to be a father and should be feeling excited and happy, not guilty for going back on what he'd promised her. So, she takes a deep breath and keeps up an icy wall. 'I explained this to Sophie. I've given her the names of other photographers who can shoot your wedding.'

'I'm not here because of the wedding.'

She knows that.

'I really am sorry,' Oliver says. 'I thought she was taking the pill. I didn't realise she'd decided to "give her body a break".' He quotes Sophie.

'Please.' Bonnie grimaces, needing him to stop. 'I don't need to know about your contraception.'

His face flushes with distress. 'My feelings for you haven't changed,' he begins.

But Bonnie quickly shuts it down. 'Don't.' Her voice is firm. 'Your fiancée is pregnant. There's nothing left to say.' The fact that she'd been floating, flying, dreaming of her future with him doesn't matter now.

Oliver clears his throat, a little awkward that she's resolutely keeping a distance between them. 'Are you going to tell me where you're going?' he finally asks.

She considers, the words are on the tip of her tongue, but she can't bring herself to tell him the truth. 'I've lined up some work,' she lies.

He accepts this but his face falls. 'You don't need to go away.'

Does he really think they can co-exist in the same town, him having a baby with someone else and Bonnie having … her business?

'Stay?' he suggests lightly.

'No,' she cuts over him quickly, terrified of where the conversation could go.

The door pushes open and Carla bustles in, her arms loaded with shopping bags. 'You should see what I got you.' She's grinning wide, but stops short at seeing Oliver. 'Oliver, hi.' Her words are sour.

Oliver takes a step back from Bonnie. 'Hi, Carla.'

'Congrats on the engagement. I hear your wedding is coming up?'

Bonnie is well aware that her sister will try to make things as awkward as she possibly can for Oliver. In Carla's mind, an engaged man shouldn't visit his ex-girlfriend, and if Bonnie is completely honest with herself she knows Oliver shouldn't be here because it offers her some kind of hope that they still somehow have a future together.

'Yeah, thanks.' He stares at the floor.

Carla's fake smile only just manages to hold on through gritted teeth. It's lucky she doesn't know Oliver and Sophie now have a baby on the way. Carla turns to Bonnie, making a big show of looking at her watch. 'Shouldn't you be locking up?'

Oliver quickly responds to Carla's not-so-subtle hint. 'I'll leave you to it.'

It's not even worth throwing Carla a look; nothing will make her ease off.

Bonnie hates how formal it feels between them and drops her gaze, crossing to the door. He follows, but doesn't reach for it like she expected him to. Instead he just takes a moment to study her face. 'Will I see you before you go away?'

Bonnie wants to say yes, of course she wants to see him again, but that would be stupid. She should be concentrating on forgetting about her feelings for Oliver, not looking forward to seeing him again.

'Look what I got for you to take away.' Carla, clearly having overheard his question, calls their attention back. She's holding up a very small piece of lingerie. Something Bonnie would never in a million years consider buying.

'Carla!' Bonnie's voice is shrill. It's blatantly clear her younger sister is trying to rile Oliver, who makes a pained noise in his throat.

'What? You'd look amazing in this. Wouldn't she, Oliver?' She's daring him to answer.

He looks between the two sisters, clearly aware any answer he provides will be the wrong one.

Bonnie turns her back to Carla. 'Good luck with everything,' she tells Oliver quietly. 'You'll make an amazing dad.' Husband too, but she doesn't allow herself the chance to fully think about that.

'Thanks,' he says, but then shakes his head, seemingly frustrated that not only do they have an audience for their farewell, things between them have gone from steamy hot to tepid formalities.

Bonnie wishes she could tell him how she longs to be in his arms, how she needs his lips on her own, that she wants more than anything to wrap her legs around his body. But instead she says, 'Bye, Ollie.'

He can barely smile as he murmurs goodbye and then walks out of her studio, and out of her life.

Bonnie gulps down on a lump forming in her throat. With her back to Carla, she takes her time locking the door. She widens her eyes to ensure she doesn't cry and exhales loudly, wishing she were alone so she could take the time to nurse her heart.

'You're doing the right thing,' Carla says steadily. 'He might have been your first love, but he's not the right guy for you.'

Maybe Carla is right.

Bonnie knows she needs to be away from Oliver, away from what's happening in his life. She just wishes it didn't hurt so much.

13

'What else have you got?' Darcy asks with a smile, trying not to stare at the girl in front of her who is posed in an extremely revealing pink dress, exactly the same dress a girl about five rooms away is wearing.

It's finally the big day. Within a few hours, each of the twenty-two girls will step out of the limo and walk down to meet Ty. In the meantime, Darcy and Mel are run off their feet approving everything.

The current crisis is that two girls both want to wear the same dress. One girl, Imogen, has outright refused to change. She purposely bought this dress to meet the suitor in, and there is no way she's wearing something else. She doesn't care if another girl is wearing it too because she knows she'll wear it better. She's got the confidence of a champion bull rider.

Darcy's now chatting to Addison to see if she wants to change. Addison has laid out every other outfit she packed on the bed to show Darcy. There is nothing but a sea of pink. Darcy doesn't wear pink herself, she's more drawn to red and navy, so has to fight the natural urge to curl up her nose.

'Can I just call my sister?' The girl turns to her. 'We went through every dress and what order I should wear it in.'

Darcy shakes her head. 'Sorry, no.' The girls had their phones and devices taken off them upon checking in to the hotel. They've been in lockdown for twenty-four hours, each stuck in their hotel room with nothing to do but watch television. 'Can you just switch dress one and two?' It's times like this that she wishes they had a bigger budget and the girls were dressed by a wardrobe department instead of having to bring their own clothes.

Addison shakes her head and looks at Darcy as though she's just suggested wearing her pyjamas to meet Ty, which is actually what another girl is doing—sexy lingerie, with the line, 'If you pick me, you get to go to bed with this every night'.

'*This* dress makes a really strong first impression. I tested out thirty dresses on a group of friends and this one was the stand-out.'

Darcy looks over the dress again. Yep, it definitely makes a statement, leaving very little to the imagination. 'If you don't want to change that's totally fine, but I want to make it clear that another girl is wearing the same dress.'

Addison gives a small nod, the tiniest flicker of doubt passing over her face.

'And this is the kind of thing the media will be all over,' Darcy goes on. 'There will probably be a comparison photo of the two of you online after it all goes to air.'

Addison gulps.

'With a *who wore it better* tagline. So, it's totally up to you.'

Addison turns to stare at herself in the mirror. Her hand runs over the dress, smoothing it down. She turns side on, stands a little straighter and sucks in her stomach, her eyes examining, scrutinising. Darcy wishes she didn't know the feeling.

'Would you change?'

Contestants always want personal opinions, most of them fretting to producers, asking if they're doing the right thing, needing to know if they'd make the same decision. What the contestants don't seem to realise is that they should never trust any of the crewmembers, especially the producers, whose job it is to create drama. Darcy would never go on a show like this and isn't really into clothes as much as other girls, so she probably would change. She doesn't think a single outfit can have that much impact, but that's not the answer for this situation. The more *The One* appears in the media, the better it will be for ratings. Darcy opts for a 'producer' reply and shakes her head. 'No, I wouldn't change either. You look great.'

Addison looks back at herself in the mirror with a satisfied smile and Darcy only feels a tiny bit bad for lying.

෴

Bonnie feels like she's going to throw up. She watches from the limousine as one by one the other four girls go down to meet the suitor. The others had been chatty; Bonnie assumes they were fuelled by liquid confidence from the champagne that flowed all afternoon back at the hotel while they were getting ready. Bonnie had been momentarily elated by their excitement, but as each of the girls vanishes down the garden path, so does her confidence. She has to put her head between her legs and is terrified she's about to pass out.

Mel, one of the producers, is sitting in the back with her, a run sheet on her lap. 'Are you okay?'

Bonnie shakes her head as she scratches furiously at her arms. She can't do this. What had she been thinking? What a crazy and idiotic decision she'd made to avoid her feelings for Oliver.

'You'll be fine,' Mel says confidently, like she's suggesting Bonnie have a routine check-up at the dentist instead of having her face broadcast on national TV.

'No, I can't do it.' Her lungs are desperate for air but her breathing has become shallow.

A flicker of concern crosses Mel's face. She looks at Bonnie properly, probably seeing the beads of sweat, the shaking hands, the panicked breathing. She talks into her headset. 'Negative. We're not ready.' Mel hasn't taken her eyes off Bonnie, and now moves to sit next to her. 'Bonnie, you look beautiful.'

Bonnie doesn't doubt that. She's had people fussing over her all day. She's never been pampered like that before. She was a bridesmaid for both Carla and Paige, but Carla's wedding had been stressful and chaotic, so Bonnie had her hair and makeup done while trying to console Carla about the flowers being not what she wanted, assuring her the best man wasn't going to say anything inappropriate about her during his speech (he did, it'd been amusing but highly inappropriate) and that her future mother-in-law's tight fluoro-pink outfit wasn't going to ruin the family photos.

'All you have to do is get down the path,' Mel goes on. 'Just think, the suitor waiting at the end might be your future husband.'

Bonnie isn't sure if that makes her feel better or worse.

'This is supposed to be exciting.' Mel leans forward and Bonnie notices one of her eyes is green, the other blue. Mel's hand moves towards her headset. 'Not yet,' she says, a slight annoyance in her voice. Her eyes are still on Bonnie, all bright and cheerful.

'Sorry,' Bonnie says, knowing the crew are waiting for her. They'd all been briefed earlier about the schedule, how many minutes each girl would be allocated, that you must wait for your cue before you got out of the limo, that a producer might step in at any point to make an adjustment.

'Take all the time you need,' Mel says. 'Just remember we can reshoot if this first meet doesn't work.'

Bonnie knows Mel means well and is only trying to reassure her, but if Bonnie trips or stutters or embarrasses herself in any way, it will, without a doubt, end up on television. She shudders, thinking about strangers watching her, criticising her, judging her. She wonders what everyone from her hometown will think of their beloved photographer Bonnie Yates putting herself on a reality television show to find love. Oliver's face pops into her mind. What will he think when he sees she's come on this show? Will he be jealous? Outraged? Will he want her back?

He's marrying someone else. He's having a baby with someone else.

She has to remind herself of that every few minutes. There is no future for her and Oliver.

This is her chance. This is it, right here. She looks up and sees the cameraman. The large camera is perched on his shoulder and it looks heavy. She feels bad that she's making him wait. But he doesn't look annoyed, he actually gives her a bit of a smile as though to say *no rush, take your time*. She wonders how he feels about working on a show like this. She doesn't know if *she* could handle working on a show like this. She starts to think about him framing her in a shot. It feels weird being on the other side of the camera. She likes being where he is—it's comfortable over there. Over here she feels like there's no air and her stomach's swirling as though she's just been on a rollercoaster. She's used to photographing nervous brides and awkward grooms, who find it impossibly hard to be natural in front of the camera. She knows what to say to them, but she can't remember a single phrase she uses.

'He's hideously good-looking,' the camera guy jokes, nodding down the pathway to where the suitor waits. 'But you're probably not into that kind of thing, more of a personality kind of girl ...?' He pauses before adding, 'I've got a good personality.'

It's enough to make her laugh and he seems pleased by this.

'What's his personality like?'

He screws up his face. 'Awful. He's one of those nice, sensitive guys that make the rest of the male race look like lazy, rude slobs.'

'*And* he's good-looking?' She smiles.

'I know, some guys have all the luck.' He shakes his head.

She notices she's breathing normally again, that her heart isn't in her throat anymore. He settled her, he used one of his techniques to calm her down and it worked. She tilts her head and smiles. 'Thank you.'

He shrugs like there was nothing to it.

She looks to Mel. 'Okay, I think I'm ready.'

As soon as she's out of the limo and waiting for her cue to walk she wonders how on earth she just thought she was ready to do this. Now she just wants to stay here and talk to the cameraman.

Mel nods at her. 'We're rolling.'

Looking down the path, which is glowing with candles and fairy lights, feels as tough as preparing to walk the plank over shark-infested waters. Her feet won't move.

'I reckon he's a nine out of ten,' the camera guy says in a low whisper. 'Tell me what you think ...'

His face is friendly with a dark, thick beard. He reminds her of a cuddly teddy bear; there's a warming reassurance about him. Bonnie knows it's another ploy to get her down there, but now she's curious and it's enough to make her take that first step. She can feel her whole body shaking with nerves, but her feet keep moving in the right direction.

She rounds the curve in the garden path and there he is. *Oh my.*

Most definitely a nine. Maybe even nine and a half. She feels a little smile form on her face.

'Wow,' he says as she approaches.

She wonders if he's struggling to come up with new things to say to every girl, but then remembers her promise to herself that she won't focus on the others.

'I know you, Bon,' Paige had said. 'You won't cope if you even think about the other girls. The jealousy will eat you up.'

'It's really off-putting when one of them mentions the other girls,' Carla had told her. 'Just focus on you and him.'

'Wow yourself,' Bonnie tells him, knowing it's not all that original but it's true. The man is gorgeous.

The ideas Carla and Paige had presented her with to make a lasting first impression—perform a poem or song, pretend to take his photo, tell a joke, dance—all fly from her mind. Carla's list had been endless; she was more dedicated to *The One* than any religion.

'I'm Bonnie,' she manages, extending her hand to shake his. Carla had insisted she should go straight in for a kiss on the cheek to immediately establish a physical connection, but to do that she has to break eye contact and that currently seems impossible.

'Ty,' he tells her, taking her hand in his own and not letting go of it.

His skin feels warm. Tingles pulse through her body and a warming in her tummy spreads rapidly. She wonders if he can feel the burn in her fingertips.

There's silence between the two of them. She feels like time could stop completely and she'd contentedly stand here, admiring him, their hands touching, desire starting to brew.

'I'll find you inside,' Ty says suddenly, with a sense of promise. His face is somewhat regretful that he's sending her on her way.

Bonnie suddenly remembers it isn't just the two of them. Her eyes fall on one of the producers, gesturing for Bonnie to move on to the house. Then she sees the cameramen and lighting guys. Her cheeks feel a little warm, her throat tightens.

'It was good to meet you, Bonnie.' He says her name purposefully, testing it out on his tongue. He holds her gaze, offering her reassurance that she'll be okay.

Bonnie knows she has to move on but as she lets go of Ty's hand she's hit with overwhelming panic, like she's Alice in Wonderland falling down the rabbit hole.

Somehow, she makes it further down the path and inside the house. The other girls seem brighter and shinier than they did before they'd left the hotel. They'd only met briefly before the limos picked them up and she'd spoken to a few of them, but it had been a blur of smiling red lips and glittery dresses. Now, their voices are loud, competing with one another, escalating at rapid speed.

'What do you think?' one of them asks her.

Bonnie can't remember the girl's name but knows she's from Sydney and works in marketing. 'A fancy name for a promo model,' another woman had whispered to her, giggling.

In all honesty, her body feels numb, in shock after a huge surge of chemicals had rushed through it. She's never felt such an attraction on first meeting someone before. Surely these aren't the kind of thoughts she's supposed to admit to the other girls?

'He seems nice,' she says finally.

'Nice?' one of them screeches with amusement. 'He's the hottest suitor they've ever had. We are very lucky ladies. Very lucky indeed.'

Bonnie is handed a glass of champagne by a waiter and she murmurs thanks, immediately second-guessing the connection she'd felt with Ty. Maybe he's the kind of guy who has that kind of power over every girl he meets.

'Are you all right?'

Bonnie turns her head and sees Darcy, the producer who had interviewed her at the auditions, clipboard in hand. Bonnie hadn't realised she'd backed herself against the wall.

'Do you need some water?' Her voice is full of concern.

Bonnie shakes her head. 'I'm okay. I think I am, anyway.'

Their attention turns to Nicole, the next girl who enters the room having just met Ty. 'He's gorgeous!' she announces, and the rest of the girls purr back in agreement.

Bonnie feels Darcy studying her. 'Just block them out. I know it's hard but just focus on you and Ty.'

Bonnie glances around the room. She knows Darcy's right, but she doubts her ability to ignore these loud, glitzy and attention-seeking girls.

'I shouldn't be telling you this,' Darcy says quietly, 'but I saw you and Ty on the monitor. There was something there. Trust me.' She squeezes Bonnie's hand and then moves away, glancing down at something on her clipboard.

Bonnie knows she has no reason to trust Darcy, but she does. Those few words are enough to give her the confidence she needs. She takes a sip of her champagne and joins a nearby group of girls.

There is something worth sticking around for.

14

'So, Ty, we've got to get rid of three tonight,' Darcy tells him as she guides Ty to a seat at the table where the photos of all twenty-two contestants have been spread out. 'Who do you want to send home?' They've just finished filming the first endearment party during which most girls drank their body weight in champagne. Hopefully some of them will sober up before the key ceremony.

'It's hard to know after only a few minutes.' He stares at the photos laid out before him. 'I can't remember everyone's names.' His eyes read over the contestants' names printed on the bottom of each one.

Darcy notices his eyes linger on Hayley's photograph. She changes tack. 'Have you got a top five?' It'd be good to know who he likes because she'll start scheduling in the single dates, planning out which girls are likely to stay around and who should be allocated extra screen time. Usually the suitor has a top five in mind but sometimes it takes a bit of prodding to get them to realise it.

'I have no idea,' he murmurs.

Darcy can tell he's overwhelmed. 'You definitely had a spark with a few.'

He looks up, relieved. 'Yeah, who with?'

Darcy goes to reach for the photos but then stops herself. 'Didn't *you* feel a spark with anyone?'

Ty doesn't say anything at first, which makes Darcy's heart pound. After all, these girls had been selected for the original suitor, not for Ty. Maybe none of them are his type of girl.

'Of course,' he eventually says. 'I'm just curious to hear what you thought.'

Darcy relaxes a little. He just wants a second opinion, which is fair. He's trying to find a wife.

'I only spoke to each of them for a couple of minutes, so how much can you really tell?'

Darcy thinks a lot can be said for a first meet with someone, but romantically speaking she's a novice—she's always been closed off to those kinds of feelings because of Drew. 'Did anyone give you goosebumps or tingles or make your heart skip a beat?'

Ty looks up. 'I've had those feelings before—the whole love at first sight thing.' He looks pained just thinking about it. 'Turns out you can't trust those feelings.'

This totally stumps Darcy. If he doesn't trust those feelings how on earth is he going to find his way through the massive journey ahead?

'Sorry, I know that's probably not what you want to hear.' He gives her a small smile before quickly averting his gaze back to the photographs.

'I know you only spoke to them briefly, but did you have anything in common with any of them? That might be a good place to start?'

Ty gives no indication that he's even heard what she's said.

'Did you feel annoyed that your time was cut short with anyone?'

Again, his eyes remain on the photographs.

Darcy finds her eyes falling on them too. She could easily point out five 'wifeys' that were specifically cast as legitimate love interests, but in previous seasons the suitor usually spotted them a mile away. Normally it's her job to insist that the catty girls are kept around for a few weeks and to kick off the dullest. But this feels very different from the previous seasons she's worked on.

'Ty?' she prods again. It's already been a long day and she knows there's a schedule they need to stick to.

He stands abruptly, his chair scraping across the floor. 'It's too much. I don't know.' He runs his hands through his hair then drags them down over his face. He turns away to the window. 'What if I choose the wrong person?'

Darcy's partly relieved to see him freaking out. Freaking out is heaps better than not caring at all and this kind of reaction is common. It's her job to stay composed, to make this very unusual situation feel *normal*. She channels her best calming voice. 'Ty, let me get you some water.' She moves to the fully stocked bar fridge and grabs a bottle from one of their sponsors. 'I'll sit down with you and we'll go through every girl, okay?'

At first he doesn't move, just stands still, almost like a statue, except his index finger scratches back and forth against his thumb.

Darcy's heart accelerates a little. All this silence feels like she's standing on the edge of a cliff. 'Ty?'

Finally he says, 'Okay.'

'What are they saying?' Darcy says, rushing into the office and plonking her stuff down on her desk after an unsatisfying amount of sleep. The first episode went to air last night less than twenty-four hours after it was filmed. Producing an episode of *The One* in such a short time is always chaotic, but Darcy has learned to thrive on the adrenaline.

Drew had missed most the show because of footy training but from what he saw he said it looked *tops*. After that phone call she'd messaged with friends for hours about what they thought of the new season and then she couldn't help but trawl the internet for articles as they were posted online. By the time she finally fell asleep it was almost time for her alarm to go off.

She flicks her computer on and while she waits for it to boot, leans over Mel's shoulder who is reading through *The One* forum to see what the latest comments are.

'Claire from Manly says Ty is the hottest suitor we've ever had,' Mel reads from the screen. 'But Olivia from Yass thinks he's too quiet and wishes he had a bit more of a public profile.'

Darcy can understand that. If Ty had a public profile there would be more articles for people to read, more photos shared across social media. As it is, there's hardly anything about Ty's past. He's just a normal guy who happened to know the right person and land himself the biggest gig in town.

Darcy still has plenty of reservations about him. He was so out of his depth choosing the first three girls to send home. She's worried how he's going to handle dumping girl after girl each week. He hasn't gone through all the psychological testing that Joe and the shortlist of suitors went through. Is he up for this after his own break-up?

Darcy's eyes glance down the screen. 'Annie from Forbes thought Imogen was hilarious and can't wait to see more of her.' She grabs her notepad and scrawls *Imogen*, making a note to give her plenty of screen time. Later today Darcy will be sitting with the editors as they put together the teaser to go at the end of tonight's episode, which is mostly pre-recorded packages about the girls, along with the arrival of the first group date card.

Mel laughs. 'She's not the only one who has something to say about Imogen.' She scrolls down the page. 'Look at the discussion going on about her.'

Darcy peers over Mel's shoulder again. It never surprises her how quickly the public get involved. Forums like this make audiences feel like they have some power over the outcome of a show, and to be honest it's true compared to a drama series. Producers definitely take notice of what viewers think of the 'characters' on a reality TV show. The reality of the suitor's love journey is always being manipulated.

'No one seems overly fussed about the girls who went home,' Mel says, still scrolling. 'A lot of them thought it was pretty ridiculous that Nicole cried so much.'

Darcy moves to her own computer and begins opening up her emails and looking at the amended schedule. 'Poor thing was exhausted. She said she hadn't slept properly in days.' Of course none of that made it into the final edit. Instead the viewers thought she was totally overreacting about being sent home. Darcy pulls out a notepad with scribbles, asterisks, ticks and crosses covering the page of the nineteen girls left. Very soon eighteen of them are going to be disappointed with the arrival of the first one-on-one date card.

Bonnie holds her mug of tea like some kind of security blanket. All the girls have been gathered together in one of the lounge rooms. Both the field producers, Darcy and Mel, are instructing crew. They've already filmed the part where Hayley rushed in, calling out to all the other girls that she'd 'found' a date card. They were told to scream with excitement, so much so that they had to do it three times 'to get it just right'.

Now they're just sitting and waiting. Bonnie looks around the large group. She's still a bit unsure on a couple of their names. Some of them look like they've just hung up their high school uniforms; they're so fresh and bouncy.

'Next time there's a date card, *I'll* read the clue out,' Imogen tells the group, stating it as a fact rather than a question.

Every time Imogen opens her mouth, Bonnie feels irritated by her. It's barely been thirty-six hours since they've been in the mansion and she's already hoping Imogen will be kicked off at the next key ceremony.

'That's not a problem is it, Bonnie?' Imogen is staring at her.

Bonnie realises she must have been glaring and shakes her head. 'Whatever you want to do.'

'Okay,' Darcy says, calling their attention. 'Hayley is going to read us the date clue first and then, Hayley, I want you to ask the group what they think the date could be.'

Hayley tosses her hair, eager for the spotlight. Bonnie exchanges a smile with Cassie, one of the girls she's actually had a decent conversation with. Cassie has a five-year-old son, who she's yet to tell Ty about. She's desperate for some one-on-one time so she can tell him without being interrupted.

'Then you can read whose name is on the card. Just make sure to take your time.'

'In other words, drag it out!' Kristy quips.

There's laughter among the group—they're already getting familiar with how everything works.

Darcy seems pleased they get the basic mechanics of the show. 'Exactly!' She looks around the group. 'Any questions?'

Bonnie wants to ask where Darcy got her blue top from, but figures that's not the type of question she's after right now.

'All right.' She glances to the crew, some with cameras, others with boom microphones, another holding a light reflector. 'Three ... two ... one ... action.'

Hayley pushes out her chest, clearly confident with all eyes on her. 'Okay, girls, I'll read the clue first.' Her voice is pitched unbearably high and Bonnie is half expecting her to burst out into cheer. Last night after a few drinks Hayley had happily done one of her cheer routines and then tried to teach some of the other girls the cheerleading moves. Bonnie had not been one of them.

Hayley reads the clue. 'Just you and me and the deep blue sea. Love Ty.' Her eyes widen. 'Oh, what do we think the date might be?'

Bonnie has to admire Hayley's ease with this. She's smooth and energetic. She could pass as a host.

'Deep sea diving?' someone calls out.

'A boat trip?'

'Secluded beach?'

And just like that, Bonnie is transformed back to a time when it was just her and Ollie. Years ago, the summer holidays after they finished school. They hadn't known what universities they'd gotten into yet, so the future was a happy haze of opportunity.

They'd driven up the coast, stopping whenever they felt like it. Oliver would surf, she'd take photographs, they'd skinny dip and make little bonfires on the sand. One day they'd found a secluded beach and hadn't even bothered setting up the tent, instead making a makeshift bed on the sand so they could watch the stars all night.

'Could you live here forever, just the two of us?' he asked her that night after they made love.

Bonnie remembers smiling at him. The notion that he could was obvious, but she still had a yearning in her heart. 'What would we do for food?' she asked, deciding to hide behind the practicalities of his suggestion.

'Well, if food and money didn't matter.'

Bonnie hadn't been able to answer straight away. She loved Ollie, she wanted to be with him and only him. But, there was still a *but*. She still wanted so much more out of her life. She wanted to travel and study and build a photography business. So, the answer was no, but how was she supposed to say that?

'Your silence says it all,' he said.

'Oh, Ollie, don't take it like that.'

But he had. He'd spent the next day sulking too.

Maybe if she had told him she wanted him by her side for all the things she was dreaming for in life, things would have been different. Maybe they wouldn't have broken up. Maybe he wouldn't have thrown himself into another relationship only weeks after they'd ended things. Maybe he wouldn't have married Amy after only one short year of knowing her. Maybe he and Bonnie would have run into Sophie Nix and gone home laughing at how much she'd flirted with Ollie. Maybe Bonnie would have felt smug, knowing that he was hers.

Maybe she never would have come on this show.

'Bonnie?'

Suddenly she's back in the lounge room of *The One* mansion and everyone is staring at her.

'What do you think?'

'You got the first one-on-one!' a voice shrieks at her.

'What?' she murmurs.

There's so much noise and commotion it hurts Bonnie's ears.

'How do you feel?' Hayley asks.

'She looks like she's in shock.'

Every single person in the room is waiting to see her excitement about getting the first date with Ty. Cassie's fixed a smile on her face, but disappointment clouds her eyes. It's now Imogen's turn to glare at her. Bonnie should be ecstatic, she should be grinning like the Cheshire cat instead of having pounding thoughts to back when she was eighteen, wishing she'd taken a different path.

Only one word springs to mind: 'Speechless.'

15

Penelope lets the water from the shower rush over her, washing away the chlorine. Before she moved from the city she'd easily been able to swim thirty laps of the pool, but today she struggled to do half that. She can't help but feel frustrated and disappointed in her body.

She wraps a towel around herself and moves into the change room. Two women are slipping out of their work clothes and tugging on gym gear.

'I loved Imogen,' one of them says, 'but he's never going to choose her.'

'I couldn't stand her.' The other shakes her head. 'All that drama about wearing the same dress as Addison.'

Penelope wants to sigh. They're talking about *The One*.

'I thought maybe the cheerleader had a chance?'

'Oh yeah, what was her name?'

Both of the women consider, trying to remember.

The cheerleader's name had been Hayley, but Penelope keeps her gaze down, pulling on her clothes.

'I liked Kristy too.'

The other agrees. 'Smart move bringing him food.'

'The key to any guy's heart is through the stomach.' The first laughs. 'But I think Bonnie is in with a chance.'

Penelope feels a little lightheaded. She closes her eyes, trying to ignore the stench of chlorine still on her skin. She'll have another shower when she gets home. She tells herself to finish getting dressed so she can get out of the overheated gym centre.

'That tall blonde one represented Australia in something, didn't she?' The woman's loud voice booms.

'Was it hockey?'

Basketball. It had been basketball.

'Excuse me,' one of the women calls to her. 'Did you watch *The One* last night?'

Their faces are bright, eager to solve the mystery of what sport Samara played. 'No, sorry, I didn't.' Penelope turns away, quickly grabbing her belongings before she's forced into a conversation she really doesn't want to be a part of.

16

'How is someone like you single?' Ty asks, his face warm. They're sitting on a two-seater lounge on a headland, facing the ocean as day becomes night.

Bonnie has no idea how she managed to score the first single date, but today has been something out of a fairytale. Ty had picked her up in a helicopter. They'd flown up the coast and then caught a private boat to go whale watching. Whales had breached right in front of them, dolphins had swum beside the boat and Ty had stood close, his hand resting on the small of her back. For most of the day things have felt quite natural between them. She doesn't feel entirely comfortable or even herself, but who could with a crew and cameras watching their every move?

'Timing, I guess.' She shrugs. 'There have been guys,' she admits, 'but the timing hasn't been right.' She isn't sure if that's completely accurate; the timing with Oliver hadn't been right, but with Dan,

Isaiah and Liam she just hadn't been the right girl for them. But for some reason she doesn't feel confident enough to tell Ty that all her ex-boyfriends married the girl they dated after her. It would only be natural to wonder what was wrong with her.

He takes in her answer, carefully analysing her words. 'So, you've been in love before?'

It's her turn to consider his words. She doesn't want to blurt out yes, even though that would be her answer. She's finding it hard to relax—every question feels like she's being judged. Thinking about him leaving their date and rating her, putting her somewhere on the leaderboard, sends a panic through her bloodstream.

'It's okay if the answer's yes,' he says, seeming to sense her anxiety. 'We all have past relationships.' He reaches out and takes her hand. It's all she needs, his touch is like a relaxant, reassuring her to just be herself.

'Yes, I've been in love before,' she tells him. 'Four relationships in fifteen years.' She gives him the smallest of smiles, her lips closed. 'And I've found myself heartbroken after every single one.' A chill rushes over her at hearing herself say the words aloud.

Something flickers in Ty's face and she knows in that instant that he's experienced heartbreak too. 'It's a horrible feeling.'

⁊

Darcy feels a bit uncomfortable watching them talk about heartbreak. All day they'd had light banter and there's plenty of footage to make them seem flirtier than they were. Darcy had actually suggested they tackle some more serious topics for the evening part of the date.

She stares through the monitor at Ty and Bonnie. Darcy has to admire the art department's ability to create romance. In the background fairy lights twinkle, candles flicker, rose petals have been sprinkled on the grass. It looks magical, a setting ready for this couple to start falling in love, not for them to be reliving relationships past. But then again, maybe they're bonding over this heartache. Darcy's unsure whether she should redirect the conversation to something else. They're always briefed on what should and shouldn't be discussed, but here in the moment it's harder to categorise.

Bonnie's hands twist in her lap. Darcy can tell she feels awkward talking about her previous relationships. Darcy wonders what types of guys she's dated before. She's taken an immediate liking to Bonnie, who seems somewhat like a fish out of water in *The One* mansion.

'Sometimes it's hard to know if you'll ever recover,' Bonnie murmurs, glancing up to the hero of the show, her face wearing the pain of heartache.

'Cut!' Darcy calls, fearful Bonnie's about to burst into tears. She approaches, trying to sound casual about the situation. 'I think you've gotten a bit off track?' It's too early in the season for them to get into heavy relationship history. This kind of conversation is best saved for the final weeks.

They look at her, wide-eyed and open-mouthed. 'Sorry,' Ty says. 'I thought you wanted serious stuff?'

Bonnie looks like she's gotten into trouble from a teacher.

Darcy feels guilty for interrupting but knows they're wasting precious shooting time talking about something that Alice won't want aired. 'How about you talk about ...' She pauses, realising she should have figured out what direction she wanted them to take before interrupting them. 'Everything happening for a reason,' she says, thinking on her feet, but immediately pleased.

Bonnie and Ty both appear to have lost a bit of momentum at having their 'scene' interrupted.

'Maybe you could go in for a kiss?' Darcy suggests lightly. Four seasons in and she still can't believe her job entails suggesting people kiss. A kiss on the first one-on-one date would set the bar high. Alice might even be mildly impressed. Darcy had stressed to Mel how important physical contact is, to always encourage Ty to sit as close as possible to the girls. 'Create intimacy!' Alice barks whenever giving date instructions.

'A kiss?' Bonnie echoes.

'You've got a connection. It's so clear on screen,' Darcy tells them, pointing to the monitor, knowing they need a push. There's already a fair bit of support for Bonnie online, mostly due to the way the editors put together their 'meet'. A bit of a slow-motion walk, a dip of charged silence before a surge of romantic music. A kiss on the first date will probably make her a fan favourite.

'It'll only be broadcast across national television.' Ty's clearly nervous himself.

'Not nerve-racking at all,' Bonnie jokes.

Darcy needs to keep things moving. If they think about it too much they'll chicken out. 'Are you ready to roll again?' She's been pleasantly surprised with how Ty appears on camera, much better than what she'd been expecting when she first met him.

'Okay,' Ty says, looking to Bonnie for her opinion. She manages a small nod.

'Great!' Darcy says, desperately hoping they're going to smooth over the conversation so it can be edited into something decent. She nods to Ben behind the camera. 'Three, two, one ...'

'Action!'

Bonnie tries not to feel suffocated by aching memories of previous relationships. Darcy stares at her, waiting for her to say something. What had she wanted them to do again?

'It's all in the past now.' Ty's voice pulls her back to him.

Bonnie pushes away thoughts of Darcy and the camera crew, turning her attention back to Ty. 'And everything happens for a reason.' She tries to sound light, but in all honesty she doesn't even know whether she believes that and from the look on Ty's face he's not sure either.

'Well, I guess we wouldn't be here right now.' He moves a strand of her hair, tucking it behind her ear. 'And today has been pretty amazing.'

Bonnie nods. 'It has.' Her mouth is dry with anticipation.

'I'm really excited about getting to know you more.'

Bonnie notices he's got beads of sweat on his temple that weren't there a few moments ago. She's comforted to see he's nervous too. 'I feel the same way,' she tells him. 'I didn't expect to be …' She stops, trying to figure out exactly what she wants to say. 'So taken by you this early on.'

A smile creases his face. 'I couldn't have said it better myself.' He leans forward, his eyes locked on hers.

She's jittery as she leans forward to meet him. Their lips touch and she almost takes a sideways glance at Darcy and the rest of the crew who are only metres away, watching, staring, leering. The cameras are so big, and all are pointed directly at them. The spotlight makes Bonnie's insides swirl, so much that she forgets she's kissing Ty. She's going to be on national television kissing a guy! And she hasn't even paid attention to the actual kiss. He pulls back slowly and her fingertips immediately touch her lips, trying to grab hold of the sensation before it floats away.

Darcy almost screams with delight. They're kissing! This will be great for ratings! She wants to high-five herself. She's always felt a bit uncomfortable 'directing' that kind of thing, but she pulled it off easily this time. And they're still kissing! She looks at Ben, who is filming the whole thing. He glances back and raises his eyebrows. He knows Darcy's very pleased with herself.

She watches Ty and Bonnie again and admires how good they look together. Maybe this kind of show can actually work.

She feels her phone vibrate in her pocket and quickly checks the message in case it's from the office. They'll be hassling her to send some footage in to make a teaser to go at the end of tonight's episode. But it's from Drew.

Okay, you win. I'll come down Friday after work. Can't wait to see you.

Darcy smiles, immediately excited. She'd sent him a photo of herself naked this morning as an incentive for him to come down for the weekend. It's going to be the first time they've seen each other since he left. She forgot how working on this show makes you crave romance. She might just throw Drew a little surprise to kick off their weekend just right …

Bonnie feels her face warming as she processes what she's just done. Ty smiles at her, but he looks just as shell-shocked by the experience.

'Cut!' Darcy calls, approaching as she slides her mobile into the back pocket of her jeans. Bonnie can hear the happiness in her voice. 'That was great! We need to wrap soon but we're just going to get one more shot,' she tells them, pointing to the setting sun. 'I'm going to get Ben to film you holding hands.'

'And gazing into each other's eyes?' Ty asks good-naturedly.

'Well …' Darcy says, 'if you don't mind?'

Bonnie's heart feels like it's beating irregularly. This whole setting is causing her more stress than she's felt in years, but then an image of Oliver and Sophie comes spiralling into her mind and she's quickly reminded of the anxiety she'd felt only a week ago.

'What do you say?' Ty says, looking to her. 'Are you up for a bit of hand holding?'

'I could be convinced,' she tells him.

And so he takes her hand and gives it a little squeeze. It's enough to make Bonnie wish she could have met this guy in the outside world.

'What do I say if the other girls ask whether I kissed him?'

Darcy studies Bonnie's face for a moment. Her producer instinct tells her that she should encourage Bonnie to tell the truth. On previous seasons it's created some great jealousy when a girl reveals she snagged the first kiss with the suitor. Darcy would like to get some footage of that this season too, but Bonnie looks so vulnerable that she can't bring herself to 'produce' as normal. 'If you don't feel comfortable telling them, just lie,' Darcy tells her. 'Sometimes the girls get nasty and they're already jealous you got the first date.' They have some brilliant footage of Imogen scowling when Bonnie's name was read out on the date card.

Bonnie visibly gulps.

'So, was he a good kisser?' Darcy can't help herself. She'd already asked her during the date interview, but Darcy wants an honest, off camera response.

'I have no idea.' She shakes her head at herself. 'I was too caught up thinking about kissing on camera.'

'Oh no!' Darcy laughs with a sympathetic smile.

'I hope it gets easier for me to switch the cameras off.'

'It will,' Darcy reassures her. 'Each day will get easier and soon you won't even notice the cameras.' She isn't sure if that's completely accurate; some contestants constantly look at the camera and so far Bonnie is one of them. Alice hates it, so it's an editing nightmare. Darcy wants Bonnie to at least try to forget them for future dates.

'I hope so.'

Darcy had imagined Bonnie would be on top of the world after a date like that, but watching her now, she looks nothing but stressed. 'Do you like him?'

Bonnie considers before rushing to answer. 'I think so, it's just so easy to doubt everything here.' She indicates around to the artificial setting.

Darcy pulls her producer hat firmly down onto her head. 'Trust your feelings, Bonnie. There's a spark between you and Ty. We can all feel it.' Darcy really needs Bonnie to believe that.

'So, your first big kiss with Mr Nine, hey?'

Bonnie turns to see Ben, the camera guy. She's supposed to be heading to the car to be driven back to the mansion, but she stops to talk to him.

'Yeah …' She draws out the word. 'Still can't believe I actually did that.' Somehow she feels like she watched someone else kiss Ty, rather than being the heroine of a love scene herself.

'You mean with the millions of viewers watching at home?'

That hadn't been her main concern, but she's suddenly swamped with thoughts of everyone she's ever met watching her make out on national television. How many of them would be judging her for kissing Ty already? 'Don't remind me.'

'Hey, you landed the first kiss, don't look so stressed. You're the cat that got the cream.'

'My head is playing games with me, but it's been a day to remember, that's for sure.'

'I guess it's lucky you got out of the limo then?'

'I have you to thank for that.'

Ben looks at her steadily before shrugging. 'I'll have to tell the bosses they need to pay me more.'

❧

Darcy is watching Ben and Bonnie chat, and makes a note that they need to capture more footage of Bonnie being natural like she is now. She moves in an unguarded way, her smile bigger than it is with the cameras on her. Darcy's phone buzzes with a call from Ed.

'Hey,' she says into her mobile.

'Hey,' Ed says. 'Still at work?'

'Just finishing up the first one-on-one date.'

'Oh yeah? Pulling out some rose petals and candles?'

Darcy laughs. 'Yep, the art department are all over that.' She watches as some of the crew pack away the props. There's a whole large box just for the candles.

'Just checking in, but wanted to say great casting with Imogen. She's going to set your ratings on fire.'

Darcy's immediately warmed. 'You've been watching?'

He scoffs. 'Of course I'm watching!'

'I like Bonnie,' Darcy admits. She'd been the one to push for Bonnie to get the first one-on-one date.

'Yeah—there was some good editing when she came on the screen. Music dipping, slow motion. Pure gold.'

'I'll tell the editors you approve.' Darcy starts shoving her drink bottle and notepad back into her bag.

'How's Drew going?'

She thinks back to her phone conversation with him last night. 'He's ridiculously happy.' Drew wanted to tell her everything—all the people he'd seen, that it had taken him an hour to get some milk at the supermarket because he kept running into people he knew.

'Back home in Kansas, hey?'

'Like you wouldn't believe.' It terrifies her how much he loves it back there.

'Don't worry, Darce. He'll be back.'

'I know.' She feels a bit silly but working on a show about love feels harder with him being away. 'He just messaged to say he'll be down on the weekend, so we'll call around for a drink.'

'Sounds good,' Ed says. 'I'll let you go, but keep your chin up, yeah?'

'I'll be fine,' she tells him. 'Honestly, there's so much stuff going on here that it'll be Friday night before I blink.'

17

'Shit, Darce. You're not about to propose to me, are you?'

The lounge room glows with candlelight, red roses fill tall vases on every surface and soft music hums in the background.

Darcy stands a little straighter, the muscles in her neck tightening. 'Would that really be such a bad thing?' She'd been so excited about surprising him with a romantic scene, inspired after Ty's string of romantic first week dates.

'Of course not,' Drew says, taking a few more steps inside the apartment. 'I just kind of assumed the proposal would be my job.'

'Job?' He may as well have said *chore*. This was not how she imagined their reunion would be going after several weeks apart.

'I didn't mean it like that.'

'How else am I supposed to take it?' They've been together for ten years and there's still no ring on her finger.

He dumps his overnight bag on the table, precariously close to a vase of roses. 'So, this is just a subtle hint?'

'Come off it.' She takes his bag from the table and makes a display of taking it the three extra steps to dump in their bedroom. Okay, so she might have made some very direct hints about the type of engagement ring she'd like over the years, but she hadn't mentioned marriage in over a year. 'You made it very clear how you feel.'

'Don't be like that,' Drew says, clearly annoyed they're going through old territory. 'I want to buy our own place first. Be set up, like our parents were.'

Darcy fiercely stares him down. 'I'll be in the grave before we can afford to buy here.' Stuff his stupid old-fashioned ideals.

'There's decent stuff on the market back home,' Drew says. 'We could buy a huge block out there for less than a unit in this city.'

Darcy suppresses a roll of her eyes. Not this again. 'And I'll what, get a job in regional television? We've discussed this, Drew. Sydney owns me.'

He gives her a resigned shrug and ruffles his hair in the same familiar way he's done since primary school. He knows the script to this argument by heart now, too. Nothing has changed. Their disagreement still stands true. 'It'll happen, Darce. We'll get there.' His light brown eyes plead with her to soften.

She knows he wants to marry her so lets her frown uncurl. 'Just so you know, this isn't the kind of thing I want.' Darcy refers to the room, feeling she needs to point that out, just in case he decides to file the scene away to recreate one day in the faraway future. She doesn't need an over-the-top romantic gesture. A walk along the beach or dinner at their favourite restaurant or a Saturday afternoon picnic with a bottle of wine would all work quite perfectly … not that she's given it all that much thought.

He sits down on the lounge. 'So what is all this about then?' He gestures to the candles and flowers.

She watches as he kicks off his shoes, pushing them under the coffee table where they'll stay until he leaves again on Sunday afternoon unless she moves them to the shoe stand at the front door. He looks up at her as he stretches his legs out in front of him. He rubs his calf muscle, his hands moving back and forth. She loves those hands; her own fit perfectly inside them. They go to sleep holding hands, and during summer, when it's too hot, their pinkies touch instead. It's only been a couple of weeks but she's missed having him in their bed. It's lonely without him. Warmth swells in her belly, contentment and longing mixing together. She doesn't want to be cranky, so decides to start over. 'I thought it'd be a nice surprise after we didn't get our weekend in the Hunter Valley.'

Drew throws an unimpressed look around their small flat. 'Really? You thought I'd like this?'

Darcy bristles. 'What's wrong with creating a bit of romance?'

Drew laughs. 'You've been on that show for too long. Red roses and candles don't equal romance.'

And just like that the warmth cools. 'Forget about it.' She moves to the closest candle and blows it out.

'Darcy,' Drew objects.

'What?' She screws up her face. 'You just said you didn't like them.'

Drew sighs, pushing up off the lounge and moving to the kitchen. He switches on a light, the candles dimming in protest. As he reaches to open the fridge he notices a bruise on his arm and pauses to examine his latest footy injury. Darcy feels like she's the last thing on his mind. He bends down to peer into the fridge, but after inspection, pushes it shut again.

'I haven't had time to do the groceries,' Darcy offers as something of an apology, but her tone is defensive.

Drew leans against the bench. 'Parko asked if I could help out with the school fete next Saturday.'

And suddenly she realises why he decided to come down this weekend. 'But that's my birthday, Drew. You were going to come down here.'

'It's not like I can say no—he's my boss.'

'So we won't see each other on my birthday?'

'I thought maybe you could drive up.'

'I don't want to spend half the day driving up there.' Their long-distance relationship officially sucks.

'If you leave really early, you'd be able to get there for most of the day.'

'Happy birthday to me,' she murmurs a little sarcastically. The last thing she wants to do is set the alarm for five in the morning and drive by herself in the car for four hours. She can't drive up on Friday night because she's scheduled to work at the endearment party and the following key ceremony. She probably won't get home until midnight.

'Oh, come on.' Drew's voice is soft, his eyes imploring. 'You always love the fete.' The school fete has been going every year since she can remember, often falling on her birthday weekend. It was probably the biggest social event of the year in Gloucester.

She did always love the fete, but she was turning twenty-six and had been hoping they could have a grown-up celebration in the city. 'I've already mentioned dinner and drinks to Ed and Sienna.'

'They'll understand.'

Of course they'd understand, but that isn't the point.

He opens the fridge again, dropping the conversation for the time being. 'Have we got any beers?'

'They were taking up too much room in the fridge so I put them in the cupboard.'

He exhales loudly at this. 'Taking up room? There's nothing in here.'

Her eyes narrow, an icy expression attempting to freeze not only her face but the entire room.

Drew gauges her reaction and offers an olive branch. 'You hungry?'

She doesn't bother trying to hide her dampened mood. 'I could eat.'

'Come on.' He tries to bolster her, finally moving to place his hands on her shoulders. 'We're going to have a good weekend together. Don't crack it on me.'

Darcy feels her mouth twisting—plenty of choice words want to come out but she doesn't let them. She doesn't know if she's got enough energy for a fight.

'Let's go grab some takeaway.'

So instead of saying anything she just gives a little nod. She can see he's trying to make an effort. But these days it seems to be nothing but an effort. 'I'll get my bag.'

In the bedroom, she blows out the candles and dumps the rose petals she'd sprinkled on the bed into the bin. Romance is clearly not on the cards.

⁂

It's late at night and Bonnie can't sleep. Her days in the house are long and boring. Most afternoons they end up drinking around the pool. Today there had been a cat fight about Imogen interrupting Addison's one-on-one time with Ty on the group date they'd been on earlier. It was like being back at high school again.

Bonnie had told herself not to get involved. For a long while she sat quietly as the bickering escalated between the two girls. But they were acting like toddlers fighting over a toy … and Bonnie simply couldn't hold her tongue any longer. 'There's no point in arguing,' Bonnie interrupted. 'I'm sure everyone will get time with Ty.'

Both Imogen and Addison had stared at her with horrified expressions.

'What's it got to do with you?' Imogen hissed, rearing up like a rattlesnake. 'Sitting pretty over there on your pedestal after already having a one-on-one date with him?'

Bonnie's single date with Ty already feels like a long time ago, despite it only being a matter of days. She'd told the rest of the girls the basics. Helicopter, whale watching, picnic at sunset. No details of the kiss or even the hand-holding despite the girls' incessant questions.

'I just think it'd be better if we all try to get along. We could have weeks inside this house together.' Bonnie had ignored Imogen's attack, instead gently trying to remind them that they were like cell mates in here.

But by this point she'd already made an enemy out of Imogen. 'Sounds like you're pretty confident that you're going to be sticking around then?' Imogen snarled. 'Goes to show how important one-on-one time is.' Imogen bolstered, clearly feeling validated in interrupting Addison's time with Ty in the first place.

Bonnie sighed at this. She had crossed the trenches and there was no return from the battlefield. Carla had warned her to keep a low profile and not make any rivals, but with cameras looming, she knew without a doubt that her 'advice' to Imogen would resemble something much more interfering.

Bonnie tosses in bed, still unable to sleep, and thinks that perhaps Imogen is right, perhaps Bonnie does already have an advantage, but she can't quite figure out if that's a good thing. She could like Ty, she really could, but her mind keeps going back to Oliver and how she'd felt when she'd first seen him again a month or so ago. At the time, she'd been completely unaware that Carla had sent in an application for her to be a contestant on *The One*. Instead, her biggest decision had come down to what flavour of ice-cream she was going to have. Bonnie's hand had been resting on the freezer handle, deciding between salted caramel or cookies and cream, when she heard, 'Bonnie!'

Bonnie turned to see Sophie Nix rushing towards her. Caught red-handed, Bonnie's hand dropped back down to her side.

Sophie opened her arms wide. 'I knew it wouldn't be too long until I ran into you.'

Bonnie wished it'd been longer. 'I heard you guys were moving back.' She tried to sound as chirpy as possible.

'We've done the Sydney thing. It's time to settle down, you know …' Sophie leaned forward to whisper, 'to have some babies.'

Bonnie almost choked on her own breath. Hadn't they been together for like two seconds?

'I hope it's not weird,' Sophie said, her face full of pity. 'You know—with me and Ollie together.'

'Of course not.' Bonnie had shaken her head like it was a stupid suggestion, but her heart twinged at hearing Sophie call him *Ollie*. Years before, Bonnie had called him Ollie. Admittedly lots of people had, but still, it stung hearing Sophie say it with a sense of ownership. 'Oliver and I dated a long time ago.' A very long time ago, but somehow she felt more uncomfortable and jealous of Oliver being with Sophie than she had of him being married to Amy for all those years. Judging Sophie on who she was at high school wasn't fair, but Oliver had known that Sophie too, and now he was with her?

'Oh, goody, that's such a relief.'

Bonnie smiled tightly and reminded herself to breathe through their conversation. 'Oliver, how is he?' Bonnie hadn't seen him in years, but his face filled her mind as though she saw him every day.

'Oh, he's great. He's such a sweetheart.'

Sophie's smile made Bonnie want to throw up.

'Here he is now.'

Bonnie turned and saw Oliver walking up the aisle, his stride faltering for the slightest second at seeing her. But then he smiled, and she'd momentarily been taken back to being seventeen, spending long summer afternoons at the beach with him. Lazing on a towel, their bodies intertwined, eyes gazing, lips touching, a constant desire for more …

She tried to swallow before speaking, but still her voice had squeaked, 'Hi.'

Oliver went in for a big hug. 'Good to see you, Bon.'

Bonnie felt a little awkward in front of Sophie but allowed herself to be swept up in his arms for a second.

He'd aged, and even though Bonnie had wanted to take her time to take in his features, she forced herself to look away.

'Did you hear we're getting married?' Sophie had taken a step closer to Oliver, linking her arm through his.

'Yes,' Bonnie had said steadily, probably one thousand times calmer than she'd been when she first heard the news. She had felt Oliver's eyes on her and wondered whether he was noticing the lines around her eyes or her grey hairs starting to show. 'Congratulations.'

'Check out my rock,' Sophie said, thrusting out her left hand for Bonnie to see her engagement ring.

Bonnie noticed Oliver grimace, and this offered her some comfort in such an awkward moment.

'It's beautiful.' Bonnie's voice was soft as her eyes almost glazed over at the large square-cut diamond.

Sophie had watched her, analysing her reaction. Bonnie felt sick.

'We better get going,' Oliver had said.

'So good seeing you.' Sophie smiled.

Bonnie had returned a look that was as close as she could manage to a smile while not looking at either of them directly.

They'd said goodbye, Sophie grabbing Oliver's hand as they walked away. Oliver glanced over his shoulder and mouthed, 'Sorry.'

She was sorry too. Sorry all her feelings for him had come rushing back the moment she laid eyes on him.

It wasn't until she was driving out of the supermarket car park that she realised she hadn't got any ice-cream.

18

Ten months earlier

'Are you going to tell me anything about it?' he asks, his eyes hopeful as he looks up from the veggies he's cutting.

Penelope shakes her head. 'Just that it's the one,' she tells him, stealing a piece of carrot.

'Hey.' He shoos her hand away. 'I thought I was the one?'

Penelope laughs, her head light, the adrenaline of buying her wedding dress making her happier than she ever thought an article of clothing could make her.

'How am I supposed to know what kind of suit to choose if I don't know anything about your dress?'

'Trust me, any suit will look incredible with this dress.' She'd known it was the one before she even tried it on. The moment her fingers touched the material, her stomach had surged and her heart had pounded fast. It had been wedged between other dresses, a hidden treasure just waiting for her to find it.

'Even a bright orange suede one?'

She knows he's teasing her and isn't going to take the bait. 'Sure, if that's what you want.' But he's a navy suit guy at his most extreme and they both know it.

She moves to the stovetop and flips the chicken pieces. She can't help but feel a little amused. 'I thought men weren't supposed to care about this kind of thing?'

'I know,' he answers honestly. 'There's something wrong with me.'

Penelope wipes her hands on a tea towel and moves to him, wrapping her arms around his broad shoulders. 'Trust me, there's nothing at all wrong with you.'

He turns, letting their lips meet, but still sulks as he draws her to him. 'I guess I just don't like there being secrets between us.'

'Aww, that's so sweet.'

For a second his face looks hopeful that she might change her mind.

She laughs, stepping back. 'But I'm still not telling you. It's bad luck, don't you know?'

19

Darcy finds herself spending her twenty-sixth birthday driving north along the Pacific Highway before turning off onto The Bucketts Way.

Drew greets her, grinning widely as he opens her car door. 'Parko offered me a full-time position to the end of the year.'

She can tell he's been bursting to tell her, so much so that he's forgotten to wish her a happy birthday.

She wants to say something but needs more coffee. The key ceremony ran late last night. Another two girls were sent home but not before hours' worth of alcohol, tears and bitchiness. She and Mel had been run off their feet with the amount of drama going on. She hopes Alice will be happy with what they managed to get the girls to say in their interviews and what the guys had captured on camera. She'd almost cried when her alarm had gone off this morning. She'd snoozed it three times before dragging herself from under the doona. Her phone had buzzed on and off the entire trip with texts and phone calls wishing her a happy birthday. Now she wishes she were out for breakfast at the cafe down the road from their unit in Sydney. Coffee, omelette, more coffee. That would make her pretty happy right now.

Instead she's here, parked on Ravenshaw Street near Gloucester High School. There's been a cold snap and the wind is whipping hard off Barrington Tops. Despite the weather, the fete is busy, the smell of the Lions Club sausage sizzle wafting through the air. She can see market stalls have been set up on the basketball courts and footy field. There's going to be lots of people she knows, lots of people she's going to have to make small talk with.

'Darce?' Drew says, still waiting for her reaction. 'Did you hear me?' His grin has only slightly faltered. He's hoping she'll be happy about it.

But she's not happy.

'Drew, it's only March,' she points out, feeling slightly bad she hasn't congratulated him on a job well done. He's clearly impressed them if they've offered him a teaching position until the end of the year. But still, her escalating nerves win out. 'I agreed to ten weeks long distance, not ten months!'

His face falls. 'I thought you'd be happy for me.'

'How can I be happy if you're going to be living four hours away? How are we going to make that work?'

Drew goes to say something but then stops, smiling hello to a couple walking past. Darcy can't bring herself to look at whoever it is. She doesn't want to be having an argument on the street. What was he thinking dumping the news on her here?

'You've only got a couple of months left on *The One*,' he says. 'After that we could pack up our unit in Sydney and you could come back here.'

'Come back here?' she echoes incredulously, as though he's suggesting checking herself into jail.

'I was dying in Sydney, Darce. I want to be here.' He looks more vulnerable than she's seen him in a long time. 'Don't you miss it?' He indicates the surroundings, showing off his paradise. The rolling green hills, the steel-blue mountains, the quaint small town.

No, she doesn't miss it. He knows how she feels.

'Think about it, we could live with our parents, save a heap of cash and have enough money for a house deposit after a year.'

Move back in with her parents? No thank you. And buying a place back here? Just the thought of living back in Gloucester makes her throat feel like it's closing over.

'What would I do for work back here?' she asks, only one of a thousand questions thumping through her head.

'Mum said she could get you some work at the post office.'

He's actually thought about it. He's thought this whole thing through. He's spoken to his mum.

Darcy's skin starts to itch. 'No.'

Drew pauses, derailed for only a moment. 'Or maybe we could talk to Mrs Winters about you doing some media studies classes at the school?'

He's suggesting she become a teacher? 'No.'

'Hi, Mr Roberts!' a voice calls out.

Drew turns, waving hello to a bunch of giggling teenage girls who quickly approach. Darcy watches as he shares a few exchanges with them before they move off.

'Drew, I work in TV. I can't live here.' They've had this conversation before. His features distort behind a watery haze. 'I can't do this right now.' Darcy pulls her cardigan a little tighter around her. 'I'm going to Mum's. I'll see you later.'

'You don't want to come in?' He gestures to the fete.

'I'm not in the mood.'

He's about to accept this and let her go but then suddenly says, 'Your birthday!' He's a bit panicked that he'd forgotten. 'Sorry, honey. Happy birthday!' He moves closer, wrapping her in a hug.

'Thanks.' Her voice is barely audible.

'I really am sorry, Darce. I just got excited. Parko told me just before you arrived. I thought it was good news.'

She can't find any words. It was in fact the opposite of good news.

His face brightens. 'I'll see you tonight for your birthday dinner?'

'Yeah, sure.' She shrugs. She'd gotten up at dawn to drive here and spend the day with him, but that didn't seem to matter anymore.

He leans in and gives her a little kiss. Putting a smile on her face requires more effort than pulling on her skinny jeans. It certainly doesn't feel like her birthday.

'You look amazing.'

Darcy spins around. Drew is standing at the doorway to her old bedroom. He's wearing a serious expression and Darcy can't help but feel a little nervous after how they ended things earlier. She spent the day trying to hold off tears that were only a blink away. Her mum knows something is up but hasn't pushed her.

'Thank you.' She smooths over her floral wrap dress that she splurged on last weekend. She's going to be too dressed up for the pub, but it's her birthday and she wants to look better than she feels.

'I thought we were meeting you there?' Darcy glances at the clock on the dresser. Their reservation is still half an hour away.

'I wanted to see you.' He moves closer, taking her hand. 'I'm sorry about this morning.'

She braces herself, waiting for his speech, wondering what tactic he'll use to try and convince her that they should move back here.

'I won't take the job,' he says, his light brown eyes staring into hers. 'I'll come back to Sydney after this term finishes, just like we planned.'

Darcy shifts, unable to let herself smile just yet. She's surprised he's given up so easily. It's unlike him. 'Really?'

He nods. 'I want to be with you, Darce. If you don't think we can make it work if I stay here, then I'll come back to Sydney.'

Darcy suddenly feels awful. 'I don't want to give you an ultimatum.'

'I know, but like you said, there's no work for you back here.' He gives a small smile. She can tell he's more resigned than excited about his decision.

'Are you sure you're going to be okay back there?' After all, he had told her he was drowning in Sydney.

'Of course.' He squeezes her hand. 'I'll be with you.' He leans in and gives her a kiss.

He's just said everything she wanted to hear. She should be soaring but instead a dull flatness moves through her body.

On the way to the pub, Drew doesn't stop talking about the fete. He gives her a detailed account of who won each prize at the school raffle. Darcy tries to concentrate on his words, but her mind keeps drifting back to Sydney, back to the weekend she would be having if she'd stayed there. She'd probably be having drinks with Ed and Sienna about now …

'You all right?' He pulls up and turns the engine off.

'Just tired.' She leans the side of her head against the backrest of the seat. 'Maybe we could just get some takeaway? Mum and Dad wouldn't mind.' Her parents were meeting them for dinner but had left earlier, her mum trying to give them extra alone time.

'It's your birthday. We're not getting takeaway! Come on, once you're inside you'll feel better.' Drew ushers her from the car. He squeezes her hand as though their earlier fight had been forgotten. And maybe it should be, but Darcy can't seem to let it go.

They walk into the pub and Darcy goes towards the bar, assuming they'll order a drink before dinner, but Drew gently pulls her hand. 'This way.'

'Let's get a drink first.' She really needs one.

But Drew doesn't let go of her hand. His stride lengthens and Darcy, wearing high heels, quickens her pace to keep up. Drew pushes open the door into the back room. It's pitch black. The restaurant seems to be closed. Darcy's about to ask whether he bothered making a reservation when—

'SURPRISE!'

At the chorus of 'Happy Birthday', someone switches the lights on. They seem harshly bright as Darcy tries to focus on the faces in front of her. Her parents, Drew's mum, her brother and sister-in-law, some cousins, school friends, people she used to work with at the supermarket when she was at school. They're all smiling, waiting for her reaction.

Her reaction. She suddenly pays attention to the horrified panic she's feeling and realises her facial expression is probably showing just that. She quickly fixes her face into a smile, trying to dig deep for a mask of delight. 'Wow!'

'Did you have any idea?' Drew is giddy, he can't keep his body still, jumping about with more energy than a playful puppy who has been locked up all day.

'None.' Her skin becomes hot and sticky. She peels off her coat. Darcy tries to match his smile, but feels it falls short in comparison. 'What a surprise.'

'Darcy, are you okay?' Lauren, her childhood friend, is staring at her, a little concerned.

Darcy shakes herself. 'Yeah, of course. I'm still trying to get my head around Drew organising all this.' She gestures around to the rest of the room.

'He told us about it when he first came back.' Lauren smiles, sipping on her champagne, obviously thinking the world of Drew for organising a surprise party. 'Made everyone promise we wouldn't give anything away.'

Darcy returns the smile, knowing she normally would have enjoyed a surprise if things were a little better between them. She's sure Drew thinks everything is okay. He had, after all, said he'd come back to Sydney for her, but Darcy can't shake the feeling that she's forcing him to do something he doesn't really want to do.

'Isn't he a doll?' Drew's mum, Sheila, bustles up behind them. Her cheeks are a little red, which means she's had at least two glasses of wine. Her bright fuchsia lipstick is a little smudged, the remnants printed on the wine glass she's holding.

'I know,' Lauren says. 'You did a good job, Sheila.'

Sheila's chest puffs out a little further. Drew is her eldest and can do no wrong in her eyes.

'Did you have any idea?' Sheila wants to know.

'No.' Darcy shakes her head. Some of the clues are now falling into place. She wonders whether he did actually have to help out at the school fete today or whether it was just a ploy to get her back to Gloucester.

'It's such a shame about the job thing,' Sheila muses, shaking her head a little regretfully. 'I would have loved to have you both back here.'

Lauren is quick to jump on this news. 'What job thing?'

'Drew got offered a position at the school until the end of the year,' Sheila eagerly shares. 'He was all keen to take it up, but Darcy thinks it'll be too hard on them.'

And Darcy knows that's exactly what Sheila will be telling everyone. They all could have had their beloved Drew Roberts back in Gloucester if Darcy wasn't such a selfish cow. She wouldn't say it directly, but reading between the lines, the message would be completely clear.

Lauren takes one look at Darcy and clearly feels a little awkward. 'Long distance would be hard,' she says, trying to offer Darcy some support. 'Especially with Darcy's kind of work.'

But this doesn't provide Sheila any comfort. 'You won't be able to work like that for good, you know,' she tells Darcy. 'When you're a mother you're not going to be able to work those long hours.'

'We might not have any kids.' Darcy shrugs, knowing there's no need to be purposely mean, but she can't help herself.

Sheila's face falls.

Darcy feels too bad to let it continue so adds, 'Not for a while, anyway.'

Sheila is visibly relieved but is quick to tell her, 'It's best to have kids young, isn't it, Lauren?'

Lauren is wide-eyed, clearly not wanting to get involved in this conversation. She stammers, unable to find suitable words to satisfy both parties.

Darcy sees her mum across the room and is just about to excuse herself to go talk to her when she hears, 'Darcy!' She turns to see Ellie and Tara, two of her closest friends from uni, charging towards her.

'What are you doing here?' They both live in Sydney. They've never been to Gloucester before.

'We got lost and didn't make it in time to surprise you!'

'You travelled all the way up here?' She caught up with them only a few days ago after work for a wine and neither of them breathed a word. Darcy hugs them to her.

'It's your birthday!' Ellie smiles.

'But it's only my twenty-sixth.' Darcy wishes Drew hadn't made such a big fuss.

'Still,' Ellie says, 'we didn't want to miss it.'

'And we thought there might be some cute country boys here,' Tara adds.

Darcy laughs. 'Oh, good luck,' she says and casts her eyes around the room to see if there are any potential suitors for her city friends, quite confident they're going to be disappointed.

'Do you know if Ed and Sienna are coming?' Darcy asks. It seems like Drew has made a point of inviting every other important person in her life. It feels weird not having Ed there.

But before either of them has the chance to answer, there's a loud *ding, ding, ding* on a glass. Drew's standing at the front of the room. 'If everyone could gather around, it's time for some speeches.'

Darcy cringes. Are speeches really necessary?

'Darcy, come out here and join me,' Drew calls to her.

There's no way she's going to get out of this. All the guests are gathering together in a warm bustle.

As Darcy reaches Drew he pulls her a little closer. 'Here's our birthday girl.'

'Cheers to the birthday girl,' Silas, her brother, calls out, charging his glass into the air as beer sloshes down his wrist. Despite being almost thirty he still drinks like he's eighteen.

The rest of the group raise their glasses. 'To Darcy!' echoes around the room.

Darcy smiles, taking a sip of her champagne, then suddenly wonders whether she's supposed to drink when people are toasting her. What's the protocol?

But Drew puts his arm around Darcy and addresses the rest of the group. 'Firstly I want to thank everyone for coming tonight. I can't believe we pulled it off.' He's grinning ear to ear.

'Cheers to that!' her brother calls out again.

There are some appreciative murmurs at this, but Darcy sees her sister-in-law, Nell, give Silas a look. A look that says he needs to slow up on the beers. Silas looks sheepish; he knows what's good for him and being in Nell's bad books is something he usually tries to avoid.

'Darce and I have been together for so long,' Drew says, glancing at her with a quick smile. 'I honestly can't really remember what life was like before her.'

Darcy can't really remember either. They were teenagers, they didn't know much about the world except for what was on offer in Gloucester.

'It's like she's always been around, kind of like a sister, I guess.'

Huh? He's comparing her to a sister?

There's some scattered laughter and Drew suddenly realises his mistake. 'A mate,' he corrects himself, then realises that doesn't sound much better. 'I mean, a best friend.' He looks at her, his face a little pale.

Darcy feels bad for him, but also feels bad for herself. She tries to ignore the feeling of annoyance growing inside her. She wants to tell him to wrap it up.

'You know what I mean, don't you, Darce?'

This is her opportunity. 'Of course.' She pastes on a smile, stepping forward to take charge of the situation. 'All right, thank you everyone for coming along to surprise me. I certainly hadn't expected a thing!'

There are a few satisfied hurrahs.

'So, let's get celebrating.' She lifts her champagne flute into the air, indicating the formal part of the night is over. *Short and sweet*, she thinks, pleased with herself.

'Hang on, hang on,' Drew calls to the group. 'I haven't finished.'

Darcy's heart sinks, and she suspects a few members of the crowd feel the same, clearly liking her idea of getting on with the night.

'Everyone just wants to have a good time,' Darcy whispers as discreetly as she can. 'I don't need you to make a speech about me.'

She's trying to be nice, but she sees his face flicker with frustration. 'I want to make a speech, okay?'

Her expression is tight. *Fine.*

The interruption has flustered Drew even more. Everyone's eyes are on him.

'Get on with it, mate!' Lauren's husband, Scott, calls from the back of the group. 'Some of us don't get out much and want to make the most of it.'

A few people laugh, well aware of his three children under five.

'Okay, I had this all figured out, but it's not going to plan.' Drew shifts from one foot to the other. 'I wanted you all here tonight to be a part of what I'm about to do.'

Darcy looks properly at Drew for the first time all night. He isn't just pale, he's sweaty, and his hands are twitchy like he gets when he's nervous. Her heart suddenly accelerates.

'I love you, Darcy Reed.' He turns to her and a few people in the crowd seem to realise what he's doing. Darcy hears some shrieks of excitement. Her heart now feels like it's beating on the outside of her body.

'I want to spend the rest of my years with you by my side.' He pulls a box from his jeans pocket, more smoothly than Darcy would have expected, and then gets down on bended knee.

Is this really happening? She looks out to the crowd, her eyes searching for her mum, but all the faces blur together. She stares back at Drew. They had a fight today. A really big fight. She spent most of the day furious with him, wondering if they were going to be able to stay together if she loves Sydney and he doesn't.

'Darcy, will you marry me?'

Darcy feels like she's going to throw up. This isn't how he's supposed to propose. Why would he think she'd want to be proposed to in front of their friends and family? At the pub? What is wrong with him?

But then she looks deep into his eyes and sees nothing but her loyal companion. He's been by her side for the past ten years. He knows her better than anyone else in the world. Their shared history is irreplaceable. She loves him. She honestly can't imagine her life without him. He brushes his hair to the side of his face. She notices his hands are a little shaky. She reaches out to steady them. He might have gotten the proposal all wrong, but she can forgive that. 'Yes. Of course, yes.'

There's hooting and clapping among the crowd.

He pushes the ring onto her finger and it takes her breath away for a moment. It's gorgeous. She feels satisfied with herself for dropping all the not-so-subtle hints about the types of rings she likes over the years.

'Wow, it's beautiful,' she tells Drew, admiring her hand.

Drew looks very pleased with himself. He stands up and pulls her in for a kiss. Darcy wishes she could savour the moment, but with all eyes on them, she pulls away before she can enjoy it.

Drew takes Darcy's newly engaged hand and victoriously charges it into the air. 'To us!'

There's more toasting and cheering and commotion. As the crowd closes in on her, she loses Drew's hand, each and every guest wanting to congratulate her.

She's engaged!

20

Bonnie watches the rest of the girls doing the 'salute to the sun' pose. Yoga has never been her thing. If she's completely honest, exercise has never been her thing. She manages a couple of walks a week with Paige, but they're normally followed by coffee and cake or wine and cheese, so she guesses that cancels out the exercise. Bonnie's tried yoga a few times but is never able to stop herself from thinking about all the things she's got to do. She's tried to keep her mind focused on the poses. One arm there, the other here, posture tall, tummy tight, all while standing on one leg, but her mind always drifts to the accounts she needs to finalise … the 'sneak peeks' she needs to post on social media … the emails she needs to respond to … what she has to grab from the supermarket … whether she has time to grab a coffee after this … And suddenly she realises her body isn't tall, her tummy isn't tight and instead of feeling relaxed she's just stressed about all the things she should be doing instead of yoga.

But now, here at *The One* mansion, there's nothing else to do. Her hands feel empty and yearn for her camera. They aren't allowed mobiles or laptops or tablets. They aren't even allowed to watch the news or read the paper. There's absolutely no contact with the outside world. The only real stimulation is reading, board games, movies and exercise. Most of the other girls dedicate the long empty days to working out. The days you don't go on a date with Ty are tedious. When a date card arrives, it gives everyone something to think about, to talk about. They spend ages analysing the clue, guessing what it could be.

'You're not joining us?' Imogen asks as she sees Bonnie staring. The makeup team are now spraying each of the girls with water to make them look like they've broken into a light sweat from the yoga.

Bonnie wants to be amused by this, but instead Imogen's voice is enough to make her snarl. She tries to avoid any contact with Imogen. She is nasty with a capital *N.*

'Not really my thing.' Bonnie shrugs.

Imogen tosses her hair over her shoulder and Bonnie suppresses the urge to roll her eyes. Why on earth doesn't she pull it into a ponytail while exercising?

Imogen's wearing a triangle bikini top and possibly the shortest shorts Bonnie has ever seen. She settles her hands on her hips. 'Too good for us, are you?' She says it lightly but doesn't quite hide the intent of her words.

Cassie looks up now from a downward-facing-dog position to gauge Bonnie's reaction. The two women had formed a fast-tracked friendship over the past week. While Bonnie just feels out of place, Cassie is missing her five-year-old son, Zac. Cassie's husband died in a motorbike accident when she was pregnant, so she's raised Zac on her own and finally feels ready for romance. This isn't the way Bonnie would go about it if she were in Cassie's shoes, but who is she to judge?

'Come on, Bonnie.' Imogen can't leave it alone and Bonnie wonders if she's had a producer in her ear suggesting she stirs some drama. 'You were the first to lecture us on getting along, but here you are just sitting there with your nose stuck up.'

Bonnie glances at Ben, who has his camera pointed at Imogen and the rest of the girls with their butts in the air. He's ready to capture Bonnie's retaliation, and offers her a cheeky smile, daring her to either join the group or flare at Imogen's comment.

But images of herself in a cat fight with Imogen jump into her head, and she knows the footage would be aired over and over again. She's not going to give anyone the satisfaction of saying a word and bites down on her lip, almost drawing blood. She gives a little shake of the head to Ben before pushing up out of her armchair and walking away, leaving Imogen and the rest of the girls watching after her.

Back in the house, she settles on the lounge. She leans back against the cushions and closes her eyes, trying to forget that she willingly confined herself to this nuthouse. Gradually, as images of Imogen and the cameras fade from her mind, she remembers back to not all that long ago when she was still in the outside world. On this particular day, Bonnie had been perched on a stepladder in her studio, pinning up a new backdrop when she heard the door push open. 'Won't be a minute.'

'Don't rush on my account.'

The voice sent an electric rush through her body. Bonnie spun so quickly that she nearly fell off the ladder. 'Ollie, hi.' She was sure her blood pressure increased immediately. It had been a few days since she'd run into him and Sophie at the supermarket.

'This place looks great,' he said, glancing around the studio. The walls were all white with large canvases and prints of some of Bonnie's favourite shots blown up. A small waiting area with purple velvet lounges was at the front, with a kids' corner of toys and colouring-in books. Bonnie's large desk was even tidy for the moment. Two areas dedicated to studio shoots were both set up, styled with distinct themes and props nearby.

'Thank you.'

'You did it,' he commented. 'You always said this is what you wanted to do.'

Bonnie remembered her teenage self spilling her deepest dreams to Oliver. She'd wanted to be a photographer, a proper photographer who didn't have to do another job on the side just to get by. She wanted her own studio, she wanted people to book her in advance. Everything she'd wanted all those years ago she'd managed to achieve. It felt good and she was proud. She'd worked hard and was good at her job. There was just that horrible niggle that it didn't feel as good as she'd thought it would. Because, when she'd been dreaming up those big dreams, she'd always imagined Oliver by her side.

'I'm stoked for you.'

Bonnie smiled, shaking away old memories and ill feelings. She wished she wasn't longing for someone to share her happiness with. She wished she were enough. She should be enough.

'Anyway, I just wanted to drop by and say hello properly, you know, without Sophie around. I hope it wasn't too awkward the other day.'

She watched the way the words formed on his lips, and suddenly a rush of euphoria overwhelmed her. 'It's good to see you.' She'd missed him. The feeling surprised her; they'd been broken up for fourteen years.

'Yeah, you too.' He exhaled. There was a look on his face that made her wish she knew what he was thinking.

'Have you got time for a drink?'

She tried to ignore her tummy flip-flopping and glanced at the clock on the wall. 'Sure, I was about to close up for the day. A drink would be nice.'

They went to the pub around the corner. The same pub they'd spent many Friday and Saturday nights when they'd turned eighteen.

Oliver returned from the bar with drinks for the two of them. 'Remember that night here?' he began.

'I was just thinking about that.' He'd vomited all over the front steps. 'Too many Sambuca shots, wasn't it?'

His face creased as though he was unsure for a moment, but then he remembered. 'Oh, not *that* night.' He shook his head. 'That was awful. Sadly not the last time I did that to myself, though.' He grimaced. 'I meant that night we played pool.' He gestured to the pool tables on the other side of the pub. 'For about five hours straight.'

Bonnie smiled, thinking back. All those years ago she'd been wearing jeans and a little white gypsy top she'd bought from a market in Byron Bay. 'I'd been so determined to beat you,' she laughed.

'And you probably would have if you hadn't had so many drinks.'

Her stomach swirled. The two of them used to drink an awful lot together. 'You could have let me win.'

'Oh, come on,' he said. 'There's no way you would have let me do that.'

That's true. She'd wanted to beat him fair and square.

'Oliver James!' a voice called, causing both Bonnie and Oliver to turn. Ryan McCann, a guy they went to school with, made his way towards them. 'I heard you were back in town.'

'Mate, good to see you,' Oliver said, standing for a moment to shake hands.

Ryan glanced between the two of them and Bonnie felt like she'd been sprung going through her parents' liquor cabinet. 'How you going, Ryan?' She tried to smile, but it was taut and unconvincing.

'Good, good,' he said, as though suddenly putting the pieces of a jigsaw together. 'You two catching up?'

'Yeah,' Bonnie attempted to say casually, but her throat tightened, squashing the word.

'Heard you're marrying Sophie Nix?' Ryan looked to Oliver, probably trying to suss out if he'd just busted the two of them doing something they shouldn't be.

Oliver's eyes flicked to Bonnie before answering. She suddenly wished she hadn't agreed to a drink. Ryan would tell his wife Emma and word would spread that Oliver and Bonnie were having a drink together. She knew what this town was like—it wouldn't take much before everyone was talking about it, assuming the two of them were involved in a sordid love affair.

'Yep, it's true. Soph's in the middle of organising the big day.'

Bonnie reached for her glass of wine, trying to seem normal, but she knew Oliver sounded a little awkward. She was thankful for the distraction when her phone chimed with a message.

I'll pick you up at 6 am. Will get you to Sydney in time for auditions.

Bonnie grimaced. Her sister was nothing but relentless about auditioning for *The One*.

Don't you dare.

She pressed send before switching her phone to silent. There was no way she wanted to be a contestant on that terrible reality show.

Ryan and Oliver made small talk for a few minutes, promising they'd catch up for a beer another day. Bonnie didn't miss the curious look Ryan threw her way before he moved off. She felt queasy.

'So, Sophie would be okay about this?' she asked once Ryan was out of earshot. 'Us having a drink together?'

Oliver smiled a little. 'Sophie's not the insecure type.'

'Yeah, I remember that from school.' An image of Sophie Nix flouncing around in her own bubble, not at all worried about other people or what they thought of her, came to the front of Bonnie's mind.

Oliver looked a little unsettled by this.

'It surprised me to hear the two of you were together,' Bonnie admitted.

'Yeah, I can understand that.'

She glanced over Oliver's shoulder, seeing more people arrive. One of the girls, Faith McKinnon, was a good friend of Carla's. Bonnie slunk a bit lower in her seat. 'So, how did it happen?' How on earth had he become engaged to Sophie Nix?

Oliver considered, his face scrunched up as though trying to isolate an exact reason. 'Alcohol,' he said eventually. 'There was a lot of alcohol.'

Bonnie returned his smile, but it didn't come naturally. She attempted to shake away the uneasy feeling and gripped her glass of wine.

'You know Sophie,' he added. 'She knows what she wants and goes after it.' He laughed a little nervously.

Bonnie was struck with an image of Sophie stripping down to a lacy G-string, the kind of thing Bonnie had never owned. She tried to remember if she was wearing her black or beige granny undies.

'Your parents must be happy you're back in town,' she said, changing the subject.

'Very.' Oliver nodded. 'Mum says she sees you around from time to time.'

Whenever Bonnie saw Dawn James she had to steady herself, because she knew Oliver would be on her mind for the next couple of days.

'That's kind of inevitable here. It's impossible to go to the shops without running into someone you know.'

'And that's a good or bad thing?'

'I'll let you decide that.' Bonnie wondered how often she would have to run into him and Sophie, like she had only days before. She felt overwhelmed knowing she had a lifetime of impromptu run-ins ahead.

'So, what about you, Bon?'

The way he called her *Bon* took her back to being a teenager, to long summer afternoons, to wearing bikinis and denim shorts, to the way it felt when he used to slide his hand into the pocket on her bum when they walked together. She suddenly felt hot and wondered if her cheeks were flushed.

'The last time I saw you, things seemed pretty serious with …' He paused, seemingly trying to remember. '… Isaiah?'

But Bonnie could tell it was just an act; he knew Isaiah's name. 'Yeah, Isaiah.' She nodded. It had been at their ten-year high school reunion. She'd thought things with Isaiah had been going pretty well. It turned out he hadn't felt the same. Two weeks later he'd broken things off. Two months later he'd moved interstate. Six months later he was engaged to someone else. 'That didn't work out.'

Oliver didn't say anything, but his eyes were full of sympathy. Sympathy she didn't want.

Bonnie shrugged, trying to make out it didn't matter, but of course it mattered. She wished she were already living her 'happily ever after'. She wished she didn't want a man to complete her life, but she did. Most of the time she wanted it so badly it hurt.

'Has there been …' He tapered off, perhaps not wanting to offend her.

'Anyone else?' She finished his question.

He nodded, his eyes full of something Bonnie couldn't quite pinpoint.

'Yeah,' she began slowly. *Liam*, the guy who she'd let herself believe was *the one*. The guy she was willing to become a step-mother for. The guy for whom she'd even contemplated shutting up her business and relocating. He was also the guy who had an affair with his ex-wife. Bonnie's heart was still bruised a year on. 'There was someone,' she finally said, 'but there's not anymore.'

'I'm sorry,' he offered.

'Yeah, me too.' Because if Liam had been at home waiting for her, there was no way she would have agreed to a drink with Ollie.

'Another?' Oliver gestured to their empty glasses.

She went to say no, but Oliver stood. 'Go on, have one more with me.'

The fact that he wanted her to say yes made her belly burst with butterflies. She told herself she had no right to be even slightly elated. 'Won't Sophie be wondering where you are?'

Oliver shook his head. 'She's at her mum's place doing wedding stuff. She won't be home for hours.' Oliver moved off to the bar before she had a chance to question it.

She realised she was having a drink with a man whose fiancée was busily arranging their wedding. What was wrong with her? But she dismissed the thought when Oliver returned with a vodka raspberry, her drink of choice when she was eighteen. Bonnie immediately smiled. 'I haven't had one of these in years.' She was slammed with memories of wearing high heels and small dresses, dancing for hours and not knowing when she'd had enough to drink.

'For old times' sake.' Oliver lifted his drink to her.

She clinked glasses with him and brought the glass to her mouth. She recoiled at the strong sugary liquid. 'That is awful!' she laughed. 'How did I ever drink these?'

Oliver took another sip of his. 'I don't mind it. I actually think it's gotten better with time.' He reminded her of a night when they'd shared a bottle of bourbon then passed out and missed her curfew. This led to talk of a night she'd drunk so much she threw up all over herself. Oliver had snuck into her house to get a change of clothes so her parents wouldn't know. There was even a brief mention of the night Carla had caught them having sex in the shower. They both became a little self-conscious, Bonnie giggling nervously like she would have done when she was seventeen. Without even realising it, she'd finished her drink and was up at the bar buying the next round.

'So, kids?' Bonnie said after another drink. 'Why did you and Amy never have any?' They were talking more freely now, the alcohol blurring the line between friends and exes.

He went quiet, his face changing like she'd winded him.

'Sorry.' She shook her head. 'It's none of my business.'

'It's fine.' But he drained the rest of his drink before answering. 'She didn't want them. I did. Twelve years later, we're divorced.'

Bonnie was sure she could hear Ollie's bruised heart thud to the ground. 'Oh, Ollie. I'm sorry.'

'The last few years were pretty rough. I kept trying to change her mind and she resented me for it. Before long every part of our relationship was falling apart. We were so angry with each other for not wanting what the other wanted.'

Bonnie felt for him. He'd make a great dad. When they were teenagers, he'd coached a young kids' soccer team and volunteered to help out with the local Little Athletics club. He had a natural way with kids. 'Didn't you talk about whether or not you were going to have kids before you got married?' Bonnie had assumed that would be a topic everyone cleared up before they said 'I do'.

Oliver shrugged, a little amused. 'We were twenty. We had no idea what we were doing.'

Bonnie remembered hearing of his engagement. The news had crushed her to the core. A few days after she'd heard the gossip, Oliver sent her a text, saying, *Just thought I should let you know I'm engaged. Didn't want you to hear it from somebody else.*

Too late, she'd typed back. *News spreads fast. Congrats.* It had killed her. They'd been broken up for over a year, but still, her heart had plummeted so hard she'd thought she would never fall in love again. They hadn't broken up on bad terms. It was mutual, both of them coming to the conclusion that it wasn't working. But Bonnie had wrongly assumed it was a relationship pause while they were living long distance. He was supposed to wait for her. They were supposed to go out with a few people and have fun, but after university was over Bonnie had thought they'd probably get back together. They certainly weren't supposed to marry anyone.

She'd stalked his Facebook page, tormenting herself by studying photos of him and Amy, but she'd become so obsessive that eventually she had to unfriend him.

Every now and again she heard what he was up to. One time she saw him walking through the car park, but he hadn't seen her. She hadn't spoken to him again until their ten-year high school reunion. She'd met Amy, who had seemed lovely, and she'd had Isaiah by her side. Their high school romance had seemed long ago and insignificant.

'Game of pool?' Ollie interrupted her thoughts.

Bonnie glanced at her watch. 'Shouldn't we be calling it a night?'

But Oliver shook his head without even looking at the time. 'I'm not ready to go home.'

There was something about the way he looked at her that made her think she should go home.

But she didn't. 'A game of pool,' she agreed. 'Let me win this time?'

Oliver smiled. 'Not a chance.'

She should have said no. She should have gone home. But instead she stayed, she drank more and let the physical attraction bubble between them. She knew it was wrong, but the spark made every inch of her body ache for more.

Bonnie heard his phone ring, saw him pull it from his jeans pocket and glance at the screen. She watched as he switched it to silent and buried it away. She knew it must have been Sophie but she looked away, pretending she hadn't seen a thing.

It became late, the publican forcing them onto the street despite their pleas to stay.

They walked together, too close, their fingers brushing.

'This has been fun,' she said, as though it was something they'd be able to do again.

'We always had fun.' His footsteps slowed, turning to face her. They were unnecessarily close, every inch of her body magnetised to his.

Their fingers intertwined. Words floated away, but their breathing was heavy, thick with anticipation.

There was a quick flicker of hesitation, but they ignored it ...

Their lips touched hungrily, starved of one another for so many years. They were greedy, grasping and forceful. Bonnie was drugged with passion, lust pulsing through her veins.

She wanted more.

She needed more.

Their bodies pressed up against one another, fitting together just like she remembered, better than she remembered.

'I want you.'

She'd nodded, breathless. 'We can go back to my studio.' It was close by, only around the corner.

He was impatient and pinned Bonnie up against a wall, their mouths finding each other, hands exploring.

Her skin prickled with expectation, goosebumps rushing over her body. 'Let's go,' she eventually whispered, winded, heart racing.

They began to walk but only managed a few steps before they were kissing again. Their mouths were hard and fervent, needing to make up for all those years apart. Bonnie was flooded with memories of exploration, experimentation and pleasure. He'd been the first guy she'd ever slept with and both of them had been eager and willing.

When they reached the door to Bonnie's studio, Oliver pulled her close for another kiss, unable to wait another second. 'Let's go inside,' he murmured into her mouth.

Bonnie reached into her handbag for her keys; she dug around but couldn't find them. She dropped her bag to the ground, collapsing onto her knees, rummaging furiously.

Car headlights cast over them like a spotlight. Bonnie looked up from her bag, holding up her arm to shield her eyes from the bright light.

'Shit.' Oliver's voice pierced the air in hushed panic. 'It's Sophie.'

Bonnie immediately wanted to throw up. 'What?' Her heart had been racing with desire, but it was suddenly pounding with fear.

Sophie brought the car to a stop and pushed open the door. 'Here you are.' She looked at Oliver with a stare Bonnie had no idea how to interpret.

'Hey,' Oliver said.

Bonnie murmured hello too, her hand finally scooping the keys out of her bag.

'You two look pretty hammered.' Sophie's tone had been terrifyingly cheerful.

Oliver laughed, nervously and too loud. 'We just had a couple of drinks at the pub.'

'Mmmm.' Sophie nodded. 'Plenty to catch up on, I imagine.'

'Years' worth.' Oliver's voice was a little shaky as he took a quick glance at Bonnie. 'How'd you know where I was?'

'I tracked your phone.' She smiled as though it was a completely acceptable thing to do.

Bonnie's eyes darted back and forth between the engaged couple, waiting, expecting Oliver to react about being tracked.

But he didn't. He just accepted it with a nod, perhaps a little frustrated with himself for not realising how she'd done it.

'I saw on my phone that you'd left the pub and thought you might need a lift,' Sophie said.

'Thanks, Soph,' Oliver managed, casting a look towards Bonnie, his eyes wide, his face white.

'I thought it would have been easier to grab a taxi from the pub rather than walk this way?' Sophie's question was loaded, her eyes like laser beams on Oliver's face.

Bonnie expected Sophie's question to be met with silence, or at least a fumbled reply. But instead, Ollie was seamless in saying, 'There were none around and Bonnie wanted to show me some of her work.'

Huh? Don't dump me in it! Bonnie fought the urge to slap him on the arm.

Sophie seemed to accept his explanation whether she believed it or not. 'Hop in, Bonnie, we'll give you a lift too.'

No! She almost screamed.

But only minutes later, she was in the back of Sophie and Oliver's car. Her head was spinning, her stomach churning, listening to Sophie chatter on about the band she'd found to do music at their wedding.

Bonnie had been moments from tearing off Oliver's clothes, moments from having his hands on her body, moments from shuddering relief.

But guilt and shame quickly replaced the feeling of euphoria.

'There you go,' Sophie said cheerily as the car pulled up out the front of Bonnie's place. Sophie commented on how homely it looked and that she'd love to come for a cuppa one day.

'Thanks for the lift,' Bonnie said, trying to open the car door, but it wouldn't budge.

'Oh, the child lock is still on,' Sophie said. 'I had Bec and her kids in here today. Help her, would you, Ollie?'

Oliver got out of the front passenger seat and opened Bonnie's door. He stared at her, his eyes apologetic.

She pushed herself out of the car, her feet unsteady as they touched the ground. Oliver reached out to her, but the moment he touched her, desire came flooding back. Her lips were raw; she could still taste him.

Bonnie gulped. She'd been moments away from sleeping with a man she knew was engaged to somebody else. What was wrong with her?

She shook herself free, giving him an anguished look. 'Thanks again for dropping me home.' She turned, smiling, to Sophie. She felt Oliver staring at her, urging her to look at him, but she didn't let herself. She knew she couldn't trust herself around him.

So, as the car had driven away from the kerb, Bonnie had gotten out her phone and sent a text to Carla. *Okay, pick me up at 6 am. I'll audition for The One.*

21

Penelope squeezes some tester moisturiser onto her hand as she waits at the pharmacy. The warm smell of caramel quickly reaches her nose. It reminds her of a candle that had been in her old bedroom, the one she left. She wonders if he'd kept it or thrown it out. She feels her teeth sink into her lips a little bit, forcing the memories away. She concentrates on the cream, rubbing it in, barely recognising her hands. She turns them over, searching for the youthful ones she remembers.

'I said no,' a drained voice sighs. A child screams in protest. 'Please, Molly, I'm too tired today.'

Penelope looks up and sees Lara pushing a pram with Molly trailing behind, clearly upset about something.

This town isn't big enough. She thought a small place would be ideal, but she would have been better off moving to another city. She could have attempted to be an invisible face among the crowd.

It seems here she can barely leave the house without running into Lara.

Penelope's natural instinct is to turn away and pretend she hasn't seen her, but the guilt wins over today. 'Lara, hi,' she calls, surprising herself by her cheery tone.

Even Lara looks a bit taken aback by Penelope's friendliness. 'Penelope, how are you?'

'Good, how about you?'

Lara's face quickly reveals she's far from good. 'Harry's got a cold and I think some teeth are coming through. I don't think he slept at all last night. I'm supposed to be at work today, but I can't send him to day care like this. My mum used to come babysit for me on days that I'd get stuck, but I had no choice today ...' She shakes her head, clearly feeling the loss of her mum today on top of everything else.

'Can I have this, Mummy?' Molly holds up a ballerina jewellery box she's found on one of the shelves. 'Mummy?'

'Not today, honey. But maybe we could get it for your birthday?' Lara's voice is light and sugary, clearly hoping Molly will be appeased by this suggestion.

But Molly shrieks, tears immediately spilling onto her cheeks. 'I want it now.'

Penelope sees Lara grimace, exhaustion tugging at her face. 'Come on, Molly. I just need to grab some Panadol and we'll go to the park for a bit.'

'Penelope Baker?'

The voice jolts Penelope for a second but she's immediately relieved. 'That's me.' Penelope indicates to the pharmacist calling that her script has been filled. She could pay and be out of here within a few minutes, but there's an expression on Lara's face that has her say, 'Do you want to get a coffee?'

Lara's face brightens. 'I'd love that. Wouldn't we, Molly? Maybe we can get you a milkshake?'

Molly smiles, finally.

So Harry sleeps in the pram and Penelope sits on a bench seat listening to Lara talk as they sip on their coffees and watch Molly play in the park. Conversation flows easily, and Penelope's surprised by how much she enjoys being in Lara's company.

She'd promised herself she wouldn't make friends, but maybe Lara could be an exception.

22

Darcy knocks on the door and waits. Ed had texted her on her way back from Gloucester, telling her to come over for a belated take-away birthday dinner. She'd thought about declining, surprised by her nerves tumbling about at the thought of telling Ed and Sienna about the engagement.

Ed opens the door. 'Welcome, Mrs Roberts-to-be.'

She feels her eyes widen. 'You already know?'

Ed shrugs with a little nod.

'You knew he was going to propose?' She tries to keep her voice steady, feeling a little cheated.

Ed nods.

'At the pub?'

He swallows before nodding once again.

'And you didn't warn me?' She would have liked to have been a bit more prepared.

'Oh, come off it,' Ed scoffs. 'I couldn't tell you.' He gestures for her to come in and then closes the door behind her.

Darcy knows he's right but she's still frustrated. 'You could have lightly suggested that maybe he do it some other way?'

'Darce,' Ed says, appalled, as he slumps on his desk chair. 'It wasn't like he asked for my opinion. He was so proud that he was organising everyone to be there.'

'You weren't there,' she says pointedly.

'I had a wedding to film,' he counters, only glancing at her quickly before tidying a few things on his desk.

'Oh.'

Ed's got a few guys trained to film weddings for him. He's used them on several occasions. She feels a little hurt that he hadn't made the effort to make it to her birthday surprise, especially when he knew Drew was going to propose.

'I couldn't get anyone to work for me,' he says, reading her disappointment, but he continues to tidy his desk, putting lids back on pens and rearranging the stack of notebooks.

'You should have just said you didn't want to see the train wreck of a proposal …'

Ed can't help but laugh, but he's sympathetic. 'Was it that bad?'

'Worse,' she confesses.

He looks a little surprised that she hasn't tried to soften the description. 'But you're happy, aren't you?'

She can see his growing concern. 'Yeah, of course.' She glances down at her ring sparkling on her finger. It still feels foreign. 'A slightly more romantic proposal would have been nice …'

'Well, I'm glad I wasn't there to film it.'

'He wanted you to?'

Ed nods, somewhat in disbelief. 'He really wanted me to come.' He shakes his head. 'But I just kept thinking of your face when you realised what he was doing—in front of everyone. I knew you wouldn't want to watch that back.'

Darcy feels her face redden at the mention of her reaction. Ed knows her so well that he'd anticipated her face falling. Ten years of being in a relationship with Drew and he thought she'd like it. 'Well, I guess I should thank you for not coming.'

He shrugs it away. 'Hey, what are friends for?'

'Bonnie, can I steal you away?'

Bonnie glances at the other girls she's sitting between, one of them being Imogen. The girls offer tight smiles but are clearly gritting their teeth. Everyone is obsessed with *time*. The more time you can spend with Ty, the more likely you'll form a connection and the more likely you'll get a key. Bonnie quickly gets to her feet. 'Of course.'

Ty holds his arm out for her and Bonnie does her best not to smile too much. She can feel Imogen glaring her down and knows that the second they walk away, Imogen will be badmouthing her to the other contestants. If Ty honestly likes Bonnie, she can't begin to grasp the idea of him genuinely liking Imogen too.

He leads her away to a private garden—well, private besides the crewmembers and cameras. 'You're quiet in the group,' Ty comments, waiting for an explanation.

Bonnie would love to moan about Imogen and tell him that he'd be doing the rest of the girls a favour if he got rid of her at the next key ceremony, but Carla's warning to not bitch about any of the girls to Ty rings loudly in her ears. 'Just trying to stay out of trouble,' she says lightly. They sit next to each other on a bale of hay set up in front of a tin shed. Fairy lights twinkle above them and a cluster of candles flicker nearby.

He reaches out and touches her hand. Bonnie's eyes flick towards the camera. 'There are a lot of loud personalities too,' he says.

Bonnie simply nods. The loud personalities are infectiously irritating, but somehow, here with him, the rest of the girls seem insignificant and annoyances fade away.

'You seem to be coping okay,' she says, 'considering you're like a hot chip among seagulls.'

Ty laughs hard, deep from his belly. 'It is a little bit like that, I guess. I'm just glad that I look like I'm coping—it doesn't feel like it all the time.'

Bonnie smiles, taking her time to take in his features and appreciate these few precious moments that they have to themselves. They'd spent the day at a farm. Bonnie can already imagine the footage the camera guys must have gotten of some of the girls literally knee-deep in cow manure. A few had been shrieking hysterically, disgusted at farmyard life. Even though Bonnie was far from an expert herself, she'd found it all very amusing.

'So, you've ridden horses before?' he asks, referring to the first part of the group date.

'I had lessons when I was a kid,' she admits. 'Begged my mum for months. I was a little obsessed—pony club and all that. I can't actually remember why I decided to give it up.' She imagines Carla writing *confident horse rider* on Bonnie's application form. 'It's been years since I've ridden.'

'You made it look like you do it all the time.'

'My legs don't agree,' she says, rubbing at them. 'I'm pretty sure I might not be able to walk tomorrow.' There had been only three on the date who could ride. The others were hopeless, needing constant attention. A ride that should have taken about twenty minutes took four hours to film. Bonnie can already feel muscles in her body that she hasn't felt in years. 'You seemed like you knew what you were doing.'

Ty laughs. 'Really? I kept thinking that I was going to look like an absolute idiot. I had some intense lessons last week,' he admits, his eyes widening as he says *intense*. 'The producers thought it'd look better if I appeared competent.' Ty seems rather amused by this.

Bonnie returns his smile. 'I don't know, seeing you clinging on for dear life would have made for some good viewing.'

'Yes, probably very true'—he reaches out and puts his hand on her thigh—'but not very manly.'

'Cut!'

Bonnie is snapped out of the moment, her focus from Ty slipping. She's suddenly staring at the camera, the big lens pointed directly at them. Ben, the camera guy, gives her a smile.

'Okay, guys,' Darcy says, approaching them from the side where the rest of the production team are watching. 'We're just going to do a makeup touch-up. Ty's looking a bit shiny.'

'Can't have that.' Ty raises his eyebrows at her like it would be the worst offence. The way he looks at her warms her cheeks. She's definitely attracted to him and her heart seems to beat faster, louder, anytime she's close to him.

'Before we do that, do you reckon you guys could give us a kiss?'

Bonnie's chest immediately tightens. She wants to kiss Ty. She wants to let herself believe in the potential of Ty, but that's hard to do in any new relationship, let alone when the guy is dating a dozen other girls. How many times has Darcy repeated that *Reckon you guys could give us a kiss* phrase? 'Reckon you guys could give us some privacy?' Bonnie says, half playful, half serious.

Ty shrugs at Bonnie, indicating it's up to her whether or not they kiss.

Bonnie glances back to the crew, the cameras … She feels like a bright spotlight is fiercely shining on her. She kissed him last time on their one-on-one date, but she'd spent the whole day with him. Now it feels rushed, and her body prickles with panic.

Ty reaches out and squeezes her hand. 'It's okay. I get it. We don't have to force anything.'

Bonnie just wants a second to think it through, but Darcy must assume her hesitation means the kiss isn't going to happen. 'We're really running behind schedule. We're going to move Ty on to the next girl now.'

Bonnie feels a cold wind whip at her heart. Her time is up. A twelve-hour day with two minutes of one-on-one time. Maybe she should have kissed him.

'If you want to head back to the girls,' Darcy says, 'I'll come get you for your interview soon.' Interviews were conducted at the end of each date in which you pretty much had to talk Darcy through the date step by step and explain how you felt at every moment. Bonnie's sure it's more boring and painful for the crew than it is for her.

Bonnie says goodbye to Ty and slowly heads back to the group of girls. On her way she sees Ben pull his mobile from his pocket and grimace, probably at the time. He steps back from the camera, well aware the simple makeup 'touch-up' will take more time than he'd like.

Bonnie watches as he scratches at his oversized beard, his fingers quickly lost from sight.

'Might be time to shave?'

He looks up and smiles. 'You wouldn't recognise me if I shaved this off.'

'Why is that? Are you hiding a baby face under there?'

'Nah, just ridiculously good looks.'

She can't help but smirk. 'Hand me a razor,' she jokes. She should head back to the group of girls, but instead stops to talk. 'How long has it been since you've shaved?'

He considers, an amused grin trying to make its way through all the hair. 'You know, I actually don't know. A couple of years?'

'Dedication.'

He seems to take this as a compliment. 'When I decide to do something, I stick to it.'

Bonnie glances back to Ty and the makeup girls leaning over him. She's now having doubts about not kissing him. Was that just a waste of her time? Will his relationships with the other girls be moving forward while theirs just took a backwards step?

'You all right?'

Bonnie knows she shouldn't say anything to Ben, but he's easy to talk to and words just slip from her lips. 'I don't know.' She lowers her voice, in case someone hears her. 'Being on here is playing games with my head. I know I barely know the guy, but then again, I feel like I kind of do.'

'I get it,' Ben says warmly. 'Time on this show is intense, relationships are magnified because you've got nothing else to think about.'

Bonnie realises she's making him listen to the same old rehashed conversations. 'Sorry, you've probably heard it all before.' Now she imagines Ben watching the suitor hook up with girl after girl, date after date. She suddenly feels just like one of many and doubts about her relationship with Ty come flooding in like a full-moon tide.

'Feel free to talk away,' he says. 'I'm all ears—and all beard.'

Bonnie laughs, but wonders if she's seen something behind his smile to suggest he isn't really interested in having her talk about kissing Ty. The poor guy must be lumped with these conversations all the time and has to be polite because he's at work. She'd prefer to stay here and talk to Ben, but she indicates towards the group of girls, still sitting down on bales of hay, glasses of champagne in their hands. 'I better get back.'

He gives a little nod and she forces herself to walk away.

❧

In a shed on the other side of the farm, away from the rest of the group, Darcy scans the list of questions on her clipboard. She's been asking Bonnie, who is sitting in front of a tractor, a stream of questions about her date with Ty.

Is horse riding with Ty something you could see yourself doing in the future?

Did any of the other girls try to steal his time?

Do you think the tension with Imogen is putting a strain on your time with Ty?

How did you find your one-on-one with Ty?

Is there a reason you didn't want to kiss him?

After seasons on this show, Darcy is used to analysing every moment and prying about every second of a date.

She's relieved to finally say, 'I think we're done.'

Bonnie's visibly pleased by this and Darcy throws a look to Ben. 'Cut.'

He steps back from the camera. 'I'm heading to the bathroom. I'll be back in five.'

Darcy is clicking her pen onto the clipboard when Bonnie draws her attention back.

'That's new, isn't it?' She points to Darcy's hand.

Darcy glances down at her ring. She feels like she's staring at somebody else's hand. 'I got engaged on the weekend.'

Bonnie's face softens. 'Oh, wow, congratulations.'

'Thank you.' Darcy toys with the ring. It still feels unfamiliar against her skin.

'You can smile,' Bonnie says. 'Just because I'm on this show doesn't mean I can't be happy for other people.'

Darcy wants to shake herself. She's working with a house full of women desperate to have what she has with Drew. She should count herself lucky. 'I think I'm still getting used to it.'

'How long have you guys been together?'

'Ten years.'

Bonnie laughs lightly and jokes, 'So it was a surprise then?'

'Actually, yes.' Over a year ago she'd wanted nothing more than to be engaged. Back then it would have felt like a natural progression. But then they had the fight. He felt buying property was more important than getting engaged. If she was being completely honest with herself, things between them changed after that. He'd drawn a line in the sand. Darcy wishes she knew what had made him change his mind about proposing. 'I thought I'd know when he was about to propose, but I didn't. I had no idea.'

'That's impressive after ten years.' Bonnie's full of admiration. 'He must have gone to some effort to get you off the scent?'

Darcy isn't about to admit that she doesn't know whether it's effort or whether it's that they haven't had much of a connection lately. 'A total surprise.' Darcy finds herself hoping that Bonnie won't ask how he proposed.

'So, you've been together since high school?'

Darcy nods. 'We got together in year ten.'

'Wow, high school sweethearts,' Bonnie says a little wistfully, her hands twisting in her lap. 'Mine recently just came back into my life.'

'Really?' Darcy's surprised Bonnie is admitting this to her.

Bonnie nods. 'He moved back to town.'

Darcy feels herself sit a little straighter, her producer ears hearing warning bells.

Bonnie seems to gauge Darcy's reaction. 'Oh, you don't need to worry. He's engaged and she's pregnant.'

Darcy doesn't know whether or not to believe that there's nothing to worry about. There's a certain look on Bonnie's face that Darcy hasn't seen up until now and for some reason it unsettles her.

'So, was it weird seeing him?' Darcy fishes, hoping Bonnie will give her an answer to shut down any concerns.

'Yes and no.'

The way those three little words come out of her mouth doesn't pacify Darcy's unease.

'We went to school with the girl he's marrying.' Bonnie shrugs. 'And to be brutally honest, I find her extremely annoying.'

Darcy can't help but laugh, immediately thinking of Zoe Eggins. 'Sounds like a girl I know.'

'They've moved back to town to settle down.' Her eyes do a little roll. 'Can't say I'm thrilled about having to see them all the time.'

Darcy isn't sure how she'd feel if she were in the same situation, but it's hard to imagine when she doesn't have an ex to begin with. Like Ed said, her six-week romance with Nick Simmons in year eight doesn't compare to this type of thing. How would she cope if she and Drew broke up and then he decided to marry another girl from back home?

She'd quite possibly be a little psycho. Probably even a lot psycho.

Unless she was in another relationship, maybe she wouldn't care then …

And it suddenly hits her why Bonnie was motivated to come on *The One*. She wants to get over her ex.

23

'So, what's the problem you couldn't solve on your own?' Alice marches into the editing suite where Darcy has spent the last hour or so with Max, one of the editors.

Darcy tries not to let her face falter at Alice's comment. 'We're not sure what angle to take with Ty and Jodie's date.'

Alice raises her eyebrows as though pained she has to use her skills and experience.

Darcy doesn't waste her words trying to explain. She looks to Max. 'Can you play it?'

Max lets the footage roll. The one-on-one date involves Ty and Jodie on a mountain hike. It's something of a non-event. They both sailed up it easily, their conversation a little dull, but the problem comes when they get to the top and sit down for a champagne picnic. Jodie gets emotional as she tells Ty the last time she hiked was with her ex-boyfriend.

'The whole way up I kept thinking he was about to propose,' Jodie says on screen. 'But when we got to the top he broke things off.'

Darcy had known this from Jodie's application form and it was the main reason she was chosen for the date. Darcy had been hoping Jodie would have a bit of a breakdown and that Ty would swoop in and be a romantic hero, comforting her.

'I hadn't even seen it coming,' Jodie says, her face in a close-up shot, her eyes brimming with tears. 'I felt like such an idiot. I was totally in love with him, ready to get engaged, but he didn't want to be with me.'

Alice looks at Darcy, annoyed her time is being wasted. 'What's the problem? This is fine, good in fact.'

Darcy wishes she could allow herself the luxury of enjoying the small compliment but indicates back to the screen. 'Keep watching.'

Ty responds perfectly to Jodie's tears. He moves closer to console her. 'I know how that feels. I was engaged, and my ex just broke things off.' He swallows a large lump in his throat and shakes his head, still in disbelief. 'It felt like the life we'd been living together had been a lie. I didn't get it. I tried to change her mind …' He trails off. 'It was like she turned off a switch.' His voice chokes and his head falls into his hands for a moment as he tries to compose himself. 'I love her so much, I don't understand why she's done this to me.'

I love her.

Present tense.

Ty is still in love with his ex, still coping with the pain of his heartache.

On screen, Jodie's eyes widen. 'Oh, Ty, I had no idea.'

This is the kind of thing that happens when you find a suitor in less than twelve hours. The suitor is still in love with someone else.

She looks to Alice, waiting for the wrath, the annoyance or even the explosion, but Alice's eyes are dancing. 'This is brilliant!'

Huh?

'Oh, the audience will love this.'

But Darcy doesn't agree. 'They'll be angry. He's on a show looking for love when he's in love with someone *not* on the show. It's wrong.' Darcy knows better than to mention that Alice had said the very same thing when Joe pulled out of the show because he was in love with someone else.

'Don't be silly, Darcy. They'll fall even more in love with him. Women love a man who has been hurt. They'll eat this story up.' Alice watches the monitors with delight as Ty confesses more to Jodie. He talks about having to cancel the wedding, that his fiancée already had a dress and that they'd sent out save the dates. It makes Darcy feel sick. How had his ex let it go on for so long if she hadn't loved him?

Ben had framed the shot beautifully. Ty's face is a picture of devastation. Darcy had thought they wouldn't be able to use any of the picnic footage, but they have so much of it that she isn't exactly sure what to cut out now. 'So, you want us to show it all?'

'Yes, yes! Fit as much in as you can.'

❧

Bonnie knows she's interrupted something as soon as she walks into the kitchen. Suddenly she forgets that she was trying to count back how many coffees and teas she's already had. She feels like she's constantly making a new one just to give herself something to do.

Katie and Hanna are huddled together, an urgent look flashing between them. Bonnie guesses they're talking about the salsa dancing group date they both went on yesterday. Did one of them kiss Ty? Maybe one of them bitched to Ty about one of the other girls. Maybe about Bonnie. Being in the mansion is making her paranoid. She knew the girls had been jealous she got the first one-on-one date. Some were outright annoyed she hadn't gone into detail about her time with Ty. She'd taken Darcy's advice and hadn't told anyone she kissed him. She knows they're all a bit threatened that Ty seems to like her, even she can tell that much. She just doesn't know whether he likes her *the most*. And if she's honest, Bonnie still has to figure out if she likes Ty *the most*. None of the girls know she spends most of her days obsessively thinking about an ex-boyfriend who is engaged to someone else.

'Thank goodness,' Katie says. 'We thought you might be one of the crew.'

Bonnie shakes her head, still trying to gauge their moods and figure out what's going on. 'Just me. Why?'

The two girls exchange a look, clearly deciding through raised eyebrows whether or not they should tell Bonnie. Hanna shrugs as if to say, 'Why not?'

'We have a phone,' Katie says in a hushed voice, then reveals the shiny silver phone that she's hidden under a tea towel.

Bonnie feels her eyes widen. All technical devices and any form of communication with the outside world are banned during their time on *The One*. There was a strict signing in of all devices and bag searches before entering the house.

'Where did you get it from?'

Another look passes between the girls before Katie admits, 'I got it from one of the crewmembers.'

'You don't want to know what she had to do to get it,' Hanna adds cheekily.

Katie throws Hanna a reproachful look.

Bonnie wonders why they desperately need a phone in the first place. Sure, it's frustrating having no contact, but it's a pretty big risk using it. If they got caught they'd get kicked out. She wants to know what's going on back home for them to risk it.

'You can keep a secret, can't you?' Katie asks.

Bonnie nods; she isn't interested in dobbing on them. 'Yeah, sure,' she reassures them and reaches for the kettle.

'Do you want a quick turn?'

Bonnie doesn't realise what they're asking at first but Katie gestures for her to take the mobile. She'd love to talk to Paige, but it'd be impossible for them to have a quick conversation and she's not even tempted to contact Carla, who wouldn't be able to keep it a secret. But then Bonnie surprises herself by reaching out to take the phone.

'Don't be too long—extra crew will be here soon to set up for the key ceremony.'

'The toilet off the laundry is probably the safest place,' Hanna says.

'Thanks.' Bonnie rushes off to find privacy, her heart pounding in anticipation.

She closes the toilet door behind her and sees her hands are a bit shaky as her fingers touch the screen. She logs into her Facebook account and taps the search bar, trying to put the word 'stalker' out of her head as she types in *Sophie Nix*. Oliver has an account but doesn't ever update it. She takes a deep breath. It only takes a moment to load. Sophie's profile comes up straight away. She should have guessed it'd be public. Sophie would probably be totally comfortable with complete strangers gawking through her page.

Her profile picture is a selfie of her in a bikini at the beach. Sophie would fit right in here at *The One* mansion. She'd do yoga, openly flirt with Ty and get drunk with the other girls. Bonnie should be the one at home in her trackies, pregnant and snuggling up with Oliver on the lounge.

But she's not.

Bonnie has to clear her throat a little, fearful it might squeeze out the last of her breath and she'll find herself crying again. She knows the whole show is built around these high emotions—twenty-two girls fixated on one guy, all living in close proximity—but Bonnie wonders if they add to it somehow by pumping oestrogen through the air vents, ensuring they're all extra emotional and grumpy and sensitive to comments they wouldn't normally be.

Bonnie scrolls down the page. Sophie's posted a series of photos over the last couple of weeks. There's a photo of a dozen red roses with the caption *Roses from my man, just because.*

Bonnie's stomach curdles.

Another photo shows Sophie's been shopping at Whisper of Lace, the local lingerie shop. It's captioned *Shhhh … someone's getting lucky tonight!*

For Bonnie, the picture of the shopping bag is even worse than seeing Sophie's new underwear. Bonnie's mind is instantly filled with skimpy crotchless lingerie bought specifically for Ollie.

She scrolls down a little further to a photo of Sophie and Oliver. They're walking along the beach and the sun must have been hanging low because part of the photo is blown out. But Bonnie can still clearly see Oliver's arm wrapped around Sophie, protective and loving. There's something about the way their bodies lean into each other that indicates a bond no one can break. The caption reads *So blissfully happy.* But Bonnie knows more than she should. She knows it means *Having a baby with this man.*

Bonnie almost gags when she realises that once the first trimester is over they'll probably do a really cutesy pregnancy post. Bonnie's seen enough of them in her newsfeed before. Photographs of his shoes, her shoes and baby shoes all lined up together. The couple proudly holding up their ultrasound photo with a caption like *Already looks like Dad*. Or maybe they'd go for something simpler, like their hands intertwined in a heart shape on her belly.

The familiar feeling of emptiness strikes hard, like a whip lashing her insides over and over. In the back of her mind, she's been fooling herself thinking that she might finish the show and Oliver will have left Sophie and be waiting for her. Now she imagines them snuggled on the lounge laughing as they watch Bonnie make a fool of herself on national television.

She was stupid to ever think she had a future with him. It's time to get over him and move on. She owes it to herself to give Ty a proper chance.

24

'Where's Sienna?' Darcy queries as Ed takes a seat next to her on the pub stool. They're meeting for Sunday afternoon drinks.

Ed pauses for only a second, ripping off his news like a bandaid. 'We broke up.'

'What?' Darcy is floored. 'When? Why?' How did she have no idea about this? Why does Ed seem so calm?

'I really should have grabbed us some drinks before I sat down.' Ed's grim, aware Darcy's going to want to dissect every inch of the break-up.

'Ed!'

'Okay, we broke up last weekend because she's in love with some other guy.'

Darcy feels her heart crumble for him. 'What?' Her head suddenly feels like muck, trying to figure it out. 'I'm so sorry. Why didn't you tell me before now?'

'You'd just gotten engaged.' Ed says. 'I wasn't sure when I should slide it into conversation.'

Darcy thinks back to last Sunday afternoon when she'd gotten back from Gloucester and told Ed every single detail about Drew's proposal, not to mention the fight they'd had earlier that day and Drew's decision to come back to Sydney once the term is finished. She had probably talked for about two hours straight. Come to think of it, she probably hadn't even asked where Sienna was. Ed had just sat there with his Thai takeaway, nodding in all the right places.

'You should have told me to shut up,' she groans. 'You must have thought I was so self-absorbed going on and on about everything.'

'Nothing new,' Ed jokes.

Darcy whacks him across the arm. 'Come on, tell me what happened.'

'All right, all right, but I'm getting us some drinks first.'

Five minutes later, Ed comes back with a tray. Two beers for him, a bottle of wine for her and a table number to indicate he's ordered food.

'Wow, it must be some story.'

'I know what you're like,' Ed points out. 'I'll tell you the story in two minutes flat, then you'll ask me a thousand and one questions. Hence all this.' He gestures to the tray of goodies.

'So?' she prods.

'Sooooo …' Ed sighs, deciding where to begin.

Darcy is waiting with bated breath.

He strangles a sigh before starting. 'She came home from work on the Friday afternoon and said she wanted to break up.'

Darcy's somewhat relieved Ed didn't catch Sienna cheating on him. 'Did she say why?'

'Not at first.' He exhales loudly, clearly reliving some of the pain. 'But when I kept saying we could figure it out, she finally admitted there was someone else.'

'Oh,' Darcy murmurs, her stomach sinking like lead for her dear friend.

'I felt more like an idiot than anything else,' Ed admits. 'I mean, I was declaring my love for her, promising I could fix whatever was broken, but she's in love with another guy. It was humiliating.' He takes a chug of his beer.

Darcy reaches out and squeezes his forearm.

'I think I went into shock because I didn't even say anything. Nothing. She kept asking if I was okay, but I just sat there.' He shakes his head at himself. 'Eventually she went into the bedroom to start packing and then the rage just hit. I flipped out, demanding to know who he was.' He drinks some more beer.

'Oh, Ed.'

'I broke the table, a vase and then I punched a hole in the bedroom wall.' He looks mortified.

'No?'

'It was bad.'

Darcy nods, imagining how horrible the whole scene must have been. They sit in silence for a little while, questions still flying through Darcy's head. 'Did she tell you who the other guy is?'

'James, another teacher at her school.'

James Winters. Darcy has seen Sienna tagged in photos with him on Facebook at different work functions.

'Nice guy.' Ed shrugs.

Darcy isn't quite sure whether he's being serious or sarcastic.

'Sadly, I'm not joking,' Ed says. 'I sat next to him at a trivia night last year. He was a good bloke.'

'Not that good if he's hooking up with somebody else's girlfriend,' Darcy points out.

'I guess,' Ed admits, his mood sombre.

'Has it been going on long?' Darcy suddenly feels cheated. Sienna is supposed to be her friend too. They only became friends because of Ed, but over the years they'd spent a lot of time together. Darcy has confided in Sienna about things with Drew, work and family.

'She said she's been "attracted" to him for quite a while.'

Darcy's gobsmacked. 'She actually admitted that?'

'I think she just wanted to be honest with me.' Sadness is etched onto his face. 'She said they didn't kiss until about a month ago.' He laughs, a little dumbfounded himself. 'Apparently that's supposed to make me feel better.'

Darcy squirms, feeling sick for Ed's sake.

'So now I keep playing back every conversation we had in that last month, trying to remember if she was acting weird.'

'Was she?'

He shrugs, clueless. 'I dunno. I mean, surely there were signs, but I was just too dumb to notice them.'

'Oh, Ed, don't be so hard on yourself.'

'Hard not to be.'

Darcy wishes she could do more than just offer him a sympathetic look. 'What can I do?'

He thinks about it for a moment, then proposes, 'Get really, really drunk with me?'

Darcy gives him a small smile. 'Sure.' She lifts her glass to him.

'To scum-cheating girlfriends!'

His words aren't even convincing, but she clinks his glass, aware they're in for a messy afternoon.

Bonnie sees him approach and her whole body tenses in anticipation. Oliver's footsteps are fast, eager to reach her. 'I left her for you.'

Bonnie smiles as the familiar images of a life with Ollie rush through her head. Somewhere in the back of her mind she wonders about Sophie and the baby, but she pushes the thoughts away. Ollie. She has Ollie. He chose her.

She reaches out to touch him but as she does—*POOF!*—he evaporates in a puff of smoke.

Amid the haze, someone touches her face and her hand moves up and intertwines with Ty's fingers. She doesn't even seem surprised that Ty so easily replaced Ollie.

Ty smiles at her. 'You're beautiful, Bonnie,' he murmurs. 'It's you. It's been you from the first moment I laid eyes on you.'

A giddiness sweeps over her. She won. She won Ty. All the other girls don't matter because he chose her. She smiles, happiness and relief warming her body.

But then she looks down and realises she's standing naked in front of a huge camera. Ben steps out from behind the lens, also naked. He walks towards her and doesn't stop until he's only inches from her face. His hands reach out for her and are firm against her waist, pulling her towards him. Their nude bodies press against each other. His lips touch hers, softly brushing them at first, but then hungry and passionate.

'Bonnie?'

She pulls him closer, needing more of him, but someone's calling her name. She doesn't want to turn away from him, but she peels her eyes open. Her body is twisted in the sheets of her bunk bed in *The One* mansion.

'You all right?' Katie is watching her from another bed only metres away.

'Just a dream,' she murmurs through short sharp breaths, but she notices that the other girls are watching from their own beds. Sharing a bedroom with six girls has never felt so humiliating. But she has a moment of relief that she doesn't share a room with Imogen.

'Looks like it was a good dream.' Hanna's eyes are suggestive.

Bonnie can't manage a reply. She turns away to face the wall, her heart still racing as the muddled images of Oliver, Ty and Ben flash through her head.

Hours later, a pool party is in full swing. A dozen girls parade their bikini bodies in front of Ty, jumping and squealing, desperate to make a lasting impression before the looming key ceremony. Two more girls will be sent home tonight. *Please let Imogen be one of them!*

Bonnie has perched herself on the edge of the pool, her feet dangling in the water, the ultimate fish out of water. Ty had come and sat with her earlier, but within seconds he'd been pulled into the pool by a few of the girls, including Imogen, who is wearing a bikini made from what looks like dental floss. Bonnie can't compete with all the flirty noise, so instead she retreats, barely speaking at all.

'You going in?' Darcy approaches from the sidelines where she'd been standing with the rest of the crew and squats down to Bonnie's level.

'Maybe later,' Bonnie says. She hasn't spent any time with Ty since the horse-riding group date when she chose not to kiss him. It feels like a mistake now. She should have just made the most of the time she had with him.

But even Darcy doesn't believe her. 'Try and get some time with him, okay? You've got some great public support.'

This should make her feel better, but she cringes at the idea of the public having any kind of opinion of her. She was all ready to fight for Ty and give their relationship a proper chance, but after her dream, her head feels all muddled again.

Darcy pushes back up and calls for everyone's attention. 'All right guys, we're going to break for fifteen minutes. Grab yourself something to eat and we'll come back and re-set with some of you applying sunscreen on Ty.'

There's laughter and squeals of interest at this. Most of the girls flock to Ty rather than the food table as they don't want to risk missing out. But Bonnie, eager as always for food, follows the crew.

She joins the end of the line, piling her plate with cakes, muffins, pastries and fruit that the caterers have set up. As she gets to the end of the line she sees Ben. Immediately she feels her face flush red and her chest grow hot. She has to concentrate on her breathing as she thinks of Ben with his shirt off, his lips on hers, the way he'd grabbed her around the waist in her dream.

'Are you okay?'

Bonnie shakes herself but doesn't manage to answer.

'You're staring at me really weird.'

'No, I'm not,' she says, a little rushed. 'Just caught up with everything that's been going on in here.' She feels like he's going to know she's lying, but he raises his eyebrows with interest.

'Yeah? Anything good for me?' The two of them naturally fall into step together, moving away from the rest of the crew.

She knows he's after dirt, some exciting footage to film. 'Oh, you know, just the usual—bitchy girls, who's got the best bikini body, who Ty likes the most …'

He looks slightly thwarted when she doesn't have any serious tips for him. 'I think you're pretty high on his list.'

'Really?' Bonnie's plagued with self-doubt, not to mention paranoia. She likes talking to Ben, but can she really trust him?

Ben shrugs. 'I've been doing this job for a couple of seasons now. You pick things up.' He bites into his muffin, his beard catching crumbs like a spider web.

Bonnie knows he's not supposed to talk about it so doesn't push for more details, despite feeling a slight smugness. She usually only allows herself that luxury for those seconds after Ty's called her name and handed her a key.

'Do you like working on this?' she asks. It seems a weird fit to her. She bites into a savoury scroll. Her tastebuds dance and she wishes she had grabbed a second.

He doesn't answer straight away, and his face stays unnaturally neutral. 'I got offered my dream job a couple of years ago—working outside broadcast on National Geographic. I had twenty-four hours to decide.'

'Okay?' Bonnie knows there must be more to the story.

'My girlfriend didn't want me to take it. It would have meant I'd be away for nine months of the year.'

'Wow, big call,' Bonnie says, unsure whether she could turn down a dream job for love. 'You're a romantic.'

Ben doesn't let the compliment settle. 'She's not my girlfriend anymore.'

'Oh.'

'I was a total prick. I resented her, and we fought every day for the next nine months. Every single day I just kept thinking, *I could be in Africa.*' He shakes his head, ashamed at how he'd behaved. 'And she knew it. I was a bastard until she finally broke up with me.'

Bonnie reads between the lines. 'Messy break-up.'

He gives her a look to suggest that it's not even worth mentioning how bad. 'She got the car, I got the cat.'

'Fair?'

'Absolutely. I didn't deserve the cat after how I'd treated her, but she knew how broken I was, how much I loved it, and let me keep her.'

Bonnie is suddenly hit with an image of Ben kicking back on the lounge with his cat on his lap. She finds herself smiling.

'You're thinking of me stroking my pussy, aren't you?' He smiles cheekily, pleased with himself for changing the mood.

Bonnie rolls her eyes at the potty joke. 'You're terrible.' But still, she laughs.

❧

Darcy guzzles water from her bottle as she follows Drew out of the gym and onto the street. She catches a glimpse of herself in the reflection of the glass window and inwardly cringes, her hand automatically reaching to her hair, which is splayed in a messy fountain on top of her head. She attempts to smooth it over, but there's really nothing she can do. Her face is red, not a rosy glow, but bright red—harsh and ugly. A lacquer of sweat coats her skin.

'I look awful,' she complains, knowing she's spending too much time with the appearance-obsessed girls on *The One*. Only a few days ago they did a segment of them doing yoga by the pool. The camera guys had been instructed to get plenty of boob and butt shots. The makeup department had even sprayed water on them to make it look like they were radiant with a light sweat.

'Just shows you worked hard.'

Darcy frowns, knowing she would have been much more comforted had he simply said, 'You look beautiful.'

Drew had driven down last night after finishing work. Darcy had hoped they could go out for a late dinner, but by the time she'd gotten home after the pool party and key ceremony he was already asleep on the lounge.

They are on their way to grab a coffee before picking up a few groceries when Darcy sees *her*.

'Oh my God,' she mutters. 'Please let the earth swallow me whole.'

'Is that Zoe Eggins?'

'Uh-huh.'

'Shit,' Drew groans. He doesn't find Zoe the most annoying person on the planet like Darcy does, but knows being in her company is always painful.

'Uh-huh.'

Darcy watches as Zoe emerges from the crowd. She's only wearing jeans and a black singlet but somehow she looks amazing, like her success is a glowing bubble of awesomeness.

Zoe catches her eye and Darcy watches her face as she registers. Her tight expression reworks itself into a fake smile.

'Darcy Reed! My goodness, it's been years.'

'Years,' Darcy confirms, wishing it had been decades instead. 'How are you?'

'Busy.' Zoe pushes her sunglasses onto the top of her head. 'Always busy.'

Darcy wishes she could pretend she didn't know about Zoe landing the producer role on *Smith Street*, but it would be impossible for Darcy to have not heard about it. 'Yeah, I saw online that you're doing really well. Congrats.' The words feel like glue in Darcy's mouth.

Zoe tosses her head. 'Oh, the media have been all over it, haven't they?' She makes a face implying she has no idea why people would be interested in her. 'It was one interview after the next for a while there. I was sick to death talking about myself.'

'I doubt that.' Darcy smiles lightly.

Zoe ignores the comment. 'Anyway, enough about me. What about you? Are you working in TV?' There's hesitation in her voice, as though she's waiting for Darcy to say she's now a check-out chick or working in hospitality, code for *waitress*.

Drew takes her hand and she feels warmed by this. 'Of course she's working in TV,' Drew says like Zoe is some kind of idiot. 'Tell her, babe.'

Zoe looks at her intently, no doubt waiting to compare their achievements. Darcy wishes for a moment she could claim to be working on *Sixty Minutes* or even a movie. 'Field producing on *The One*,' Darcy says as brightly as she can, waiting for the judgement. She partly feels angry with herself for not just being proud. She loves her job.

Zoe smiles, clearly satisfied. 'Oh, reality television. I've never done that. I imagine it's a hoot.'

Darcy knows that by 'hoot' Zoe's implying it's not a serious TV job. And honestly, who else their age uses the word *hoot*?

'Not everyone is cut out for reality TV,' Drew comments, with an expression that suggests he doubts Zoe would be any good at it. Darcy almost laughs.

'So, you two are still together?' Zoe asks. 'Dean, wasn't it?'

'Come on, Zoe, you're not that important that you can't remember my name,' Drew says, more amused than offended.

Darcy's a little surprised by Drew's comment and by the look on Zoe's face, she's been taken off guard too. These days she probably isn't used to anyone challenging her.

'Drew, of course. It must have just slipped my mind for a moment.'

Darcy feels herself smile. Seeing Zoe even slightly flustered for half a second is still as enjoyable as it was at university.

'We're engaged, actually,' he tells her.

Darcy wants to puff out her chest proudly—marriage is, after all, a grown-up thing to do—but instead she feels her neck tense. Zoe probably views marriage as some kind of failure, that instead of concentrating on her career, Darcy has been sidetracked by a relationship.

'Congratulations then, I guess.' The way she says *I guess* confirms her opinion of marriage is fairly low.

'Thanks,' Drew murmurs, but his tone has changed. He's realised that trying to impress Zoe with their engagement was the wrong tactic. 'Did you know this is Darcy's fourth season field producing on *The One*?'

Darcy cringes. She knows he's trying to help, but it sounds like he's clutching at straws. Bragging that Darcy has worked on the same show for four years isn't going to impress Zoe. Frankly, nothing is going to impress Zoe. She's going to walk away knowing she landed the superior job whereas Darcy is marrying her high school boyfriend.

'Field producing for four years? Wow ...' Zoe manages, somewhat polite, somewhat patronising. They both know she should have been promoted by now.

'Anyway ...' Darcy begins, desperate for their little reunion to be over. She wishes she could walk away and not give Zoe a second thought, but Darcy already knows she'll be replaying their conversation in her head late at night.

'Do you still see anyone from uni?' Zoe asks suddenly.

Darcy's a little thrown—from anyone else it'd be a normal question, but at university Zoe had never been interested in maintaining relationships of any kind. 'Um, yeah. We see Ed all the time and I catch up with Ellie and Tara every few weeks.'

Zoe's expression tightens. 'That must be nice.'

Huh? She sounds genuine, possibly even envious.

'I've fallen out of touch with everyone, but I'd love to see them again.'

Darcy swallows a lump in her throat.

'Aren't a whole lot of you catching up next weekend?' Drew looks to Darcy.

Darcy shoots him daggers. Even if Zoe is feeling left out, Darcy doesn't want to hang out with her. 'Yeah, Tara's just organised a bit of a catch-up through Facebook.' Darcy tries to play down the reunion as best she can. 'I don't know how many are going, though.' Pretty much everyone who lives in Sydney will be going and even a couple who are now based in Melbourne are flying up for the weekend, but she doesn't want Zoe to know that. The whole vibe will change if Zoe Eggins is there, parading around her success.

'That sounds great,' Zoe says. 'When and where?'

Darcy's heart sinks.

25

Penelope stands on the front doorstep, listening to the hurried footsteps approaching.

Lara throws open the door. 'Hello. Come in, come in!' She beckons, urging Penelope to follow. 'I'll just be a moment,' Lara tells her, running down the hall, her arms loaded with washing. 'Molly wet the bed last night, so I've got to get another load out on the line.'

Penelope tells Lara to take her time and finds herself moving to the hutch to look at one of Lara's wedding photos. Lara wore an extravagant white dress, nothing like the one Penelope had chosen for herself almost a year ago, yet it still reminds her of the feeling she'd had when she'd tried it on. Absolutely beautiful, head over heels in love and ready for her wedding day. Penelope's heart stings, causing her to gasp for air.

Lara comes back and sees Penelope looking at the photo. 'Look how skinny I was!' She picks up the frame. 'What I'd give to be that size again.'

'You look just as beautiful now.'

Lara laughs. 'What nonsense—I'm about twenty kilos heavier. It's a shock Nate hasn't left me!' she jokes.

'You've had two kids. I think you should give yourself a break. Life's too short to be obsessed with weight.'

Lara smiles, clearly appreciating the kind words, but Penelope imagines it's a little tough to take from someone like herself who barely weighs sixty kilos.

'Is that your mum?' Penelope changes the subject, pointing to another photo.

Lara nods, a fondness sweeping over her face. 'Yes. Taken at Christmas.' Tears mist her eyes. 'I had no idea that it was going to be our last Christmas with her.'

Penelope gives a sympathetic smile, remembering her last Christmas with her own mum. They'd gone to the beach, had a picnic and all got terribly sunburnt. It wasn't long after that her mum got the diagnosis.

'I ended up getting cranky with her because she kept sneaking Molly lollies even though I'd asked her not to. So now that's my last Christmas memory of her.' Lara's voice shakes, her mouth sloping downwards.

'What's your favourite Christmas memory of her?' Penelope asks.

Lara seems a bit taken aback. 'Oh, I don't know.' She chews on the inside of her lip. 'Maybe when we were little, and she and my dad surprised us with a dog on Christmas morning ...'

'Well, that's the one you should think about,' Penelope says, all too familiar with this. 'When you want a Christmas memory, think of getting that dog, or how her face looked when she watched you open presents …'

'Or how she'd hum along to Christmas music when she was putting up the decorations …' Lara was getting it.

'Surround yourself with the beautiful memories. Of course the other memories will come to you every now and again, but some days are hard. In my experience, you don't want to make them harder on yourself.'

'I'll remember that.' Lara smiles, then points to another face in a frame. 'That's my brother. Haven't seen him in two years.'

'What about your mother's funeral?' She immediately wants to stuff the words back into her mouth; it's unlike her to ask prying questions.

Lara shrugs. 'He was travelling.' Distaste colours her words. 'Said to have the funeral without him.'

'Oh …'

'He said Mum wouldn't mind—that the funeral wasn't going to change anything for him. But still …' Lara clearly thinks he made the wrong decision.

'I guess we all have to make peace with the choices we make.'

'Well, he's right. Mum wouldn't have minded. She would have told him to keep travelling and have a good time. She hated to inconvenience anyone.'

'My sister was like that.' The words are out of her mouth too quickly. Penelope doesn't know why she's being so careless.

A faint line of concern rushes over Lara's face at hearing *was*. 'Your sister?'

'She died, a few years ago now.' Penelope prepares herself for it—the sympathy and horror.

'You've lost both your mum and your sister?' Lara doesn't even wait for her to respond, she just throws herself forward, wrapping Penelope in a hug. She smells of Weet-Bix and laundry powder. 'You poor thing.'

Penelope surprises herself by sinking into the hug and, for the first time in a long time, she lets herself be swept away in the sadness.

26

The clue for today's group date is *Food Appreciation* and Bonnie feels nothing but relief. A few days ago, half the girls went on an athletics carnival group date. Bonnie had almost been sick as she'd waited to see if her name was going to be called out. Physical competition is not her strong point. She was lucky with the horse-riding date but doubts there'll be another sports activity she can actually do. A date revolving around food is definitely her kind of thing.

But when they arrive at the date, Bonnie feels the colour drain from her face. There are six kitchen workstations set up. She isn't going to be eating food, she's going to be making it. A clear memory of Carla opening her freezer stocked full of frozen dinners pops into her mind.

'Bonnie,' Carla had said, horrified. 'I have three kids and manage to put something healthy and nutritious on the table every night.'

'And I work seven days a week,' she'd bitten back.

Carla had just frowned. 'It wouldn't take long to throw together a healthy stir-fry.'

'I'd end up having to eat it as leftovers for the next week, or throw it out—you wouldn't want me to *waste* it, would you?' Bonnie had said it seriously, knowing Carla had a thing about wasting food.

Bonnie watched as Carla thought about it for a moment, waiting for her next plan of attack. 'Surely you could make some lasagnes and shepherd's pies and freeze them in single portions? It'd be much healthier than the store-bought stuff.'

Bonnie had been exhausted, Carla draining the last of her energy. 'I'm sure I could.' But she wasn't going to.

Carla hadn't said another word. But the next day she had filled Bonnie's freezer with fresh and organic homemade meals.

Now Ty stands in front of them with a big grin on his face. He's clearly excited about the date. Bonnie wishes the ground would swallow her whole. The only relief is that she has a few precious hours away from Imogen, who only that morning viciously accused Bonnie of using too much detergent while washing up the dishes. Bonnie has never seen Imogen do the dishes in the first place but she held her tongue to avoid ensuring herself more screen time.

Mel, the field producer on the date, calls action and Ty launches into his spiel. 'For today's group date, I thought it would be fun if you each made me your signature dish. I'll sample each one and whoever cooks my favourite will join me tonight for a special treat.'

Addison, dressed in pink as always, squeals with delight. When she isn't exercising, she's in the kitchen cooking. She has a very good chance at winning, but there's also Kristy, who apparently brought Ty spicy soup on the red carpet, so there's going to be some competition. Bonnie just isn't going to be in the running. She groans so loudly that the rest of the girls turn to laugh. They all know she's hopeless in the kitchen, so they're probably thrilled that she won't be a threat. Ty stares at her a little quizzically and goes to say something but Mel calls, 'Cut!' and promptly approaches to run through what will happen next.

They're taken to a supermarket and given five minutes to choose their ingredients, but it's closer to three hours by the time each of them is given time to walk around the supermarket with Ty to explain what they're going to make.

When it's finally Bonnie's turn, she and Ty fall into step with each other. 'So, what are you going to make me?' he asks, a cheeky grin on his face.

'Do you feel more like eggs or baked beans on toast?' Bonnie deadpans.

Ty's expression immediately changes. 'I thought you liked food?'

'I do, I love it,' Bonnie enthuses. 'I'm just terrible at making it.' On their first date they'd talked about all their favourite foods. She feels bad that he'd assumed she could make any of it herself.

Ty laughs but seems a little disappointed. 'I really thought this would be your kind of date.'

'Hey, if you were cooking for me, then it would be perfect.' Bonnie feels herself relaxing in his company and tries to ignore the crew who are standing less than a metre away. 'I should have told you that my freezer is usually stocked with Lean Cuisines and that I also have a terrible addiction to drive-through takeaway.'

He smiles, but she can tell he's unsure whether she's exaggerating.

'Sadly, I'm not kidding.' They are walking fairy-step slow down the supermarket aisle, Ben the cameraman expertly taking backward steps with the large camera resting on his shoulder.

'Maybe another time I can cook for you,' Ty says, so genuine that Bonnie tingles with hope.

'I'd offer to be your apprentice, but I'm pretty sure I'd just get in the way,' Bonnie says. 'I can keep your glass full of wine?'

'Sounds like a deal to me.'

Bonnie smiles. She wishes again that she had been able to meet Ty outside of *The One*, where they could just date like normal people.

'You had me fooled. When we were talking about food on our date, your whole face lit up. I assumed you must have been a bit of a gun in the kitchen.'

'Yep, fooled you.' She grins as she reaches for a carton of eggs.

'You're actually going to make eggs on toast?'

She can tell he doesn't know whether to be amused or appalled.

'I was going to try an omelette thingy that I've watched my sister make.'

'The fact that you call it an "omelette thingy" is concerning.'

Bonnie winces, already anticipating the disaster she'll create.

'You can't be that bad.' He has too much faith in her.

'Oh, you're going to be *so* let down,' she says, laughter on her breath. 'But I'm sure watching me in the kitchen is going to be very entertaining. Probably something you won't forget in a long time.'

A few hours later and back at her cooking station, Bonnie has burnt two pans, has ingredients splattered all over her workspace, has a dish that resembles rubber and is feeling totally dishevelled. Bright studio lights are set up, the heat causing sweat to run down her back.

Ty approaches her station for taste-testing. The other girls have been ushered off for more touch-ups. 'You weren't lying.'

Bonnie grimaces. 'I honestly don't think I can let you eat this.' She screws her face up just looking at the plate she's presenting. The omelette looks a lot more 'thingy' than omelette.

Ty looks down at it. 'I think they're going to make me try it.' He gestures to Mel standing next to Ben and his camera.

Bonnie puts her hands up in defeat. 'I did warn you I was terrible.'

'You did,' he agrees. 'And you were right—I don't think I'll ever forget watching you in the kitchen.'

Laughter tickles the air between them.

Bonnie shrugs. 'Anytime you want to watch a stressed-out girl try to make something that should take ten minutes ruin an entire kitchen, you just let me know.' That's the closest she gets to flirting.

Ty stares into her eyes, studying her. 'I don't know what it is about you, Bonnie Yates, but I like being around you.'

Her stomach contracts, urgent for breath. 'I feel the same way.'

∽

'You did what?' Ed's face is a mix of annoyance and amusement as he learns of Zoe Eggins coming to their university reunion.

'I had no choice,' Darcy tells him, shifting her bag of fruit and veggies to her other hand as they move through the farmers' market on Sunday morning. 'She invited herself.'

'She did,' Drew agrees as he drains the last of his coffee. In only a few hours' time he'll be driving back to Gloucester. Their weekend together is almost over.

'She hasn't changed.' Darcy's rather satisfied that Zoe's still exactly the person she was at university. It makes it easy to keep her feelings the same. Darcy likes the consistency of that.

'Everyone's going to be so pissed at you,' Ed says. He shoves an arancini ball into his mouth. He makes it his mission to eat the entire time they are there.

He's right. One of their favourite pastimes at such events is to bitch about how much they all hate Zoe.

'It's Drew's fault.' She turns to him accusingly. 'You're the one who mentioned it to her in the first place.'

But he's not about to take the blame for it. 'I was just trying to keep the conversation going.'

'Well, maybe you need to learn to keep your mouth shut.' Her tone is much harsher than she'd intended.

'Whoa.' Ed's eyebrows jump high onto his forehead. He gives Darcy a look to suggest that maybe she should cool it.

Darcy knows it's not really Drew's fault, but she'd been looking forward to the reunion. She doesn't want Zoe to come.

'I need a drink,' Ed says, now finished with his arancini balls. 'And probably some macadamia nuts. Anyone else?'

'I'm going to go grab some chilli jam to take home to Mum,' Drew says.

'*Home?*' Darcy parrots. Isn't his home in Sydney, with her?

Drew goes to say something, to adjust his words, or maybe to justify them, but just shakes his head and walks off towards the jam stand.

'Are you trying to make things really awkward, or am I just imagining things?' Ed asks as he leads the way towards a fresh lemonade stall.

Darcy lets out a groan. 'I don't know. I'm just frustrated.'

'It's not Drew's fault that Zoe's coming. And you know what she's like—she probably won't even come.'

Darcy knows he's right, but deep down she also knows it isn't either of those things causing her mood. 'I'm just over doing long distance.' Her fiancé should be referring to the house they share as 'home'. It makes her jaw clench tight, but is she overreacting?

'He'll be back in Sydney for good soon, Darce.'

She nods, not trusting herself to say anything else for fear she might start crying in the middle of the farmers' market.

Ed slings his arm around her. 'Come on, I'll buy you a lemonade.' As they join the end of the line, there's a child having a massive tantrum in front of them. Ed doesn't seem to notice the child lying on the ground kicking and screaming, instead he points out a sign announcing a new raspberry-flavoured lemonade. 'Shouldn't lemonade be strictly lemon flavour?'

But Darcy can't draw her attention away from the child, who now has snot hanging from her nose, her cheeks red and blotchy. The parents are unsuccessfully trying to reason with the distraught little girl. The task looks harder than dealing with any of the highly strung contestants on *The One*.

'How does anyone want one of those?' she whispers to Ed, her eyes like magnets on the child. The mother looks up, somehow having heard Darcy's hushed whisper despite the piercing noise her child is making. She sends her a look that fills Darcy with guilt.

'Maybe I should try the raspberry,' Ed debates, flavour of utmost importance, somehow still oblivious to the scene unfolding in front of them. 'Oh, look, she got the raspberry.' Ed points to a girl turning away from the stall with freshly purchased raspberry lemonades in hand.

But then Ed makes a gurgling sound in the back of his throat, as though he's drowning in his own saliva.

Darcy manages to peel her eyes away from the outburst in front of them and sees what Ed is looking at.

Sienna. Sienna holding two raspberry lemonades. She's alone, but clearly not at the market alone.

'Hey,' Sienna says, panic washing over her face.

Darcy wishes she hadn't been paying so much attention to the screaming child. Maybe she would have seen Sienna in the line and been able to suggest a fresh juice instead.

'Hi.' Ed's body has become stiff next to her. Darcy glances at him. The pain of the recent break-up with Sienna is rushing to the surface of his skin in the form of sweaty patches. Darcy hasn't seen Sienna in over a month, since before she knew she was a cheater. She feels a swell of protectiveness for Ed rush through her body.

'Sienna, hi.' Darcy knows she should take control of the conversation to spare Ed the pain, but then isn't sure what else to say. Sienna used to be her friend too. Darcy wants to know when she started having feelings for some other guy. Had Sienna dropped clues into conversations they'd had? Had Darcy just missed all the signs? She wonders where she's living now. What did her parents say? They always loved Ed, like any parents would. How do they feel that their daughter left him for someone else? And deep down Darcy wants to know if Sienna's okay too. Even though she'll forever be on Ed's side, she wants Sienna to be happy. Darcy should know what to say; asking people questions about awkward situations is a big part of her job. But instead she sweeps away all hard questions and settles on, 'Is the raspberry lemonade any good? Ed was just deciding whether to get it.' She feels Ed's eyes on her. She isn't sure whether he's grateful she's making conversation or annoyed she's talking about lemonade.

Sienna also seems thrown by the question. 'Umm … yeah. It's good for something different.'

Ed exhales loudly, trapping a sound in the back of his throat. 'I don't need to try something different. I'm happy with traditional.'

They all know he's not talking about lemonade.

Darcy notices the family with the child has disappeared and wishes for the noise and distraction instead of the awkward silence.

'You said yes!' Sienna suddenly exclaims, excitement in her voice as she points to the engagement ring on Darcy's finger. 'We knew Drew was planning …' She looks to Ed but then freezes, realising she said 'we' and knowing she has no right to do that anymore.

'Yeah, he's around here somewhere …' Darcy glances around but instead of seeing Drew's familiar face in the crowd, she sees *him*. Sienna's new guy. She recognises him from the photos on Facebook. Darcy's tummy tumbles in anticipation. She feels like she's just been in a car accident, but is still stuck in the car, waiting to be rescued, and now a semitrailer is about to ram into their vehicle and she can do nothing but wait to be hit.

Both Sienna and Ed see him approaching too. Darcy's sure she hears Sienna swear under her breath.

'Hey.' He bounds towards them. His friendly smile indicates he has no idea who Sienna is talking to, which somehow makes it worse. He stands close to Sienna, two plates of Dutch pancakes in hand. 'I'm James,' he says, perhaps assuming the prolonged silence is because Sienna can't remember the names of the people she's talking to and is saving her the embarrassment of admitting it. If only that were the case.

'This is Darcy … and you've met Ed before …' Sienna throws James a pointed look, avoiding any eye contact with Ed or Darcy.

Blood rushes from the boyfriend's face, his smile melting away like ice-cream on a sweltering day. 'Right ...' Darcy can see plain as day that James wants the ground to swallow him whole. 'Hi.' He gives a small nod, guilt quickly replacing the friendliness he was wearing only moments ago.

Darcy looks at Ed again. His face is unreadable, but his gaze is fixed on Sienna and James. She's sure this has just chiselled away another piece of his broken heart.

'We better go find Drew,' Darcy says, touching Ed on the arm. 'Good to see you,' she says to Sienna, even though they both know it isn't true. Maybe if the two girls had bumped into each other one-on-one, it would have been completely different. Maybe they would have gotten coffee, maybe Sienna would have broken down in tears and explained how hard it was for her to break things off with Ed. Maybe Darcy would have assured Sienna that Ed would be okay ...

'Good luck with the wedding,' Sienna says, a harmless comment, but one that reminds Darcy that a month ago Sienna would have been on their guest list and now simply isn't.

There are murmurs of goodbye as the two pairs walk off in opposite directions, Ed and Darcy without any lemonade.

She glances at her friend. It's like seeing a loveable teddy bear with stuffing spilling out of it. 'You okay?'

Ed just shakes his head. 'I should have known not to come here.'

'You can't avoid every place you and Sienna ever went together.'

'I can for a couple of months. Just until it doesn't hurt so bad.'

Darcy wraps her arm around him as they walk silently through the markets to the chilli jam stand.

27

Six months earlier

Penelope looks at the man who is staring at her. Skinny, pale, thick beard. He waves but it isn't until he offers a smile that she recognises him.

'Jon, hi.' She reaches out to hug him before stepping to the side to let other people on the street pass them. It's been a while since she last saw him, which feels odd. He was someone she used to see at least every week.

His whole face is saturated with loss. He stares at her, his mouth frozen for a moment. He finally shakes himself. 'Sorry, Penny, you just look so much like her.'

Penelope feels guilty and wishes she could hide her looks. She pushes her hair off her shoulders but knows it'll make no difference; she'll always be a photocopy of Miranda.

'I'll let you go,' Penelope offers, assuming her presence must be painful, but Jon's face falls.

'I was hoping we could get a coffee?'

Penelope glances at her watch, but figures she has time before her appointment.

Ten minutes later, they are seated at a cafe Penelope has never been to but has walked past a thousand times. It's small from the front, but there's a gorgeous courtyard out the back, with greenery and flowers on every table. She thinks to herself that she should bring him here. He'd like it.

Penelope orders a green tea and expects polite chit-chat while they wait for the drinks to arrive, but Jon launches into his grief straight away.

'Some days I just think, fuck it, why bother, and I don't even get out of bed.'

It had been over four years since Miranda died. Penelope still thinks of her sister every day, but Jon is still going through horrific pain and loss.

'What about work? How's that going?' Penelope hopes to steer the conversation in another direction.

'I've dropped my hours. I do what I can to get by most weeks.'

Jon, a university lecturer, was always enthusiastic and inspiring, but now his face is dull, the spark hidden, maybe even extinguished. 'But you loved your work, Jon.'

'I used to love a lot of things.'

Penelope feels let down; she'd expected more from him. She senses he knows that.

'Everyone copes with grief differently, Penny. I tried to throw myself into work, I tried obsessive exercise, I tried meditation.' He shakes his head. 'Last year I even tried dating. None of it has worked for me. All I can do to get through each day is let myself feel the pain.'

Penelope closes her eyes for a moment, knowing Miranda would hate him living like this. She'd hate to know he was consumed with nothing but grief.

It's a life Penelope wouldn't wish on anyone.

28

Despite the layers of makeup applied to her face, Bonnie still feels like she's flaming red with embarrassment. Today's group date had been a photoshoot for *Scoop* magazine. Bonnie had been one of five girls on the date who had to pose with Ty in 1950s swimwear. Walking out in a polka-dot one-piece with frills around her waist had nearly brought on the same anxiety levels that she'd felt on the first night when she had to step out of the limousine. Wondering about how she's being portrayed on TV makes her insides feel as though they're being wrung out.

'I couldn't help but notice that things with you and Imogen were a bit tense today?' Ty rests back on the two-seater lounge, his arm slung around the back of her. It's finally Bonnie's one-on-one time, which will last about fifteen minutes if she's lucky, and he's bringing up Imogen?

Nothing in particular had happened, just their usual terseness with one another. Bonnie wonders if Darcy had suggested to Ty that he ask her about it. Or maybe with fewer girls on the date, he just had more of an opportunity to notice their interactions.

So many words hang from Bonnie's tongue. Part of her wants to vomit out the vicious complexities going through her head. Oh, she can imagine what Imogen would say about her if given the chance.

'We're just very different people,' Bonnie offers as an explanation, her eyes darting to the camera as though the equipment, along with Ben, would know she's making a very large understatement.

'O-kay.' Ty's mouth twists and Bonnie's sure she sees a flicker of amusement.

'Anyway, I'd prefer to not spend *our* time talking about Imogen, or any of the other girls for that matter.' She tries to smile breezily but hears the irritation in her voice.

Ty looks to Darcy as though waiting for her permission.

'Yep, move things along,' Darcy calls out. 'Let's get things focused back on your time with Bonnie.'

Ty nods at this. He looks at Bonnie for a moment before speaking, as though giving the two of them just a moment to forget about everything else and concentrate on their connection instead. Bonnie's heart flutters under his gaze and a calmness settles over her.

'So, you don't like being in the limelight, or cooking, or doing physical activity?'

Bonnie sounds far from the ideal partner but she can't lie about who she is. 'I don't even like yoga,' she admits. 'I know it's supposed to be relaxing, but …' She shakes her head as she trails off, indicating it's anything but relaxing.

'I tried it once,' Ty says. 'I was awful. The instructor said she'd never had anyone as inflexible as me.'

Bonnie grins, imagining him in his sports gear attempting a downward-facing dog. 'How did you get conned into doing that?'

Ty hesitates for a moment. 'My ...' He begins, but stumbles on his own breath before steadying himself. 'My ex. She used to do it a couple of times a week. She begged me for months to go with her. One day I finally did. Afterwards she told me I never had to come again.'

They haven't talked about specific exes before, so Bonnie isn't sure exactly how to tread. 'Are you sure you weren't purposely bad?'

He almost laughs at this. 'You're giving me too much credit. I wasn't smart enough for that.'

There's silence for a moment. Bonnie doesn't think it's necessarily awkward silence, but the atmosphere has shifted. She sees movement out of the corner of her eye, causing her to take a sideways glance. Darcy is moving closer to the monitor, whispering something to Ben behind the camera.

'Wrong direction, guys,' Darcy calls to the two of them. 'Let's go back to Ty's comment about not liking the limelight, cooking or physical activity.' They will clearly edit out the bit about Ty's ex.

Bonnie feels suddenly nervous, especially when she sees Ty's closed his eyes for a moment as though trying to push away old memories.

'Ready when you are, Bonnie,' Darcy calls, trying to get the conversation going again.

'Yep, okay.' Bonnie nods, forcing herself to focus on the prompt. *Limelight, cooking, physical activity.* 'I hate being in the limelight and I'm a terrible cook, but some physical activity is okay ...' It takes a split second for her to realise that the phrase sounded far from how she'd intended. 'Oh my God, I can't believe I just said that!' She clasps her hands over her mouth.

Ty laughs, seeming grateful for the distraction. 'Hey, I've got no problem with that.'

But Bonnie looks to Darcy standing beside Ben and the camera. 'Can you cut that out?'

Darcy and Ben are both laughing too. 'No way,' Darcy chimes. 'They'll definitely be using that in the promo for tomorrow night.'

Bonnie buries her head in her hands. 'You do know my grandmother will be watching this.'

'We're still rolling,' Darcy calls, indicating to keep the conversation moving.

Bonnie grimaces but knows there's no point in being annoyed at Darcy and Ben when they're just doing their jobs. It's her own stupid fault for making embarrassing comments.

'My grandmother would probably really like you,' Ty adds to the conversation. He has a fond expression on his face.

'Are you close to your family?'

He nods, shrugs. 'My dad died when I was five. I don't remember much about him. After that it was always me, my mum and my grandparents.'

They hadn't really talked family before. 'No siblings or cousins?'

Ty shakes his head, needing to clear his throat a little. 'Both my parents were only children too.'

Bonnie doesn't miss the sense of longing. She can't imagine growing up as a single child when so much of her life has Carla weaved all the way through it.

'I think that's why I've always wanted kids—lots of them.'

'Lots?' That makes Bonnie tense. She's always wanted two. Just two.

Ty looks at her and laughs. 'Have I scared you off?'

'Well, that depends on what qualifies as *lots*?' She smiles, but there's certainly some truth to her answer.

Ty shrugs. 'Five or six.'

Her eyes bulge. 'You're crazy.'

But he just smiles. 'Imagine how amazing it'd be to have that much love in your life.'

Bonnie's done enough photoshoots with large families to turn her off the idea. 'I think the word you're looking for is chaos.'

Ty is unwavering. 'I was always so lonely growing up. I'd look at friends who had brothers and sisters and, sure, they'd complain about how annoying their siblings were, but whenever I was around I just thought how awesome it was. Someone to play with and to talk to.'

Bonnie tries to picture herself with Ty and a brood of babies, but the image isn't clear.

He reads her face. 'I have freaked you out.'

Not exactly, but the concept jars in her head. She shrugs. 'I'm thirty-three. Even if I wanted five or six kids, I don't think it's going to happen.'

Silence settles between them. Is this a deal breaker? Does this mean Bonnie will be the next to go home? Do other girls simply tell him yes—they'd love to have five or six babies with him? A bit of bile comes into the back of Bonnie's throat. *Don't think about the other girls,* she tells herself. *Don't think about it being a competition for love. Don't think about being on a TV show. Don't think, don't think, don't think!*

'Do you want kids?' Ty asks, a tightness in his throat.

Bonnie nods. 'Yeah.' Her own voice is shaky. 'But I've started to realise it might not happen for me.' *Oh no … please don't cry.*

'Bonnie.' Ty cocks his head to the side, affected at seeing her close to tears. 'Don't say that.' He gazes into her eyes as his fingertips dance across her neck. They lean in and their lips touch. Bonnie wants to let herself be swept away in his kiss, but instead her heart aches for dreams she may have to give up on. She feels his hand brush hair from her face and she suddenly wonders whether this is a pity kiss. Had he not known what else to say and the best way to get around the awkwardness was to kiss her? Are the viewers at home going to think her emotional outburst was just a ploy to get sympathy?

Bonnie pulls away, a little abruptly. She wants to be away from here, away from the spotlight. She feels like she needs to have a good cry in her bath at home with a block of chocolate and a very large glass of wine.

Ty's hand moves to hers and gives it a bit of a squeeze. He hasn't seemed to take it personally.

Bonnie looks to Darcy, urging her to call cut, but Darcy is watching through the monitor, waiting to see the moment play out.

'Are we done?' Bonnie asks, eyes focused on Darcy, too shaky to look back at Ty.

Darcy meets her eye and after a moment's consideration says, 'Okay, cut.'

Ty leans in, concern on his face, but Bonnie pulls her hand free. 'My time's up. I won't keep you.' With her emotions swirling inside her, she's relieved to be able to escape. Why did she think she could do this? She's wearing her heart on her sleeve, but it feels more like she's circulating a photograph of herself naked for the whole country to see.

'Thanks, Bonnie.' Darcy sends her a kind smile, but Bonnie knows she'll be pressed about this later.

The makeup girls swarm over to Ty, ready to set him up for the next one-on-one.

'Six kids?' Ben murmurs, stepping back from his camera as Bonnie moves past him. 'He's an idiot.'

Bonnie finds herself smiling though her eyes are still teary. 'I guess it's lucky he's a good-looking idiot?'

'Well, yeah, he does have that going for him.'

She gets the feeling he wants to say more, but he probably feels awkward that he's just seen her cry. She cringes. All of Australia is going to see her cry.

9

'Nice work with the fifties swimsuit date.' Ed smiles as they make their way to the pub to meet the uni crew.

Darcy laughs. 'I thought you'd like that one.' Five gorgeous women in sexy classic swimwear.

'Bundles of footage to choose from when Imogen's on a date, I imagine?'

'She barely even needs prompting—she comes up with so much of that nastiness herself,' Darcy explains. 'But it might be time to get rid of her soon.'

Ed makes a mock-horrified expression. 'You mean she's not going to win Ty's heart?'

Darcy giggles at this. She loves that Ed pretends the show is all magic.

'How's Bonnie doing?' he asks now. 'She was a bit of a wreck.'

'I talked to her afterwards, but she kept insisting she was okay and didn't know why she got so emotional.'

'Umm, maybe because she's on a reality TV show?'

'She seems kind of normal.' She's not like most of the other girls and Darcy actually likes her. In all honesty, she's kind of rooting for her. 'I'd like to see her get a happily ever after.'

Ed's face contorts. 'I know you're paid to believe that, but do you really think relationships can survive once the cameras stop rolling?'

Darcy shrugs; she still hasn't figured that out yet. But survival rates of couples from previous seasons of *The One* aren't all that great.

'Have you heard from Zoe?' Ed changes the subject.

Darcy wants to cry as she sidesteps an elderly man walking his dog, her mind bombarded with thoughts of Zoe Eggins. 'Yes! She messaged me on Facebook, asking for all the details. It's not like I could lie.' Even though she'd considered it. Darcy had hoped Zoe would forget about the little university reunion, but she'd tracked Darcy down through social media to say she'd definitely be there tonight. She'd even used a smile emoji, which had made Darcy want to reply with a gun to the head emoji.

Her relationship with Drew is surviving through text messages and the occasional phone call. He seems fine, which only leaves her frustrated that she's not coping. It's been a massive week of work and all she really feels like doing tonight is bitching about how crappy her boss is to all her other university mates who would reply with equally sucky stories about their own lives. But having Zoe Eggins there will change the whole vibe—it'll be a night of fake smiles and pretending everyone is over-the-top happy with their lives.

'I wonder how many people will be sucking up her arse trying to land a job on *Smith Street*?'

Darcy screws up her face. She can't think of anything worse. 'Surely not?' Her mind quickly starts scanning through the guest list. 'I don't think anyone could be that desperate.'

An hour or so later, Darcy finds herself glaring across the pub courtyard. The surrounds are gorgeous, with greenery covering all the walls, long wooden tables and funky-coloured stools. Fairy lights hang overhead and music from a live band hums from inside the pub. Despite this, Darcy's eyes are fixed on Ed and Zoe. Most of their friends are milling around together, but Ed and Zoe are off to the side by themselves at a small bar table. Ed's hand is clutched around his beer as he listens to Zoe speak. She's using her hands, flamboyantly throwing them around, her mouth moving at an annoyingly fast speed.

Ed looks captivated rather than repulsed. It makes Darcy want to throw up. Instead she just rolls her eyes and fights the urge to spit.

Zoe leans forward, touching Ed on his shoulder. Darcy waits for Ed to shrug her hand away, but he just laughs, like he's actually enjoying himself.

Ed starts talking now, a smile on his face.

A *real* smile.

Zoe laughs, tossing her hair.

Pathetic.

Ed keeps talking, as though the rest of the room doesn't exist.

Darcy can't quite figure it out. Is he flirting or trying to get a job? God, Darcy doesn't know what's worse.

Darcy tries to involve herself in other conversations. There's plenty to talk about. Friends ask her about work and her engagement, but Darcy keeps finding herself tuning out, her eyes drawn back to Ed and Zoe.

'What's he doing?' she mutters to herself, not realising Ellie's listening to her.

Ellie follows Darcy's eye and shrugs it away. 'Oh you know what Ed's like. He's too nice to be rude to her.'

But Darcy knows if Ed was having a miserable time, he'd find a way to remove himself from the conversation. He could excuse himself to get a drink, go to the bathroom, or call someone else over to join them. There are plenty of ways Ed could get out of talking to Zoe Eggins.

He must *want* to be there.

'He's doing us all a favour,' Ellie says. 'Guarding us from the troll or something.' She laughs, amused at her own joke, but Darcy can't meet Ellie's level of jest.

The two girls watch Ed and Zoe for a moment.

'I hate that I love her dress,' Ellie says.

'And her shoes,' Tara chimes in, joining them, a glass of champagne in her hands. 'I saw them last week. Six hundred bucks.' She shakes her head. 'Can you imagine having enough money to spend that much on a pair of heels?'

Darcy glances down at her own heels, the best she owns. She had to buy them when she was a bridesmaid for her cousin about three years ago.

'Should we save him?' Tara asks. 'I think I've had enough of these,' she holds up her champagne glass, 'to find Zoe amusing.'

Ellie looks at her and giggles. 'It could be a bit of fun.'

'Let's do it.' They link arms in unison, waiting for Darcy to join them. 'You coming?'

Darcy hesitates, knowing she should just slink away to another group, but she can't stand Zoe having Ed any longer. She links arms with Tara. 'Wouldn't miss it.'

'Hey, Ed,' Tara calls as the trio make their way towards Ed and Zoe, who are lost in their own private conversation, apparently oblivious to the rest of the pub. Darcy feels a mixture of anger and distress. She's not exactly sure why, but she feels betrayed by Ed. Not that she has a personal vendetta against Zoe Eggins—no one from their course is supposed to like her. He's breaking the rules.

'Tara, hey.' Ed stands to give her a kiss on the cheek.

Darcy notices Zoe sit a little straighter on her bar stool. Her face tightens and there's definitely a whiff of disappointment. Darcy feels a sense of satisfaction.

'I haven't had the chance to talk to you all night,' Tara says pointedly to Ed, glancing at Zoe.

'I thought your arse must have become glued to the seat.' Darcy tries to say it lightly but knows she sounds petty and harsh.

Ed shrugs, not buying into any of it. 'Just been chatting.'

'So, Zoe, how *are* you?' Ellie asks.

'Couldn't be better.' Zoe's face contorts into a smile, making Darcy feel a little queasy. She should stop drinking. 'I'm making some real changes at *Smith Street*. The network are really happy with my work.'

The group responds with silence. Darcy knows Ellie, currently being slammed as a travel coordinator on a film, and Tara, doing her third season on a game show, do not really want to hear anything about Zoe's success as a producer on the country's most successful television serial. At uni, they'd all found comfort in assuring one another that no one in their right mind would hire Zoe, that she was too annoying, too self-righteous.

'I'm surprised you have the time to socialise,' Ellie comments.

'You never had the time at uni,' Darcy adds.

Ed throws her a look as if to say *settle down*.

Her jaw clenches.

'There's always networking opportunities.' Zoe glances at Ed, a genuine smile on her face. 'I just offered Ed a job, actually.'

Darcy almost laughs at the idea of Ed agreeing to work for Zoe. But then she gauges Ed's reaction and her heart drops to the floor. 'But you already have a job.' She stares at him hard, stepping a little closer, demanding he look at her. 'Love Lens—your business?'

'Yeah, thanks Darce, I'm well aware of my self-employed status.' He's unusually short with her. 'It doesn't hurt to mull things over and weigh up my options.'

'A couple of years editing on *Smith Street* and Ed would be in demand to do features,' Zoe chimes in.

Edit feature films. That had been Ed's dream job when they were at uni. Darcy hadn't forgotten, but she hadn't thought about it in a while. Love Lens started off as him shooting a wedding for one of his mum's friends when he was on uni holidays. That one led to another, then another. Soon he had bookings for most weekends. When they finished university, Ed had gone back to Sydney and dug himself deep in his business while everyone else partied for the summer.

'Like I've been telling Ed, I've got some great connections now,' Zoe offers with another hair toss.

Darcy has to fight the urge to scoff in her face. How can Ed even be contemplating working for her?

'I'm after someone who can offer me a new spark and I'd be happy to help a friend out.'

Oh my God. Is she hitting on him? And referring to him as a friend? Darcy looks to Ellie and Tara, who seem just as shell-shocked as she feels. She exchanges glances with them. This hasn't been as fun as they'd been hoping. Ellie and Tara make excuses to leave for the bathroom, but Darcy can't bring herself to walk away. She wants to shake some sense into Ed.

'Another drink, Ed?' Zoe asks, grabbing her clutch purse from the table. 'Oh, Darcy?' she says as an afterthought.

'I can grab them.' Ed goes to move but Zoe touches his arm.

'Please, let me.' She smiles, eyes only for Ed as she heads off to the bar.

Darcy tries to steady her breath, a thousand thoughts slamming around in her head. She watches Ed, hoping he'll offer a place to start.

But he says nothing.

'So ... you're actually considering her job offer?' She tries to sound calm, as though he were considering a job offer from anyone other than Zoe.

'Yeah, I am.'

Darcy's stomach surges as she thinks about Ed and Zoe laughing at the water cooler.

'I've been doing Love Lens for over five years now,' he says. 'I don't know, after the whole Sienna thing, I feel like maybe I need something else. A new challenge or something.'

'I didn't know you were feeling like this.' She feels a little cheated he hasn't mentioned anything.

'Neither did I until tonight.' He shrugs innocently. 'Zoe pointed out I could hire people to keep Love Lens going and just give *Smith Street* a go for a few months.'

'I'm sure she did.'

Ed tilts his head to the side, a little smirk on his face. 'You're taking this very hard.'

How can he joke about this? 'Zoe Eggins would be your boss! Are you out of your mind?'

'Yeah, I get it, Darce. She was a real pain in the arse at uni, but she's not that bad now.'

He's going to take the job.

She glances over Ed's shoulder and sees Zoe making her way back towards them with two drinks in hand. She can't stick around to watch. 'Please just promise me one thing?'

'What's that?'

'Don't go home with her.'

But Zoe's back at the table before Ed has a chance to reply.

29

Darcy glances down at the list of questions she has to ask Ty about the date he's currently on. Ty and Samara have taken a rowboat out from Lane Cove National Park and are currently midway through the more serious part of the date—a romantic picnic. Ben had struggled getting decent footage of them on the rowboat. Samara is tall with broad shoulders and really long limbs. They had to do a few takes because she'd looked ridiculous perched on the little seat with her knees up in front of her face. Ben managed some good long-distance shots that will look more romantic than they actually were with a bit of music and editing. So far there's been no kiss and zero chemistry. Alice isn't going to be happy.

'Hey,' Ty says, approaching and taking a seat in the chair opposite her. Samara is down with the girls from hair and makeup, getting touch-ups.

Darcy greets him with a smile and without really thinking says, 'Having fun?'

Ty stalls, running his hands through his hair, and gives her a little look as though to say *not so much*.

Poor Samara will be going home at the next key ceremony.

Darcy offers a sympathetic smile. It'll be over soon. 'Ben shouldn't be too long.' He's over at the van, sending through footage he's already taken so the editors can use it as a teaser at the end of tonight's episode. Thankfully it only has to be a quick grab because there won't be much to choose from. Darcy's already texted Mel saying they're going to need extra footage of the girls in the mansion to pad out tomorrow night's episode. It was stupid for Samara to get this one-on-one. But Alice had insisted on Samara after seeing how competitive she'd been on the athletics carnival group date. Alice is trying to secure a sports brand sponsorship deal and is confident that Samara is the right kind of incentive.

'Have you got a boyfriend?'

Darcy's thrown by Ty's sudden question. 'Yeah,' she tells him and then remembers that isn't completely accurate and holds up her hand. 'Engaged actually.'

'Congrats.'

'Thanks.' She looks down at her ring and twists it back and forth. She hasn't even spoken to Drew today. After all the years they've lived together, their engagement feels nothing like she thought it would. When they first moved in together he used to drive her crazy by never replacing the toilet paper and always putting the carton back in the fridge with only a teaspoon of milk left and she couldn't stand that he would take his clothes off for a shower and leave them on the floor at the entrance of the bathroom. But as the years passed she's either trained him or learned to tolerate his habits. She misses him being away, she misses the companionship, the conversation, their hands touching while they sleep.

'Where'd you meet him?'

Darcy's surprised he's bothering to ask her questions. He's currently dating ten girls, so he really doesn't need to worry about getting to know her.

'High school.'

He nods, somewhat disappointed. 'I went to an all-boys school.' His chances of meeting a girl were clearly limited.

'Yeah.' She feels a bit weird that she already knows this because of all the background research she's done. She probably knows more about him than she does most of her friends.

'Do you really think you can meet "the one" on a reality TV show?' This question is quite common for the suitor. The situation is constantly overwhelming, and they start doubting themselves, the girls and also the whole premise of the show.

Four seasons in and she still doesn't know whether she believes 'the one' can be found this way, but it's pretty much in her job description to wholeheartedly believe that true love can be found on television. 'Of course.'

But he doesn't meet her enthusiastic and over-the-top smile. He looks more vulnerable than she's ever seen him.

She glances over at Ben standing near the van. He's on his phone now. She wishes he'd hurry up.

'I'm starting to wonder if I made a mistake coming on here.'

Darcy doesn't panic. She knows he's having a tough date. 'Maybe Samara's not the one, but you still have lots of other great girls to explore things with.'

'Samara's not the one.' His voice is low as he hangs his head. 'I don't think any of the girls here are right for me.'

Darcy had thought they were having a stock standard freak-out, but her heartbeat quickens at an image of Alice's face screeching at her for being an incompetent field producer. If the suitor walks on her watch, she'll never get another job in TV.

'We all have those kind of days,' Darcy begins. 'Some days I wonder if I'm doing the right thing marrying Drew.'

He looks quizzically up at her. 'Really?'

'Yeah.' And she's being honest. 'Some people think high school sweethearts have an amazing love story, but in reality we were just two fifteen-year-olds who hooked up and never broke up.'

Ty seems to be mull this over. 'Yeah, but you're obviously together for a reason?' He isn't buying into her angle. 'I mean, if you weren't meant to be together, you would have broken up by now.'

His words hit her hard. There had been times over the years where she'd considered breaking up with Drew. 'It hasn't been all smooth sailing.' In year eleven, she'd had a bit of a crush on Mick Phillips. He was in her maths class and there'd been weeks of playful banter between them. There was a party coming up and Darcy kept fantasising about kissing him. She'd decided it was time to break things off with Drew; they'd only been together for just over a year and she was ready for something new. But then Mick got himself a girlfriend and suddenly Darcy's motivation to be single disappeared, so she just stayed with Drew. Then there was a night at university when she'd told Drew to get stuffed after seeing him all flirty with another girl who was visiting for the weekend. Darcy had gone to bed crying hateful tears, but the next day the other girl had gone home, and Drew had turned up with his tail between his legs. A few years later, when they'd first moved in together, they'd had a massive fight about doing the dishes. They didn't speak for three days. Darcy thought it was over, but somehow, they started talking again and within a few days the fight had been forgiven.

'All relationships have their ups and downs.' He shrugs. 'I like the idea of that—sharing your whole life with someone. I think that's why most people believe there's something so romantic about marrying your high school sweetheart. You know everything there is to know about one another.'

'Well, he's definitely seen me at my worst. I don't know about you, but I certainly did the awkward and gawky teenage thing.'

Ty laughs, and Darcy realises it's the first time she's seen him laugh all day. If only Ben had been filming, they could have used the image as a cutaway shot after Samara had said something.

'Some days I just wish I got the big romance,' she admits. It was hard not to think about, working on a show where every date was set up and scheduled by a production team.

'I had that,' Ty says, the words catching his breath. 'Love at first sight.'

His ex. Darcy closes her eyes for a moment, trying to remember the ex's name. She had scribbled it down when she was ringing around, doing background checks on Ty before he'd officially been signed to the show. She can see the broken-heart picture she'd absentmindedly drawn when she'd been on the phone. She'd even sent the girl several emails in hope of getting her opinion on Ty being on the show but never got any replies.

'I accidentally ran up the back of her leg when I was riding my bike,' Ty goes on. 'She turned around and my heart skipped a beat.' He shakes his head, wistful. 'I'm not joking, my whole life changed in that moment.'

Darcy feels goosebumps prickle her arms.

'Everything happened so fast, but at the same time it didn't feel fast enough. We moved in together, got engaged, we were planning our wedding and then …' He swallows hard, the memories clearly hard to take. 'Well, she decided it was over.'

'Why?' Darcy can't help herself, though she knows she should be shutting down the conversation about his ex and redirecting him to the willing and wanting women who are desperate for him to fall in love with them.

'I don't know.' His face is sad, but it's etched with some bitterness too. 'She said she couldn't do it anymore.'

Darcy remembers talking to Mel about Ty's mysterious break-up in the production office. No one they'd spoken to had been able to give them a proper explanation. All his friends and family had said they'd been really surprised by the break-up. Darcy and Mel had tossed around different reasons, guessing why the girl had called things off, but Darcy had always assumed that Ty knew the real reason. 'Do you think it was cold feet?'

Ty looks up and holds her gaze longer than normally comfortable. 'I honestly don't know.' His face pales. 'Sure, maybe?'

There's more he isn't saying, and Darcy chews the inside of her mouth, becoming invested in the mystery. 'But you don't think that was the reason?'

'No, I don't think it was,' he confirms. 'But I can't come up with anything else. I thought I knew her, but in those weeks after she left I kept realising I mustn't have known her as well as I'd thought. She was a private kind of person, but I just hadn't realised she'd kept stuff from me.'

Darcy remembers how angry she'd felt at Drew for talking to Parko about a job without talking to her first. She'd felt so cheated.

She can only imagine how hurt Ty must have felt. 'Did you tell her about coming on the show?'

He nods but his mouth twists awkwardly. 'She wished me luck.'

It was clearly still a hard pill to swallow. Seeing how unguarded Ty is being right now, Darcy suspects he might have gone to his ex in hope that hearing he was going on a dating show would change her mind and make her want to get back together.

'Is there a way out?' Ty stares at her steadily. 'Can I get out of the show?'

Oh God. *Oh God*. Darcy wants to press an eject button on this conversation.

'You've signed a contract, Ty,' she reminds him. 'We're more than halfway through filming the show.'

'But I could break it?' He won't make eye contact now, instead looking down at his hands.

She doesn't say a word, and silence brews as a thousand thoughts go off like fireworks in Darcy's head. She can't keep track of a single thought as new ones keep exploding in the forefront of her mind, expanding and shattering. She's never had a suitor get this serious about walking before. Is Ty about to quit? Is he about to leave the show? There are still a few weeks of television to be made. She has to do something. She has to save her job. She has to save the show. She has to save this guy from walking out on a chance at love. She decides to ignore the question and try a new tactic.

'You deserve to be happy, Ty. And I believe that one of the girls still here will give you everything you want. Someone to stand by you and create a life with. House, kids, the whole shebang.' Darcy catches herself wondering if she's ever used the word *shebang* before. 'I've seen you with some of the other girls, I've seen there's something there with a few of them.' She wants to ask about his feelings for Bonnie, she's sure there's potential there, but stops herself.

'The girls are great,' Ty agrees.

But his heart belongs to someone else.

'I feel bad for all the women who are here for me.'

'Oh Ty,' she stammers, truly starting to freak out. Can anyone compete with his ex? She has no idea if they can, but she feels like she has no choice but to shake some sense into him. 'You said yourself that things with her are over. She'd be with you if she wanted to be.' Her lips feel dry, her heart racing. If anyone else had confessed they were still in love with their ex she'd be full of sympathy, but her job is on the line. 'You've got to get over her. This is your chance to move on.'

'Sorry,' Ben calls as he approaches from the van. 'Technical issues.'

Ty stands abruptly, the moment interrupted. 'I'm sorry,' he says in a hushed voice to Darcy, a horrified expression on his face as though he's realised what he's confessed. 'Shit! That was really out of line. Forget it, okay?'

Ben reaches them, unimpressed with what he's just been dealing with. 'This equipment is a load of ...' He trails off, but they get the idea.

Darcy can't be more relieved that the momentum of their conversation has been broken. She feels like she's standing knee-deep in mud and doesn't know how to get out.

Ben looks between Darcy and Ty, sensing he's interrupted something. 'So ...' He pauses. 'Are we right to go?'

Darcy looks to Ty. 'Are we?' She's desperately hoping he isn't about to throw in the towel.

He takes his time to reply, but finally meets her eye. 'Yeah.' He nods. 'The past is in the past. Let's get on with it.'

Darcy exhales the breath she's been holding, looking down at the questions she has to ask him about Samara, but a seed of worry has started to grow.

30

Twelve years earlier

'… My fault … the coffee.'

'Sorry, Mum? What did you say?' Penny looks up from her textbook, thrown by her mum's voice. She's barely spoken over the past few days.

'It was all that coffee,' her mum manages, her voice husky and dry.

Penny reaches for the ice. Her mum goes to wave it away, but then tilts her head so Penny can place a few chips in her mouth.

Penny waits, putting her book to the side. She has a maths exam the next day and after months of neglected study is struggling to make sense of the numbers and formulas in front of her. Her mum suddenly panicked last week and said Penny needed to keep her studies up. She's in year eleven and her mum insists she needs to be thinking about university. Penny doesn't want to think about university, she doesn't even want to think about next week, but if trying to study makes her mum happy, she'll do it. So here she sits, by her mum's hospital bed, trying to care about simultaneous equations and differentiation.

Penny watches her mum suck on the ice chips, letting her mouth moisten.

'I read an article in a magazine a few years ago.' Her voice is low, and Penny has to concentrate on each word. 'About coffee increasing your chances of getting cancer.'

A shooting pain seizes Penny's heart.

'I read it and laughed, thinking *what bullshit*, and went and made myself another cup.'

Penny almost laughs at her mother swearing like she'd always done. She's barely uttered more than three words at a time over the past week.

Her mother looks up and meets Penny's eyes. 'It's not so funny anymore.' Her face is grim, nothing but sadness left.

'It wasn't the coffee,' Penny urges.

'Coffee was my thing,' her mum says. 'I love you girls but when you were young and it was just me looking after the both of you, coffee got me through the day.'

Penny's dad had taken off about two months after she was born. Miranda was four at the time and had been a difficult child, while Penny had reflux and spent most of her time crying. Their father had told her mum he couldn't do it anymore, so their mum was left to look after two small girls all by herself.

'At first it was just "get out of bed and you can have a coffee",' her mum explains. 'But then it was "breakfast is done, and everyone is dressed, have another coffee!"'

Penny takes her mum's hand, which is dry and scaly, unfamiliar to what it used to be like. Penny reaches for the moisturising cream and begins rubbing it gently into her mum's hand.

'Somehow I went from having a couple of coffees a day to having …' She trails off. 'Well, you know what I was like.'

For as long as Penelope can remember, her mum always had a coffee on the go.

'And look what I've done to myself.' She gestures to her decaying body, destined to spend the last of its days bedridden.

'Mum, the coffee didn't do this to you,' Penny says.

But her mum speaks as though she hasn't heard her. 'Could have had more years with you girls if I'd just drunk green tea instead.' Her mum shuts her eyes, exhaustion taking over again.

Penny's throat closes over and she suffocates a sob as it tries to make its way out of her throat.

The end was too close.

31

Hanna is sunbaking by the pool wearing dark sunglasses when Bonnie approaches and perches next to her on the pool chair. Bonnie doesn't say anything to begin with, needing more courage than she thought she would.

Hanna glances up. 'You okay?'

Bonnie can't even pretend that she's not agitated. As each day passes, it's getting harder to live in the house. She gives a quick shake of the head. 'Have you still got the phone?' she asks in a hushed voice.

Hanna props herself up a little, quickly turning her head to check if anyone's listening to them. With Hayley on a one-on-one date with Ty, the rest of the girls are using the time to hang out by the pool. Once Hanna realises no one else is paying attention she confirms, 'Yeah, it's in my red bag. There's an inside zipper that has a safety pin on it. Just make sure you put it back.'

'Thank you.' Bonnie smiles and is about to get up from the chair when Hanna says, 'If you need to talk …'

They probably wouldn't be friends outside of the house, but Bonnie is becoming fond of Hanna. Bonnie nods but doubts she'll ever breathe a word of all the tumbling thoughts that won't stop going around in her head. There are cameras everywhere, people listening. Nothing, not even her private thoughts, feels safe.

She climbs the stairs to the bedroom. It takes her a while but she eventually finds Hanna's bag and the phone inside. She's about to head back downstairs to the laundry toilet when she pauses at one of the windows. She counts heads; all remaining girls are down in the pool. It'll probably be quicker to look at the phone up here in the bedroom rather than risk walking down the stairs, then back up again. She switches the phone on and sits on the edge of her bed.

She's been trying to focus on moving forward in her relationship with Ty, but since their horrid 'how many kids do you want?' conversation she's questioning everything again. She knows there's a connection between them, but is he really going to choose her as opposed to someone like Addison, who is twenty-six and talks constantly about wanting babies?

The phone finally comes to life. Bonnie finds the Facebook icon and logs into her account. In her search history Sophie's name is on the top. She clicks for her page to load and feels her foot tapping as she's forced to wait. The page loads but when she scrolls down she assumes it hasn't refreshed. Everything looks exactly the same as last time. That was a couple of weeks ago.

She refreshes the page, yet all the content stays the same. It doesn't make sense. Sophie usually posts on a daily basis, sometimes even an hourly basis. Why hasn't she posted in so long? It's puzzling and she finds herself annoyed. For a split second she wonders if Ollie and Sophie are fighting. Maybe Oliver told Sophie about kissing Bonnie ... She imagines Sophie's face twisting into terrifying anger.

Oh gosh. Poor Ollie.

Bonnie types into the search bar, taps at the screen and scrolls until she finds what she's looking for—his mobile number listed on his business website. She taps it without even thinking through what she's doing.

Brring, brring. Brring, brring.

Bonnie should feel nervous, but she doesn't. She has to make sure Ollie is okay. And maybe she can offer him some hope.

Or is it hope for herself that she's looking for?

'Hello?' a female voice answers the phone. But it's not just any female, it's the unmistakable voice of Sophie Nix. 'Hello?' she says again.

But Bonnie has frozen. It hadn't crossed her mind that Sophie might answer Ollie's phone and now she's struck with a sinking feeling. Maybe Sophie somehow found out that Bonnie has been stalking her Facebook page. Maybe Sophie has restricted her privacy settings so that Bonnie can't see everything anymore. Would Oliver know? Would they be talking about Bonnie? Are Oliver and Sophie actually in a good place and has she stupidly jumped to the wrong conclusion?

'Hello?' Sophie's getting annoyed now.

Bonnie's stomach twists like a dishcloth having water squeezed out of it. Oliver probably wrapped his arms around Sophie and told her she had nothing to worry about. He was with her and Bonnie meant *nothing* to him.

'Bonnie?'

Bonnie jumps and the phone fumbles out of her hands and lands on the floor. She looks up and sees Ben with the camera rested on his shoulder, but he's looking at her around the side of it and not through the lens. She finds some relief in that—he hasn't filmed the moment he caught her red-handed with the mobile.

He looks down at the phone and then back at her.

A faint yet irritated 'hello' comes from the phone's speaker.

Bonnie picks it back up and ends the call, drowning out Sophie's voice. 'Please don't tell anyone,' she says hurriedly to Ben.

Without missing a beat, he says, 'Tell them what?' Ben is stone-faced in his reply, so much so that it takes Bonnie a moment to realise that he's purposely chosen to ignore seeing anything.

She's about to smile her thanks but Ben moves abruptly, his head turning towards the stairs. 'Hey, Darcy,' he calls, his voice louder than it had been only moments ago as he moves away from the bedroom.

Bonnie's heart begins thudding in her throat as she realises that Darcy has arrived at the house and is now only metres away. Bonnie quickly shoves the mobile under the blankets.

'Hi, Bonnie,' Darcy says, appearing in the doorway. 'Did Ben tell you we're going to shoot some footage with all the girls?'

They're probably going to ask the group what they think of Hayley's relationship with Ty. *Do you think Hayley is the right kind of girl for Ty? What do you think Ty sees in Hayley? Do you think Hayley's here for the right reasons?*

They've done this a couple of times before when someone has been out on a date. Bonnie cringes at the thought of the others being asked the same questions about her when she's been on a date with Ty. Bonnie can't even answer the questions truthfully about herself.

Am I the right kind of girl for Ty?

What does Ty see in me?

Am I here for the right reasons or am I just trying to bury the feelings I have for Ollie?

'Yeah, umm, he did,' Bonnie fudges, knowing that Ben had been momentarily sidetracked.

'Can you change into your swimsuit?' The words roll out of Darcy's mouth as though she's suggesting Bonnie put shoes on.

Usually Bonnie would at least grimace at such a suggestion, but today she'd do just about anything to get Darcy away from the bedroom and the illegal phone that's almost burning a hole into the mattress. 'I'll just get changed and I'll be right down.'

'Great. I've got the guys setting up on the lounges by the pool.' Darcy goes to walk away, but at that moment a humming sound palpitates through the room.

Omigod.

It's been so long since Bonnie has even heard that beloved sound, but the noise immediately fills her with dread. She feels like someone has weighed her down with bricks and thrown her out to sea. Somewhere in the back of her mind she knows she needs to distract Darcy from the noise. But she's frozen as vibrations pulse against the mattress, causing the hairs on her arms to stand on end.

Darcy's eyes widen and her mouth falls open, her lips forming a little 'O' shape. 'Have you got a phone in here?'

Too late.

Bonnie tries to speak, which would probably help dull the incessant buzzing, but instead shakes her head with an expression to suggest that Darcy is crazy for even suggesting such a thing.

Oh, God. Did she really just try to lie about this?

Darcy takes a step closer, her expression tight and her narrowed eyes already a blaze of fury. She reaches the bed and pulls back the blankets without any hesitation. The black mobile stares up at them, the screen bright with an incoming call.

Bonnie hears herself whimper.

Of course Sophie would be her undoing.

$$\sim$$

'I have to give you an official warning.' Darcy is surprised she doesn't choke on the words. When on earth did she become the principal, reprimanding someone for doing the wrong thing? A decade ago she'd been dragged into her principal's office for wagging class and heading down to the river. A few times they'd even driven over to Forster for the day. She has a sudden longing for when her life contained no responsibility.

'Okay.' Bonnie's voice is meek and she won't meet her eye.

'When you entered the house, you signed an agreement,' Darcy goes on. The agreement is close to a one-hundred-page document about all the conditions of being a contestant on *The One*. Some of the clauses are a little ridiculous, but the use of mobile phones is surely a straightforward one. 'You've broken the contract.'

'I really am sorry.'

Never make friends with the contestants. Darcy has had enough experience on the show to know this, but somehow she'd let herself get friendly with Bonnie. She had seemed different to the others. And while she had never thought of her as a friend, Darcy had liked her, had even been rooting for her.

And now she feels like she's been betrayed.

'What happens now? Do you want me to leave the show?' Bonnie asks.

The drama of a contestant being kicked off the show would be good for ratings, but Bonnie has a good fan following and the backlash of kicking her out wouldn't be worth it. Darcy's also fairly confident that Ty likes Bonnie, whether he realises it or not, and doesn't want to take away a legitimate love interest for him, especially after his meltdown about wanting to leave the show on Samara's date. 'No, but any other incidents like this and our agreement will be terminated immediately. Understand?'

'Yes.'

Darcy turns the mobile over in her hands. It was an older model, but clearly still did everything anyone needed it to. 'Where did you get the phone from?'

Bonnie's mouth opens but it takes a moment for any words to come out. 'I'd rather not say.'

Darcy feels herself bristle with frustration knowing that Bonnie is protecting someone else. Another contestant or a crewmember? She hopes it isn't the latter. She'd told Ben in exasperated outrage that she'd caught Bonnie with a phone and he'd seemed as shocked as she was. 'Well, who were you contacting?' She stares at Bonnie. 'Or should I give the number a call myself?' Oh, geez, now she's threatening her?

'I tried to call my ex.' Bonnie seems defeated and offers up the information without protest.

This isn't the first time they've spoken about Bonnie's ex. 'The same ex who is engaged and having a baby with someone else?' Darcy could hear the judgement laced through her words.

Shame appears on Bonnie's face. 'Yep, stupid, I know. I wasn't thinking.'

Darcy studies Bonnie, searching for the answer without having to ask the question, but in the end she has to make sure. 'Is anything going on with you and your ex?'

Bonnie's quick to reply, and if she's sad about the fact, she's quick to hide it. 'No, nothing at all. It's over. One hundred percent.'

'So, you want to be here?'

There is only the slightest hesitation before Bonnie says, 'Yes.'

Knock, knock, knock.

Last night Darcy told herself she'd talk to Alice first thing this morning about the conversation she had with Ty on Samara's single date, but from the moment she arrived this morning she'd let herself get busy, and now after the drama at the house she also has to report Bonnie's use of an illegal device. She can't put off the conversation she needs to have with Alice any longer.

'Mmm–hmm?' But Alice doesn't even look up from her computer.

Darcy steps in. 'Hi!' She immediately curses herself, knowing she sounds too cheerful. Alice's eyes are fixed to the screen. Darcy reminds herself that Alice isn't interested in pleasantries, just professionalism.

'I caught Bonnie using a phone in the house and have given her an official warning.'

Alice finally looks at her, which Darcy had hoped would make her feel better, but the intense gaze is unbearable.

'She was in one of the bedrooms when a call came through. I heard the vibrations and caught her red-handed.' Darcy delivers the bothersome news. There are rules when contestants sign on to the show. Why can't they just obey them?

But she realises Alice isn't annoyed, but rather interested. 'Who was calling her?'

Darcy's thrown that Alice isn't furious. 'I didn't answer the call.' But she clearly should have. 'Bonnie said she'd tried to contact her ex and it was his fiancée calling back.'

Alice's face lights up like a kid who has received everything on her Christmas list. 'Oh, what drama! Can we get them on the show?'

No! Darcy wants to scream at her. 'He's engaged to someone else, I doubt he'd agree to it.'

'It's worth looking into.' Meaning, it's worth Darcy looking into.

'Okay.' Though Darcy knows she'll put it on the very bottom of her to-do list and hope that she never makes it that far down.

Alice is bored now. 'Is that all?'

Darcy wishes she could run straight from the room. Being in Alice's office feels like being sent to Antarctica in a bikini. 'I also wanted to have a chat with you about Ty. I don't think he's in the right headspace.'

'What headspace are you expecting a guy who is dating half a dozen women at one time to be in?'

Darcy immediately falters, shifting weight from one foot to the other. 'Umm,' she stammers, wishing she didn't feel twelve years old whenever she was in Alice's presence.

Alice raises an eyebrow, suggesting she either get on with it or leave her alone.

Maybe Alice is right—just because he's not like the other suitors they've had doesn't mean she should raise the red flag. He's dating more girls at once than some people date in a lifetime. But Darcy knows it's more than that. She has to trust her gut. 'He's said a few concerning things and—'

'I don't have all day,' Alice cuts over her quickly before Darcy's even finished talking.

'He's worried he shouldn't be on the show at all and admitted he still loves his ex.' Exes are clearly nothing but trouble.

Darcy's waiting for Alice to look shocked or worried or even appalled but she just looks annoyed. 'Our fans want to see him end up with someone on our show, not his damn ex. Surely you've been doing this job long enough to know you're the one who has to make sure he believes he's falling in love with one of the women on our show?' She exhales loudly, as though talking to Darcy causes her physical pain. 'You do understand what your role involves?'

This seems very hypocritical seeing that Alice just wanted Darcy to contact Bonnie's ex.

'Yes.' Spoken barely loud enough for a mouse to hear.

Alice stares at her with even more doubt than normal. 'Surely you know to talk about journeys and soul mates and all that drivel?'

Darcy swallows hard. 'Of course.' She tells herself not to let the words sink in too deep.

'Honestly, Darcy,' Alice scolds, 'you expect me to give you a promotion when you come to me about stuff you should be handling with ease?'

She wishes she could let the cruel comments fall away, but instead they hit her to the core. 'Sorry for troubling you.' Her voice squeaks before she rushes out of Alice's office and straight to the bathroom.

Hours later, she's still trying to forget how Alice's words sliced at her like a razor blade. She's purposely kept herself busy since she got home. A lasagne is cooking in the oven, she's got Ed's favourite chocolate brownies ready to bake for dessert and she's now chopping up a salad.

She invited Ed over for dinner to clear the air after last week's uni catch-up. She doesn't know what ended up happening with him and Zoe; they only exchanged a few texts during the week and Darcy hasn't been game enough to ask him outright.

There's a knock on the door. 'Just me,' Ed says as he pushes it open. He's carrying a bag that is clearly very heavy.

'What have you got in there?'

'Goodies for you,' he replies, heaving the bag up onto the bench for her to take a look. 'Smells amazing. You didn't have to go to all this trouble.'

She enjoys impressing in the kitchen and he knows that. 'No, trust me, I did.' With Drew away, she hasn't been making proper meals. Sometimes she bothers with a salad or a stir-fry, but more often than she'd like to admit she just has toast. She wipes her hands on a tea towel and peeks inside the bag, which is full of wedding magazines. 'Where did you get these?'

'A client,' he says as he settles on the barstool. 'I told her a good friend of mine had just gotten engaged when she was picking up an extra DVD copy. She came back the following day with all these.'

Darcy peers back into the bag again. There are easily over two hundred dollars' worth of magazines. 'Wow.'

'She said a few of the corners have been dog-eared but she hasn't gone at them with scissors or anything.'

'Should I buy her a thank-you?' The woman was clearly very generous.

Ed shakes his head. 'I didn't charge her for the extra DVD.'

Darcy tilts her head, smiling her thanks to Ed, but he shakes it away and indicates to the chopping board. 'What can I do to help?'

'Nothing.' She slides the garlic bread into the oven. 'It'll be ready in about fifteen.'

'Wine?' He holds up the bottle he'd brought with him.

She points to her half-full wine glass. 'I couldn't wait until you got here.' She gets a glass from the cupboard and passes it to him.

'Bad day?'

'Just another day working for Alice.' Resentment hangs from each word.

He gives her a sympathetic look. 'Anything new or just the usual stuff?'

'Just the usual, but I'm starting to feel like I'm going to be stuck there forever, doing the same job. I honestly don't think she has plans to promote me.'

'I'm sure she knows how valuable you are, Darce.'

Darcy isn't so sure about that.

'You could always leave, try something else?'

'Yeah, that's what Drew said.' But Darcy knows that when Ed says 'try something else' he means another TV job in Sydney, while Drew means 'take a break and come live in Gloucester'.

'You'd be snapped up. You've got some great experience behind you.'

Darcy knows she could find a new job but isn't sure she can leave *The One*. Despite Alice, she loves working on the show.

They move to the lounge. Ed brings a couple of magazines and hands her one.

Darcy sits with the magazine in her lap, staring down at the model wearing a slinky white dress, looking over her shoulder with her back to camera, one arm bent, her hand positioned near her face showing off a large diamond ring, with the other hand down by her side holding a bouquet of white roses.

'Is that the kind of thing you like?'

Darcy snaps her head up; she hadn't realised she was staring. 'What kind of thing?'

Ed peers at the cover. 'The dress, the hair, the flowers?' He's used to talking about these kinds of particulars with his clients, who give specific details of what they want him to cover when filming.

'I don't know,' she tells him honestly.

Ed's amused. 'Have you even thought about what you'd like at the wedding?'

Darcy considers for a moment. 'I'd like tulips.'

'So, a winter wedding then?'

She stares at him blankly.

'That's when they're in season.'

'Oh.' She considers. 'I guess.' Does she really want to get married when it's cold? Do brides base their entire wedding date around what flower they want?

'Have you and Drew talked about the wedding?'

'He's talked about all the people he wants to invite.'

Ed doesn't say anything, which makes Darcy feel like she has to explain. 'We just haven't had the chance. We talk every night but it's not usually for long. I'm always buggered after work and Drew seems to be helping coach every Gloucester High sports team so some nights we only manage five minutes before one of us has to go.'

'Well, there's no rush,' Ed says, seemingly trying to reassure her. 'There will be plenty of time to plan a wedding once he gets back.'

'Yeah.' Darcy nods, feeling a little bit better. She should just admit that planning a wedding with someone she's barely seen since she got engaged just feels really weird but instead she purposely changes the subject. She's ready to find out what happened with Zoe Eggins and *Smith Street*. 'So, you took the job?'

'Start Monday,' he says with a nod.

Darcy knows she should be happy for him, but the whole thing just makes her feel uncomfortable. 'What's happening with Love Lens?'

'It's all sorted.' Ed takes a drink. 'I've lined up people to film and others to edit but I'll still do as much as I can.'

Darcy wants to comment that he's going to burn himself out if he works full time on *Smith Street* and then has to come home and edit wedding videos late into the night for Love Lens, but she forces herself to bite her lip.

Ed senses she wants to say something, so adds, 'I've told Zoe I'll give it a go for three months then decide what I want to do.'

She nods but another question is niggling away in her mind. She has felt unsettled all week because of it. 'Did you go home with her?'

'No, Darce, I didn't go home with her.'

He seems a bit annoyed, which raises a red flag. 'But you wanted to?' She can't help herself.

Ed takes a deep breath, as though trying to calm himself so he won't snap at her. 'She's my boss. I won't be getting involved with her like that.'

Darcy knows she has to drop the subject, but she doesn't trust Zoe Eggins. She doesn't want Ed to have anything to do with her, but now he's going to be working for her, seeing her every day. The niggling she's felt all week hasn't gone away. Instead she fears she's going to feel like this for the next three months.

32

For Ty it's been another week of dates, but for Bonnie it's been a week of solitary confinement in the house. A week for her to do nothing but think; to drive herself crazy with every thought flying through her head.

Another endearment party is in full swing, another key ceremony looming. Bonnie knows how important it is for her to spend time with Ty, but tonight she feels like she's sitting back watching everyone around her in a movie rather than having the ability to interact herself.

She sees Ty walk across the grass after some one-on-one time with Addison. Bonnie knows she should go over and grab him before someone else does.

But she doesn't. She just sits there and watches until Jodie sees him and races over in hot pursuit.

'You waiting for an invitation?'

Bonnie's head turns. Ben and his camera have probably just filmed her watching Ty. Her heart tenses as it always does when she wonders how she's being portrayed. Ben lowers the camera so he can talk to her normally.

'I thought Darcy told you girls tonight was the night to pounce?'

That's exactly what Darcy had told them at the start of the night—to make the most of the limited time left. Whoever Ty picked tonight would get to take him to their hometown. 'Yeah, she did. But everyone wants a piece of Ty so it feels greedy interrupting.'

'Damn it,' Ben says, 'I should have filmed you saying that—it'd make a good dialogue grab.'

She shrugs, indicating he missed his chance. Bonnie's seen Ben a couple of times since he caught her with the phone, but there's always been people around, preventing her from clearing the air. 'I'm sorry about the other day up in the bedroom—'

But before she's even finished her sentence Ben gives a quick shake of the head; he clearly doesn't want her to mention it.

She wonders how much trouble he'd get in if his bosses found out he not only knew about an illegal phone in the house but also failed to film it. Has Darcy suspected he covered for her?

'All okay with you?'

Bonnie stares at him, searching his face to know how to answer properly. Her gut instinct is to say no, that she's not okay. But can she really trust Ben? Sure, they're friendly enough, but she doesn't really know him. He has a life away from the house. He gets to go home, talk to other people, be in his own space. Longing swells inside her. 'What did you do last night?'

The question seems to throw him. 'What do you mean?'

'I'm stuck in this place like a prisoner. I need a taste of the outside world. What did you do after work yesterday?'

Ben's face crinkles with an amused smile. 'I picked up some pizza and hung out with Sofia.'

She imagines his simple life—pizza, girlfriend, lounge—and feels envious.

'Sorry,' he says. 'I feel like I should have done something to impress you.'

She smiles. 'Hey, to me that sounds like the perfect night in. This is probably the longest I've ever gone since leaving home without eating takeaway. I wish I could say I don't miss it, but I do.' She feels a bit pathetic admitting this, but Ben laughs.

'Well, I guess when you screw up making an omelette, you would need to rely on takeaway.'

He's teasing her about the meal she made for Ty on the *Food Appreciation* date. It feels weird that Ben's been there for almost every date she's had with Ty. He's seen how she acted, heard what she said.

'I would have thought you'd be craving some Indian?' He's waiting for her to respond but she doesn't get it.

'Huh?'

He gestures to her outfit, a Bollywood-inspired costume that all remaining girls are wearing tonight. Hers is a dark olive green, with a beaded crop top and a long flowing skirt. Her stomach is bare and her arms are covered in gold bangles. Her dark hair has been curled and a gold headpiece sits in the middle of her forehead.

She shakes her head. 'I love Indian food, but I don't love wearing this.' She doesn't like dressing up. She's happiest in her trackies and a T-shirt.

'Only a couple more days in the house,' he says. 'Then you can have as much pizza and Indian as you want.'

Bonnie nods. They haven't been informed of the schedule yet, not until it's revealed who Ty is picking for hometown visits. Her chest tightens thinking about the key ceremony tonight. Will she be chosen? Will Ty want to go to her hometown? Does he see a future with her?

'You okay?

'What?'

'You're staring at me.'

Bonnie drops her face into her hands. 'Sorry, my head is just going around and around.'

He seems a bit concerned now. 'Do you still want to do this?' He nods in the direction of Ty.

Her feelings for Ty yo-yo up and down. The sensation makes her feel constantly queasy. She wants to believe that she has a future with Ty, but can she really let herself believe that when there are still four other girls left in the competition? Can she expect him to choose her when he wants a brood of kids and she doesn't? He seems like a nice guy, but does she really even know him? All the words inside her head are on the tip of her tongue and she feels like she could let it all pour out. She craves that kind of release instead of the tightness across her chest but instead she says, 'Yeah, of course. I was just thinking of all the takeaways I'll be getting when I leave this place.'

❧

Darcy moves away from Ty and Jodie's one-on-one time. It's already been decided that he'll give her a key. The audience loves her. They seem like a ready-made match. She also lives in Sydney, a suburb away from his place on the Northern Beaches. He designs furniture, she designs interiors. They both want lots and lots of kids.

But Jodie isn't the only girl left in this race, and Darcy knows Ty's heart is still yet to be won. Well, won away from his ex, anyway.

Darcy needs to find Bonnie and give her a pep talk about approaching Ty. Bonnie is also a fan favourite, a bit of an awkward and vulnerable underdog. Things between them have been a little stilted since the illegal phone incident, but Darcy is committed to doing her job properly and isn't going to avoid Bonnie just because it makes them both uncomfortable. She'll suggest Bonnie interrupt Ty's time with Jodie and she doubts Bonnie will refuse her after everything that's happened.

As she rounds the corner she sees Bonnie talking to Ben, who has his camera resting off his arm. Once again Darcy has a longing to film Bonnie in a natural conversation like the one she's having now. Her whole body seems relaxed, her facial expressions raw. So often footage of Bonnie with Ty has her looking blatantly nervous and unsure.

Bonnie and Ben both turn as they notice her approaching. Ben looks mildly guilty for talking on the job, but it's a common occurrence. With only five girls left and three camera guys working, there's not all that much for them to film.

'Was it your idea to have us dress up?' Bonnie eyes Darcy, clearly feeling self-conscious and totally unaware that she actually looks stunning.

'Sorry, I can't take credit for that one.' The costume department had come up with the idea after learning they could secure the costumes for free in return for a decent credit at the end of the show. Darcy had called in a media contact and gotten photos taken of all the girls before the party started to appear online with an article after the episode airs.

'Want me to go set up for the ceremony?' Ben asks.

Darcy glances at her watch. It's still probably a bit early but she wants to be able to talk to Bonnie without Ben around. 'That'd be great, thanks.'

She waits a few moments as Ben walks away, watching as Bonnie plays with the gold bangles around her wrist.

'How are you feeling?' Darcy asks, trying to clear the air between them. She's also well aware that Bonnie has withdrawn since her last one-on-one time with Ty. 'It's getting close to the end.'

'I'm okay,' Bonnie says, but the words sound high in her throat and aren't overly convincing.

'You should go talk to Ty.'

Bonnie glances over to where Ty and Jodie disappeared into the garden. 'I don't want to interrupt. Everyone wants time tonight.'

'You've been quiet since the last one-on-one time you had with him,' Darcy fishes, purposely not mentioning the phone.

Bonnie shrugs. 'It was the big *babies* conversation. The fact that I'd biologically struggle to give him five kids is only a side issue to the fact that I know I don't want that many.'

Darcy had worried that this had been eating away at Bonnie and wondered if it had been the thing that spurred her to contact her ex in the first place. 'All relationships have a bit of compromise.' Darcy knows the truth in that, with her own fiancé living four hours away.

'Of course,' Bonnie agrees. 'But I don't know what other conversations he's had. I don't know if everyone else has said "I'll give you as many babies as you want!"'

Darcy can see the stress of the competition is eating away at Bonnie. This is common; Darcy has had this conversation with plenty of girls before. 'You have to have faith in the relationship you've formed with Ty. Don't think about the other girls. I've seen there's a connection between the two of you. You can feel it, can't you?' Darcy is being genuine. Something sparked between Bonnie and Ty from the moment they met on the red carpet. But the fact that Darcy knows Ty still has feelings for his ex sits like lead deep in her guts.

'Yeah.' Bonnie nods, but she's still troubled. 'Being in this house is just really getting to me.'

Darcy's familiar with this conversation too. It's like the women start becoming suffocated. 'Only a couple more days, I promise.'

Bonnie swallows hard and nods. The prospect of a couple more days must still feel like a lifetime to her.

'You're the only one who hasn't approached him tonight,' Darcy says gently. 'He's choosing hometowns, Bonnie. You want one, don't you?'

Bonnie stands straighter, turning a little to watch Addison, Hayley and Cassie sitting on the patio with their champagne flutes. 'Yeah, I do.'

'Well, the key ceremony is going to start soon. You better go make the most of the time you have left.'

༄

Bonnie makes her way to Ty and Jodie, who are coupled up on a two-seater lounge. They look like they fit, like they should be together, but Ty smiles a welcome to Bonnie and she realises that maybe she still does have a chance.

'Do you mind if I steal Ty away?' she says to Jodie.

Jodie's face drops, disappointed of course, but her voice remains pleasant, always pleasant in front of Ty. 'Of course not.'

Ty gives Jodie a hug goodbye, forcing Bonnie to look away as she tries to give them some privacy in this unnatural situation.

Ty turns his back on Jodie and takes Bonnie's hand, leading her towards another part of the garden. Bonnie feels the usual buzz whenever Ty touches her. She just wishes the large intruding camera wasn't following them.

'I feel like I haven't seen you in ages.'

Bonnie wants to laugh at this. 'Yeah, well, you've been pretty busy.' He's had a constant stream of dates while she's had nothing but endless days in the house. Thank goodness he got rid of Imogen at the last ceremony. Bonnie had let out an audible sigh of relief when Imogen's name wasn't called out to receive a key. For a second Bonnie had thought she was about to get a punch to the face. Luckily one of the other girls had stepped in to give Imogen a goodbye hug. At least Bonnie's endless days in the house had been Imogen-free.

'I've been thinking about you, though,' Ty offers as they slowly walk through the garden.

Bonnie feels herself smiling. It mightn't be true, but she finds herself taking comfort in this and suddenly doesn't know why she was so reluctant to spend time with him.

She notices Darcy approaching. Ty does too, and both of them pause, waiting to see if she's about to give them an instruction or a conversation prompt.

'Ty, can you ask Bonnie about her hometown, please?'

Bonnie's body stiffens. She wishes their conversations could flow naturally rather than be directed by a producer.

'Sure,' Ty says. He seems to have gotten used to this process. He looks back to Bonnie and squeezes her hand before asking, 'How do you feel about introducing me to your family?'

Ugh. That dreaded question. She wonders if she should warn Ty about Carla and how draining her sister can be. How Carla will not only drill him about his intentions but also try to extract his past demons too. Carla would demand to know if Bonnie is the one, when clearly that's something Ty wouldn't be able to tell her. Bonnie chooses to sidestep the question. 'I'd love to show you around my hometown. Port Macquarie is a beautiful place and it'd mean a lot to be able to share it with you.' Suddenly images come tumbling into her head of Ollie and all the places back home that she's been with him. She bites down on her lip, pleading with her mind to let such thoughts slip away. She can't be here and thinking about Ollie anymore. He has a life with Sophie and she needs to see this thing through.

'Where would we go?'

Bonnie can't help but look up at Darcy, who helped her outline her 'ideal' hometown date weeks ago. The field producers had to plan the dates well in advance even though only four will go ahead. 'I'd love to show you my photography studio,' she tells him. 'It was a large empty space when I first bought it, pretty run-down and not much to look at, but I've been in there almost eight years now and I'm pretty proud of what I've done.'

'I'd love to see your studio.'

Bonnie wants to know if that means he'll give her a key or whether he's said something similar to all the girls tonight.

'I must say, I've been worried about how you're feeling,' he admits. 'You kind of rushed off last time we spoke. It made me think that you were doubting things here.' He gestures between the two of them.

The anxiety she'd been feeling earlier comes rushing back. Bonnie glances at Darcy, painfully aware that she knows Bonnie tried to contact Ollie after that. 'I freaked out.' There's no point lying to him. 'I kind of assumed the whole baby thing would be a deal-breaker for you.'

He stares at her blankly for a moment.

She's waiting, hoping he'll say that of course it isn't a deal-breaker, but his expression looks so unsure that maybe he's still trying to figure that out himself.

'Sorry, can you excuse me?' Ty's whole face has become ghostly white.

'Sure,' Bonnie says, looking between him and Darcy.

'Is everything okay, Ty?' Darcy asks, looking as perplexed as Bonnie feels.

He stands, walking straight past Darcy as he heads towards the house. 'I need to talk to you.'

∽

'What if that was it?' Ty says. 'Maybe she broke up with me because she found out she can't have kids.'

Darcy's heart sinks. Ty had been in the midst of some good one-on-one time with Bonnie when he abruptly ended things to talk to her instead. They've gone to one of the production rooms in the house for privacy. He hasn't said it yet, but she already knows he's talking about his ex.

'I didn't think to ask her at the time, but it seems so obvious now. I've always wanted kids, so maybe she thought it'd be a deal-breaker, like Bonnie said.'

Darcy feels weary. The night is supposed to be wrapping up. The rest of the crew are set up and ready to film the key ceremony. She really doesn't feel like she has the energy to talk Ty down off the ledge of 'what-ifs' about his ex. She promised Drew they would have a long talk on the phone when she got home tonight but who knows how long this is going to take? She closes her eyes and takes a deep breath. 'I don't think that's what we should be talking about right now.'

Sadness tugs at Ty's face.

'Do you know who you want to send home tonight?'

But he ignores her question. 'If I could just contact her. Just ask if that's why she broke up with me.'

Darcy quickly shakes her head. 'That's not going to happen.'

'Please, Darcy.'

She meets his gaze and her heart aches for him as she sees the desperation etched into his face. Despite this, she forces herself to remain firm. 'I can't let you contact your ex-girlfriend, Ty. I could lose my job.'

'She's not just an ex-girlfriend, she was my fiancée. I wanted to marry her, I wanted to spend the rest of my life with her.' He's not afraid to plead.

Swear words fly through Darcy's head. This isn't a normal suitor freak-out, this is something she should be calling Alice in to deal with, but asking for help seems to only make it less likely that she'll get promoted. *Step up*, she tells herself. *Deal with this problem and prove to Alice how invaluable you are.*

'I could just use your phone to call her and ask if that's what it is.'

Darcy does the only thing that she knows might get Ty to focus on the girls in the house instead of the girl who dumped him. 'Okay, Ty. I'll make a deal with you. I'll let you make one phone call. You've got five minutes to talk, to sort out whatever you want with your ex.'

Ty's face lights up, relief almost choking his breath.

'But in return I'll need you to finish off the season,' Darcy goes on. 'It's only a couple more weeks. I'll need you to pick one of the girls at the end and stay with her for three months after the show wraps.'

The brightness that had so quickly filled his face now dims. 'What if ...' he begins to ask, but Darcy shuts down the question as quick as she can.

'Do we have a deal or not?'

He's reluctant for a moment, clearly thinking it over, but his eyes remain focused on her phone sitting on her clipboard. 'Deal,' he confirms, leaning forward to shake her hand.

She offers him her phone, which he takes and quickly keys in the number. She's surprised he even knows the number off by heart. She barely knows her own.

He holds the phone to his ear. She can see his chest rising and falling, the lump in his throat, the shakiness of his hands.

She feels a bit bad for him, waiting for the devastation.

And then it happens. His face falls. Ty presses the loudspeaker so that Darcy can hear the mechanical voice say, 'The phone number you have dialled is no longer connected.'

Darcy had tried calling his ex enough times when Ty first signed on to the show to know the phone had been disconnected.

'If I could just contact her boss and get her new number?' He's expecting Darcy to say yes.

'Sorry, Ty.' She extends her hand for him to give her the phone back.

'You said five minutes.'

'I also said one phone call. I gave you that. Now it's time for you to hold up your end of the deal.'

He's annoyed she cheated him into a bad deal and whacks the phone back into her palm.

Darcy can feel her emotions begin to waiver, but she reminds herself that she needs to prove her worth to Alice. 'Ty, if she's changed her number she clearly doesn't want you to be able to contact her.'

He looks winded by her harshness, but Darcy pretends she doesn't notice. Instead, she gestures to the photos of the remaining five girls. 'So, do you know who you want to send home, or should I pick someone?'

⁓

'It's taking a long time,' Addison says, craning her neck to look for Ty. Some of the crew have taken to playing a card game while they wait.

Bonnie shifts from one foot to the other. She can't stop fidgeting with the bracelets around her wrist, which creates a jingling noise that she imagines is annoying the others. The five remaining girls have been put in the ceremony room, all waiting for Ty to come and hand out four keys. One of them is about to be sent home.

'I hate this part of the night,' Jodie murmurs. She smooths over her Bollywood outfit, much the same as Bonnie's but a soft lilac colour.

Cassie, in electric blue, agrees. 'I start to analyse every word I said to him.'

Bonnie feels the same. She'd thought their conversation had been going okay. He seemed happy to see her, he said he'd been worried about her. In that moment she'd taken it as a good sign that maybe there was a future for them. But then he abruptly ended their time together, right after she'd asked whether the whole baby issue would be a deal-breaker. It doesn't feel like he's about to give her a key.

'They won't make us wait too much longer.' Hayley, a true cheerleader, is forever bolstering everyone.

'I just really hope he gets to meet Zac,' Cassie says, playing with the locket around her neck, which holds a photo of her five-year-old son.

Bonnie reaches out to squeeze her hand when Darcy suddenly appears, striding towards them, holding her clipboard as usual.

'Sorry about the hold-up, girls. Anyone need a toilet break or a drink before we get things going?'

They murmur no. Everyone just wants to get this over with and know who Ty is sending home.

'All right,' Darcy calls loudly, 'everyone into position, please.' The crew abandon the cards for their equipment. The girls move to the five small marks that have been set out on the floor for them.

Bonnie can feel her stomach twisting in knots. Her legs are unsteady as she tries to ignore the sensation that she's standing on a boat in the middle of a rough sea. She watches as Darcy casts one last look around the room and then calls, 'Action.'

They've been told hundreds of times not to look at the cameras, but Bonnie finds her eyes drifting to Ben, his back slightly hunched as he looks through the lens. But her attention shifts as Ty enters the room. He's pale and distaste brackets his mouth; clearly he's more than a little unsettled about what he's about to do.

He stands in front of them next to a small table holding the four keys.

Bonnie finds herself closing her eyes for a moment, wondering which one of them will be going home.

Ty looks to Darcy, whose expression is fixed and serious. She just nods, indicating for him to begin when he's ready.

He takes another moment before looking up at the five of them. 'I want each of you to know that I really appreciate you being here for me and letting me get to know you. I'm truly touched that you've all opened your hearts.' He visibly swallows down on a lump in his throat, his head dropping. 'I don't deserve it.'

'Keep rolling,' Darcy says to the crew. 'We'll edit that out.'

It's common for the camera guys to be told to keep filming but Bonnie feels her jaw dropping at Ty's comment. What does he mean?

'Just like we rehearsed,' Darcy tells Ty. She wants him to keep it moving.

Ty stares at Darcy with a hardness Bonnie hasn't seen before. Finally he drops his gaze before looking back to the girls. 'We're getting close to the end now and I really didn't realise how difficult it was going to be.' He rubs his face, looking tortured by the position he's in. 'I really didn't want to hurt anyone but now I realise that I was naive and stupid.'

'Rephrase please, Ty,' Darcy calls, feeding him the line back. 'I really didn't want to hurt anyone, but I now realise that it was inevitable.'

He looks at Darcy again and is about to say something, but then turns back to the girls and repeats the line before reaching for a key.

Bonnie's chest tightens. Something doesn't feel right, but maybe it's just because they really are getting towards the end.

He waits, like he's been told to do, drawing out the drama of the moment before finally saying ... 'Addison.'

Bonnie feels Addison's breath exhale with relief beside her as she rushes forward to Ty.

'Will you accept this key?'

Addison accepts, of course.

So does Jodie.

And then Hayley.

There's one key left. Bonnie and Cassie take a step closer to each other, closing in the space where Hayley had just been standing. They offer each other a heartfelt smile, knowing that one of them is about to be sent home. One of them has lost in this competition of love.

Bonnie watches as Ty picks up the last key. She prepares herself for the rejection, reminding herself to not let her face fall when he calls Cassie's name.

Ty can't look at either of them. Instead his eyes remain focused on the key in his hand. It feels like it's taking longer than it normally does. Nerves have imprisoned Bonnie's body; her own breath kept captive in her throat.

And then her name passes through his lips. 'Bonnie.'

She stands still as she tries to make sense of what this means. She feels Cassie slouch beside her and knows this should help with her own reaction, but still she remains frozen.

Ty is staring at her, his face warm.

Cassie squeezes her hand, offering Bonnie a smile despite her eyes being clouded with disappointment.

Guilt clamps at Bonnie's heart as she realises Cassie is being sent home. Cassie, the single mum, hasn't won Ty's heart. Cassie, who has sacrificed two months of her life to be away from her son. Bonnie embraces her friend, aware she can't really offer any real comfort. But Cassie steps back so Bonnie can have her moment.

Bonnie now looks to Ty as she steps towards him.

There's a softness in his face, yet he still looks worn. This process seems to be getting harder for him.

'Will you accept this key?' he asks, holding out the golden antique key, a symbol of hope and the possibility of love.

There are still things to be discussed, still decisions to be made, but she nods. 'Of course.' Her chance for love isn't over yet.

33

'Hello! Come in, come in!' Lara says, her arms outstretched, her voice loud. There's already a general buzz of women, which makes Penelope feel uncomfortable. She didn't realise other people had been invited. 'It's just about to start.'

'What's about to start?' But she already knows. Of course Lara would be into it.

'*The One*,' Lara says. 'You're watching it, aren't you?'

'I've seen bits and pieces.' Which isn't a lie. She's tried to watch it several times but always ends up having to turn it off.

She follows Lara into the lounge room. A pile of toys has been pushed to the side and the house is in a general state of disarray. Penelope has to give Lara credit for not caring what other people think. There is no way she'd ever have people over if her house looked like this. Mind you, she doesn't have kids, won't have kids, so it won't be a problem. Instead, her place is immaculate, and since moving in no one except herself has set foot inside her unit.

'This is Penelope.' Lara proudly presents her new friend to the group. 'This is Natalie, Nicole and Melinda.'

Pleasantries are exchanged. They all seem nice enough, but Penelope immediately wishes she hadn't come. This isn't her kind of thing.

A platter of cheese, dips and chocolates is set up on the coffee table, along with wine glasses. Without asking, Lara pours Penelope a glass and hands it over. It's been a while since Penelope's had alcohol, but she's grateful it gives her something to do with her hands.

'What a spread,' Penelope comments, more to make conversation than anything else.

'Oh, this is nothing!' Lara picks up the platter, thrusting it towards Penelope so she feels like she needs to take something. 'You should see how much there is when it gets to the finale.'

Penny bites into a cracker but the taste of bile comes up the back of her throat.

'Oh, shh! It's starting!'

'Oh, he's so dreamy,' Melinda purrs as the opening credits roll. 'I love this shot of him with his shirt off.'

'This shot?' Lara remarks. 'He gets his shirt off nearly every episode!' She leans forward to cut herself a piece of cheese and sips on her wine. 'Not that I'm complaining.'

Penelope gulps her wine.

'I think Bonnie's going to win,' one of the girls declares, possibly Natalie but Penelope can't be sure. 'I think she's the one.'

The one.

Penelope has to take a deep breath. Is that even a thing? Her mum died without having a great love while Miranda died leaving her great love behind. Neither situation seemed fair. But that isn't something she can bring up. These women aren't here for a deep and meaningful conversation. They're here for laughs, eye candy and hope in a happily ever after.

'I don't know.' Lara shrugs. 'He's good-looking, but he's not like the other suitors. Sometimes he seems really hot and cold. I wonder if he's genuinely into any of them.'

Penelope turns her heard sharply at this.

'Imagine walking away from this and not finding anyone.'

'It happened in one of the American seasons.'

'He'll choose someone. Look at him, he's like sex on legs. The girls will all be dying to get into bed with him.'

'Stop,' Penelope murmurs. She can't listen to this. She can't hear them talk like this.

'Sorry?' Lara turns to look at her, her mild expression indicating she hasn't heard what Penelope said.

Penelope swallows down the tennis-ball lump in her throat. 'I've got to go.'

'What?' Lara protests. 'But tonight we find out whose home-towns he's going to. Don't you want to see who he sends home?'

'Cassie.' Penelope's confident. 'He'll send Cassie home.'

'No way,' Nicole crows. 'He's into her.'

Penelope is pleasant as she says her goodbyes, telling them it was lovely to meet them all, and tries to leave before Lara can make too much of a fuss. But just as Penelope is about to escape out the front door, Lara catches up to her.

'Is everything okay?' Lara's face is painted with concern.

'Of course, it's just not my thing,' she says.

'Oh, I'm sorry. I just thought you might want to meet some other people. We try to get together once a week to watch it. It's a good excuse to have some wine and a bit of a laugh.'

It sounds so normal, so reasonable, and of course extremely generous that Lara was willing to invite her into her group of friends. And for a split second Penelope considers telling her everything.

'It's back on!' one of the voices calls from the lounge room.

And then she shakes herself. She promised herself she wouldn't tell a soul. 'I'll let you go.'

Lara nods, clearly eager to keep watching. 'I'll give you a call in a couple of days.'

Penelope nods, but knows she'll have to start dodging her calls. She's letting herself get too close. It's dangerous.

34

It's the night before hometown visits and Darcy is quickly trying to pack her bag before she heads out for a drink with Ed and Mel. Darcy asked Mel if she wanted to tag along before they knocked off work, and Mel had clarified that Ed was single before agreeing. She wasn't going to waste her time hanging out with men already coupled up.

Her phone buzzes to life with an incoming call from Drew. She grabs it. 'Hey.' She doesn't want to fob him off, they've barely spoken all week, but she glances at the clock, knowing she'll need to keep the conversation quick.

'Got time to talk?'

'For a bit,' she tells him as she drops a few pairs of socks into her suitcase.

'I've been thinking,' Drew says. 'We need to set a date.'

'A date?'

He immediately recognises her confusion and laughs. 'You're far from the typical bride-to-be, Darce.'

Darcy can't help but laugh too as it clicks. She'd honestly had no idea he'd been talking about their wedding. Most of the time she forgets she's engaged. 'We've got plenty of time to set a date.'

'Everyone up here is hounding me.'

'Tell 'em to get a life.' Darcy shakes her head as she chucks a few more things into her suitcase. 'We're both flat out with work. We don't have time to organise a wedding.'

Drew doesn't say anything but the silence down the phone line is deafening.

'What is it?'

'Well, the thing is, Mum and I were thinking a New Year's Eve wedding could be good?'

Great. So Sheila has gotten involved. Darcy tries not to let it bother her. 'New Year's?' she echoes, trying to think of a reason against it. 'People might not like having to go to a wedding on New Year's Eve.'

'Are you kidding? People would love it. A massive party with free booze.'

That is true.

'Most people are on holidays then too, so they wouldn't have to worry about getting time off work to come away for the weekend.'

Another good point, but still she challenges, 'Come away?'

'To Gloucester.'

She doesn't say anything. Of course Drew wants to get married in Gloucester. The sweeping countryside and mountains make a pretty iconic backdrop for wedding photos—she's seen enough of them. They hang in just about every house in Gloucester.

When the silence goes on for too long, Drew asks, 'I thought you wanted a wedding back here too?'

She had when they used to talk about it, she'd always imagined it there, but now it doesn't feel right. 'Maybe we could have it here in Sydney?' She hasn't actually pictured her wedding in Sydney before, but they will be living there. It makes sense.

Drew scoffs, somewhat amused. 'We can't afford a wedding in Sydney.'

No, probably not, but Darcy isn't going to let that stop her from arguing the point. 'If we have something small we could.'

'I've done a rough guest list with Mum and we're up to about a hundred and sixty.'

Darcy almost screams. How could he do a guest list without her? How could he do a guest list with *his mother*? And how on earth could he think that she would want that many people at their wedding? 'One hundred and sixty?!' She collapses onto her bed, lying back against the pillows. Since Drew's been gone, she's started sleeping in the middle of the bed, sprawling her body out like a starfish.

'Family, school friends, uni mates, work people, footy guys, some of the girls you used to work with. It all adds up.'

'No.' Her voice is tiny, her heart racing.

'I'll email it through. Have a look over it, but I don't think there's anyone we can really cull.'

Darcy can't say anything; no words want to come out. There's a knock at her door and she's actually relieved. She flings it open to find Mel standing there and gestures for her to come in.

'Darce, you still there?'

'Yep but I've got to go,' she says hurriedly. 'Mel's here.'

Drew doesn't say anything. He's annoyed with her.

'I'll talk to you tomorrow.'

'Yep.'

Something is wrong with her. Her fiancé wants to set the date and start organising the wedding and she can do nothing but oppose him. She tries to push the feelings away as she smiles at Mel. She only has one shoe on, hasn't put any makeup on yet and will have to finish packing in the morning. 'Sorry, I'm running late.'

'No rush,' Mel says, then asks, 'Do I look all right? I changed about five times.'

She's wearing a cute little black dress. 'You look great,' Darcy assures her.

Mel looks a little nervous as she smooths over her dress, clearly hoping to impress Ed, who she hasn't even met yet.

'Make yourself at home,' Darcy calls as she hobbles back to her bedroom to find her other shoe. It's the first time they've hung out together outside of work. The lines between colleague and friend have started to blur.

Darcy pulls on her other shoe and heads into the small bathroom, glancing to the living area only steps away where Mel is looking at photo frames on a bookshelf.

'So this is Drew?'

'Yeah,' Darcy says as she quickly whisks some mascara over her eyes. 'That's Drew.' She's probably looking at the photo taken of them at their year twelve formal. They both look like babies in it. Hard to believe it was over eight years ago.

'You guys are cute together.'

Darcy smiles as she picks the clumps of mascara off her lashes. She really needs to stop using this brand.

Mel laughs, causing Darcy to wonder if it's at her hideously tacky maroon dress or Drew's haircut and high-waisted pants. She hastily applies some lip gloss before rushing back out to find out.

'I love this one.' Mel points at a photo that Darcy had forgotten was up on the shelf. It was from a toga night during their final year of uni. Ed and Sienna are in the photo too. 'That's Ed,' Darcy points out.

'Cute,' Mel replies, satisfied.

Darcy smiles at Ed's familiar grin in the photo. He and Drew are dressed in amusingly small gladiator togas. She remembers the material had barely been long enough to go around them. The girls had laughed so hard as they all got ready with a few pre-drinks. Darcy and Sienna had gone as pussycats, though she can't remember why. Probably something to do with being *sex kittens*— everything seemed connected to sex at uni, a contrast to the life she's leading now. She feels a slight twinge thinking back to her friendship with Sienna. She'd thought about messaging her after the awkward meeting at the farmers' market but it didn't feel right. Darcy and Ed were friends before he started going out with Sienna and that's where her loyalties lay despite the four years of friendship she and Sienna shared. She wonders whether she should take the photo down now that Ed and Sienna aren't together anymore.

Mel gasps. 'What are all these?'

Darcy looks up to see what Mel has moved on to. 'Oh, just some wedding magazines Ed dropped off for me. A client passed them on.' She's still thinking about the photo. 'Hey, maybe we should do a toga party on one of the group dates next season.' Knowing Alice, no promotion will come, and she'll still be doing the same job.

'Yeah, good idea,' Mel murmurs, but she's clearly mesmerised as she flicks through the pages of one of the magazines. Her whole face is bright, her eyes dancing. 'Oh, I love that dress ... wow, that cake is amazing ... aww, look at the little flower girls.'

Darcy realises this was probably the response Ed had been waiting for when he'd given her the magazines in the first place. She still hasn't flicked through them since that first night. She glances at her watch. 'We should probably go.'

'Okay.' But Mel looks like she could happily curl up on the lounge and flick through the magazines for the rest of the night.

Darcy's left with the unsettling feeling that her single friend is more interested in the wedding magazines than she is.

'I'll get the next drinks,' Mel says, touching Ed on the arm as she moves from the bar table the three of them are sitting around. She stares at him for a loaded moment, a playful smile dancing on her face.

Darcy almost laughs but instead manages, 'Thanks, Mel.' Mel had been outright flirty with Ed from the moment he met up with them.

'Are you trying to set me up?' Ed eyes Darcy suspiciously once Mel moves to the bar.

'No, of course not. She didn't have any plans tonight and was keen to do something. You don't mind I asked her along, do you?'

'I wish you'd told me it was "bring a work mate" night. I could have brought Zoe.'

Darcy scowls. She knows he's teasing, but she bites anyway. 'Arsehole,' she mutters.

Ed throws his head back and laughs, satisfied she took the bait like she always does.

'Mel's really nice. I think you'd like her,' Darcy says, watching Mel up at the bar as she starts talking to a group of young guys. 'She looks hot in that dress, don't you think?'

Ed frowns. 'She's not my type, Darce. You should know that.'

'What's your type?' Before Sienna he hooked up with a few girls at uni, but it was nothing serious and certainly nothing to signify a particular type.

'I don't actually know.' Ed muses. 'But she's definitely *not* my type.'

'What's wrong with her?'

Ed shakes his head. 'She's got that look in her eye.'

Darcy has no idea what he's talking about.

'You know, the desperate for marriage and babies look.'

'That's a bit harsh, isn't it?'

Ed shrugs.

Mel saunters back to the table with two drinks and places them on the table. 'I used to go to school with some of those guys. I'm going to go hang with them for a bit.'

'Sure,' Darcy says. 'You'll come back later, right?'

Mel looks to Ed. 'Yeah, of course.'

Darcy notices Ed makes quite an effort to stay stony-faced. He clearly doesn't want to give Mel the wrong idea.

'Where's Mel?' Darcy asks suddenly an hour or two later as she tips the wine bottle in an attempt to fill her glass, but it's empty. How many bottles have they drunk? Darcy had welcomed the distraction of alcohol to numb the pain of her earlier phone conversation with Drew.

Ed seems amused by this. 'She left ages ago with one of those blokes she was hanging out with.'

'Oh.' She tries to remember this, but all traces of memory seem currently unavailable. 'Was that safe?'

'You took a photo of him and also of his licence, so you could hunt him down if for some reason Mel disappears,' Ed informs her.

Darcy feels quite satisfied with her drunk self. 'I'm a good friend.'

'Yeah, you're a good friend,' Ed assures her. 'But, what do you reckon, should we call it a night? You're out.' He gestures to her empty wine bottle.

'No, not yet!' She reaches for Ed's glass, then tilts her head back and lets the last of his drink slide down her throat.

Ed checks the time on his watch. 'Come on, it's late and you have to get up early tomorrow.'

She's headed to the first hometown date. 'I only have to go to the Blue Mountains. I'll be right.'

He eyes her warily. He knows her too well. 'What's going on?'

But Darcy doesn't want to talk about it, isn't ready to talk about it. 'I just want to have a good time.' She goes to put the glass back down on the table but misses it completely and it smashes to the ground.

'I'm fine, I'm fine,' Darcy says, pretty sure she just heard herself slur.

Ed has drunk with her too many times to find it amusing. 'Let's get some air.'

'No, let's dance!' She moves to the dance floor, knowing he'll follow her. Partly because he loves to dance, but mostly because he'd be too concerned to let her out of his sight after all those drinks.

They've only just reached the dance floor when a song Darcy loves comes pounding through the speakers. 'I love this song!' Darcy tilts her head back and pushes away all thoughts, letting her body move to the music.

Ed breaks out some of his familiar yet always impressive moves. Darcy tries to better him. She rarely attempts this because Ed's not only got confidence but skills that make his moves look choreographed.

Ed's feet glide across the dance floor and his arms move effortlessly through the air. As he does this, people step back, allowing him more space. He's a natural and entertaining to watch. Usually Darcy laughs, amused and impressed, but tonight she's had too much alcohol to shuffle from side to side on the outer circle. So instead she lets her body contort and thrust in moves she didn't even know she could do.

Ed smirks as Darcy does a high kick, then spins around really fast before repeating the move with the other leg. 'Whoaa! Go, Darce!'

She twirls again. Her balance is a little off, but she laughs, tilting her head back and throwing her arms in the air.

She hears noises of reaction around them. She doesn't know if they're cheering her on or laughing at her, but she doesn't care, and it feels good.

Dancing like nobody is watching is cathartic and she definitely needs this kind of release tonight. She feels weightless and free from responsibilities and commitments. Suddenly she flings herself to the ground, the urge to incorporate floor moves into her routine overtaking her. She goes to leap up, envisaging herself doing an impressive star jump, but as she does, her foot trips on … air? … and she finds herself tumbling back to the ground. She goes to spring back up but—

No!

Her knee thumps in pain.

'Are you all right?' Ed extends his arm to help her up, the music still thudding, plenty of people watching on.

Darcy looks up at him and instantly tears spring to her eyes. It hurts, it really hurts.

'Come on, let's go.' He wraps his arm around her and she leans into him, hobbling as the pain in her knee throbs.

'What about Mel?' she asks suddenly. 'We can't leave without her.'

'Oh, geez, you are drunk. We've already been through this.'

'Oh.' How much has she had to drink?

When they step out into the street, the cold air feels harsh but good against her face.

'You've been holding out on me for all these years.'

Darcy isn't sure what he means.

'Those moves ' He shakes his head, smiling. 'I wish I'd filmed you.'

'Was everyone watching?' She wonders if Ed feels like everything is swaying too.

He laughs, amusement thick on his breath. 'It was quite the show.'

'Speaking of shows, how are things with Zoe?' It's been on her mind all night, especially after he joked about bringing her earlier, but she hasn't had enough confidence to ask until now.

'Darcy.'

'What?' She acts innocent.

'We've been through this. She's my boss.'

'Your boss who wants to rip your clothes off.'

Even Ed can't help but smirk at this.

But a wave of nausea suddenly hits. 'I think I'm going to be sick.'

She leans against a shopfront as Ed pulls her hair back. 'If you must.' He rubs her back. 'Better out than in, I say. You'll feel better for it tomorrow.'

But the urge to throw up disappears. Just having him rub her back is nice. Ed is so nice. He's always so nice to her. She turns and, without another thought, leans in and kisses him.

Ed jerks back, as though startled by this, but then he responds, kissing her back, their lips exploring uncharted territory.

Ohhhh …

This is good.

Why haven't we done this before?

But then Ed yanks back, his hands still holding her around the arms. His face is confused. 'What are you doing?'

Shit!

What is she doing? She tries to concentrate but thoughts float away before she can focus on any of them.

'Is this about Zoe?'

Zoe. Huh? 'No, I don't think so.' It's about … Drew. Oh God. She's engaged. She has a fiancé.

'Darcy? What's going on?'

What is she doing? Ed's her best friend. 'I don't know. I wasn't thinking.'

'Shit, Darcy.' He steps away from her.

Darcy knows she hasn't thought this through. She's not thinking at all. Is she? Does she like Ed?

Of course she likes Ed. He's her best friend.

Exactly. He's her *best friend*. Why is she trying to kiss him? Is she an idiot? Is she trying to ruin everything? 'Shit, sorry!'

He shakes his head. He's annoyed with her, really annoyed. They've always only ever been mates. There's never been any almost-kisses or sexual tension, but she knows that those few moments they just shared have stuffed all that up. They can pretend it didn't happen, but it did.

Ed turns away from her. Her head continues to spin as she watches him hail a taxi. He indicates it's for her but won't look at her. 'I don't know what's going on with you and you might not want to talk about it, but you need to sort yourself out.' Without another word, he puts her into the back seat of the car, tells the driver her address and hands over some money. Only then does he look at her. 'I'll see you when you get back from the hometown visits.'

Her eyes lock with his and she's surprised that a sense of longing to have his lips on hers takes over her entire body. She gulps down, a tightness expanding across her chest. Can she really blame alcohol for that?

35

Bonnie almost laughs when she pushes the door open to her photography studio. Candles have been placed on every available space. She looks to Ty. 'Ta-da.'

He smiles back at her, knowing too well the production team's love for candles.

'Something I prepared earlier,' she jokes.

'Where are the rose petals?'

Bonnie chides herself. 'I knew I forgot something.'

They both laugh but she's still not completely comfortable in his company. The first part of their hometown date, a walk along the breakwall, had been even more nerve-racking than normal with a crowd of locals watching from a partitioned area. All the rocks along the wall were painted like an outdoor gallery. There were pictures, tributes to loved ones, commemorations of anniversaries or holidays. One rock had been painted white for Bonnie and Ty to repaint with something to symbolise them. They'd stared blankly at each other when they were supposed to come up with a concept. It had been Darcy who eventually suggested they write, *May everyone find The One.* Bonnie had tried to block everyone out, but found herself glancing up, searching for Ollie in the crowd. Even in Ty's company she can't seem to get him out of her head.

'Show him around the place,' Darcy prompts from the side, standing close to Ben and his camera.

It's been nearly a week since Bonnie and Ty last saw each other at the key ceremony, when he'd abruptly ended their one-on-one time, so she knows it's only a matter of time before Darcy suggests they readdress the whole 'how many kids do you want' subject. Her neck immediately stiffens.

'You took all these?' Ty's looking at the canvases covering each wall space.

'Yeah.' She nods, quite proud. She hasn't been in her studio for over nine weeks and it feels good to be back; she can feel herself relaxing. 'That's my sister and her family.' Bonnie points out one of the canvases.

'Cute kids.'

Bonnie nods, looking at her niece and nephews. She's missed them but feels her body tense in anticipation, assuming the 'kids' conversation is coming.

But Darcy doesn't say anything, and Ty takes a few steps, admiring all her work. He stops at one piece. 'Wow, that's awesome.'

Relieved for the moment, Bonnie smiles at the photograph. She'd taken it a couple of years ago now, but it is still one of her favourites. It was taken early morning on the beach, with breathtaking light, the sun bursting up from the horizon as six very flexible women positioned themselves into different yoga poses.

'I didn't join in,' she jokes, referring to their conversation where she'd admitted she didn't like yoga. But Ty barely smiles in return. Instead his mind seems preoccupied as he continues to stare at the photo in front of them. Bonnie swallows hard, thinking she may have made a mistake in mentioning that conversation, the same conversation where Ty had spoken about his ex.

Bonnie finds herself looking to Darcy, but she has her head tilted to the side, her clipboard clutched in her hand as she stands just away from Ben. It doesn't appear that Darcy is concerned or going to offer any direction, so Bonnie decides to take matters into her own hands. 'This is where I do all my editing,' she says, pulling his attention away from the wall and instead to her large desk. 'And where I eat way too many takeaway meals.'

Ty takes a few steps towards her desk. 'Wow, this is a beauty.' He bends down to inspect it more closely. 'What a piece of work.'

Bonnie shines with pride. The oversized desk had cost her a fortune, but she'd fallen in love with it from the moment she saw it. And she loves that it is the centrepiece of her studio. She watches as Ty takes in the space, which is all so familiar to her even though she hasn't sat at this desk for a couple of months. She sees Ty reach for a book, one she hasn't seen before. He picks it up, turns the cover over.

'Did you like it?' he asks.

Bonnie shrugs. 'It must be my sister's. Carla's been coming in to take bookings and do some paperwork for me.'

Ty doesn't say anything, causing the conversation to fall flat. Bonnie knows the date isn't going as well as it could be. Things are too stilted.

'Have you read it?' She tries to spark something up.

'Yeah.' He nods, the word coming out slowly. 'My ex, she commissions books.' His eyes only glance up at her for a second before looking back at the book. 'She was reading this manuscript when I met her.'

A metallic taste develops in the back of Bonnie's throat.

'She spent every day hunched over manuscripts,' he volunteers. 'Yoga was her out.' He gestures to the photograph up on the wall and Bonnie knows he had been thinking of her earlier.

Bonnie feels like she should say something, but Ty continues on, seemingly not realising that this is already an awkward conversation.

'She'd always have piles of manuscripts around the house. I'd get home from work and she'd be reading, pen in hand, jotting down notes.'

Bonnie watches him remember, still unsure what to say, waiting for Darcy to interrupt and redirect the conversation. Desperately hoping Darcy will redirect the conversation.

'Most of the time she could tell if the manuscript was going to be any good from the first page.' Ty shakes his head, a little smile on his face, clearly still in awe of his ex's brilliance. 'But she'd always read the first three chapters. Always, even if she knew it was total rubbish. She'd sit there twisting her hair, her eyes narrowed, totally absorbed in another world.'

Bonnie glances at Darcy again, hoping she'll somehow know how to steer this back on track, but Darcy's eyes are blank, her expression unreadable.

'I never used to read before I met her, but now I'm hooked on action-adventures. Can't get enough of them.'

Bonnie wants to say something, that she wishes she had more time to read, or that she'd hate to have to read books that were rubbish, but ideas of what to say fly out as quickly as they pop into her head.

'Why did you break up?' The words surprise even Bonnie as they spill from her mouth, but she feels like she needs to know.

'Penny broke things off,' he murmurs.

Penny. His ex has a name. Bonnie's stomach clenches in reaction to the way he said it. Bonnie waits for Darcy to call cut, expects that it will come at any second.

'Four months before we were supposed to be married,' he goes on, his eyes never leaving the book in his hands. 'It was supposed to be our wedding this weekend.' Ty's whole face has become consumed with heartbreak. He'd been hiding behind a mask for the last couple of months, but he's taken it off and now everything is so clear.

He still loves her. He's still in love with his ex.

Oh God.

Bonnie's throat suddenly feels dry. She picks up one of the champagne glasses and drains it.

Stay calm.

But her heart is racing, and a darkness pierces her heart as she processes what this means for her.

'Cut!' Darcy finally calls.

Ty's head turns sharply to look at Bonnie, like she's snapped him out of a hypnotic spell. He's confused at first, but as his eyes meet hers, he seems to realise what he's been talking about and where he is. His eyes are apologetic; he knows what he's inadvertently done.

For Bonnie, this is over.

36

Four months earlier

Penelope has been sitting on the edge of the lounge for about forty-five minutes when she finally hears Ty arrive home. She braces herself, standing to greet him, but then sits down again, unsure what she's going to say. Her stomach aches, her hands shake.

The door pushes open. 'Hey,' he says, a smile filling his face as he sees her.

Oh, she's missed him. She has no idea how she's going to do this.

'I don't think I'm going to have a bucks,' he moans. 'I can't do another weekend like that for at least five years.' He dumps his bag on the floor and she sees his face as he takes in her bags, packed and waiting. The rest are already in her car.

'Are you going somewhere?'

Everything is about to change. She wishes she could hold on to what they have for another day, but she doesn't trust herself. If she doesn't do this now, she'll trap him into a life he doesn't deserve.

'I'm leaving.' The words sound clunky and unnatural and not at all what she'd planned.

'What?' Ty eyes her, trying to figure out what she means.

'I can't marry you.' Her heart cracks as the words slip from her lips.

'What's happened?' Instead of being angry, his eyes are wide with worry. It reminds her of the first time she met him. It had been a Sunday afternoon and she'd been walking back from the beach, her hair still wet, sticky and salty, her bag weighed down with the latest manuscript she'd been reading. She was dreading going home to the flat she'd shared with Laine, who had a very healthy sex drive and extremely messy living habits. A couple pushing a pram stopped abruptly in front of her and Penelope had tried to sidestep around them when a shooting pain clipped her heel.

'Arghh!' she'd shrieked, turning to see a man quickly swinging off his bike to see if she was all right.

'I'm so sorry,' he'd said, his eyes just like they are now, wide and concerned. 'Are you okay?' He bent down to examine her ankle that he'd clipped with his bike wheel.

Penelope had been lost for words. For a moment Ty hadn't said anything either.

Zap! Just like that they'd connected and the whole universe looked different.

Now, when Penelope doesn't answer, Ty asks, 'Is it cold feet?' His voice is still gentle, but she knows it won't last for long. 'We can postpone if that's what you want?'

She shakes her head, her voice escaping her.

His face falls. 'What have you done?' He sounds terrified.

Penelope knows what he's implying and partly wishes all this was about her stuffing up and sleeping with somebody else.

'Whatever it is, Pen, we can work things out. It's not as bad as you think.'

If only that were true, but there's no way to work through this confession. Penelope can see his concern and can't stand to look at his winter-crisp blue eyes, all vulnerable and willing.

'I forgive you.' He urges her to look back at him and the moment she does, she immediately regrets it. 'Just talk to me.'

Part of Penelope is furious he thinks she's cheated on him but another part loves him more for being so understanding. She wants to tell him everything. She wants to let him take her in his arms and hush her while she breaks down into relentless sobs of fear and anger and sadness.

'Penny! Please, talk to me?' He's on the verge of breaking down. He reaches out and touches her, but she shakes him off, causing his face to drop.

'Ty, it's over.' She sounds firm, stronger than she feels.

'This is bullshit.' He's frustrated, his anger building. 'Our wedding is booked. We sent out save the date cards.'

Penelope's relieved that the formal invitations haven't been sent yet. They've been ordered, but she'll have to try and cancel them. 'I'm sorry.'

He scoffs, moving away, rubbing at his head that is no doubt still pounding after a weekend of boozing with his mates.

'So, you're just going to move out?' He eyes her bags by the door.

Penelope nods, not trusting herself to speak, remembering how excited they'd been when they first got this place together. They'd only known each other for ten weeks when they signed the lease.

'I won't be able to afford it without you.'

She knows that, but she didn't think she could very well pack up his things and kick him out. 'I'll help with the rent until you find someone to move into the spare room.'

'Your office?'

She tries to ignore his dig, but it had been at her insistence that they got a two-bedroom place. She had wanted a workspace that wasn't going to take over their kitchen table as it had in every other place she'd ever lived.

'Where will you go?' He turns around abruptly, knowing she doesn't have close friends or family to run to.

'I've booked a room for a couple of nights.'

'You're going to stay in a hotel?' Ty's exasperated. He turns away, running his hands through his hair.

She longs to go to him and wrap her arms around him. She longs to ease his pain, but knows she'll only make it worse.

He turns back to her. 'This is crazy. I don't understand why you're doing this. Please, don't leave.'

She swallows a lump that continues to grow in her throat. 'I'm moving. I head off in a few days.'

'Where are you going?' he's quick to ask.

She looks down, realising she shouldn't have offered that information.

He studies her. 'You're not going to tell me?'

'I'm not exactly sure yet.'

'Is that what this is all about? You want to travel? We can do that! Let's just take off.' His eyes are bright again and suddenly dancing, as though he's just figured it all out.

She's crying now, tears making their way down her cheeks. 'I'm so sorry, Ty.' And without another word, she picks up her bags. She looks back to see his whole face shattered with grief. 'I'm sorry,' she whispers and slips out the door.

37

Bonnie's feet are cemented to the spot, her eyes locked on Ty. Her heart is beating so hard that she can feel the vibrations in her head.

'Okay, guys, we might move you over to the lounge,' Darcy suggests to them a little breathlessly. 'Bonnie, if you could tell Ty a bit about your sister and who else he's going to meet tonight.'

Bonnie's eyes dart hastily towards Darcy and she feels her face crease with irritation. How can Darcy even be suggesting that? She'd remained silent for that whole time and now she wants to instruct them to simply move on with the date?

'Can someone fill up Bonnie's champagne glass?' Darcy calls to her crew.

If only champagne was the answer to this problem!

But Bonnie lets her glass be filled and actually has to resist the urge to take the whole bottle. The throbbing realisation that has started to settle in her mind needs something to numb it.

Bonnie's eyes settle back on Ty. His expression is one she's never seen before. He visibly swallows a lump in his throat.

And it is suddenly all so clear.

'You still love her. You still love Penny.'

Ty's whole face crumbles as he admits, 'I do.'

Bonnie sees the relief wash over him that he's finally being honest about how he feels. He might feel relief, but Bonnie feels stupid as she tries to fully grasp the situation. She's spent the past couple of months trying to fall in love with a man whose heart wasn't ever on offer. She feels her face warm as she remembers all the ridiculous things she's done on national TV: the swimsuits, the costumes, the silly dates.

Is it possible to die from embarrassment?

'Ty, Bonnie?' Darcy's voice interrupts her thoughts. 'Just don't say anything else for a minute. I'm sure we can figure this out.'

Bonnie's voice is low. 'I can't do this anymore.' What on earth was there to figure out? Ty is in love with someone else!

Darcy goes to say something, but Bonnie puts her hand up to silence her. 'There's nothing you can say. I can't pretend I don't know that.'

'But it's over with your ex, isn't it, Ty?' Darcy says, the words rushing out of her mouth.

Ty nods, sadness woven through every inch of his skin. 'Yeah, it's over.' He looks back at Bonnie. 'I told her I was coming on here and she wished me luck.'

'See,' Darcy says, bright-eyed, to Bonnie, 'there's nothing to worry about.'

Bonnie almost laughs at how pathetic the suggestion is. 'I know Ty's dating four of us at the moment, but him being in love with someone who isn't on the show *is* a concern to me.'

But Darcy doesn't give up. 'I think Ty just got caught up in the past. We've all had relationships like that, haven't we?'

But Bonnie ignores Darcy's feeble attempts. Instead, her attention is focused on Ty, emotion spreading over every inch of her skin. 'You shouldn't even be on the show, Ty.'

The words seem to hit Ty like a slap across the face. Bonnie sees him start sinking into himself. He steps away, his shoulders slouching and his eyes looking at the ground.

'Bonnie?' Darcy touches her on the arm. 'How about we just get some fresh air for a few minutes and talk it through?'

Is this woman crazy? 'You did see how he was when he talked about her?'

Darcy falters at this and Bonnie wonders whether she had been paying attention during Ty's heartfelt ramblings.

In Bonnie's mind, there is no other option. 'I'm sorry, but I can't be part of the show knowing that. I quit.'

❧

'Shit!' Darcy curses herself as she stands beside Ben, watching the footage back. Their suitor has been filmed admitting he's in love with someone else!

Shit! Fuck! Crap!

'What a train wreck.' The worst part is there were plenty of times where she could have called cut. She could have prevented the whole thing. In the end it had been Ben who saved her butt, pinching her arm and gesturing for her to call it. 'What the hell was I doing?' But she knows exactly what she'd been doing. She'd been thinking about Drew and Ed and the whole mess she'd got herself into.

She's been on the road with the hometown dates for almost a week. She's spoken to Drew each night, briefly as usual. Neither of them have brought up setting the date, instead filling their conversation with dull occurrences from their day.

But she hasn't heard from Ed at all. Normally he sends her a text every couple of days to check in. Darcy has composed about a hundred messages to him but hasn't managed to send one. Nothing feels quite right so she keeps leaving it, aware that the extended silence is only making things worse.

So instead of paying attention to the actual words coming out of Ty's mouth, she'd been playing out a conversation in her head of what she'd like to say to Ed. She'd been doing exactly that while the 'Ty still loves his ex' footage was recorded. She'd momentarily forgotten she had a job to do. And now one of the contestants has quit!

'Alice will fire me over this.'

'They can edit around it?' Ben suggests.

That's true, they could cut the whole conversation after Ty comments on the photo of Bonnie's niece and nephews, but then where would they go from there? They have a bit of footage from Bonnie and Ty's walk along the beach but not enough to hold a segment together. And they still have to explain why Bonnie is leaving the show.

After calling cut in Bonnie's photography studio, Darcy had been sweaty and breathless as she'd desperately tried to save things. She'd had faith she could do it, but watching the footage back now, she realises how naive she'd been to believe that she could have rectified anything.

She knew things were falling apart, but she couldn't think quickly enough. Darcy had cringed at herself as words fell from her mouth. She'd been clutching at straws, trying to talk Bonnie around, but it had been pointless. Bonnie was ashen but firm in her decision.

There would be no coming back from Bonnie's resignation.

'I'm going to have to send the footage in.' Ben gets her attention back and points to the time.

They're behind schedule. 'I have to call Alice.' It's the last thing she wants to do. Any hope of a promotion is going to disappear into thin air.

Darcy knows they'll use Bonnie's exit to grab ratings, and if Bonnie was leaving due to her feelings alone, Darcy could feel okay about it, excited even about the drama. Instead, she's worried the whole thing is going to blow up in her face. Is Ty going to continue his downwards spiral? Will there soon be no suitor on *The One*?

Darcy's career has never looked so dire.

❧

'Hi,' Carla purrs when she opens the door. Her eyes widen and her smile pauses at finding Bonnie on her doorstep. The arrangement had been for Darcy to arrive with the camera crew before Bonnie and Ty. Carla is bright and smiley. She's had her teeth whitened, hair done, and Bonnie suspects a touch of Botox.

The drive over had been a blur, a thousand thoughts going through Bonnie's head. One of the most persistent ones was that Carla had redecorated her entire house for this and now it wasn't even going to be on TV.

Carla looks past Bonnie, her eyes searching, clearly trying to remain calm. 'Where are the cameras?' She leans forward and cranes her neck to look down the street. 'Where's Ty?'

Bonnie's face twists, not sure what to say. Where should she begin?

But Carla reads her expression. 'He's not coming?'

Bonnie gives the slightest shake of the head. 'I just quit the show.' Numbness outweighs tears for the moment.

'Oh, Bonnie.' Genuine concern rushes over Carla's face as she opens her arms to hug her older sister. She directs her to the lounge as Bonnie explains what happened, that Ty is in love with someone else. As the words spill from her lips, tears glaze over her eyes.

But Carla's emotions opt for outrage instead. 'How can the producers let this happen? They're supposed to pick a guy who isn't hung up on somebody else!'

'I'm pretty sure he hadn't told anyone.'

'We should sue!'

Bonnie almost laughs as she curls her legs up underneath her. 'For what?'

Carla falters for a moment. 'Humiliation, for one! You've put your entire life on hold for a guy who never should have been given the privilege of being on *The One*.'

'Privilege?' Bonnie wants to smirk at this suggestion but quickly reminds herself that Carla is a diehard fan of the show. There are going to be plenty of other people who will be just as horrified as Carla. Poor Ty. He'd had his heart broken and was just trying to get over his ex. Bonnie knows how that feels.

'Want to stay the night?' Carla offers.

But after her time in *The One* mansion, company is the last thing Bonnie feels like.

A few hours later Bonnie is snuggled on her own lounge, a glass of wine in one hand, ice-cream in the other, trying to determine if she's treating heartbreak or humiliation.

She flinches when there's a knock at the door. She should have known better than to expect Carla would be able to stay away. Bonnie had seen how her sister's face had fallen when she had turned down her offer of staying over. Carla would have wanted to stay up all night, badmouthing Ty of course, but also interrogating Bonnie about every behind-the-scenes element of *The One*. Bonnie wasn't up for any of that. Can't she just be a bear and hibernate for the next couple of months?

Ha! She smiles at the thought. Carla had been panicked that Bonnie would be without her mobile until she officially signed off the show. Darcy will be coming over in the morning with all the paperwork and to brief her through the exit interview. She doesn't even want to think about what she'll be encouraged to say to the cameras. Darcy had said they still weren't sure what angle they were going to take as to why Bonnie was leaving the show. Apparently, they don't want Bonnie to say that Ty is still in love with his ex. Bonnie swallows the sour taste in her mouth. She's disgusted that the whole production team seem to be okay with turning a blind eye. How would Addison, Hayley and Jodie feel if they knew?

Bonnie doesn't even know how she feels!

She's sad for herself because she'd had a glimpse of a future with Ty, but she's also sad for him, still deeply hurt and mourning his last relationship. But then, if she sweeps all the sadness to the side, she's really pissed off with him. Why did he decide to come on a show when he's still pining over someone else? But then she reminds herself not to climb too far up on her high horse. After all, she's spent an awful lot of this 'journey' thinking about Ollie.

There's another knock.

Bonnie yawns as she makes her way to the door. She had reassured Carla she'd be fine. *Fine* probably wasn't the right word. She'd had a cry, but she wasn't devastated, just empty and disappointed.

She always knew it was a competition and that he could be falling in love with the other girls, she just hadn't expected him to be in love with a girl who wasn't 'in the running'. The way he'd looked when he talked about Penny reminded her how she wanted to feel about someone and how she wanted someone to feel about her.

She pulls open the door.

'Ollie?'

His hands are shoved in his pockets, his face drawn as though he hasn't slept in days.

'I didn't know if you'd be staying here.' But he looks relieved that she is.

Bonnie is supposed to be staying in a crappy motel about twenty minutes out of town like she had for the past couple of nights but today she told Darcy she was going home. She needed to sleep in her own bed. She'd assumed she'd be left alone, that no one except Carla would know where she was. She hasn't even called Paige yet. 'What are you doing here?' she asks Oliver.

'I don't know. I knew you were back in town and I just had to see you.'

Her heart does a flip. She wants to smile but doesn't allow herself the luxury. 'Does Sophie know you're here?'

There's a small shake of the head.

'Ollie, don't do this,' she urges. There's a sound on the street, which unsettles her. 'I think you should go.'

'Please, Bon, I need to talk to you.'

She knows she should say no. Her head feels like mush. She knows hearing whatever it is that he has to say will only complicate things, but looking into his eyes, she finds herself crumbling. 'Five minutes, okay?' She steps back, letting him inside. He smiles gratefully and squeezes her hand for just a second as he walks by. She forces herself to ignore the tingles left in her fingertips.

She sits opposite him in the lounge room, not trusting herself to be any closer.

'I saw you today, down at the beach.'

He had been there. He'd been watching her.

'Pretty full on crowd.'

Bonnie nods. 'Yeah, it looked like half the town were trying to have a stickybeak.'

He doesn't say anything for a moment and Bonnie wonders if he's forgotten where he is.

'So, this guy,' he manages. 'You really like him?'

'Ollie, I can't talk about the show.' She knows it's a bit of a cop-out, but she has no idea where to begin. Her feelings for Ty are irrelevant now. She knows she's a bit of a hypocrite telling Ty he shouldn't have been on the show because he was in love with his ex, when she'd committed to the show despite her feelings for Ollie. She wants to tell Oliver that for her *The One* is over. It'll only be a night or two and something will be aired about her leaving. She's pretty sure Darcy and the producers will do everything to get Ty to stay until the series finale. Bonnie can't help but feel for the other three contestants who still think they have a future with him.

'Sophie had a miscarriage.'

The words throw Bonnie. She feels winded as she watches him. He looks like he's been punched in the face. 'I'm so sorry.' She knows how much he wants to be a dad.

'It happened a couple of weeks ago now.'

'How's Sophie?' Bonnie finds herself asking, quickly remembering Paige's devastation after she miscarried.

'She's taking it pretty bad,' Oliver says, looking up to meet her gaze.

'I really am sorry, Ollie.' She's sympathetic. 'I imagine it's a horrible thing for any couple to have to go through.'

Oliver nods his thanks and they sit in silence for a moment. Bonnie wants to ask him why he's here, but she's scared. After today, does she want to hear the reason?

Until finally he says, 'We called the wedding off.'

38

Three months earlier

Penelope pauses before she reaches the cafe and the lady behind her is forced to sidestep at the last moment, her handbag banging against Penelope as she walks past.

'Sorry,' Penelope murmurs as the lady passes by, but her eyes have already found Ty. He's sitting alone at their table. He's staring down at his phone, but his leg is tapping up and down nervously, waiting for her to arrive.

This is a bad idea. She shouldn't have come. But when her boss had emailed saying Ty wouldn't stop harassing her, Penelope knew she had to put a stop to it. Well, she told herself that anyway. Really she'd wanted an excuse to see his face again. Just one more time.

She'd emailed back to Monique. *Tell Ty I'll meet him. Eleven o'clock, Monday at Berts.* Now she realises she should have chosen somewhere else. Berts has too much history. It had been their favourite place to get coffee, their favourite place for weekend brunch, their favourite place to talk wedding plans.

It's a stupid idea to see him again.

Penelope's about to turn to leave when Ty looks up. Their eyes meet, and she's instantly taken back to the day when they first met. Sun soaked and hopeful. But now it all feels like a dream. Too good to be reality.

He holds up a hand to say hello and goes to smile, but stops himself mid-expression.

She walks towards him, not giving herself time to fumble or back away. 'Ty,' she says, her voice almost escaping her. It's only been a month since she walked out the door, but her heart has ached every day since.

He stands to hug her. She braces herself, taking a breath. She'd prepared herself for this. She needs to be numb and not feel his body against her own. But the moment he touches her, a jolt runs through her entire body and she quickly steps back, not trusting herself.

He looks hurt, his mouth sagging. 'I just ordered us some drinks. A green tea for you.'

Penny's heart stings at her old order but her mouth is watering at the thought of caffeine touching her lips. 'I might just go change mine for a coffee instead.'

Ty's surprised. 'Since when do you drink coffee?'

She'd always avoided the stuff, drinking more green tea a day than water. It used to drive Ty crazy that she'd leave half-filled mugs of it around their place. But it had always given her a small sense of satisfaction that she was like her mother. 'It's just a new thing.' She shrugs, purposely avoiding eye contact, knowing he'll be able to tell there's more to it than that. She can feel him studying her face, trying to figure out what she's not telling him.

'Let me,' he says, indicating he'll go change the order. 'Flat white?'

'Thanks.' She smiles. She would have ordered a latte, but she already feels bad enough. She should have just stuck to green tea.

As he moves past her Penelope feels her breath suddenly escape like a blown-up balloon being let go. She sits down and watches Ty at the counter. Every inch of her body longs to be in his arms. She forces herself to look away and notices a waiter carrying a piece of hummingbird cake to a nearby table. Only a few months ago she'd shared a slice with Ty as they flipped through wedding magazines. She'd had a list of things they needed to decide on and it kept getting longer and longer. He'd joked that they should just escape to Hawaii and elope. She'd said, 'Yes, let's do it.' He'd stared at her for a moment, unsure, but knowing she was serious. She had no significant friends or family that she needed at their wedding. He'd finally said, 'We can't elope, Penny, Mum would never forgive me.'

If they had eloped, they would have already been married. It would have been too late to protect him.

He arrives back to the table. 'Did you want any food? I didn't order anything, but I can go back?'

It's weird to see him so unsure. 'Coffee is fine.' She doesn't know if she can be around him for the length of a meal.

'How've you been?' he asks.

But Penelope can't go through the torture of small talk with him. 'You told Monique you needed to talk to me about something?'

His nostrils flare, slightly taken aback that she's chosen to ignore normal pleasantries. He takes a deep breath. 'I've made a pretty big decision and thought I should tell you before it's all over social media.'

Confused, her mind immediately starts ticking. 'What do you mean?'

He's nervous, which unsettles her further. 'I've signed on to be the next suitor on *The One*.'

Penelope's mind goes blank for a moment, the words not making sense. Had he just spoken in English? She has to force herself to connect the dots. 'The reality TV show?' She's pretty sure she's heard one of his mates, whose dad is a big TV executive, talking about *The One* before.

He nods, only the tiniest bit embarrassed, but clearly still unsure.

All the air chokes out of Penelope's lungs and there's a tightening across her chest. She has an urge to stand up out of her chair and shake it off, if only that were possible. 'Why would you want to go on a show like that?' How could someone she wanted to spend the rest of her life with be willing to do that?

'I'm ready to get married, Penny.' He stares at her, his eyes burning, desperate to break through the barrier she is only just managing to keep up. 'I want to share my life with someone and start a family.'

Penelope almost lets out a sob. She wants that too. She wants all that with Ty. Her heart sinks. *He's going to marry someone else.* She wishes she could feel happy for him, but she wants to kick and scream and cry and curse the world.

'Have you changed your mind about us?' There's no mistaking his hope.

Penelope fights every urge in her body. 'There is no us, Ty.' She stands and sees his whole body sink. It kills her. 'Good luck.'

39

'I never should have agreed to come on this show,' Ty says, his face drawn, his hand wrapped around a beer as he leans against the wall in Darcy's hotel room.

'You're not wrong.' Darcy can't help herself. Phone conversations with Alice were never nice, but the one she'd had this afternoon was the worst of all. Alice had belittled her and made it abundantly clear that she was to blame for Ty's love confession being filmed. Darcy knows that she should have called cut way before Ty declared his feelings, but she can't help but feel furious with him. Her career could take a serious beating from this so she's trying to stop herself from screaming at him for being such an idiot.

Ty looks a little horrified by her brutal honesty.

'Sorry, Ty, but this is bad. The whole premise of the show relies on the suitor wanting to fall in love with one of the contestants. We filmed you starry-eyed and talking about your ex.'

'I thought she'd take me back when I told her I was coming on here.'

Penny, the love of his life, the woman he wanted to spend forever with. The same woman who dumped him.

Ty's mouth twists, the pain of rejection quickly flashing onto his face. 'But it was like she didn't even give a shit.' He's loose-lipped after the couple of beers she gave him to try to ease his anxiety. 'I was so pissed off that I thought I'd show her. I thought I could fall in love with someone else, that I could forget about her ...'

But he can't.

Darcy knows she should be sympathetic, but she can't muster it. She clicks open her phone at hearing a message arrive. It's from Drew saying he'll call after footy training. Her heart sinks a little at seeing there's still no message from Ed.

'Get Ben in here with one of the cameras and I'll confess every-thing. I'll take total blame and say I can't go on with the show anymore because I'm still in love with Penny.'

'The last thing the network wants is for you to walk,' Darcy says, slumping into a chair.

'But you agreed I shouldn't have come on the show.'

'Yeah, I agreed that you shouldn't have come on here, but you're well and truly on here now. The season is nearly finished. We just have to figure out how to minimise Bonnie's exit and coast to the finale.'

'So they want me to stay and just pick one of the other girls?'

Darcy nods. 'Yes, that's exactly what they want.'

Ty takes a swig of his beer then rests his head back against the wall. 'But I'm not in love with any of them.'

'You don't have to be in love to be in a relationship with one of them.' Darcy is implying that love could develop with time but as she hears the words come from her lips her mind flickers to Drew. A heavy thud of guilt lands squarely across her shoulders as she remembers the feeling of her lips pressed against Ed's.

'Well, that's romantic.' Sour sarcasm seeps from his mouth.

'Welcome to reality TV,' Darcy replies steadily.

Ty shakes his head in disgust. 'I don't want to do it. I can't string the girls along anymore. They deserve to know the truth.'

Of course he's having a crisis of conscience now. 'Ty, let me be frank. You've strung the girls along for over two months. Two more weeks isn't really going to make a difference. Jodie, Hayley or Addison. Tell me which one you want, and I'll organise the rest.'

'I'm not doing it. I want to walk.' Ty's expression has become hard and certain.

But Darcy is under strict instructions that under no circumstances can Ty leave the show. 'Ty, Penny doesn't want you and if you walk the network will sue you for more money than you could earn in a lifetime.'

His eyes flash up to hers as though she's brutally attacked him.

She turns her head away, shame reeking from her skin. She just threatened someone's livelihood. Who has she become?

40

'You're sick?'

Penelope looks up and finds herself swearing under her breath. She'd known it was a bad idea booking in with a local doctor, but she'd had no choice. 'Lara, hi! How are you?' Oh dear, her voice sounds too perky, too fake. Very unlike her.

But Lara's face is aghast. 'Is everything okay?'

Penelope had been avoiding her phone calls and only sent one measly text message back in return saying she'd been busy. Now, she wishes words would come fast, something convincing and believable, but the fight is becoming harder. Her head can't think straight, she's scared to tangle herself in more lies. She only came to get something for the pain and she knows Lara's seen the sign.

Dr Owen Mills, Oncologist boldly sits on the building she's just walked out of.

Penelope clears her throat. There's no point in hiding it now. 'I've got stage four cancer.'

41

Bang, bang, bang.

Bonnie is embedded in a deep sleep, as though a heavy weight has been placed on her chest. She's tumbling around and around, happy and unaware. She'd tossed and turned for hours with thoughts of Oliver and Sophie calling off their wedding and of being on set with Ty, Ben and his big camera leering at them.

BANG, BANG, BANG!

Bonnie's eyes peel open as she hears, 'Bonnie!'

She groans as she swings her feet over the side of the bed. She catches a glimpse of herself in the mirror and almost laughs.

BANG, BANG, BANG!!!

Quickly followed by another, 'BONNIE!'

'Coming!' she calls back, annoyed, trying to pick the familiar voice. It certainly isn't Carla or Oliver.

She pulls open the door to see Darcy, who looks like she's had no sleep at all.

'Who the hell is this?' Darcy thrusts her mobile towards Bonnie.

Bonnie's insides somersault as she reaches for the phone, her mind spiralling at the image. The screen is filled with a photo of Bonnie and Oliver on Bonnie's doorstep, taken last night. It's grainy and dark, but it's still easy to recognise who they are. The frame shows Oliver touching Bonnie's hand as he moves into the house.

'Is he still here?' Darcy looks past Bonnie, implying he might be in Bonnie's bed.

'What? No!' Panic rushes over her. 'Where did you get this from?' They were being watched? She feels sick. She wants to sit down.

Darcy must recognise this and glances over her shoulder. 'Come on, let's go inside.'

Bonnie, still clutching the phone, makes her way to the lounge. Darcy follows and perches next to her. Somewhere in Bonnie's brain she knows Darcy hasn't been here before and she really should offer her a drink but she can't seem to connect any words to her mouth.

'It's already online,' Darcy says, clearly stressed. 'All the major gossip sites have posted it. Comments and shares are coming in fast.'

'How?' Bonnie utters, finally managing one word.

Darcy pushes back some hair off her face. 'Someone must have been watching your house last night.' She shrugs. 'They've probably just made themselves a few thousand dollars.'

'A few thousand dollars for this?' Bonnie knows a little bit about how the paparazzi work, but she can't quite get her head around the fact that they want to take photos of her. She stares down at the photo on the screen again. She can still feel Oliver's touch against her skin.

'As far as everyone is concerned, you're still a contestant on *The One*,' Darcy says. 'People are already outraged—some think you've gone behind Ty's back.'

Bonnie grimaces. 'Just what I need—the whole country to hate me.'

'It gives us a good angle for why you're leaving the show.'

'No!' Bonnie rushes, panicked at the ramifications of that.

Darcy studies her face for a moment. 'Look, we'll do what we can to try and spin the story, but I need to know what we're dealing with. Who is the guy?'

She wishes she could lie. She wishes she could protect him, but there's no point, it's already too late. 'My high school boyfriend. His name is Oliver.'

'Shit!'

Darcy didn't think life could get much worse after yesterday, but she'd barely had any sleep when Alice had called her, outraged. 'Bonnie is supposed to be in lockdown. Why is there a photo of her with a guy all over the internet?'

Darcy's stomach had sunk like lead. She had no idea what photo Alice was talking about, but gut instinct told her she'd made a terrible decision letting Bonnie go back to her own place instead of the cheap hotel they were staying in.

That decision might cost her job.

'Is something going on between the two of you?' Darcy looks at Bonnie, wondering how many people they went to school with. It's likely that old photos of them will start circulating within the hour. Darcy can imagine the headlines now: *The One contestant leaves show for ex-lover.*

'Uh …' Bonnie says slowly, her eyes closing for a moment before shaking her head. 'He's got a fiancée … or a girlfriend at least. He came here last night to tell me they've called off the wedding.'

Darcy inhales sharply at the thought of another wedding being called off. 'Because of you?' Darcy isn't about to have to justify a cancelled wedding along with everything else, is she?

The One contestant breaks up wedding of ex-boyfriend.

'No,' Bonnie says quickly, but then adds, 'well, I don't think so. I kind of shoved him out the door before he had a chance to explain.'

Darcy doesn't say anything. She doesn't know what to say. She doesn't know what to do. She needs her brain to think—to come up with a plan. She feels herself become very still. She wants to breathe a little deeper, she needs more air in her lungs, but the more she thinks about air, the more she starts gasping.

'Are you okay?' Bonnie stares at her.

Darcy tells herself to get a grip. She needs to concentrate on work, but it seems impossible because she has one thought that won't stop replaying over and over in her head. 'I want to call off my wedding,' she blurts without even meaning to. It's the first time she's admitted it. The relief is momentous, like she's been walking around in a suit of heavy armour and has just taken it all off. And even though it feels liberating, she suddenly realises that she won't ever be able to fit into the armour again. Her heart squeezes tight, her throat closes over and tears come flooding until she's snotty and barely able to speak. She needs to pull herself together. 'Can I use your bathroom?'

'It's through there.' Bonnie points, clearly not sure how she should be reacting.

Darcy closes the door behind her, her chest still contracting from lack of breath. In the mirror, her face stares back at her all red and blotchy. She quickly turns on the taps and begins splashing water on her face. Her body longs to break down and let the emotions pour out. The realisation that she wants to end things with Drew is devastating. Ten years of history together only to call it quits? Another whimper escapes her mouth.

'Stop it,' she reprimands herself. She's technically working. Imagine if Alice knew she even *thought* about her personal life during work hours. Her personal life is on pause until she figures out what to do about Bonnie leaving the show *and* Bonnie being caught on camera with her ex.

She pats her face dry with the handtowel. She wishes she had some makeup to try to make herself look semi-respectable. She reaches for Bonnie's top bathroom drawer, but it squeaks violently and Darcy freezes. She doesn't want Bonnie to know she's gone searching through her drawers, so she has to go back out there barefaced with nothing to hide behind.

She makes her way back to the lounge room to find Bonnie sitting on the edge of the sofa. 'You okay?' she asks.

Darcy gives her a tight smile. 'Sorry about that. So unprofessional.' She shakes her head, disappointed in herself. 'I'm fine. Not enough sleep.'

And instead of pressing Darcy about it, Bonnie seems to accept her excuse and instead brings the conversation back to herself. 'I need my phone back. If that photo is all through the media, I'm sure there'd be a fair few people trying to contact me.'

Darcy assumes Bonnie is referring to her ex in particular. 'It's in Sydney. All the phones were put into a safe in the production office after you guys were put in lockdown.'

'Can you get it couriered up here or something?'

Darcy considers the logistics of this, trying to ignore the throbbing headache forming behind her eyes from her crying outburst. 'It might be an option, but I don't know that Alice is going to okay it. Technically you're still signed on to the show. Legally we don't have to give your phone back until after the season finale.'

Bonnie groans and buries her head in her hands. 'How is this happening?' she mumbles.

Darcy finds herself feeling sorry for Bonnie. Yesterday she woke up being a fan favourite to win *The One* and now, only twenty-four hours later, she's facing a media frenzy, the latest villain in reality TV. 'Can you sit tight and I'll try to sort this stuff out?' Darcy asks. 'I'll see what I can do about your phone, but I also have to go see Ty.'

'How is he?' Bonnie's expression is stiff, as though she's unable to decide whether she's concerned or pissed off.

Darcy pauses, reminding herself that she needs to be careful about what she says. 'He's okay.'

'So he's still doing the show?'

He has no choice in the matter, but she can't tell Bonnie that. 'Yes.'

'What a joke.' Bonnie rolls her eyes. 'He's still in love with his ex. He shouldn't be on the show.'

In the name of love Darcy wholeheartedly agrees, but her personal opinion can't come into play here. 'I have to remind you, Bonnie, that you've signed confidentiality forms. You'll be told what you can and can't say as to why you've left the show.'

'That hardly seems fair.'

Darcy can't help but feel for her. 'I'm hoping to spin the friendship angle, that your relationship with Ty moved into the friend zone before a romance could truly take off.'

But this doesn't seem to appease her. 'The public won't know anything about Ty's ex and his feelings for her?'

'No, the public won't know about Penny.'

42

Four months earlier

'What if we just drop back your hours? Even to a couple of days a week?'

Penelope knows it's a generous offer. Monique would never normally agree to anything like this.

'That wouldn't be fair on you. I'm not going to be in Sydney anymore.'

'Where are you going?'

Penelope swallows hard, considering lying because she knows the truth will just create more questions. But Monique will see through a lie and demand an address or at least more details.

'I'm not sure yet.'

Monique eyes her, clearly trying to figure out what's going on. 'I know you've heard of email and phone.' It's said more as a statement than a question. 'We can courier the manuscripts if you want hard copies.'

'Monique, thank you so much for the offer, but I want to make a clean break.'

'Have you been offered another job?' Monique knows there's more going on.

'No, not at all,' Penelope says. 'I'm going to take a break from working altogether.'

Monique doesn't say anything, just watches her, as though she'll be able to figure out what's going on if she stares at her intently enough.

'And Ty's happy about relocating too?'

'I've broken up with Ty.' Penelope can't meet her eye.

'Why? What's happened?' Monique's voice rushes with concern, too much concern. Their relationship has always been more professional than friendly.

Penelope can't speak, knowing tears are close.

'Penelope, tell me. What's going on?'

She'd promised herself she wouldn't utter a word. She'd promised herself she'd stay strong, but these promises are becoming increasingly unrealistic. Her willpower is slipping from her grasp at rapid speed.

'Has he done something?' Monique's blunt.

'No, no.' Penelope shakes her head quickly. Ty would never cheat. That seems so simple compared to the reality.

'Well, is it cold feet?'

Cold feet. That's what everyone will think. Everyone will assume she doesn't want to spend her life with Ty, which couldn't be further from the truth. She'd happily live to a hundred with

Ty by her side. She feels a flash of guilt for making Ty face them without a proper explanation. But they're mostly his friends. She's never been good at keeping people close.

'I know it's daunting, with one in two marriages ending in divorce,' Monique says, waving the fact away, 'but you and Ty, well I've seen the two of you together. You're meant to be.'

Penelope almost lets out a sob. A breath of air escapes her mouth before she clamps it shut, feeling the lump in her throat try to make its way out.

Monique studies her face again, seeing how hard it is for Penelope to hold herself together. 'Just tell me, Penelope.'

And Penelope can't hold it in another second. 'Cancer. I've been given twelve months.'

Monique doesn't say anything. Penelope sees the words hit her hard, throwing her back in her seat. She hadn't been expecting cancer.

'No.' Monique knows her well enough to know both her mum and sister died from cancer. 'You can fight it. There's got to be treatment …'

But Penny shakes the familiar conversation away. 'No, I'm not doing that. It's spread, just like Mum's, just like Miranda's.' Aggressive and fast.

Monique is still full of hope, like anyone when they first hear of cancer. 'But treatment could still give you more time.'

'What's the point? Six more months if I'm lucky.'

'It's still six months!'

'No.' This is why she didn't want to tell her. She doesn't want to have this conversation. She just wants to live her last year in peace, not fighting. 'Ty has no idea. You can't tell him, okay?'

Monique's face contorts, confused. 'You have to tell him.'

'I saw what it did to my brother-in-law, having to watch Miranda die. I won't do that to Ty.'

'So you've just broken up with him with no real explanation?'

Penny shrugs, nods. She isn't proud, but that's exactly what she did.

'Oh, Penelope. That's unfair on him. He's going to think you don't love him anymore.'

Penelope can feel herself become a little defensive. 'I'm giving him a clean break. If I tell him any of this, he won't leave my side. I don't want him to have to go through it.' Penelope keeps thinking of Jon's grief-stricken face. 'This way he can move on quicker.'

It's clear Monique doesn't agree.

'It's my decision, okay? I don't want him to know.'

Monique gives a small nod, promising her word.

Penelope finds some comfort in this. She knows Monique well enough to know that she won't break her word. Penelope's secret is safe.

43

Bonnie waits about thirty seconds after Darcy leaves to grab her keys, but just as she's about to head out the door she reconsiders and rushes back to her bedroom to change out of her PJs and brush her hair ... and add a smidge of makeup.

It isn't until she's driven across town and standing on the doorstep, face to face with Sophie, that she really registers what she's doing.

'What are you doing here?' Sophie's face is pale, her eyes red and puffy. Irritation visibly creates tension in her neck. 'Don't you think it's enough that a photo of you and my fiancé is sprawled all over the internet? Now you think it's okay to show up at our house?'

Guilt rushes through Bonnie like icy water entering her veins. She really should have thought this through. 'I'm sorry. I didn't mean to upset you. Oliver said you'd called the wedding off and I'd just assumed ...' She trails off, a little unsure where to go with the sentence. She assumed they'd broken up, but standing here now, she realises they might have just scaled things back to deal with the grief of the miscarriage.

Sadness comes crawling onto Sophie's face, as though she'd forgotten about the cancelled wedding. 'Yeah, I guess he's not my fiancé anymore.' Tears fill her eyes and Bonnie instinctively wants to reach out and touch her, offer her some comfort.

'I'm sorry about the baby,' Bonnie says, honestly feeling like it's the right thing to say, but Sophie looks up, eyes glaring, swatting Bonnie's sympathy away.

'He told you.' She clearly feels betrayed.

Bonnie realises she shouldn't have said anything, but more words seem to pour out of her mouth, which is apparently no longer connected to her brain. 'I imagine it's been a tough time.'

'But here you are? Ready to sweep in and take him away from me?'

'No, it's not like that,' Bonnie rushes to say. But is it? Is that why she's here? To get back with Ollie? Bonnie tries to grab hold of one of the many thoughts flying around in her head, but they zoom past, impossible to catch.

'He'll take you back,' Sophie remarks. 'Apparently I'm too sad all the time. Too hard to talk to.'

Bonnie wishes she had given it some more thought before coming over here. Last night she'd kicked Ollie out of her place moments after he'd told her about calling the wedding off. 'I can't deal with this now,' she'd told him, her mind swelling like a raging sea after everything with Ty.

Ty. Was all that only yesterday?

'You'd think losing a baby would have brought us closer together, but he wants me to just move on, get over the fact I had our child growing inside me. A little us, growing right here.' Her hand settles on her belly, a longing to feel her baby inside.

Bonnie's never seen Sophie like this before. She's always been perky and fake, but she sees none of that now. Harsh and raw emotions have peeled away her former self.

'I know what you're thinking.' Sophie wraps her arms around her body, which Bonnie notices seems much smaller than when she last saw her. 'That it's not that big a deal. People lose actual babies and I was only ten weeks pregnant.'

'That's not what I'm thinking at all.'

Sophie's chin trembles. 'I feel like I've had the biggest loss in my life and people are just expecting me to get over it. No one understands.'

'Where's Ollie—Oliver?' Bonnie quickly amends. Using his nickname feels too personal. 'He should be here with you.'

'He's never here. He goes to work, goes out to the pub, plays footy and squash … bike rides. Anything to get away from me.'

Bonnie gets it. Oliver's let his life go on, but Sophie is still embedded in her grief.

'Give him a call, I'm sure he'll answer if he sees it's you calling.'

Bonnie doesn't miss the snide tone. She goes to say she doesn't have her mobile, she wouldn't be *here* if she had her mobile, but decides against it. 'Look, I don't want to make things harder for you and Oliver.'

'Are you saying you don't have feelings for him?'

That isn't what she's saying, and Sophie knows it. 'I've been away for a couple of months. I just expected I'd come back and Oliver would have moved on from what happened.'

'So, something did happen between you two before you went away?' There's cockiness to her remark, some satisfaction that she's right about a previous conversation.

Bonnie's heart squeezes tight realising what she's just done. She tries to swallow but the lump in her throat stubbornly lodges itself. Had Sophie suspected things earlier? Had she asked Oliver? Had he lied?

Sophie's eyes burn into Bonnie, waiting for an answer. 'Is that why you went on the show? To get away from him?'

Her feelings for Ollie were one hundred percent why she agreed to go on that show. She'd feared if she stayed in town, she wouldn't be able to fight the attraction.

'I couldn't believe it when I saw you get out of that limousine,' Sophie says. 'I called out to Ollie to come see. He nearly fell over at first and then his face went green.'

Bonnie drops her head, imagining how Ollie must have felt when he'd seen her on screen.

'Bonnie Yates on a reality TV dating show?' Sophie shakes her head in disbelief. 'It doesn't seem like a very *you* thing to do.'

No, it's much more of a Sophie thing to do.

'You went on there to get away from Oliver, didn't you?' She's clearly not going to give up until Bonnie confesses.

'There were some old feelings there when you guys moved back to town,' Bonnie admits, 'but I knew he was with you.'

Sophie laughs, wicked but also amused. 'You actually expect me to believe that?' She closes her eyes for a moment, as though trying to get a grip on her emotions. 'I honestly don't know whether to laugh or scream.'

Bonnie's heart is beating so hard that pain thuds through her body.

'I thought you were a decent person. I honestly thought I could trust you but you're both as bad as each other. Pathetic liars.'

Bonnie finds herself feeling a little defensive. She isn't the one who was engaged. She isn't the one who cheated. But she also feels ashamed, because she thought she was a decent person too, but a decent person wouldn't kiss a man who was engaged to someone else. 'I'm sorry,' Bonnie hears herself mutter. 'Please believe that I really am sorry.' She turns away, unable to meet Sophie's gaze before rushing off to her car.

As she drives away, her whole body is drenched in dirty, mucky guilt.

44

'Did you have a good flight?' Darcy asks as she greets Alice through the taxi window. She'd flown up from Sydney to Port Macquarie's regional airport.

Alice doesn't even bother replying and instead just offers her familiar icy gaze.

'Do you want me to help you with your bags?'

'I'm not an invalid.'

The polite smile on Darcy's face aches. Once the photo of Bonnie and Oliver had gone viral, Alice had made it very clear that she didn't feel Darcy was equipped to deal with everything on her own and would be flying up immediately to ensure Bonnie's exit interview went smoothly. Darcy's sure Alice thrives on this kind of drama, it's like fuel for a dragon.

'What has the network decided to do about the photo of Bonnie and her ex?' Darcy asks. When Darcy had spoken to Alice last night it still hadn't been decided.

'We'll address the photo after Bonnie's exit interview is aired tonight. We're going to say Bonnie had already left the show when the photo was taken, and an old friend was comforting her.'

'I'm glad they agreed with what I suggested.' Darcy can't help herself. She's sick of continually getting no credit for ideas she puts forward.

But Alice ignores the comment. 'Has everything here been arranged?'

'Yes.' Darcy has been flat out finalising paperwork, securing a location and writing the script for Bonnie's exit interview. Alice herself had spoken to Bonnie via Darcy's phone to double and triple check that she didn't want to give Ty another chance and stay on the show. Under no circumstances would Bonnie even consider this.

Ty's flown back to the city and is in lockdown. Darcy and Ben have already filmed an interview with him. If Bonnie says what has been written for her, then the two interviews will be cut together. It'll look like a mutual parting of ways, that their friendship had become stronger than romance ever would.

They arrive at a private garden Darcy had secured.

'Are you sure you're capable of running things here?' Alice's mouth is downturned. 'I can take over.'

Part of Darcy wants to lie down and admit defeat, curl up under a blanket and enjoy endless cups of tea. But she isn't going to give Alice the satisfaction. 'I'm more than capable,' Darcy assures her.

Bonnie's waiting, her hair and makeup already done.

'Are you ready?' Darcy asks as she approaches.

There's no trace of a smile on her face. 'I know what I have to say.' What they've asked her to say. She's made it abundantly clear she doesn't agree, but will fulfil her contract requirements and confidentiality clause.

Darcy can feel the tension. They may have been friendly in the past, but it's nothing but professional now.

'Are you sure we can't tempt you to stay?' Alice's cool voice cuts the air. 'We can assure you the win?'

Disgust washes over Bonnie's face. 'I won't be someone's second choice.' Why would Bonnie settle for a life with Ty when she knows Ty's heart belongs to Penny?

Naturally Darcy's thoughts go to Drew and she wonders if she'd be settling if she stayed with him.

'Is that where you want me?' Bonnie indicates towards a chair.

Darcy buries her feelings about Drew and nods to Bonnie, watching as she sits nervously in the chair. Darcy moves to stand next to Ben, who is waiting by his camera. He offers Bonnie a little hello and Darcy is surprised that Bonnie returns his smile in spite of everything.

'Okay, Bonnie. Just like we rehearsed and straight to camera,' Darcy says. 'Rolling in three, two, one …'

⤳

Bonnie watches as Darcy's finger slices through the air and gestures to the camera. It's time for Bonnie to speak.

You can do this, she tells herself. *Just like you practised.*

She stares down the barrel of the camera, Ben's body perfectly still behind it. She closes her eyes as she exhales a long breath, finding courage from deep within to just get this over and done with. 'Being a contestant on *The One* has been an experience I'll never forget.' Even though right now she desperately wants to forget the whole thing. She wants to forget that she put herself on television for all of Australia to see, she wants to forget that she let herself believe she had a chance with a guy that she never had a future with.

Darcy offers an encouraging smile and gestures to keep going.

Darcy had written something about forming special friendships with the women she'd met on the show, but Bonnie isn't going to say that. Sure, some of the women were great, but she probably won't talk to any of them ever again. 'Living in the house was harder than I thought it would be. I'm looking forward to getting home and living a normal life again.'

She notices Darcy lean in to Ben and whisper something to him. Bonnie feels her head drop, wondering how she looks on camera. How has Ben framed her? Can they see how depleted she's feeling under all the makeup?

'I feel lucky to have spent time with Ty. It was easy to be in his company.'

Darcy had wanted her to say that Bonnie knew he wasn't the guy for her, but Bonnie had argued, insisting on saying, 'But I believe Ty's feelings for someone else are stronger than they are for me.'

She can see Darcy's boss Alice standing with her hands on her hips, her lips thin, an air of terrifying importance about her.

'He's a great guy and I wish him the best of luck in finding the one.' She holds her smile to camera for a few seconds, giving them enough time to call cut. 'Is that all you need?' she asks, already half out of her chair.

'It'd be good if you could say the bit about knowing the right guy is out there for you?' Darcy says.

Bonnie doesn't miss the hope in Darcy's eyes. It would clearly make Bonnie's exit look more favourable if she's optimistic for her own future. But Bonnie doesn't know what expectations she should have. Ollie showing up at her house announcing he's called his wedding off has her second-guessing a life with him. She'd like to think it's all going to unfold naturally, but can it when he's still living with Sophie?

Bonnie notices Ben tilt his head to the side so he can see her around the camera rather than through the lens. 'Still rolling.' He shrugs. 'If you want to say something else?'

There's a calming presence about Ben and she finds herself sitting back down despite herself. She takes a deep breath and focuses on the camera. 'I really hope the right guy for me is out there,' she says. She's surprised that amused laughter bubbles from the bottom of her throat. 'It'd just be nice if he hurried up.' Once again she holds her smile before letting it drop, ready for this to be over.

'Cut,' Darcy calls and approaches. 'Thanks so much, Bonnie. That was great.'

Bonnie knows it wasn't great, but appreciates Darcy saying so.

'That's all you need?' She's already signed the official paperwork.

'Yep, you're free to go.' Darcy offers a smile with a look of acknowledgement that Bonnie's about to escape the crazy TV world.

Bonnie gratefully pushes out of her chair. She can't wait to get home and scrub the makeup off her face and change into something comfortable.

'I've arranged for your mobile to be couriered up. It should be delivered to your place this afternoon,' Darcy says.

Bonnie's heart beats a little faster, the anticipation of getting her phone back higher than she'd ever thought it would be. 'Thanks.'

'Good luck,' Darcy says. 'I really do hope the right guy finds you soon.'

Bonnie nods. 'I hope you figure everything out too.' It was only yesterday that Darcy had been crying about wanting to call off her own engagement.

Darcy forces a smile, but a stricken look crosses her face, something she's managed to hide at work and in front of her boss. 'Me too.'

Bonnie is making her way across the room when she hears a voice. 'Heading straight for the drive-through?'

She smiles as she turns to face Ben. That hadn't crossed her mind but … 'Yeah, I think I might.'

He laughs and is about to say something else when Darcy's boss, Alice, crosses to him. 'I need to review the footage.' She clearly isn't going to wait until Ben finishes his conversation with an ex-contestant.

'Of course.' He nods at Alice, but his face drops as he turns back to Bonnie. 'See you.' He waves goodbye.

Bonnie waves back, her smile falling at their conversation being cut short. But she's eager to leave. She's a free woman and there's a hamburger calling her name.

'It's not terrific, but it'll have to do,' Alice says tersely as they watch back Bonnie's exit interview.

'It'll work,' Darcy assures her, a little disappointed but not surprised by the piece. Bonnie had only read the very basics of the script Darcy had written for her and she'd remained quite emotionless throughout the whole thing. It's going to be dissatisfying for the viewers, but what could the production team really expect when the poor woman had witnessed Ty's admission to still being in love with his ex?

They'll try to minimise Bonnie's exit and instead create hype about the three women left. Max has edited together an impressive package of Ty with Addison, Jodie and Hayley. This will run straight after Bonnie's exit interview. 'We'll blow up the online buzz for the other women,' Darcy adds. Bonnie fans will be disappointed, but hopefully there won't be too much damage.

'Who are you pushing for the win?'

Darcy's throat tightens. She'd hoped Bonnie would win. 'I think Jodie's our safest option.'

'You don't sound confident.' Alice is far from impressed.

Darcy is far from confident. Getting Ty to commit to any of the remaining women in the end is going to be a massive feat.

'We're relying on you, Darcy.' Alice's eyebrows furrow, causing a thousand lines to wrinkle across her forehead. 'You're the one who has formed a working relationship with Ty.'

Her relationship with Ty has been damaged since she threatened the network would sue him if he walked. 'He's still not keen about finishing the show.' Darcy has relayed this message several times, but Alice continues to ignore the gravity of it.

'We both know that's not an option.'

Darcy wishes she could concentrate on just this rather than being on the brink of her own break-up.

'You do realise that if you don't pull this off, I won't be able to promote you?'

It doesn't even surprise her that Alice is willing to blackmail her with this. 'This isn't a normal season,' Darcy tries to point out. It's hardly her fault that they got stuck with Ty as their suitor. Alice's boss Nigel should be taking the blame.

But Alice isn't going to be making any special considerations. 'I can't take your name forward to the network if the show doesn't get the normal height of ratings.'

'I'll do my best,' Darcy says through gritted teeth, hoping that will be enough.

Alice's serious gaze doesn't falter as she gathers her things to leave. She's about to be picked up by a taxi to be taken back to the airport while Darcy drives back to Sydney. Darcy's at least grateful she doesn't have to spend five hours in the car with her. 'Is there anything else?'

Yes, there is, but asking anything remotely resembling a favour won't go down well with Alice. 'What time do you need me in the office tomorrow?' There's something she wants to do on her way home and she would love the luxury of not having to rush back.

'You'll need to take Ty to the breakfast show interview in the morning.' Alice casts a quick look in Darcy's direction.

Darcy had already checked the schedule. 'I thought Mel was taking him to that?'

'I want you to take him,' Alice snips. 'That's not a problem, is it?'

Darcy gives a quick shake of her head. 'Of course not.' There's no point mentioning her personal life is falling apart. Personal time is a luxury she won't have until this season is over.

45

Miranda was seven when she lost her first tooth. Penny, only three at the time, had been jealous. She wanted to lose a tooth, she wanted the tooth fairy to visit her, she wanted the gap in her mouth like her big sister. Her mother told her that when she was seven she might lose a tooth too.

Years later, the day after Penny turned six, she lost her first tooth. The same thing happened with getting her tonsils out, the chicken pox, even getting her first period. Penny always did it a year earlier than Miranda had. It became a bit of a family joke, so much so that when Miranda broke her wrist at sixteen, they all laughed and said that when Penny was fifteen, she'd break one too.

And sure enough, weeks after Penelope had turned fifteen, she tripped over her school bag at lunch and broke her wrist.

So Penny had been ready. It had been six months since her last check-up when she'd been told she was all clear. But this time was going to be different. This time she was going to get the 'I'm sorry, but there's nothing we can do' conversation. The same talk Miranda had received a year later in her life. The same talk their mother had received before her thirty-ninth birthday.

Both cancers had been referred to as aggressive. Penny had wondered at the time whether any cancer was considered peaceful or calm or even complacent. Cancer is, after all, cancer.

She was so ready that she didn't even think she'd cry. She braced herself as the doctor settled into his seat and ran his hand over his salt and pepper hair. But then, when he delivered her results, Penny had cried. She'd sobbed and sobbed. *All clear.*

She'd escaped the cancer. How had that happened? Why had it taken Miranda and not her?

Two weeks later she met Ty.

A diagnosis had been hanging over her head for the past few years, but with that all clear, she'd let herself think that her future had changed, that her life would be different. She wholeheartedly let herself be swept away in falling in love. So much so that she missed her next check-up and had to reschedule.

She grimaces now as she thinks back at herself stupidly thinking she was going to get her happily ever after.

Of course her future was destined for cancer.

46

'How'd it go?' Paige asks as she steps into Bonnie's lounge room, ready to comfort her after her exit interview with *The One*. In one arm she's carrying a bucket of fried chicken and in the other a bottle of wine.

'You're a good friend,' Bonnie says as they squeeze together for a long hello hug. She then takes the chicken and leads Paige through to the kitchen. 'It went okay,' she says. She knows they weren't entirely happy with what she said, but she doesn't care. 'It felt weird after all these weeks to be able to walk out of there and be a free woman.'

'I can only imagine.' Paige holds up the wine. 'Too early for this?'

Bonnie hesitates; they haven't tackled the IVF conversation yet. She now realises that the fact Paige has brought wine isn't a good sign.

Paige is quick to register Bonnie's indecision. 'It didn't work.'

Bonnie feels her face fill with sympathy. 'I'm so sorry.' She moves closer and holds her friend tight.

When they pull apart, Paige's face is indented with heartache. 'I've cried so much already. I don't think there are any tears left.'

She gives Paige's hand a squeeze. 'How's Andy coping?'

Paige gives a quick shake of the head. 'Not good.'

He's never coped well, shutting himself in the garage to tinker away with his small tool collection, pretending to be busy despite everyone knowing Andy is a finance man who feels proud when he changes a lightbulb or the batteries in a clock.

'I really thought it was going to work this time.'

Bonnie is scared to ask, 'So what does that mean?' They'd said it would be their last shot.

'I don't want to give up hope, but maybe I don't have a choice.'

Bonnie's stomach drains to hollowed emptiness. She has no idea what words to offer her dearest friend.

'I can't talk about this anymore.' She shakes the conversation away. 'Tell me more about the house.'

Bonnie feels her eyes sting with tears as she watches Paige pour them two very large glasses of wine but she knows Paige is relying on her to keep the conversation moving. So, the two friends quickly ease into a conversation about Bonnie's time on *The One*.

The freedom of seeing her best friend feels like a luxury after being locked away for over two months. Talk spills easily between them, desperately needing to share the words that have been kept captive. After weeks of forced friendships, it's more comfortable than putting on her favourite tracksuit pants.

'I have to confess, Bon, I didn't think Ty was for you from the beginning,' Paige admits as they're halfway through their second glass.

'Really?' It feels weird that Paige has a perception of her relationship with Ty. Bonnie has no idea what footage the public has seen.

Paige shakes her head. 'He's gorgeous and seems nice but there's something about him that isn't you. A bit serious or something? I don't know. Every time I watched, I couldn't quite put my finger on it.'

Deep down Bonnie's pretty sure she knew Ty wasn't the guy for her either, but she tried hard to believe that he could be … 'Maybe the fact that he's still in love with his ex has something to do with what you were picking up on.' Bonnie had already explained the whole Penny situation.

'True.' An amused smile dimples her friend's face. 'So, what are you going to do about Oliver?'

Bonnie had also filled Paige in on Oliver announcing they'd called the wedding off and Bonnie's awkward conversation with Sophie on their doorstep.

'I don't know.' Bonnie wishes she had let Oliver tell her more before pushing him out the door. 'If he was coming to tell me because he wants us to be together, why hasn't he ended things with Sophie?' Even saying those words makes Bonnie feel icky. Is she really okay with him jumping from his life with Sophie into hers?

There's a knock at the door. 'Carla?' Paige guesses.

'Probably,' Bonnie says as she unfolds her legs and moves to the door. Her sister will no doubt want to hear as much as she can about Bonnie's last moments on *The One*. But it's a courier. 'My phone!' she exclaims, immediately buzzing as she signs for the package and rips open the envelope.

'Expecting a message or two from Oliver?' Paige doesn't miss a thing.

Bonnie nods, hoping there will be something from him to offer her hope for the future. She's so confused about how she's feeling, let alone how Ollie's feeling.

Her phone comes back to life and the flood of messages starts. There are messages from people she hasn't spoken to in a long time and more missed calls than she can even fathom, but her eyes can only focus on one message.

You talked to Sophie about us?! What the fuck is wrong with you???

The hope she'd been letting herself hold on to explodes into a thousand pieces.

47

'What are you doing here?' Drew smiles, surprised but clearly pleased to see her. He leans in for a kiss and hugs her. She lets herself soak up the embrace for a few moments. After what she's got to say he won't want to hold her like this again.

He pulls back and begins moving into the kitchen, expecting her to follow him.

'Is your mum around?'

With a shake of the head he says, 'Still at church.'

Darcy feels relieved at this.

'I'm just getting ready to go around to Lauren and Scott's for a barbecue. They'll be stoked to see you.' He's got an esky on the bench. He opens the fridge and pulls out a six-pack of beers.

She thinks of Lauren and Scott's place and knows her feelings of confinement are in opposition to Drew's wistful longing for a life like theirs. 'I can't stay.'

This gets his attention. 'How long are you here for?'

'I have to get back tonight.' It's already the afternoon. 'Ty's got a guest spot on *Good Morning* first thing tomorrow and Alice wants me there.'

'You've been working ten days straight.'

She shrugs. 'Reality TV doesn't fit into nine to five.'

A groan vibrates in the back of his throat. Drew's a traditionalist and Sundays should be nothing but a day of rest. 'So, what, you're here for twenty minutes, an hour at the most?'

Pretty much.

'Geez, Darce. Why did you even bother?'

Darcy remembers reading a saying once. *Be with someone who would drive five hours just to see you for one.* Maybe they were that couple once, but they're not now.

'Drew, we need to talk.' She recoils as the clichéd words spill from her lips. She'd practised hundreds of alternative opening lines during the car trip here.

But those few words say it all and he's quick to shake his head. 'Darce.' *Don't.*

She's surprised and wonders if he already knows what she's going to say.

'I shouldn't have pushed you about setting a date,' he says, quickly addressing the tension from their phone conversation. 'If you don't like the idea of a New Year's wedding we can come up with something else.'

'Drew, it's not just the wedding date.'

He looks up at her, his eyes a mixture of dread and fear. 'We'll figure things out,' he tells her, but he quickly averts his eyes as though looking at her might reveal a truth he doesn't want to see. 'Only a couple more weeks and I'll be back in Sydney.'

Maybe he's right. The school term is ending soon, and he'll be moving back to their place in Sydney. Their place that's started feeling like *her* place. At first it was lonely without him, but that's eased. Part of her feels sad. She wishes she'd been longing for him to come home every day. It'd be easier than having this conversation.

'I don't think we should be together anymore.' Her throat contracts, choking her breath. Tightness grabs at her chest. It hurts so much that she wonders whether she's doing the right thing.

He grimaces, his eyes shutting for a moment as though he's about to be in a car accident and is preparing himself for the collision. There's nothing for him to do but wait for the impact and pain to pierce his body.

She stands mute, wishing she could think of something better to say than *I'm sorry*.

But then he shakes his head, wanting to whitewash her words. 'You're just stressed about work and I haven't been around. We're not spending time together, so of course it feels weird to be planning a wedding.'

He's been preparing himself for this. It hasn't come as a complete surprise, and that surprises her. She'd imagined he was oblivious to them drifting apart. She's been trying to ignore the fact that they're on different paths, but maybe he's been doing the same thing.

'We don't have to do anything about the wedding. Let's just hit pause.' He glances at her again, but quickly goes on before she has a chance to say anything. 'Once I get back, things will go back to normal. We'll sort everything out.'

She thinks about him coming back and sharing the flat again. Of course she can imagine it because them coexisting has been second nature to her for the past ten years. But somewhere along the way they've become more friends than lovers. The idea of him coming home doesn't spark excitement in her. The idea of going to sleep without him doesn't even make her body ache. The yearning and desire has faded, but to tell someone this outright would be like a slap in the face.

'I don't want things to go back to normal.' Her voice is barely audible. She wills herself to look at him, she owes him that much.

Sadness swells in his eyes, yet all hope hasn't faded. 'Please, Darce. Can we just see how everything is once I get back?'

Part of her understands that this would be the easier option. Just go with it, live with the dull comfortableness of their relationship rather than face the pain of breaking up. The hurt is already flowing through her veins. She forces herself to breathe. 'Don't come back, Drew. Stay here. Tell Parko you can teach until the end of the year, like you wanted.'

That is what he wants. They both know this is the life he's supposed to be living. But still he says, 'I don't want to break up.' His face is crumbling, pleading with her to not put him through it.

Except Darcy believes otherwise. 'You just haven't realised it yet.'

He doesn't know what to say to that. But there's no escaping the truth. She's a career girl, she'll stay in the city, she might even be okay with never having kids. Now that she's given him the out, Drew will stay here in the country and be happy. The fresh country air, the small town and sense of community will offer him everything he wants. He'll marry of course and have kids and even though the idea of him being with someone else stings her heart, she knows one day she'll be able to smile about it.

'So, you just swung by on your way back to Sydney to break up with me?' He's not being malicious, just saddened as he's slumped himself at the kitchen table, knowing the decision has been made.

'I didn't want to do it over the phone.'

He nods, his mouth twisting, quite possibly to stop himself from crying.

Darcy wants to tell him that they can still be friends, but she knows that will end up being a lie. She wants to tell him that she'll always remember him. But instead she tells herself to shut up.

And so, there's silence.

Even though it's not uncomfortable, there's a feeling in the air that they need to carefully step through these next moments. For one word, one look could have a colossal effect on how their relationship ends.

'You should have this back.' She twists the beautiful engagement ring from her finger.

He waves it away. 'Keep it.'

She shakes her head. 'I can't.' For that would be a reminder of a life she could have had, a life she chose not to have, and she doesn't want to let herself dwell on the past. She settles it on the table next to his hands. His very familiar hands that will no longer touch her. 'I'll miss you.'

He looks up and nods. 'I already do.'

48

'It's completely live?' Ty asks. 'They don't review footage or anything before it's broadcast?'

Darcy's surprised that Ty seems worried. 'They're just going to ask you the questions we've already been through. They know they have to stick to the script. And I've got the cue cards ready if you can't remember what you're supposed to say.'

Ty gives a little nod as the makeup artist from *Good Morning* applies some more powder to his sweaty face. She'd hate to see what her own face looks like. Even though she knows she did the right thing in breaking up with Drew, she'd spent most of the night crying, mourning the ten years they spent together. She'd layered her face with foundation and drowned her eyes with drops, but she imagines she's not hiding her swollen face or her red eyes from anyone.

'Okay, Ty, we're ready for you now.' A floor manager wearing a large headset approaches. She guides him over to the lounges where Kiel and Janine, the breakfast hosts, are already sitting. Darcy hears the floor manager give some quick introductions and instructs Ty where to sit.

A sound guy hovering nearby adjusts Ty's microphone. Darcy moves next to the cameraman where she was told she'd be able to stand and hold up the cue cards. Before there's a chance for Darcy to give Ty any encouragement, the floor manager calls across the studio floor, 'And we're live in three, two, one ...' She gestures to Kiel and Janine.

'Janine is very excited about our next guest,' Kiel says, looking down the barrel of one of the cameras. 'We all know she's a sucker for all things romance and she's a big fan of the latest season of *The One*. That's right, folks, we have the star of the show, Ty Peterson, joining us on the lounge this morning.' Kiel moves to face Ty. 'Welcome, Ty.'

'Thanks for having me.'

It's obvious to Darcy that he's nervous, which surprises her, because he's become quite natural on the set of *The One*.

'So, Ty, you're down to the final three.' Janine smiles. 'You've just been on hometown dates, but how have you found the journey to find love so far?'

Darcy and Ty went over this question; the cue card is ready for him. Darcy had insisted there was to be no specific mention of Bonnie's exit.

But Kiel decides to add an extra comment. 'Dating twenty-two women at once can't be all that bad?' He laughs, amused with himself.

Janine smiles through her teeth, clearly used to her co-worker going off script.

'It's been harder than I thought it would be,' Ty says. 'There's been so many great women and it's hard sending them home when they've put their lives on hold to meet me.'

Darcy changes cue cards, ready for the next question.

'There have been lots of loud personalities in the house,' Janine comments. 'How did you cope with that?'

'Some of them were outright painful, weren't they?' Kiel adds his own comment once again and Darcy bristles that he's trying to coax more drama out of the interview.

Thankfully Ty ignores Kiel's comment and reads the cue card. 'I tried to get to know all of them, but some connections form more naturally than others.'

'The finale is fast approaching. Can you tell us if you're planning on proposing?'

Darcy knows Ty's cue card by heart: *Anything is possible.* They don't want to give too much away, but still offer a hook.

'I don't think so,' Ty says, his attention on Janine.

Oh God. Darcy waves the cue card around frantically, trying to get Ty's attention.

'Oh.' Janine's clearly surprised by his answer.

Kiel eagerly jumps on the new comment. 'What are you saying, Ty? None of these girls are *the one*?'

Janine laughs a little nervously, knowing repercussions for the show and network are at stake. 'You're not going to disappoint *The One* viewers nationwide, are you, Ty?'

Ty now looks up at Darcy, his expression nervous and apologetic. He looks back to Kiel and Janine. 'The truth is, my heart still belongs to someone else. Someone not on the show.'

This can't be happening. Darcy wants to scream cut, but she has no power on this set.

'Oh, Ty,' Janine murmurs, now on the edge of her seat.

'My ex broke off our engagement and I thought this would be the best way for me to move on, but as it turns out, I was wrong. I can't stop thinking about her.'

Fuck! He wasn't nervous about being on live TV, he was nervous about revealing the truth. Darcy dumps the cue cards and rushes to the floor manager, panic climbing fast. 'Can we go to an ad break?'

The floor manager relays Darcy's request into her headset to the *Good Morning* director, who is in the control room. But the floor manager shakes her head. 'There's still thirty seconds until the ad break.'

'It'll ruin our show if he keeps talking!' But Darcy knows deep down that the damage has already been done.

The floor manager offers a sympathetic shrug; her hands are tied.

Darcy knows she's supposed to remain a silent spectator, but her career depends on ending this. She can't have Ty ruin the show. 'Ty!' she calls out loudly to him across the set. 'Don't do this!' Her heart is pounding in her chest. 'Ty!'

The floor manager grabs Darcy by the arm. 'I'll have security remove you from the studio if you don't remain quiet.'

Ty ignores Darcy and turns to the camera. 'Penny, if you're out there, I still love you. I want to be with you. I need to know if there's any future for us.'

Darcy's phone starts vibrating in her pocket. She knows who it's going to be before she even reads *Alice* on the screen. Her throat tightens, suddenly desperate for water. The phone continues to pulsate in her palm. The floor manager looks over, gauges that Darcy's contemplating answering the call and shakes her head. Darcy was told her mobile was to be switched off before coming on set.

'Is there anything else you'd like to tell Penny or the Australian public?' Kiel asks Ty, a buzz in his voice now that the interview has become more than what he'd expected it to be.

'I'd like to say I'm sorry,' Ty admits. 'I know I've hurt people along the way and I didn't mean to do that. It was all very last minute that I became the suitor and the truth is that I shouldn't have signed on to do the show.'

Darcy wonders if she should start crying. There is no way of backtracking after a comment like that.

Janine reaches out and touches his arm. 'We're sorry to hear that, Ty. There will be disappointed fans out there, but if your heart is already with someone else, I'm sure everyone hopes you'll get your happily ever after.'

Darcy can't help but be impressed with Janine's quick response. She notices the floor manager finally giving the hosts a signal to wind things up. She should be relieved, but honestly is there anything worth saving?

'Thanks for coming on the show, Ty.'

Ty gives a small nod. 'Thanks for having me.' His face is white despite the hot lights of the studio shining down on him.

Kiel looks back to the camera. 'You heard it here first. Ty Peterson, star of *The One*, is still in love with his ex-fiancée.'

'And we're out,' the floor manager calls out, indicating filming has stopped. 'Three minutes to re-set.'

There's a general buzz as Ty farewells the hosts, who clearly want to have a bit more of a chat to him, but the sound guy takes the microphone off him and the floor manager herds him off the set. Darcy remains frozen to the spot as her phone starts buzzing again.

Ty approaches. 'I'm sorry, Darcy. I just miss her so much. I can't pretend anymore.'

He planned the whole thing. He knew he was going to confess his true feelings on live TV and screw over *The One*. But Ty knows he could be sued for doing something like this. Did they push him to this cliff edge?

Darcy musters a smile for him. He's nothing but a heartbroken guy pining for his love.

49

'Are you sure you're feeling okay?' Lara asks for about the hundredth time as they enter the first dress shop.

'I'm fine,' Penelope insists. She agreed to go shopping with Lara weeks ago to help her find an outfit for a wedding—before the whole 'I've got cancer' announcement. Lara had said they didn't need to do it anymore, but Penelope wants to do things like this, she wants to at least try to feel normal even though it's becoming increasingly hard with a cloud of tiredness trying to weigh her down.

'Okay, but tell me when you've had enough,' Lara tells her as she starts shifting through a rack. 'I pulled absolutely everything out of my cupboard again last night and I haven't even got a backup outfit. Nothing fits anymore.'

Thankfully Lara's kids are in day care. Sometimes they're cute and funny, but most of the time they're just grubby and whingy.

'We'll find something,' Penelope assures her. She used to go shopping with Miranda all the time. Miranda would know if something was going to work when it was still on the hanger and always had an uncanny ability to find bargains. Penelope, on the other hand, has always had a knack of falling in love with the latest full-priced items.

'What do you think about this?'

It's red and high-waisted, not the right colour or shape for Lara. Penelope nods. 'It's nice.' But then she hears Miranda's honesty in her head. 'But I think we can find something better.'

They pop in and out of shops, Lara trying on several dresses, but nothing being quite right.

'It's hopeless,' she sighs. 'I'm not going to find anything. Everything is either too tight or too old-fashioned. How did I let myself put on this much weight?'

'Lara, you're beautiful. We're going to find you something. Come on, let's go in here.' Penelope looks up at the *Dress Me Up* sign at the front of the shop and wills it to have the perfect dress. She doesn't want to have to let Lara go home feeling depressed.

'Okay.' Lara's reluctant. 'But if I don't find anything, I'm calling it quits.'

They're only a few steps in and instantly both gasp. An emerald wrap dress hangs at the end of one of the racks.

'Oh, I love that.'

'Try it on.'

Lara is hesitant as she takes it, smoothing her hand over the fabric. 'It probably won't fit me.'

Penelope sits down outside the change room, weariness starting to take over. She notices two women arrive. They look like mother and daughter. The mother gets straight to business, quickly flicking through clothes hangers while the daughter sighs and pulls her phone from her pocket, staring down at the screen.

Lara pulls back the curtain to the change room, a smile wide across her face. 'It fits!' She twirls in the dress, laughing giddily.

'It's perfect!' Penelope agrees.

'I never want to take it off!' She admires herself in the mirror and they discuss how she should style her hair, what shoes she could wear with it, that she's already got a perfect little clutch to go with it.

Penelope finds herself smiling. She hasn't had this much fun in a while. She hasn't had a friend like this before. The only people she's ever let herself be close to were her mother, her sister and Ty.

Lara shuts the curtain to the dressing room and Penelope pushes off her seat and begins looking through the shop.

'Oh, look at these,' she says, holding up a pair of white peep-toe shoes as Lara emerges from the change room. A warm and fuzzy feeling sweeps over her. 'I bought a pair just like them for my wedding.'

'You're married?'

Penelope chastises herself for being so careless. 'No, I'm not.'

Lara looks at her expectantly.

Penelope feels like she's about to pull a bandaid off a gaping wound. 'I called the engagement off a few months before the wedding.' She hopes it won't bleed too much.

Lara's face drops. 'Oh no! That must have been horrible.'

She can feel the blood rushing to the surface, the pain immediately raw and brutal, like she remembered it. 'It was hard,' she admits, trying to keep her voice steady despite it feeling as though she's trying to balance a book on her head as she walks down a dirt road with potholes. She's suddenly aware of her heart beating very loudly. She can see Lara's mind ticking over with questions.

'How did you go?' An eager sales assistant interrupts, staring at Lara who is still holding the dress.

The moment is gone. Penelope lets her breath exhale slightly. But Lara glances at her a little wistfully, as though she knows the momentum of their conversation has been lost.

'I'm going to take it,' Lara says, handing the dress over, following the assistant to the register.

Penelope takes a moment to stare again at the peep-toe shoes and imagine how she would have looked and what it would have felt like to become Mrs Ty Peterson.

'Excuse me, is this you?'

Penelope turns to see the girl with the phone. She holds up the phone screen and Penelope sees an old photo of her and Ty locked in an embrace, smiling at each other.

Panic jolts through her. Why would this girl have an old photo of her and Ty? 'Where did you get this?'

'It's all through my newsfeed.' She scrolls down to show her more. There's an image of Ty talking on some kind of talk show. The headline reads, *Suitor star still in love with his ex! Ty pleads for ex-fiancée Penny to come forward.*

'You were engaged to Ty?' Lara's now standing next to her, peering at the girl's phone, her face awash with shock. 'From *The One*?'

But Penelope can't answer. She looks back to the girl. 'What else are they saying?'

'He wants you to give him another chance. He shouldn't have gone on the show.' She shrugs. 'There are heaps of stories about it on here.' She indicates towards her phone. A few moments later she clicks a button and footage of Ty talking begins to play. The girl holds it out for Penelope to see.

'Penny, if you're out there, I still love you. I want to be with you. I need to know if there's any future for us.'

Penelope's body begins to shake, blood draining away from her head.

'Hey, reckon I could get a photo with you?' The girl grins. 'That'd be so cool.'

Penelope feels like she's going to be sick, no words come out, but she rushes off, terrified the rock she's been hiding under is about to be overturned.

50

'This is awful,' Darcy murmurs. She's scrolling through the online articles that have quickly flooded the internet since Ty's interview with *Good Morning* only hours earlier. She assumed everyone would be furious with Ty and there are plenty of 'Ty haters' commenting on what a low act it was to go on a dating show when he was still in love with someone else, but there are plenty of Ty supporters as well.

Let's find Ty's true love. Penny, where are you?

Team Penny!

Ty and Penny must reunite!

'What makes them think that she's even interested in Ty anymore?' Mel wonders. 'She broke off their engagement. Clearly there was a pretty big reason she didn't want to be with him.'

Darcy hasn't mentioned she called off her own engagement to Drew. It's a conversation she isn't ready to have yet. 'It's his heartfelt speech,' Darcy says, focusing on Ty's heartache rather than her own. 'They're all suckers for seeing a guy broken-hearted.'

'If a woman had done what he did they'd say she was desperate.'

'He is desperate,' Darcy confirms. She'd just seen how desperate on the *Good Morning* set. He wants to find Penny more than anything else.

'Do you reckon the network will sue him?'

Darcy shrugs. 'I guess that depends how the next week pans out.' Addison, Jodie and Hayley are all in lockdown, so they have no idea any of this has happened, but all their families and friends would have seen it. How are they going to feel once they're out of *The One* mansion and know that this was kept from them?

'All the sites are replaying that footage of Ty's date with Jodie,' Mel comments, scrolling through articles on her computer.

Darcy remembers the hiking date well. It was weeks ago now, but Ty's emotional speech about his fiancée breaking up with him is raw. It was the footage she'd shown Alice with great concern. The footage Alice insisted they use. Thankfully it was the only real hint to his feelings for Penny that had been aired. His conversation with Bonnie had been sent straight to the bin.

Alice storms into the office. She's slightly dishevelled, her appearance not as immaculate as usual, but she's still terrifying as always. 'I've had the executives on the phone all morning. We don't want there to be Team Bloody Penny.'

'Unless ...' Darcy is staring at a photo of Ty and Penelope that is being shared all over the internet.

'Unless what?' Alice glares at her.

Even as the words are about to leave her lips, Darcy isn't sure about it. 'Unless we can find Penny?'

Alice is waiting for more of a sell.

'We could bring her onto the show and film the reunion with Ty. For all we know Penny doesn't want to be with him anymore. Hopefully she'll dump him. Either way it'll pull ratings.' Darcy feels weighed down with guilt. Penelope might still love him or want to give him another chance and where does that leave their three remaining contestants? But maybe Penelope won't want him at all and in that case, he might be convinced to explore a relationship with one of the others.

Without saying a word, Alice puts her phone to her ear. 'Nigel, it's sorted. We're going to find Penny and shoot the whole reunion.' She pauses, not even bothering to cast an eye in Darcy's direction. 'The public will eat it up and no doubt pull the ratings we're looking for.'

Darcy's heart is racing, already anticipating the pressure that's about to be lumped on her. She'd tried to contact Penny several times before the show started. She'd called and emailed and received not one single reply. She won't be able to give up this time.

Alice hangs up the phone and looks to Darcy. 'Get a team together and find out everything you can on Penny. We needed her here yesterday.'

Darcy nods, feeling slightly ashamed that she's buzzing off the adrenaline suddenly pumping through her body. She's going to ensure Ty and Penny come face to face again.

51

Bonnie's getting ready to close up for the day when there's a knock at the back entrance to her studio. This throws her as she's usually the only person who uses it. With some hesitation she crosses to the door and opens it a little warily.

Ollie stands in the darkened shadows of the business car park. She hasn't seen him since he turned up on her doorstep after her last day on *The One*. The same night the photos were taken of them.

'Look at you.' Oliver's deep voice fills the air between them and immediately awakens butterflies in her belly.

She takes a few steps backwards, allowing space for him to come in.

'I've always loved you in that colour.' His eyes meet hers a little daringly. 'Very sexy.'

Bonnie's wearing a purple peasant top, more pretty than sexy, but her cheeks warm all the same. 'Thanks.'

'You got the flowers?' He gestures to the over-the-top bouquet that is sitting on her desk.

'You shouldn't have.' A courier had dropped them off yesterday with a note saying, *I'm sorry.* Her eyes had kept wandering to them all afternoon and when she'd opened the studio first thing this morning, the fragrance had filled her with hope.

'I wanted to.' He shrugs. 'I shouldn't have sent that text. It was out of line.'

She feels grateful that he's realised this. Bile had crept up her throat when she read the words. She'd tortured herself with what to write back in response, but in the end she hadn't written back at all.

'I didn't mean to make things worse,' she tells him. She honestly hadn't set out to hurt Sophie or damage Ollie's relationship with her.

'You only told her what she already assumed.'

Bonnie can't bring herself to ask how much Sophie told him of their conversation.

'I think she knew something was going on before you went away, but she didn't ask if anything had happened between us until after she lost the baby.'

Bonnie can't help but notice that he said 'she' and not 'we', as though the miscarriage was something that happened to Sophie alone rather than to the both of them. Bonnie can understand Sophie choosing not to mention things earlier—after all she'd had a baby to keep Oliver by her side—but after the miscarriage, the threat of him leaving might have brought out insecurities she'd previously been able to ignore.

'Suddenly she was furious, accusing me of having feelings for you, insisting something happened before you went away. I know she needed someone to blame for the miscarriage but ...' He shakes his head, a little flippant about the situation.

'Well, she was right ...' Bonnie's voice is soft. 'Something did happen between us.' She can't quite meet his eye. Even though they didn't sleep together, they did kiss and there was a promise for a future together. In some ways Bonnie believes it was more of a betrayal than a sex-ridden affair.

'Yeah, but it's not like I was going to admit that to her.'

Bonnie's throat constricts at the reminder of his feelings for Sophie. It should be obvious—he is, after all, still with her—but somehow Bonnie had convinced herself that his feelings were stronger for her than they were for Sophie.

'You want to turn out the lights?' His eyes are suggestive, his mouth arched in a grin. The implication is clear that he wants the studio darkened so they can enfold themselves in pleasure.

'You're still with Sophie, aren't you?'

But he dismisses the comment as he reaches for Bonnie, his hand settling on her waist.

He wants her. But he's still with Sophie.

Is this the kind of guy she wants to be with? Usually his touch sends nothing but desire through her body, but she backs away. She doesn't want this. She doesn't want a relationship where the man she loves has to come see her after hours, through the back door, away from prying eyes. She doesn't want secrecy about spending time with him, let alone having to hide her feelings for him.

'This isn't going to work.' She shakes her head, finally letting herself realise it.

'You want me to break up with Sophie?' His expression is serious but not surprised.

But that isn't what she wants. Instead she wants him to *want* to break up with Sophie. She wants him to want her more than anyone else.

When she doesn't answer, Ollie offers, 'I will, I promise I will, but it's just not the right time.'

Bonnie's head drops and her stomach sinks. He hasn't offered her the reassurance she needs. Suddenly her mind clears, a fog lifts and she feels liberated at finally seeing the truth. 'It's never going to be the right time.'

He looks at her as though she's dealt him a low blow. 'Sophie's still not over the miscarriage,' he says a little defensively. 'I can't break up with her when she's in such a bad way.'

'Do you love her?' Bonnie studies his face as she's really not sure of what his answer will be.

His eyes narrow a little, a crease forming between his eyebrows. He seems annoyed that she's asked him the question. 'Don't do this.'

Bonnie can't quite figure out if he's pleading with her to drop it or threatening her.

'We can make this work,' he urges.

But Bonnie shakes her head. 'I don't want it to.' She deserves more than this. She may have got caught up in old feelings for her first love, but what they had all those years ago doesn't exist anymore.

'You're making a mistake.' He looks bewildered. 'This kind of chemistry doesn't happen every day.'

'What we have is lust,' she assures him. 'What I'm after is love.' She moves past him and opens the back door for him to leave.

He shakes his head as he walks past her into the carpark. 'You're going to regret this.'

'You know what? I don't think I will.' She closes the door after him, finally feeling a lightness that she hasn't felt in a long time.

52

'Is there any chance that there's a future for you and Ty?' Darcy has the phone to her ear, enjoying the small victory that she managed to secure this phone call with Penelope. While Penelope's former boss had been very tight-lipped about Penelope's whereabouts, her new assistant had been more than happy to help when Darcy concocted a story about it regarding money being left to Penelope via a will.

Work is the only thing keeping Darcy going. She still hasn't sorted things out with Ed. She's picked up the phone on several occasions, wanting to call him or at least text him, but then she finds an excuse. She's pretty sure she has feelings for him and that's not really okay seeing that she was engaged to another guy only days ago. So she's just going to embrace this chapter of her life: Darcy Reed, career woman.

There's a long pause before Penelope answers. 'No.'

Darcy wishes she could see Penelope's face. This isn't an ideal phone conversation. 'Are you sure?' There's definitely some kind of hesitation.

'Yes, I'm sure.' Penelope sounds more confident this time.

'Okay,' Darcy says, glancing back down at her notes, scribbling around *Ty and Penny reconcile*. 'Have you managed to see any of the show?'

Darcy's pretty sure she hears Penelope sigh before answering, 'Bits of it.'

'So, you're aware that Ty still needs some closure over your break-up?' A total understatement, but she's hoping she'll be able to reel her in this way.

'What are you asking?'

Darcy likes that this girl is so straight to the point. 'We'd like you to come on the show and tell Ty it's over, once and for all.' She knows what a big request it is given the lengths Penelope has gone to in order to hide from Ty and any media attention.

'I don't think so.' Penelope sounds almost amused by the idea.

But Darcy remains focused; she's good at her job. She can do this. 'He needs to know it's over. I've gotten to know him over the last couple of months and even though he's got women desperate to win his heart, he won't let himself fall for any of them because he hasn't given up hope on you.'

Penelope doesn't say anything, but Darcy can hear she's still on the phone.

'I don't know anything about your break-up, but did you say something to make him think you might change your mind?'

'No,' Penelope murmurs.

Darcy doesn't know whether to believe her or not. 'Ty talks about you as though you're the great love of his life …' Darcy purposely lets the words dangle in the air for a moment before adding, 'He most certainly hopes you feel the same way.'

Darcy hears Penelope take in a deep breath, and feels satisfaction in knowing the conversation is starting to evoke some emotion.

'The whole country is behind him. They're all hoping you'll change your mind.'

'I'm not going to change my mind,' Penelope says, a little rushed and perhaps louder than she intended. 'And the last thing I want is media attention.'

'Look, Penelope, I'll be honest with you. We're trying to make a TV show about finding love. Ty still having feelings for you— someone who's not on the show—is making it a little bit difficult for us.'

'I'm sorry, but that's not really my problem.'

Darcy reminds herself to stay calm, this isn't lost yet. 'Haven't you realised that this isn't going to go away until the show is over? Ty's made a public declaration. People all around Australia are rooting for the two of you to be reunited.'

'Well, they're going to be disappointed,' Penelope says, but her voice has started to quiver, her breathing muffled.

'I know you still care for him. I can hear it in your voice.'

Penelope doesn't even try to argue it. 'Of course I do.' Darcy can feel the conversation shifting as she imagines waves of emotion sweeping in and trying to knock Penelope off balance.

'Don't you think you owe it to him to tell him once more? He needs to hear it. Please help him move on,' Darcy urges, feeling as though her career relies on convincing this woman to come on the show. 'We've still got three women left who want to spend the rest of their lives with him. Give one of them the chance to have a happily ever after.'

There's silence on the other end of the phone. Darcy tingles with hope.

'What exactly do you want me to do?'

Darcy manages a victory fist pump before professionally launching into their plans for the reunion.

A few hours later, Darcy is standing at the door to Ed's apartment trying to work up the courage to knock. After her successful day at work she figured she'd try to smooth things over here. Her plan had been to show up with Chinese, hoping that everything would go back to normal. But standing here now, her insides are twisted, her throat dry, and it feels far from any normal she's ever experienced with Ed. She's never been nervous to see him before. Maybe she should go home and just send a text. She turns abruptly to leave and sees Ed walking down the hall, arriving home.

'You didn't knock?'

She gives a shake of the head, feeling a little stupid. 'You haven't called.' She's defensive, hoping it masks some of the sadness in her voice, but it undoubtedly shakes as the words slip from her mouth.

'Neither have you.' He turns the keys over in his hand, the rattling sound the only noise in the hall.

Well no, she's hasn't. Has he been waiting for her to make contact? She wants to tell him she's been busy, that *The One* has been somewhat hellish to work on and that she broke up with Drew, but she feels like if she says either of those things he'll think she hasn't thought about him. Because that would be a lie. She's thought about him every day.

'You got Mongolian lamb in there?' He gestures to the takeaway bag from the Chinese place on the corner.

She nods. 'Honey prawns too.'

'I was going to make a salad, but I guess you could come in and I could help you eat it?'

Darcy cracks a smile, knowing full well that he had no plans to make a salad. 'I'd like that.' She moves out of his way so he can unlock the door and feels an unexpected desire to reach out and touch him. Before the kiss it would have been normal for them to hug hello but she's pretty sure that any form of physical contact is going to seem weird or at least become overanalysed. So she fights the urge, forcing her arms to remain stiffly by her side.

Ed switches on some lights and moves to the kitchen, grabbing bowls and cutlery. As they begin dishing up the takeaway he makes a comment about how nice the weather has been, and Darcy finds herself in a horrible small-talk situation that feels so unnatural with her best friend. She should have brought some wine; this conversation would be much easier with her hand wrapped around a vino. 'You got any wine?'

Ed frowns. 'I'm on a detox.'

'What?' This is new. Ed is not a detox kind of guy.

He shrugs. 'It was getting bad so I'm cutting myself off for a month.'

For Ed to admit it was getting bad makes Darcy wonder if something happened. 'What day are you on?'

'Six.'

Still weeks' worth of conversations for them to have with no alcohol.

Ed hands her a glass of water and they perch at the bench on bar stools rather than sink into the lounge like they normally would have done.

'How's work?'

'Fine.' He gives no real indication of his enjoyment level. 'I'm busy but *Smith Street* is a well-oiled machine, so now that I know what's expected I'm managing to get through the footage and deliver to all the deadlines.'

Before the kiss, Darcy would have made a snide remark about Zoe being pleased, but their world has spun off its axis and now she isn't sure how to make her way through normal conversation.

'I usually spend a couple of hours each night putting together the wedding vids for Love Lens.'

'You must be exhausted.'

A look confirms he is but he's surviving. 'I think all the work has been a good distraction.'

Darcy gulps. Is she one of the things he's needed to keep himself distracted from? She finds herself pushing around the food in her bowl with her fork.

'So, there's been some pretty heavy stuff going down in lover's paradise, huh?' Ed comments.

Darcy loves that Ed somehow makes time to watch the show, but she shakes her head; that doesn't even begin to cover it. 'There was so much crap going on I thought I was going to lose my job.' She's tempted to fill the conversation with work talk. She could easily distract herself from awkwardness and dish out all the drama from the show, but she can't keep the conversation going without telling him her biggest news. *Rip it off like a bandaid!* 'I broke up with Drew.'

Ed has a forkful of food on its way to his mouth but his hand freezes midair, his mouth gaping wide. 'What?'

She gives a little nod. 'I drove to Gloucester on my way back from Bonnie's hometown date.'

'Things were that bad?'

'I kissed you, Ed. I wouldn't have done that if I was happy.' It's the first time either of them has mentioned the kiss. Part of her had wanted to pretend she'd been too drunk to remember it, but she can still feel the tingle on her lips when she thinks about it.

Ed swallows hard, his eyes casting down to his bowl for a moment. 'How did it go?' After all, Drew was his friend too.

Part of Darcy wants to tell him word for word what happened. She'd love to dissect it, analyse all the things that were said and all the things that weren't. But instead she simply says, 'Okay. I think deep down he knew it was the right thing to do.'

'Did you tell him ...?' He trails off, not saying the words, but she knows he means their kiss.

She shakes her head. Maybe it was wrong of her—she had cheated on him—but the kiss wasn't why she broke things off; it was simply the catalyst for her being honest with herself.

Darcy's relieved that she's told Ed, but the heaviness of the moment still hangs in the air, like a big rain cloud squashed into the small space of Ed's apartment.

'So, what does this mean?' His eyes flick up to meet hers. She wonders if he's asking what it means for them. Is he expecting her to confess feelings after their kiss? Darcy's felt the glimmer of such emotions but has locked them in a box at the bottom of her heart. She can't bare them to Ed. What if he doesn't feel the same way? What if a few precious words ruin their whole friendship? It's hard enough already trying to recover from that kiss.

'It means I have to find a new place to live.' She decides to concentrate on the logistical problems rather than the emotional ones. She can't afford the place on her own, and she'll be glad to get a new space, one that's not connected to all her history with Drew.

His eyes dim. There's an expression on his face that she can't quite figure out. 'Yeah, of course. I'll keep my ear out for you.'

'Great, thanks.' And just like that they reforge their friendship, pretending nothing has changed, but aware everything has shifted.

53

Penelope hasn't told the producers the truth. Despite her better judgement, she's agreed to go on the show and tell Ty one last time that they're over. As far as the producers are concerned, she just doesn't want to be with him anymore. Darcy tried to push for more details, but Penelope had purposely been evasive. Lara had tried to convince her to be honest with Ty, but she wasn't going to be talked around. She would speak nothing of the cancer, nothing about dying. She's simply there to tell Ty that there is no future for them and to let him move on.

But in the back of her mind she wonders if he'll notice a difference. Will he know just by looking at her?

She knocks on the door and waits. She can't help but look at the camera—with the lens pointed directly at her. Darcy, the producer, catches her eye, offering her a warm smile and encouraging her to look back at the door.

She hears footsteps. Her stomach, already twisted, knots a little tighter. She thought her heart would be racing, but it feels like it's stopped altogether.

Ty pulls open the door wearing only board shorts. His face is weary, as though he hasn't slept in days.

She can see the flood of shock hit him. She's the last person he expected to be on the other side of the door. But then the happiness and relief come soon after. 'Penny ...?'

'Hi.' She can feel her whole body shaking.

She sees the tears sting his eyes. 'You came?' There's apprehension in his voice. He doesn't want to get carried away.

She goes to speak but feels herself falling, lost in his eyes.

He takes her in properly now and concern rushes over him. 'What's happened? Are you all right?'

She shakes her head, she doesn't want to tell him. Her heart starts to ache ...

'Ty, how about we go inside?' Darcy suggests, indicating for him to lead them into his hotel room.

Ty looks surprised by Darcy's voice. 'Yeah, right, okay.'

Penelope wonders if he'd forgotten about the cameras and crew. She follows him into the luxurious hotel suite. Her hand reaches up to touch her neck; she's sure she can feel the lump in her throat.

'How about you guys sit there?' Darcy points to the lounge.

It feels weird to have their conversation interrupted, paused and redirected, but she supposes this has come to feel normal for Ty. He simply does as she suggests.

Penelope doesn't know how close to sit to him. There's a natural magnetic pull that makes her grip the side of the lounge as though she's clinging to a branch trying not to be swept downstream.

Darcy nods to Ty. 'Okay guys, whenever you're ready.'

'What's going on?' His eyes are wide as he stares at Penelope.

Penelope swallows hard. Why did she agree to do this? She hopes the producer, Darcy, is being paid well—she had been very convincing on the phone.

'Penny,' Ty says, staring at her, his expression fixed. Somehow he's learned to block out the rest of the room.

But her heart is racing. She can hear it thumping, she can feel it trying to escape her chest.

'It's okay,' his voice soothes. He reaches out to take one of her hands. Her own are freezing, like always, and she can see he's slightly warmed by the familiarity of this. It could be a thirty-degree day and somehow her hands would still be cold. He cups hers in his own, like he always did, attempting to warm them.

An unexpected sob escapes her mouth. His touch after the last few months feels so natural, she wonders how he could have possibly acted this way towards anyone else. 'Why did you do this?' She gestures around the room to the crew and cameras. It wasn't what she planned on saying to him at all, but the script she'd prepared for herself, and for the producers, has suddenly disappeared. 'How could you come on a TV show looking for love?' All the frustration she's been feeling comes bubbling to the surface.

Ty jerks like a whip has lashed his face before his whole body washes with pain. 'You left me. I begged you to stay.' His words are raw and anguished. 'What did you expect me to do?'

She shakes her head; she still doesn't know what she wants him to do. She told herself she wanted him to move on and find love with someone else, but she hadn't realised it was going to hurt so much.

'I even told you about this, hoping you'd change your mind.'

Penny has to lower her gaze. She can't bear to see his vulnerability. She's been watching him for the past two months on television, but he's had such a wall up. Finally she sees the real him.

And he's aching. A throbbing pain pulses through his whole body.

'I laid everything on the table for you, Penny. I wanted nothing but a life with you.' He looks away and for a moment Penny thinks he's about to get up and walk away. But then he looks back, sad and defeated. 'I thought you wanted that too ...'

She realises now that he's questioning whether she ever loved him in the first place. 'I felt the same way. Honestly, you were everything to me.'

He's annoyed, possibly not believing her. 'Well, what changed?'

She has a longing to reach out and touch him, but she's too scared he'll bat her hand away. She's certainly hurt him enough to warrant rejection.

'What changed, Penny? What did I do?'

The facade she's been trying to hide behind comes crumbling down at this. She imagines him tossing and turning at night, blaming himself for the break-up. 'Nothing. You did nothing.'

His eyes are locked on hers, waiting ...

She can't stand it anymore. 'I'm sick, Ty,' she whispers. The words leave her lips and she feels the breath knocked out of her for a moment. She wasn't going to tell him, but the relief tingles on her skin. It's like standing at the bottom of a waterfall, letting the water cascade over her body. She wants to tilt her head back and savour it. There's been so few of these moments ... but instead she watches as he absorbs the words.

'What do you mean?' His mind is clearly racing.

Her throat instinctively wants to close over, but she knows she can't stop now. 'Cancer.' It's funny how one word can wipe out all others.

His face drains, his eyes widen. Everything sinks in. 'No.' His voice is low. 'No …' Disbelief takes over.

Penelope gives him a look of sympathy as she sees him digesting the news, processing what she's already told him about her mother's battle, her sister's fight. How cancer had taken everything. She'd told him it had been like one person fighting an army. That the cancer was unstoppable, that it was always going to win. He'd argued of course. Everyone always did.

His eyes glaze over. *At least he knows the truth now*, she reminds herself.

Finally some words spill out. 'You didn't tell me?' He's angry, which doesn't surprise her. 'You kept it from me?' He's angrier than she first thought.

Penny's confounded. She'd felt such relief by telling the truth, but she's quickly filled with regret. She should have kept the lie. Now it's too late. 'I'm sorry, Ty. I wanted to spare you the pain.'

He shakes his head in disbelief. 'You have no idea.' He buries his head in his hands.

Penny's hands twist in her lap.

'Cut!' Ty stands abruptly, turning to the crew. 'Cut!' He's louder this time. He knocks over a chair, looking as though he wants to punch the wall.

Penny had almost forgotten about the crew, but her eyes glance over to the producer, Darcy, standing next to one of the cameras. Her eyes are wide, her teeth bearing down on her bottom lip as she clearly tries to decide what to do. Penny sees the cameraman look to her, waiting for her to call it.

'I'm not having this conversation with the bloody cameras rolling.' Ty's voice echoes around the room.

'Yeah, okay,' Darcy says. 'Cut.'

54

'We got it,' Darcy murmurs to Ben and immediately feels horrified. How can her first thought be about the footage captured rather than Penny's death sentence? The phone call she'd received from Drew this morning asking if he could come and get his things from 'the' unit, specifically not 'their' unit, seems so insignificant now.

Ben had glanced at her from behind the camera, floored by the reveal. Darcy is just as shocked. Penelope hadn't given any indication that she was sick. Darcy had just assumed she didn't love him anymore and agreed to make it clear to Ty that they were over for good.

'Reckon we can have a bit of privacy?' Ty's fixated on Darcy, gesturing to the rest of the crew. He reminds her of a bull, rampant and aggravated in a room full of red flags. He can't keep still, as though trying to decide which flag to charge at. 'I don't want to hear any bullshit about my contract and what you'd like to get footage of.'

Shame washes over Darcy as she wonders what he thinks of her. She's always been eager to capture insecurities and ugliness throughout Ty's quest for love. She knows Alice would want her to keep filming, because the drama isn't over. The scene is currently *in medias res*—in the middle of things. Everyone will want to see what happens next, but Darcy feels she owes them the respect to do it alone.

The truth is she feels overwhelmingly sad. Penelope has cancer. Penelope is going to die. She doesn't even know the woman, but that doesn't take away from the sadness. It seems the only reason Penny broke up with Ty was to offer him a way out. She clearly still loves him. That's a love story.

But she isn't the producer of their love story. She has three girls still vying for Ty, still hoping they're 'the one'. There's a crashing reality that none of them could be after this kind of footage. The repercussions start flowing through her mind. What will the audience want? They've spent the past two months getting to know Ty and the contestants on *The One*. Viewers will have picked their girl to win. But will this change everything? Will they want Ty and Penelope to end up together? There's a bit of 'Team Penny' momentum but how will the franchise cope with that as a result?

'All right guys, let's clear out,' she calls to the rest of the crew.

They all begin to shuffle out but Darcy pauses, feeling as though she should offer some support to Ty, or to Penelope, who is bent over herself, her hands wringing in her lap. Darcy studies her a moment longer and when Penelope looks up to meet her eye, it's clear she hadn't planned on telling Ty the truth. There's a tight gauze of regret wrapped around her entire body.

'If there's anything you need,' Darcy begins.

But Ty cuts over her quickly. 'We need to be left alone.' Tears are brimming in his eyes, his words caught in his throat. He looks like he's just lost ten years of his life.

Darcy has to force herself to leave. She pulls the door to the hotel suite shut and stands in the hall.

Ben's waited for her. 'I think there's a four-letter word you're looking for about now.'

Darcy laughs awkwardly, not knowing how to handle this. 'Love?'

Ben's forehead creases, somewhat amused by her weirdness. 'Yeah, not the word I was thinking.'

Darcy sighs, letting her body slide down the wall and onto the floor. She knows she should be racing back to the edit suites to review the footage and figure out what angle to take, but she just has to have a moment …

'Fuck!'

55

The room is silent. The crew vanished quickly, all equipment still set up. Penny remains in the chair, as though she's still on set, but Ty can't stop moving which only adds to the tension. She's filled with regret. She shouldn't have said anything.

'How long have you got?'

She knows what he's asking. 'Maybe six months.'

His body flinches, her words like a bullet to his heart.

She feels like she should comfort him but fears she'll only make things worse.

'Have you had treatment?'

She shakes her head. Her mother and sister had both tried that. They'd spent their last days battling for more. After her sister died, she vowed to herself that if she ever got the cancer diagnosis she'd just enjoy the days she had left.

'And I guess I'm not going to be able to convince you otherwise?'

She shakes her head again. She won't be talked around. Lara had tried, arriving breathless at Penelope's unit one morning, her arms full of pamphlets and information on treatment options.

Ty slumps into the chair beside her. She can see him letting the truth sink in—that she left him because she's dying, not because she didn't love him. She hopes he can find some comfort in that.

'So, what have you been doing?' he asks finally.

'I'm living down the coast. Just trying to be kind to myself.' She meets his eye and sighs with relief. 'Reading, yoga, beach walks.'

'I could have been there with you.' He reaches out and takes her hand.

Penny closes her eyes as her body soaks in his love. She wants to let herself relax with images of him by her side, but forces herself to shake them away. She promised herself she'd protect him. 'I want you to be happy, Ty. I hope you'll let yourself find love with one of the girls left on the show.' That was just a snippet of what she was supposed to say instead of telling him she has cancer.

He's so shocked that she's said this to him that his mouth gapes for a moment before he speaks. 'You want me to be with one of those girls?' He shakes his head. 'I don't love them. I love you.'

Penny drops her head at this. Hearing him say those three words evokes something deep inside her. He used to tell her all the time that he loved her. She hadn't realised how much she'd missed hearing it. She can't hold the tears in any longer.

'I want to be with you,' he pleads.

She shakes her head, wiping at her face. She can't even look at him. He's staring at her with such longing. This is exactly why she didn't tell him the truth in the beginning. 'No, I can't do that to you.'

'Why, Penny?'

'Because I'm going to die.' She clutches her heart; saying it aloud hurts more than the soft whisper she allows to float through her head. 'And I don't want you to have to live with that grief. It hurts, it hurts so much that I don't want you to have to suffer.'

'Don't you get it, Penny?' Ty asks. 'I'm suffering now.'

She looks into his eyes and sees the raw pain. The pain she's causing him.

'Let me be with you. I want to spend whatever time you've got left by your side.'

She can feel herself crumbling. Of course she wants Ty by her side. She's never stopped loving him. Her heart has continued to ache for him the whole time they've been apart.

'I know losing you is going to crush me, but don't rob me of any more time.' Ty reaches out for her and she feels herself fall into him. Her body relaxes against his. This wasn't what she'd decided, but it's what she wants. To be with Ty. To love him with every ounce of herself. 'I love you,' she whispers.

She feels his relief against her body. 'I love you too. So much, Penny.' He holds her closer to him. 'Please, let me look after you.'

She's scared, terrified, of what's to come. More pain, loss of functions and, inevitably, death.

His hand touches her face, tilting it so she looks up at him. He looks at her with adoration as he leans down, letting his lips touch her own. Her body is filled with an ecstasy better than any of the drugs she's been having for the pain. Their love is a therapy like no other.

'Okay,' she finally says. 'Please, be with me until the end.'

56

'Can I show you something?'

Darcy is walking down the hall, having just left Ty. He's leaving the show. He doesn't care if the network sues him. Penelope doesn't have much time left and he wants to be with her. Darcy had barely been able to speak. What do you say to someone who has just found out that the love of their life is dying?

She looks up to see Ben standing in the doorway of the hotel room where he's been packing up the equipment. 'Sure,' she says, willing to stall for as long as possible before she has to go back and tell Alice that they don't have a suitor for the final week of *The One*.

'I was reviewing the footage we took earlier and, well …' He indicates for her to watch the small monitor.

Darcy looks at the screen showing Penny sitting on the lounge and Ben turns up the volume.

'How long have you got?' Ty's audio is clear, but his head is out of frame.

Penny's hands wring in her lap. 'Maybe six months.'

It takes a moment for Darcy to realise that this isn't the footage they filmed earlier. Her heart starts beating faster. She hasn't seen this before. 'You didn't stop filming?' Her head turns sharply to Ben.

His expression is unreadable. 'I thought I had.'

Darcy doesn't know whether to believe him or not, but her head turns back to the monitor. She stands open-mouthed as she watches the scene play out in front of her. The love between Ty and Penny is mesmerising. It's so real compared to the months of dates they've filmed with Ty over the past couple of months. Darcy realises now that of course none of the other girls were ever really in the running. His heart belonged to Penny.

Darcy has to wipe a tear away when Penelope eventually concedes and tells Ty he can stay with her until the end. She closes her eyes, feeling a wave of exhaustion dragging her down.

'No one else knows about it.' Ben's voice is steady. 'The footage is yours if you want it use it, otherwise I can just ...' He trails off.

'Delete it?'

He shrugs; the decision is up to her. Can she delete it? Can she just let this footage go? This could be a heart-wrenching, tear-jerking ending to *The One*. This kind of footage would be a huge ratings grab. It'd impress Alice and the network executives. It'd secure her a promotion.

But as she takes in the images on screen, she sees what a private moment it was for Ty and Penelope. Penny's the love of Ty's life. She is the one. But she's dying, and they won't get their happily ever after.

She'd be inviting all of Australia, possibly even all of the world, to have a part in Ty and Penny's intimacy. Could Darcy live with herself if she let this footage go to air?

57

'Bonnie!' A voice propels through the air. 'Bonnie, over here!'

Bonnie's arm is outstretched, ready to take the bag of breakfast goodies from the drive-through window, but without thinking her head turns at her name being called.

A photographer has wound down the window of his car and quickly snaps photographs, no doubt satisfied that she's looked at him.

She puts her hand up to cover her face but knows it's too late. He would have gotten the shot already.

She's had constant media attention since her exit interview aired. She had no idea how popular *The One* was. It makes her feel constantly nauseated that people are watching her, taking photographs of her, yelling out questions across the street, asking why she really left *The One*, wanting to know about her relationship with Oliver James. A few journalists have even approached her at work, coming into her studio.

Yesterday she screamed at one of them to leave. 'You're trespassing! Get out of here!' The media frenzy has brought out an ugly and embarrassing side to her. She wants to forget about Ty and *The One*, but the constant spotlight is making it hard to leave behind.

Bonnie digs into the paper bag and pulls out a hash brown as she makes her way to work. She lets herself be comforted by the golden fried potato; it might just be the happiest moment of her day.

Not long after she arrives at work, the door pushes open and Bonnie knows who it is without having to look up. Carla's perfume infiltrates Bonnie's photography studio before she's taken more than a few steps inside. Bonnie shoves the Maccas breakfast wrapper into the bin, then rams the bin further under the desk.

'I brought you breakfast,' Carla trills, clutching a container of no doubt organic, low-carb, sugar-free muesli. Her blonde ponytail swishes from side to side as she bounces towards Bonnie.

'You shouldn't have.' Bonnie turns her head and the two sisters kiss on the cheek. 'You've got enough meals to pack without worrying about me.'

Carla is dressed in her tiny gym gear, likely heading off to a Pilates class and then coffee, her three kids already dropped off for the day.

'What's one more? And you'd probably eat rubbish if I didn't look after you.' It's a loaded comment and Carla holds her gaze, waiting for Bonnie to crack.

Bonnie really shouldn't be surprised that Carla's seen the paparazzi photos. It's the kind of thing she would obsessively seek out. 'I don't need a lecture,' Bonnie says, anticipating the assault.

But Carla clearly sees this as permission to launch. 'Bonnie, you have a problem.' Carla pulls her mobile from her bag and begins scrolling through the photos. 'Six of these photos are of you at different takeaway places.' She holds out the phone to show her. 'What are you doing to your body?'

Bonnie can see that rather than being outraged that her sister is being stalked by the media, Carla's actually quite pleased that they are helping her keep track of Bonnie's eating habits.

'I know you've always found comfort in eating, but this really isn't the time to be hitting one fast food place after another.'

She means because of the photo evidence. Carla would much prefer to hide in the pantry and binge rather than be caught out in public.

'We really need to get you on a cleanse,' Carla says. 'It'll make you feel so much better.'

The idea of drinking nothing but juice and forbidding herself carbs, sugar, coffee or alcohol would actually be a form of torture right now. 'I'm not doing a cleanse.'

Carla eyes Bonnie up and down, examining her outfit—jeans and a T-shirt from the dirty wash pile. 'Even making a bit of an effort with what you wear would make you feel better.'

There's no time to even respond to Carla's comment because the door to the studio pushes open again, a cameraman entering first with the same journalist as yesterday only a step behind.

'What are your thoughts on Ty and Penny's reunion?' the journalist probes.

Bonnie knows Penny agreed to appear on *The One* and even though the reunion itself would have been filmed already, it won't be aired until tonight. She forces herself not to think too much about it. Feelings of anger and sadness and frustration are all bound together and she doesn't want to feel weighed down with it. 'Please, just leave me alone,' Bonnie urges. She used to believe everything happened for a reason, but she can't see how going on *The One* was guided by any higher powers.

'How do you think the remaining girls would feel about Ty coming face to face with his ex again?'

'Go away,' Bonnie murmurs, feeling completely incapable of dealing with this today.

'You heard her, get out!' Carla shrieks. 'Leave us alone!'

The journalist and cameraman slink away, Carla almost pushing them back out the door.

'It's disgusting.' Carla shakes her head as she stands at the window watching them, arms folded like a bodyguard.

And while Bonnie takes the slightest comfort in her sister's protectiveness, she can see that the whole situation has given Carla the biggest thrill and will be recounted to every one of her friends.

Bonnie hangs her head. She invited this ugly mess into her life by agreeing to go on *The One*. Is she going to regret that decision forever?

58

'What's this?' Alice looks up sharply as she takes the envelope Darcy's handed over.

'It's my resignation.' Darcy's voice is steadier than she thought it would be.

'Don't be ridiculous.' There's annoyance in Alice's voice, as though Darcy is wasting her time with theatrics. 'I thought you wanted to build yourself a career here?'

'I have built a career here,' Darcy says confidently. 'And I thank you for that. I've been pushed hard and become very good at what I do.'

Alice frowns. 'I haven't trained you up just to have you walk away now.'

Darcy feels the slightest satisfaction in having Alice view her as some kind of investment. But deep down she knows Alice is more likely irritated that she'll have to spend time instructing someone new, someone who can't anticipate her many demands.

'I'll finish out this season, of course.' There is only a week until the show technically wraps and she's already guided Max in editing together the package for Ty and Penny's reunion. No one will ever know about the extra footage Ben captured of them. Darcy had watched as Ben deleted it. As badly as she wants to move up the ladder and gain credibility within the industry, she realised she would never be able to forgive herself if she aired the footage. Her emotions and conscience are satisfied in knowing she's managed to give Ty and Penny the tiniest bit of privacy. 'It'll give you plenty of time to find someone else before the next season starts.'

Alice's face is tight.

The silence should make Darcy feel nervous, but instead she feels a sense of freedom in seeing the finish line ahead. 'I've scheduled one-on-one scenes to be filmed with Addison, Hayley and Jodie for today.' Darcy moves the conversation back to the job she's prepared to see through to the end. The interviews will be aired before an edited version of Ty and Penny's reunion. 'Ty's agreed to tell them all separately about his feelings for Penny.'

'Will he apologise to them?' The network is in fear of being sued by the girls once the truth of Ty's feelings for Penny are revealed. Alice's eyebrows raise, waiting for the answer.

Darcy nods. 'We've gone through what he's going to say and if he sticks to the script, I think the network will be satisfied.'

Alice turns back to her computer and Darcy assumes that their conversation is over. She doesn't wait to be dismissed and instead turns away, the feeling of dread returning as she remembers her next task is to go and watch Ty break up with three different women.

'Darcy?'

She's surprised to hear Alice call her back.

'Are you sure you can walk away from this?'

Darcy knows that somewhere behind Alice's question is a hint of a compliment and that in itself is satisfying. She can't deny that she has loved working on *The One*, but she developed tunnel vision. She'd forgotten that the world has other jobs on offer. This isn't the only place she can grow. It's going to be hard walking away from familiarity, just like it was hard walking away from Drew, but she knows something else is out there for her. 'It's time for me to move on.'

After a long afternoon of break-ups and tears and apologies, Darcy finishes up for the day. Her hands are shaking as she shoves her water bottle and phone into her bag. She had convinced herself that she could squash down the feelings for Ed that have been hovering like a second shadow. But now that she's made the decision to leave *The One* she can actually take a breath and let herself think about what she wants for a second. Her feelings for Ed keep creeping up on her. She needs to tell him how she feels; she doesn't want to waste any more time. Penelope tried to protect Ty from pain, but instead she just robbed them of time they could have spent together.

Darcy wants to speed through the Sydney peak-hour traffic but it's a slow crawl to Ed's place. She tries to stay calm and focused, but frustration quickly builds, her desire to see him increasing by the second.

Her usual parking spot has been taken up with a limousine, and Darcy curses as she has to go around the block and park at the bottom of the hill.

She's puffed by the time she reaches Ed's apartment block and tells herself she'll start going to the gym more. She strides down the hall, ready to launch her mission.

Without hesitation, she knocks and waits …

But female laughter from behind the door chills her entire body. Panic rushes through her and natural instinct makes her want to run. But Ed flings the door open too quickly. He's dressed in a suit and her knees go a little weak. She wants to swoon or at least hold her heart.

'Darce, hi.' Ed's eyes are wide and it doesn't take Darcy very long to figure out why.

Over his shoulder stands Zoe in a sparkling gown, drenched in makeup and shiny hairdresser hair. The female laughter had come from her. What is Zoe Eggins doing dressed up in Ed's apartment?

Ed's face washes white. 'Zoe asked me to go with her to an awards night.'

Ed is Zoe's date?

Darcy feels sick. Is that a tumor she feels in the pit of her stomach?

Zoe smiles, but it's fake and infuriating, her eyes narrowed. 'Hi Darcy.'

'Hello.' Darcy's body stiffens, her hands clenching by her side.

'Is everything okay?' Ed asks. She used to show up on his doorstep unannounced all the time, but *the kiss* has really screwed up what's normal for them.

All the words that were ready to come pouring out are now hiding, terrified of Zoe Eggins getting even a sniff of the truth.

But she doesn't get to reply, because Zoe says, 'I saw all that stuff going on with the show you're working on. Can't be good if the guy publicly declares his feelings for his ex?'

Zoe doesn't even know the half of it yet. The last the public has seen is Ty's interview on *Good Morning,* and that isn't even the tip of the iceberg. 'Any publicity is good publicity, right?' Darcy doesn't believe that but there's no way she wants Zoe to feel vindicated in her comment.

Zoe forces a laugh that is laced with judgement. 'That's what they say.'

Darcy looks to Ed. His eyes are carefully watching her, trying to gauge her response. He's possibly wondering if she's going to make a scene. All her feelings towards him that were ready to come tumbling out are now stuck, the great wall that is Zoe Eggins firmly preventing any from bursting through.

'Ed said you broke up with Drew.' Zoe moves forward, closing in the space between her and Ed. 'Sorry to hear.'

Darcy wants to scoff in her face, but instead she simply says, 'Thanks.'

'We better get going, Ed.' Zoe touches him on the shoulder, her eyes meeting Darcy's as though declaring ownership over Ed. An ownership Darcy used to have as his best friend but somehow lost.

Ed glances at his phone, checking the time. 'Yeah, don't want to be late.'

Darcy has no choice but to back up and step into the hall.

'I'll give you a call tomorrow?' His eyes urge her not to make a scene but she can see a hint of worry too, as though he's still trying to figure out if she's okay.

Darcy nods, not trusting her voice.

'Don't expect a call too early—I think it's going to be a late night.' Zoe's words float like poison through the air, trying to sweep Ed under her spell.

'Good luck surviving it without alcohol,' Darcy murmurs to Ed, feeling as though she has well and truly lost her best friend.

'You're not drinking?' Zoe's head snaps to Ed.

'He's banned himself for the month.' Darcy's happy to relay such news. 'Still have a while to go, don't you?' Her eyes settle on Ed, her voice light, pretending she doesn't know for a fact that he's still got a long way to go.

'Yeah, still a while.' But there's a look to indicate that he's perhaps reconsidering his self-inflicted ban.

'Oh well, you don't need alcohol to have fun, do you?' But it's helpful if you're hoping for inhibitions to come down and Darcy doesn't doubt for a second that Zoe wants Ed relaxed enough to fall into bed with her at the end of the night. 'I'm really proud of you, Ed,' Darcy continues. 'It's so good that you're sticking to it.'

He nods but doesn't say anything, his face dripping with self-doubt.

The three of them walk down the hall and onto the street. It's now that Darcy realises the limousine is here for them. A driver appears and opens the door of the luxurious vehicle for Zoe and Ed.

'Bye Darcy,' Zoe calls over her shoulder, linking her arm through Ed's. He doesn't shake it off, but he does look back and give Darcy a little smile. He's sorry she caught him with Zoe. Darcy wonders if he would have told her if she hadn't shown up at his place. Darcy feels a panic starting to spread that maybe he does like Zoe. Maybe Darcy missed her chance to tell him how she feels. Maybe everything for them has already changed.

59

'You're leaving?' Bonnie feels panic seep through her body as she tries to digest the news that Paige and Andy are moving. The sushi roll she just jammed down her throat has now wedged itself in her chest.

Paige reaches out and squeezes her hand. 'We need the distraction of something new.' She glances out to sea for a moment but then leans back against the park bench they're sitting on. 'I was pushing Andy to do just one more round, but ...' She trails off.

Bonnie's heart stings. It feels like IVF has been a part of their conversation for so many years now. Bonnie had hoped and believed her friends would have a success story to tell.

'Andy can't do it anymore.' She shrugs. 'We've been focused on having a baby for so long that we've let it take over. I can see it'll destroy us as a couple if I insist we do another round.'

Andy once confided in Bonnie that the reason he finds it so hard is that it's unbearable to see Paige's devastation. He doesn't want her to feel that loss over and over again.

'Once upon a time *we* were enough. We've just got to learn to find that again.'

Bonnie remembers Paige and Andy in the early days of their relationship. He'd moved to town for work and had instantly been taken with Paige. He swept her off her feet. Paige had been like a giddy schoolgirl, giggling all the time. The two of them couldn't keep their hands off each other. Bonnie hadn't been sure whether to be amused or sickened by it.

'You'll find it.' Bonnie can't bear the idea of her friends not getting through this.

Paige gives a small nod, her faith in their relationship still there. 'When Andy got the job offer in Hong Kong it just felt like a chance to start fresh and make some new memories. Just being somewhere else will keep my mind busy. When I'm here doing the same thing day in, day out all I think about is falling pregnant. I'm obsessed with babies and wondering what kind of mum I'd be.' Paige momentarily closes her eyes and with a deep breath she leaves that conversation behind. 'You'll have to come visit.'

Bonnie feels devastated at the prospect of losing her best friend but knows she can't show how sad she is. Paige has enough going on without having to worry about upsetting her too. 'Of course.'

Later, as she walks away from lunch and back towards her studio, she wonders how she's going to survive living in this town without Paige. She knows the media attention she's faced over the past few weeks will die down, but she's never felt so alone. It's hard to mourn a relationship with Oliver when she now realises he was never hers to begin with.

Bonnie reaches into her handbag in search of her shop keys as she walks past a good-looking stranger. But on second glance, he looks familiar, and he's smiling at her ... And just like that it clicks.

'Ben, wow!' She shakes her head. 'I didn't recognise you.' She stares, taking in his face.

'Thought it was time to shave that extra layer off.'

Bonnie finds herself a bit mesmerised, breathless even, which makes her want to laugh. 'Well, it suits you.'

He grins and without the facial hair she notices he has a dimple in his cheek. It's funny how she spoke to him every day for over two months but didn't know that about him.

'I like the new look,' he says, gesturing to her haircut.

Her hand immediately reaches up to touch her hair, which she had cut off to her jawline. She'd had a typical 'my relationship is over, I need a makeover' moment. 'Thanks, I thought it was time for something a bit different.'

'Looks good.'

'What are you doing here?' She smiles as she finally yanks the keys free from her bag, forcing herself to break eye contact for a moment.

Ben pauses, then says, 'Work. I had to come see someone about a story I might be covering.'

She's surprised they'd get him to come up from Sydney for something like that but knows when the regular gigs dry up freelancers are pushed to travel more. 'So, you're all finished on *The One*?' She feels a bit nervous bringing up the topic. She doesn't know why, it's not like she has anything to feel bad about. She didn't do anything wrong.

'Yeah, it wrapped up sooner than we thought.'

'I read a bit about what happened,' Bonnie admits. Her heart had ached for Ty when she learned that Penny was dying. That the love of his life was soon going to leave him. 'It's really sad.'

'Yeah.' Ben nods. 'I think it affected a lot of people.'

Bonnie feels at ease in this conversation with him; she'd forgotten how much she enjoyed being in Ben's company. She gestures to her studio. 'Have you got time to come in?'

'Yeah, sure.'

She unlocks the door and they move inside to the lounge. Ben puts some bags down at his feet.

'It's a great space,' he comments, as though it's not the first time he's told her. She tries to think back to the day they filmed her hometown date with Ty. Ben had been here, he'd filmed the whole thing, but the whole day seems blurred. Had Ben told her back then that he liked it? She can't remember.

'So,' Ben begins, drawing out the 'o' sound. 'I need to be honest with you about something.'

She turns, giving him her full attention as she settles against the lounge. She gets a sinking feeling, wondering what's happened behind the scenes on the show. Maybe he was the one who leaked the photo of her and Oliver to the media. She's always liked Ben, but has she misjudged him? Or maybe it's something else—what if *The One* team has sent him up here to do a follow-up story on her? Her body tenses, waiting for Darcy to spring out with more confidentiality forms.

'I've kind of had a massive crush on you from the first day I saw you.'

Bonnie's so startled by this that she's momentarily winded. She tries to think back to the first time she met Ben. 'In the limousine?' Her mouth is dry, her cheeks warming like someone is flaming them with a blowtorch. How on earth could he have a crush on someone who had been practically hyperventilating? But their conversation comes crashing back to her. He'd made a joke, or so she'd thought. He'd said he had a good personality; he'd implied she should date him. She shakes her head, bemused. Had he really liked her back then?

'That was the second time,' he tells her steadily. 'I first met you at the casting day.'

It takes her a second but then an image of Ben standing alongside his camera pops back into her head. She remembers their eyes locking, and even though the bottom half of his face had been hidden by the camera she'd known he was smiling. Had he spoken to her that day? Surely she'd remember? But maybe she wouldn't …

'There was something about you.' He shakes his head. 'You were just so different to everyone else.'

She feels very self-conscious but can't help but laugh at the understatement. 'Older and brunette for starters?'

Ben laughs, his dimple transforming his face. She suddenly has a longing to reach up and touch it, to feel his skin on her fingertips. She wonders if he shaved freshly this morning, if she'd be able to feel the prickles of his regrowth yet.

'Comments like that,' he says with a shrug, pleased that she's made it so easy for him to point out. 'They just sucked me in. I knew I wanted to get to know you. I didn't want you to fall in love with Ty, but I didn't want him to send you home either because then I wouldn't get to see you every day.'

Bonnie suddenly considers the key ceremonies in a different way, imagining Ben standing there behind his camera, hoping she'd be chosen just so he could spend more time with her. Images of their interactions keep flickering into Bonnie's mind as she tries to pin-point a moment where she might have seen this coming. Had his feelings been obvious and she'd just been too caught up with Ty and Ollie? She wants to bury her head in shame at having so many guys on the go at once, but she concentrates on Ben standing in front of her. 'So, you just decided to come and tell me?'

'No,' he says, very matter-of-fact. 'I've come here to ask you on a date.'

She smiles. She can feel it widening, taking up her whole face. Being asked on a date makes her feel young and beautiful and desired. And the idea of going on a date with Ben, who has always been nothing but lovely to her, is very appealing. But she can't let herself be swept downstream in the giddiness. 'What about Sofia?'

'What has Sofia got to do with this?'

This throws her for a second. 'Well, is she still your girlfriend?' There's no way she's even going to entertain the idea of getting involved with a man who is in a relationship again.

But Ben laughs, his head tilting back. 'Sofia's my cat.'

'Your cat?' Everything suddenly shifts in her mind. Ben hadn't been going home each night to cuddle on the lounge with his girlfriend. Instead, he'd been at home with his cat, possibly even thinking about her. Bonnie can feel her cheeks reddening.

'I haven't had a girlfriend since that ex I told you about.'

He's been single for a couple of years. Unlike Bonnie, who feels like she's been jolting from the possibility of love from one guy to the next. 'And you're sure you want to get involved with me?'

He nods. 'Believe it or not.'

It's enough to make her grin, so much so that she bites down on her lip because she feels a little ridiculous smiling so much. 'Okay, so what kind of date did you have in mind?'

He reaches down and grabs the bag at his feet. Her head cranes, eagerly watching. He pulls out two pairs of tracksuit pants and holds them up to show her. One is clearly for her, the other for him. 'I hope you're okay with grey?'

She laughs, immediately knowing where this is going, but elated to watch it unfold.

'And I got these.' He holds up a handful of takeaway menus, fanning them wide for her to see. 'What's good here? Thai, Indian, Mexican, Italian?'

Bonnie points to one of the menus. 'The Thai is amazing.'

He settles the menu on top of the tracksuit pants before reaching back into his bag. This time he produces a bottle of wine. 'Look, I don't know much about wine, but the guy at the shop told me this was a good one.'

Bonnie's nose tingles and her throat tightens; she can feel the tears building.

'I'm just hoping you can help me out with Netflix?'

She can't believe he's remembered what her fantasy date would be from that first day of casting. She nods and laughs. 'We'll probably spend half the night debating what to watch.'

'I tell you what, you can choose whatever you want, because I'm going to be happy just sitting next to you.'

Bonnie moves closer to him. Her heart beats a little faster, the space around them suddenly closing in. She's sure she can feel the blood in her veins racing around her body, the vibration propelling her forward. She looks up into his eyes before letting their lips meet. His hand brushes her cheek, his touch so gentle that her whole body quivers. Feelings are expanding in her mind. What she'd been looking for had been right in front of her. He pulls her closer, she lets herself lean into him, and at once she feels like she's found a place she might never want to leave. She feels herself crumble, the ecstasy of his kiss taking over.

60

One month later

'What's this?' Ty asks as Penny hands him a professional-looking cardboard folder with embossed writing across the front.

She watches as his face falls, his mouth quickly turning downwards as his eyes take in *Leigh Family Funerals.*

The cracks in Penny's heart fracture a little more as an image of Ty standing at her funeral comes spiralling into her head again. Alone, lost, heartbroken. 'All the details are in there.'

A soft whimper escapes the back of his throat. 'Penny ...'

But she charges on. 'Everything has been finalised and paid for. It's all quite simple and straightforward. There's a poem in there that I'd like read. My mum had it at hers and then Miranda had it too.' Her heart squeezes as she immediately remembers standing at her mum's funeral, her sweaty hand in Miranda's as the unforgiving summer sun blazed down. Then, years later, at Miranda's funeral, a cool autumn day where the wind had slashed the air. But she only takes a moment to pause, knowing such silence will bring with it tears. 'You can read it, but if it's too much Barbara from the funeral home will do it. She knows the situation. You'll just need to contact them to organise a date after I ...' She chokes, the word catching before it reaches her mouth.

Ty's eyes glaze over with tears. 'Don't say it, Penny. We don't need to talk about it yet.'

She wishes she didn't have to talk about it, but the end is closing in on them. 'It's important to me that you know what I want.'

He shuts his eyes, gaining strength before nodding at this. 'Okay.'

So they sit there, Penny leaning her head back against his chest as she gets him to open the folder, pointing out the details, letting him read the poem, explaining how she wants the funeral to proceed. She can hear his heart beating and wishes hers would beat alongside his forever, but she knows this is a wish only a genie would be able to grant. As the pain from her cancer increases, so will the morphine, and then it will only be a matter of time.

'No music at all?'

She shakes her head. 'It's too sad. Music makes everything so much worse.'

'It's a funeral. It's supposed to be sad.'

She gives a quick shake of the head, remembering how silent tears had fallen until 'Tears in Heaven' had played at Miranda's funeral, at which point she'd wept loudly and uncontrollably.

'I've told Barbara that I want the whole thing kept short.' Barbara from Leigh Family Funerals had been professional, sensitive and understanding. She hadn't looked at Penelope with the usual sympathy that people did once they found out about her death sentence.

This wasn't the first time Barbara had been given specific funeral requests from someone terminally ill.

'Can I say something at the funeral?' His eyes remain on the paper in front of them rather than meeting hers.

She'd feared he might ask this, imagining the words he'd say about her. Imagining him having to stand there shaky and broken. 'I've told Barbara I don't want a eulogy.'

His mouth twists. 'Okay, but what about a brief acknowledgement of how you've made my life a better life just for knowing you?'

Tears sting her eyes, the unfairness of it all tumbling towards her like a wave. She feels her legs shake as her body is swept under the water. Her head goes under, she struggles for breath.

Ty reaches out, takes her hand and squeezes it tight. That single moment rescues her from going under and she steadies her breath.

'I'd like to say something,' Ty says. 'I think it'd be good for me.'

She gives a small nod. She owes him that much. 'Okay, but nothing too over the top.'

'Wouldn't dream of it,' he teases steadily.

Penny moves on, going through the paperwork, explaining she's bought a crematorium plot to be with her mother and sister.

He stares at her for so long that her procedural manner wavers again. 'What is it?'

He breathes loudly out of his nose, his eyes downcast. 'I was just wondering if I could buy a plot there—for me, you know, when …'

For when he dies?

Her throat dries at this. Of course Ty wants to be buried with her now. But he's thirty-two. Realistically he could have another fifty years ahead of him. How do you tell someone who is deeply in love with you that they won't feel this way forever? That he will probably fall in love again, that he might have a long marriage, a happy family … a life that goes much further than an early chapter titled 'Penelope'. She doesn't want him buying a plot and then having to deal with the guilt of not wanting to be buried there after years have passed and his life has moved on. 'I don't think that's something you need to decide on yet.'

'Okay.' His voice is soft, his face pale.

'Not many people will be there,' she says, focused back on her funeral. She knows Lara will be there and doesn't know whether to feel warmed by the friendship she's made or guilty that she's brought more grief into Lara's life. Lara calls her every few days to check up on her and each time Penny finds herself wishing that her new friend didn't have to be sad again so soon.

'Penny,' he begins, perhaps worried that she's offended by the thought of not having a mass of people to send her off, but that isn't the case at all. There have been three important people in her life and two of them have already gone. 'I think you'll be surprised.'

'Well, people will be there for you. Lots will be there to try and support you. But I don't have very many friends, Ty.'

He stares at her for a moment, for this he knows is true. 'You've never really let anyone in.'

They both know this has been a conscious thing. 'I let you in,' she counters.

This makes him smile. 'Well, yes. And I'm going to be a selfish bastard and not share any of the time we have left with anyone else.'

Penelope isn't going to argue with that. 'I'm entirely yours, Ty Peterson.'

61

Darcy tosses and turns. Her bed usually feels like a cloud but tonight it feels like she's lying on a pile of sticks. She kicks back the twisted sheets from her body. It's useless; sleep isn't going to be her friend tonight. Her new job as a segment producer on *Lifestyle* should be the only thing on her mind, but she can't stop thinking about Ed.

She finds herself pushing out of bed. Her new room is half unpacked, with boxes and suitcases carpeting the floor. She digs around until she finds a jumper to pull over her pyjamas. She opens her bedroom door and tiptoes quietly so she doesn't wake Tara, her new flatmate sleeping in the other room, who has an early call time tomorrow.

Darcy grabs her keys and wallet and tells herself not to think about what she's doing. She has to keep reminding herself to breathe as she manoeuvres her car through the darkened suburb. She parks, blocking out the fact that it's very late at night. Much too late to go knocking on someone's door.

She walks down the hall of the apartment block. A sliver of light peeks from under the door. Despite all the pretending, her heart is racing high in her throat. She lifts her hand and knocks.

After a few moments the door flings open. Ed's in trackies and a T-shirt. The computer in the background is bright, frozen on a close-up of a wedding cake. He's been working.

'Darcy? Is everything okay?'

She wonders if she can trust her voice. She shakes her head a little. No, everything is not okay. She has feelings for him she can't contain anymore. 'Is Zoe here?'

'What?' He shakes his head, a little annoyed she's asked him such a question. 'It's the middle of the night. Why would Zoe be here?'

Darcy feels stupid for asking now. 'I thought there might be something going on between the two of you ...'

'So, you were going to pounce on us in the middle of the night and do what?'

She hangs her head. She's not sure what she would have done if Zoe had opened Ed's door in her pyjamas.

He sighs. 'I told you, she's my boss. Nothing's going to happen.'

'But she wants it to,' Darcy urges. 'Call it women's intuition, but she likes you.'

He groans and shrugs at the same time. She knows she's frustrating him, but she can't help herself. 'If she wasn't your boss would you be interested in her?'

'Darcy, no! What's gotten into you?'

She can hear herself—she knows how crazy she sounds. She stares at him and his familiar eyes stare back. He's been her friend for seven years. She's terrified she's about to lose his friendship, but she needs to tell him. She has to risk it all. 'I'm pretty sure I'm in love with you.'

Silence falls.

She waits for alarm, but a little smile climbs onto his face.

'You're not surprised?' She'd expected him to be floored by her declaration. Maybe even annoyed.

'That kiss kind of changed everything, didn't it?'

She's missed his honesty. All their recent conversations have been behind a protective wall but revealing her feelings like this seems to have pulled it down.

'I tried pretending it was nothing.' He laughs at himself. 'But all I've wanted to do since then is kiss you again.'

'Really?' It's Darcy's turn to be flattered. Heat rushes over her face as she grins back at him. 'Why haven't you?' She steps closer, her body shuddering with hope.

'I wasn't sure whether you'd punch me in the face or not.' He moves closer too, their bodies almost touching.

Darcy laughs. She can actually imagine herself doing that before she'd kissed him. But she's the one who made the move and now she knows what it's like to have his lips on hers. 'I promise I won't punch you.'

They both lean in. Darcy tingles, her body starting to float off the ground as he kisses her. It's soft at first, a few precious moments as their lips delicately rediscover each other. But hunger and desire quickly take over. They grasp at each other frantically, needing to make up for lost time. They stumble to Ed's bedroom, their lips barely leaving each other. He picks her up and her legs wrap around his waist. She feels lightheaded with anticipation. They yank at each other's clothes, pulling and ripping them away until their bodies are bare. They fall into his bed and heat quickly radiates, sweat rising to the top of their skin. He pulls her closer still, his firmness causing

Darcy to groan. She finds herself arching back with a pleasure she's never felt before.

They lie there staring up at the ceiling, hearts still pounding, breaths unsteady.

'Wow.'

'Uh-huh …'

'I was going to suggest we take things slow?' She raises her eyebrows, amused.

'Are you kidding me? There is no going back from what we just did.'

She laughs and takes a peek at Ed lying beside her. She greedily wants to stare, which feels weird, because Ed's her best friend. He was her *mate*, but now all she wants to do is explore his body.

But then Ed props onto his side, his fingers finding their way onto her stomach and gently tracing a map of their own. The sensation causes her breath to catch in her throat. He senses this and lowers his head, gently kissing her on the shoulder. His big eyes look up at her, somewhat cautious.

'You were so angry that night,' she says, remembering Ed's face after she'd kissed him. 'You basically shoved me into that taxi. I thought you hated me.'

'I was furious with you,' he admits, 'because that kiss was bloody amazing, and I knew it was going to be pretty hard going back to being your best friend and watching you marry someone else.'

Drew.

They're both silent for a moment.

'Is he all right?'

There's a lump in her throat. She tries not to let any guilt take hold. 'He will be.'

'About this?'

Them.

Us.

Darcy's eyes meet Ed's. Her heart clenches at the thought of having to tell Drew about him. 'Maybe, with time?'

Ed gives a small nod. She imagines he's going through the same feelings she had when he and Sienna split up. Darcy and Ed had met on the first day of university and immediately hit it off. Drew had been Darcy's boyfriend and therefore Ed and Drew became mates too.

She turns, propping herself up to match him. 'Let's not think about that today.'

'Agreed.' He leans in, their faces almost touching. 'What do you propose we do?'

She bites down on her lip, a burning hunger raging through her body. 'I was thinking we could do a bit more of this ...' And as she pushes her body on top of his, her words drift away ...

62

'How's the pain?' Ty asks as he settles next to her. The warm sun streams through their large window. They've spent weeks curled up here on the lounge they chose together, back when they thought they had forever ahead of them. Neither had realised the practical dark-coloured fabric they'd chosen with kids in mind wouldn't matter. No kids of theirs would climb over the lounge or spill food on it. Instead Penelope has lain propped against cushions listening to Ty read her passages from some of her favourite books, both of them trying not to think about the end approaching at rapid speed.

'Okay,' she murmurs from dry lips, her pain constant but oddly bearable for the moment.

He brushes back hair from her face, his fingers gentle and soft against her skin. Her breathing is shallow, but she inhales his smell. She wishes her body would allow her a deep breath so she could take the sweet scent to the pit of her stomach. She's glad he's here with her now. She'd been focused on believing that he didn't need to go through this. But maybe he did. Taking care of her with such devotion might offer him some peace once she's gone.

'You look beautiful,' he says.

She wants to swat at him or even laugh at such a ridiculous suggestion, but she doesn't have the energy. 'You're deluded,' she finally manages.

'That might be the case, but I still think you're the most beautiful woman in the entire world.'

She can't resist a smile at this. She reaches for his hand, needing more of him. Her chest aches at the knowledge that she's leaving him behind. They could have had forever and her heart is still wrestling with accepting that what she's had is better than not having him at all.

'Thank you for everything, Ty.'

He chokes at hearing these words, tears brimming as he brings his lips down to kiss her hand.

She wants to keep looking at him, to take in every feature of the man she loves, but her eyelids are heavy. She can feel something trying to pull her away. Her eyelids flutter to the darkness.

Her own whimpers wake her, with the pain now overwhelming. Her eyes try to adjust to her surroundings and panic jolts through her body when she realises she's not at home anymore. Just like her mum and just like Miranda, hospital confines her.

But the warmth of Ty's hand as it wraps around her own immediately calms her. The fingertips of his other hand lightly dance across her skin. She concentrates on the feeling, not just the physical sensation but the emotion. Pure, good, and whole.

'It's okay,' he tells her gently, giving her permission to leave him.

Quietness settles around them, Ty's hand forever holding hers, offering a safeness like no other.

Time warps, the concept vanishing altogether. But Ty stays by her side.

The pain dulls as she wraps herself in his love, in all his affection, in the knowledge that what she had with Ty was better than she ever imagined.

Her breath slows …

… slows …

. . . s l o w s . . .

Until there is no breath at all.

ACKNOWLEDGEMENTS

It is a dream come true that this book is being published and there are so many people in my life who deserve heartfelt thanks.

To Alex, I hit the jackpot with you. I'm so thankful for the life we have.

Biggest love to my three little cheerleaders, Leo, Minnie and Cherry, who are always close by, sometimes on my lap, or nestled under my arm as I write the words. You inspire me every day. Special mention to Leo, who said I'm his favourite author, ahead of J.K. Rowling—which is the greatest compliment in the world from my obsessive Harry Potter fan.

My mum, who has read all the pages numerous times, along with discussing the characters and story arcs in depth on our beach walks. Your support and encouragement have meant the world to me.

Thank you to the team at Harlequin for bringing this book to life. A special thanks to Rachael Donovan for believing in me and this book after I pitched to her at the RWA conference. I will be eternally grateful. Also, huge appreciation to my editor, Julia

Knapman, for her insight, patience and editorial brilliance at making *The One* a richer story.

My cousin, Sharon Hammond, who took me onto the set of *E Street* when I was ten years old. I still have vibrant behind-the-scenes memories that I know spurred me on to have a lifelong love and fascination for film and television.

I must make note of the English teacher who gave me full marks for a creative writing piece when I was about fourteen and commented, 'You have a vivid imagination.' Those words have stayed with me all these years.

Thank you to Toni Fatherley for pushing me in the classroom. Your knowledge and brilliance are astounding.

A huge hurrah to all those involved in my days at Charles Sturt University, Wagga Wagga. TV Land and the Res Scheme are four years I'll never forget and have certainly armed me with plenty of stories to tell.

Thank you to Bevan Lee, who gave this country girl her first big break and dream job as a storyliner on a brand-new television show when I was fresh out of university.

I'd also like to acknowledge the mentors and friends from the world of television, especially the story masters from the script departments. There are too many names to mention, but I value all your guidance and appreciate the story skills you helped me develop. Being in a plotting room is such a thrilling experience—and I still pinch myself for the time I spent in there.

Special mention to the Romance Writers of Australia. Joining this organisation was a critical step in my writing journey and I feel overwhelmed by the tribe's love and support. Also, to Writing NSW and the Australian Writers' Centre for all the courses and festivals

I've attended over the years. These have been hugely beneficial for writing growth.

To the inspiring friends I have made along the writing journey: Christine Ratnasingham, Maya Linnell, Clare Atkins and Faith Mckinnon.

A big shout-out to my Book Club girls, who make every fourth Sunday afternoon delightful with delicious foods, drinks, book talk and friendship. The hours we share are never long enough but always cherished.

Thank you to Mike Luke's gruelling boot-camp sessions, along with (Sara) Everitts Fitness classes for keeping blood pumping through my veins and making me feel so much better about all the hours I sit at my computer.

To my fellow *Bachelor* fans for our ongoing analysis of each episode. It certainly helped spark ongoing drama in this book. Special mention to Natalie Kavanagh for coming up with the title *The One*.

I need to mention my local MidCoast Library, which continues to stock fabulous books, put on events and keep a beautiful place to not only read, but write too.

Love and appreciation to Ian Forrest and Madison and Quin McClintock for their encouragement. And a big thank you to the friends and family, near and far, that I feel lucky to have in my life.

And, finally, a shout-out to the community of Old Bar, who I know are cheering me on! I absolutely love where I live.

BOOK CLUB DISCUSSION QUESTIONS

1. Which of the three main romances was your favourite, and why?
2. Which character did you most identify with?
3. Do you think the book accurately described what a reality TV show is like behind the scenes? Were there any aspects that surprised you?
4. Do you feel like Darcy behaved ethically in her job? Do you think it's possible to do a job like that in an ethical way?
5. What were your feelings towards Bonnie when she kissed Oliver despite knowing he was engaged to someone else?
6. What did you think about Bonnie's relationship with her sister, Carla? Do you think it was acceptable that Carla logged into Bonnie's email and banking accounts, and sent in an audition tape without her permission?
7. Darcy and Drew ended up more like friends than lovers after ten years together. Do you think that's inevitable for couples, or do you see things going differently for Darcy and Ed?
8. Sophie starts off as a villain, but we have a lot more sympathy for her by the end of the book. Did you change your mind about any of the other characters as you learned more about them?
9. At what point did you realise how Penelope was intertwined in the story?
10. Penelope withholds the truth from Ty to save him from heartache and in hopes he will move on faster. What's your opinion on this? How do you think you would have reacted if you were in Ty's position?
11. The book poses the question whether we need 'the one' to be truly happy. What is your opinion on this?
12. What did you think about the way each couple's story ended? Which wrap-up was the most satisfying?

Turn over for a sneak peek.

by

KANEANA MAY

Available April 2021

FICTION
H Q

1

'Maybe the podiatrist?' Olive pulled the CV to the top of the pile.

Bree rolled her eyes. 'She was even more boring than you.'

'I'll try not to take offence to that.'

The interviews had lasted a few hours. A psychologist, a herbalist, a podiatrist, a physiotherapist and three psychics. All of them had applied to rent out a room in Healing Hands. Seven of the applicants were female. The only male was a herbalist from the hills of Elands. He arrived almost an hour late for his interview with no shoes and couldn't provide them with any formal qualifications. Olive knew she was supposed to embrace the alternative in their line of work, but no shoes to an interview? It made her shudder.

Their receptionist, Nia, came into the room. 'A man has just arrived—he hasn't sent in a proper application but he's happy to interview right now. I had a quick look over his CV and he's worth seeing.'

'Why hasn't he applied properly?'

'He only saw the advertisement this morning. Drove straight here,' Nia explained.

'You did say a man would be good for business,' Elsie reminded her.

Their clientele at Healing Hands was predominantly female.

'And he's quite good looking,' Nia assured them with a grin.

'Definitely send him in,' Bree said.

A few moments later, Nia led him back up the hall. 'Oh, listen to that,' Bree murmured. 'Strong, manly footsteps. It makes me go a bit weak at the knees.'

'Oh, behave yourself,' Elsie said, the only married one of the three.

Olive threw Elsie an appreciative look; she liked it when she didn't always have to be the stickler.

Nia was a bit flushed when she re-entered the room. 'This is Tom Henderson.' She stepped to the side.

Olive felt all the air in her lungs evaporate at the sight of him.

'Olive Atkins?' His face broke into a smile. He was clearly pleased to see her. 'It's been years.'

Thirteen years in September. Olive wouldn't ever forget.

She could feel the other women watching on with great interest. At school she'd always thought he was cute, but he'd definitely grown into his looks. She found the gaze of his dark blue eyes unsettling.

'You're one of the owners?'

'Yes. I'm the dietitian.'

He smiled but couldn't hide that he clearly wasn't expecting that answer. 'Wow. I thought you would have been off on the other side of the world ...' He trailed off, as though realising he was probably at risk of offending her.

Olive cleared her throat as she tried not to think about the fact that living a small life in Wingham, a country town with the population of no more than six thousand people, would have been the last thing that people from school expected of her.

'How are your parents?' he asked.

'Yes, fine,' Olive said, scared her voice would give away too much.

'Are they still in Laurieton?'

She could feel her cheeks warming. She barely talked about her parents, or her hometown, despite them both only being an hour away. She visited when she had to—birthdays, Christmases, that kind of thing. But otherwise she avoided it. Memories haunted her from the moment she walked in the front door. 'Yes, still there,' she finally managed, wondering if he was imagining her childhood brick house with the large frangipani tree out the front too.

'How do you guys know each other?' Bree's eyes danced with devilry.

Olive ignored the tightening in her chest and tried to wave the topic away. 'We went to the same school.' And while they were never really good friends, Olive knew her description wasn't quite accurate.

'How was your big trip? The last I heard was that you were going around Australia.'

Sweat prickled her temple. 'It was fine.' Until it wasn't.

'I didn't know you went travelling,' Elsie mused.

She hadn't spoken to them about the time she tried to rebuild her life only to have it destroyed again. Olive gestured for Tom to take a seat. 'Anyway, we better get on with this interview.'

'Yes, of course,' he said, but not before she caught a flash of disappointment fall across his face.

Olive could feel the others looking at her. She was usually the one to take them through the interview, but she was momentarily floored, her heart fluttery and her arms jittery as though she'd drunk too much coffee. She tried to suck in more air. She felt Elsie trying to meet her eye. Olive flashed her a panicked look.

Elsie took the hint. 'So, Tom. Why don't you tell us a bit about yourself?'

Olive threw Elsie a small smile. She had to pull herself together.

Tom cleared his throat. 'I'm a massage therapist.'

Her breath quivered in the back of her throat. Of course he was a masseur. She found herself staring at his hands. Large, capable, healing …

'Oh, how lovely.' Bree's voice was as sweet as honey.

Tom went on to tell them about his training and credentials, all impressive. The more he talked, with his deep soothing voice, the more obvious it became that he was the perfect candidate for the position.

'So you've just moved here?' Bree asked with interest.

'Actually, I don't live anywhere right now. I've packed up my place on the Sunshine Coast. My dad recently passed away and I want to be closer to Mum.'

It was a good hour's drive to their hometown of Laurieton but career prospects anywhere on the mid north coast were pretty slim.

Olive could see both Bree and Elsie were a little taken by this man. She wanted to scream. She wanted to find a big fault, or at least one tiny reason why they shouldn't hire him. She also wanted to say that she was sorry to hear about his dad. Mr Henderson had been a teacher at their high school and she'd particularly liked his science classes. But somehow her voice couldn't quite manage the words; she was terrified her condolences would lead to another conversation she didn't want to have.

'We're still interviewing,' Elsie told him, 'but we'll be in touch.'

Olive stood, signalling the interview was over. She was eager for him to leave the room so she could breathe properly again.

'It was good to see you.' Tom held her gaze, causing heat to spread from her face to her neck and all over her chest.

Once he had left the room, Bree and Elsie turned to her, their eyes wide. But she just shook her head and words she barely ever said spilled from her mouth. 'I need a drink.'

Twenty minutes later, the three women sat at a table in the beer garden of their local pub. Elsie and Bree looked at her expectantly, waiting for Olive to fill them in on her relationship with Tom Henderson.

'There's not much to tell,' Olive began, knowing she was balancing on a tightrope of truth and lies. 'We were in the same year at school.'

'And did anything ever happen between the two of you?' Elsie asked.

'No, nothing at all.'

Elsie stared at her. Olive knew she didn't believe her.

'So, you don't like him? You know, like *that*?'

'No,' Olive said, a little rushed, knowing Bree was definitely interested in him. But Bree was always interested in any new male, so Olive tried not to let it bother her. She took a large gulp of wine and noticed Elsie was still watching her thoughtfully.

'Oh my gosh!' Bree whispered across the table. 'Look who it is …'

Olive turned and there was Tom Henderson for the second time that day. Her stomach dropped to the floor as she saw Bree wave him over.

'Bree!' Olive muttered under her breath.

He approached, a flustered expression across his face. 'Hello, again. A lovely afternoon for it.' He nodded, indicating the drinks around the table.

'We were just talking about you,' Bree said, a cheeky glint in her eye.

Olive fought the urge to kick her under the table.

This looked like it knocked the wind out of him. 'Good things?' He looked hopeful.

'Of course,' Olive said professionally, ignoring the sweat on her neck.

'I imagine you all had a laugh over the Valentine's Day card I sent Olive all those years ago?' He laughed nervously.

Olive silently groaned, her eyes dropping as she reached for her glass of wine.

'No,' Elsie said. 'We know nothing of any Valentine …'

'But please join us.' Bree moved to give him space next to her on the bench seat. 'We'd love to hear more about Olive's mysterious school days.'

'Ah …' Tom's eyes fell on Olive, perhaps waiting for her to support Bree's invitation. But when she said nothing, he shrugged. 'I better not. I'm meeting a mate soon.'

Olive was barely able to make eye contact with him as he politely excused himself.

Once he walked away, Bree frowned at Olive. 'Well, that was rude.'

'I don't think it's appropriate to mix business with pleasure. It's very unprofessional—we still haven't decided who we're hiring yet.'

'Yes, we have!' both Bree and Elsie chorused.

'No one even comes close to Tom.' Elsie leant in closer. 'We'd be silly not to hire him.'

Olive exhaled loudly. She knew they were right.

'And what's this about a Valentine?' Bree smirked as though they'd gotten to the bottom of Olive's secrecy.

Olive shook her head. 'We were in primary school. I honestly have no idea why he'd even bring that up.'

'Don't tell us he's been pining over you for twenty years!'

'Don't be ridiculous.' Olive pushed out of her chair. 'Anyone for another drink?'

An old Valentine's Day card from Tom Henderson was the least of her worries. It was the fact he could reveal secrets she'd been hiding for over a decade that was scaring her senseless.

talk about it

Let's talk about books.

Join the conversation:

 facebook.com/romanceanz

 @romanceanz

romance.com.au

If you love reading and want to know about our
authors and titles, then let's talk about it.